THE INDESTRUCTIBLES

by

Matthew Phillion

Lizy!
Thanks for everything!
[signature]

The Indestructibles

PFP, INC
publisher@pfppublishing.com
144 Tenney Street
Georgetown, MA 01833

April 2014
Printed in the United States of America

First PFP edition © 2014

ISBN-10: 0991427521
ISBN-13: 978-0-9914275-2-9
(also available in eBook format)

Front cover photos:
"Damaged Radiation Sign" © Peter Zelei - Getty Images
"Downtown Minneapolis" © Dan Anderson - Getty Images

Back cover author photo: © Kayt Silvers
www.bowkerhousephoto.com/the-photographers/kayt-silvers/

Acknowledgements

This book could not have happened without a spectacular group of people who kept me honest and kept me inspired during the writing process.

First and foremost, Stephanie Buck and Lea Ann Dziurzynski, you have my infinite thanks for the hours you put in editing the first, second, third, fourth, and beyond drafts. I'm a better writer for your efforts. You kept me honest and kept me going, and you deserve all the credit in the world for the work you did.

I need to thank Peter Sarno and PFP Publishing for the opportunity to bring *The Indestructibles* to life. We're in an era where the signal to noise in publishing is deafening, and it is an incredible thing to find not only a publisher to put their faith in you, but to find one with as much respect for authors and their craft.

My test subject/readers: Bec Gianotti, Colin Carlton, Christian Sterling Hegg, Elisabeth "Calibama" Brazil, Kate Carlton, all of you made me realize these characters were real enough and important enough to tell their stories and bring them all to life, and your genuine enthusiasm for the story kept me writing every single night. There's more to come for all of these little heroes, I promise.

Robert Alan, Nynia Chance, T'Lera Elkins, none of us knew it at the time, but all of you helped me test out almost all of the voices in this book over the years. They've gone by different names and lived different lives, but they all got their sparks from our time together, and certainly Entropy Emily would never have existed without our super-heroic testing grounds.

To my family: thanks for letting me be a weird little comic book loving kid growing up. You never got in the way of my imagination, even when I was lost in my own little world. It only took thirty-six years to realize it was okay for grown-ups to use their imaginations, too. And yes, I'm still sitting at the kitchen table writing stories. Some things never change.

- Matthew Phillion

This book is dedicated to my father, who is and always has been my own superhero, and to my mother, who still believes I can fly.

PROLOGUE:
ONCE, ON A FARM

Doc Silence touched down in the cornfields behind the farm, dropping from the sky like a falling star. Dressed in street clothes, a long black coat, old boots, and a college tee shirt, he looked nothing like a hero, which suited him fine. Doc never wanted to be a hero in the first place.

He walked slowly through the cornstalks, pushed his rose-tinted glasses to rest better on the bridge of his nose, and surveyed the burned out ruin of a storage shed behind the sun-bleached red farmhouse. It had been extinguished hurriedly and ungracefully, and still bore the blackened scars of a recent fire.

I waited too long, Doc thought. He had been mourning his lost friends, and this was never meant to be his responsibility. This wasn't his role. But Doc was the only one left, and someone had to take responsibility.

Doc always stood by his obligations.

Old John Hawkins waited for him on the back steps, thick farmer's arms folded across his chest like a pair of rawhide bones. He nodded when he reached the foot of the stairs.

"Been a while."

"I know. Sorry."

John shook his head. "No need to apologize. Hell, was hoping this day would never come. Doris and I started to think — "

" — That she might stay forever?"

"She's a good kid. A wonderful girl."

1

I'm sure she is, Doc thought. A child can't help but turn out right, raised by John and Doris Hawkins. But nothing good lasts forever.

He followed John into the living room, where Doris sat primly on the sofa, wearing an apron. Who still wears aprons? He'd been away too long from here, spent too much time in dark places. It weighs on you after a while, and you start forgetting that places still exist where good people live ordinary lives.

Next to Doris sat a teenage girl. Her hair the color of late afternoon sunlight. She wasn't much to look at, a slender little thing, sunburned, hair falling in her eyes.

"Doris," Doc said.

The older woman smiled, stood up, kissed him on the cheek.

"Jane, this is an old friend of ours," John said. The girl didn't look up. "He's come to talk to you about what happened in the barn."

Jane locked eyes with Doc for just a split second before returning her gaze to the floor. He sat down across from her on an ottoman, resting his elbows on his knees. Then nodded to the Hawkins, and the couple left quietly.

"I don't know what happened," she said.

This broke Doc's heart; her earnestness, her honest confusion.

"Of course you don't," he said. "Have your . . . Have the Hawkins ever told you how you came to live here?"

"They adopted me."

"True," Doc said.

He wished Annie were here. She was better at this than he was. But Annie was gone and the only one left who could help this girl was Doc Silence. How unfortunate for Jane, he thought.

He exhaled.

"When you were an infant, there was a plane crash."

She raised her eyes again, trying to stare through his colored lenses. He wished he could take them off, but now was not the time to scare her.

"There was a crash. Every person on the flight died, including your birth parents. A terrible, terrible accident."

Doc ran a hand through his hair. He felt old and insensitive, awkward and strange.

"Every person on that flight died, except one. A little baby girl. When we found you, you didn't have a scratch."

She studied him then. Smart kid, looking for clues. She waited.

"We knew you were special. Knew that you'd only become more special the older you got, and that if the wrong people found you, they'd want to take you away. So my friends and I hid you here."

She shook her head, almost imperceptibly. Her eyebrows drew together tightly.

"You've come to take me away."

"I have," Doc said. There wasn't much use in lying. Annie, why'd you have to leave this all up to me? He thought. What am I going to do with this kid?

"I don't want to go."

Doc smiled.

"I don't blame you. But your powers have started growing, and you might not be safe here anymore."

"Mom and Dad might not be safe from me anymore is what you mean."

"That too," he said. "But I'm going to try to help you learn how to make sure you don't have to worry about that."

Doc reflected on the file they'd created for her. She was a little solar-powered energy cell, impervious to most injuries. Probably never had a broken bone or a scratch in her life. There was potential for unassisted flight. Strange heat signatures — that's where the problems arose. According to John, the girl set the barn on fire when her hands burst into flames as she tried to lift a crate.

Jane had the potential to be a huge handful. Except that she was raised by John and Doris Hawkins. They raised good kids. Some of Doc's best friends had grown up in this house.

No wonder they looked so sad when he arrived. All those children, now dead or returned to the stars.

Doc extended his hand.

Jane hesitated, then took it in her own.

"I bet you didn't know you could fly," he said.

CHAPTER 1:
THE GIRL IN THE CLOUDS

§he looks like a corpse," the cyborg said, glaring down at the girl in the glass jar. All color had gone out of her, eyes gummed shut, wires and tubes in her arms disappearing under the covers of the hospital bed she lay on inside the clear coffin. The cyborg, who went by the name Agent Black and who had not been called by his birth name for so long he barely remembered it, found himself vaguely uncomfortable with what he was witnessing.

Black wasn't particularly sympathetic to the girl, but, the science he was being made privy to gave him pause.

"She's a vegetable," said the woman with an eye patch who stood next to him.

The woman, Rose, also gave the cyborg pause, and for entirely different reasons. She was, and always had been, the most ruthless person he'd ever worked with in all of his years of mercenary villainy. In this line of work, there were paid professionals, there were maniacs, and then, there were the utterly merciless. Rose fell into the latter category. Agent Black used to think that the maniacs were the ones who were the scariest, because you never knew what a truly insane villain would do. But the older he got, the more the merciless ones made him nervous. Madmen could be counted on to do something stupid or self-destructive. The merciless ones were too smart for that.

"Where'd you get her?"

"We paid off a physician in Florida to sign her death certificate," Rose said. "Her family thinks her organs were donated, her body cremated. Instead, they scattered someone's golden retriever in the Gulf."

That's awful, the cyborg thought. But he kept it to himself. Nobody benefits from empathy in this line of work.

"What happens next?" he asked. He'd been briefed on what was actually being done, but no one had fully explained exactly how they planned to accomplish the science fiction lunacy his employers had been talking about.

Rose stepped up to a computer terminal beside the girl. She tapped a few keys, and the wall behind the bed opened up like venetian blinds. Behind it was a massive pane of something clear, not quite bulletproof glass but similar, a pane of clarity. Beyond that, sat a large chamber, clearly reinforced, lit by red emergency lights. The room was empty except for a thin gray mist.

After a few seconds, sparks of lightning crisscrossed the mist, like a distant storm. It reminded Agent Black of a huge thunderstorm hovering on the horizon of a Midwestern plain.

The sparks flashed in increasing succession. And then, the mist charged the glass like an animal unleashed.

The cyborg jumped back.

Rose laughed.

"We captured her off the coast of Norway," Rose said.

"*Her?*"

"An adolescent sentient storm. Her mother was responsible for the flooding in Southeast Asia last year."

"Her?" Black asked again.

"It's female."

The cyborg stared at Rose, half-expecting her to tell him she was joking.

She fixed her remaining eye on his own red-lensed artificial one. Dead serious.

"A sentient storm."

"Weather agencies say they name them for historical purposes, but the truth is, some storms have thoughts. They're feral things, though. Sources of chaos. They truly know not what they do."

"How do you capture weather?" Black asked.

"I don't fully understand the science behind it myself," Rose said. As she spoke, the sliding doors behind her opened. Two anonymous guards — masked and armored, chosen by Black himself because they were so similar as to be unidentifiable from any of the other guards on the premises — led a little man in front of them. He sported a hippy's ponytail, a receding hairline, small glasses, and wore a blue chambray shirt under his white lab coat.

"What's he doing here?" the little man asked.

Black looked at Rose, raised an eyebrow, silently asking the same question.

"Agent Black is here to slit your throat if the next step doesn't work, Doctor Wegener," Rose said. She laughed again, and Black smiled with her, but he knew there was no joke there. He didn't particularly want to kill the scientist, but money was money. His job was compliance. Stand there, be scary, force the scientist to do what Rose asked.

"You realize there is no guarantee this will work," Wegener said. "The process is entirely untested."

"It's your one shot, Doctor," Rose said. "The likelihood that we'll capture another sentient weather pattern is nil. So there's really no reason to keep you alive if this doesn't work."

Wegener attempted to stare her down.

Black gave the scientist credit — he lasted almost three seconds before turning away. It was better than most could handle when looking into Rose's dead eye.

Wegener pulled a wheeled stool to sit on, then took Rose's place at the terminal. He tapped commands. Inside the chamber, the sentient storm tested its boundaries, touching corners and hinges with fingers of lightning. The light inside the chamber changed from red to blue. Wegener glanced over at the girl in the glass jar, her bed looked — for all intents and purposes — like a colossal syringe. The scientist caressed the glass lightly.

"I'm sorry," he said, softly. He turned away, entered one last command, and the glass jar began to move forward.

Black hadn't realized it before, but the coffin-like hospital bed was embedded in the wall, the same wall as the cage holding the storm in. The girl was, bed and all, injected into the chamber with the brewing storm. Black moved closer, looking through the glass, and saw that the comatose girl was no longer surrounded by glass, but exposed to the storm, silently suspended in mid-air. The blankets of the bed fluttered in silent wind.

And then lightning struck.

A blue bolt of light lanced into the girl's comatose body with such power that Black was positive he saw the outline of her skeleton, and before he could finish his thought: *I swear I thought that only happened in the cartoons* — lightning lashed out again and the girl woke, moving, her arms pushing up off the bed, head thrown back, mouth open in a silent scream.

"What the hell's happening?" Black said.

"We're trying to force the storm into the girl's body," Wegener said.

"Why?"

"Because it's a lot easier to control an alien sentience when you can shoot it in the head," Rose said. She was watching the process intently, one hand pressed against the glass.

More lightning lashed out, this time from the girl's eyes, striking the walls, dancing across the giant windowpane. And then she was in the air, drifting, hospital gown fluttering in the wind, her hair flowing all around her, changing color, bleaching out from dark brown to pale, silvery blue. Her skin was changing, too, first to an even more deathly white, and then darkening, turning gray, the color of a storm cloud.

The girl looked Agent Black right in the eyes.

His stomach clenched and he reached for the high-tech sidearm strapped to his thigh, knowing full well he couldn't kill a storm with it. Reflex. Fight or flight. A life spent battling and killing, and now he stood staring into the eyes of a teenage girl with a thunderstorm invading her veins.

The girl, the storm, the combination of the two slammed into the glass, palms outstretched, streams of electric light lashed out in all directions, her eyes filled with it, her body surrounded by fog. It began to rain in the chamber then, really rain, a pounding, unyielding downpour.

"Looks like your lucky day, Doctor. You get to live," Rose said. Then the lights went out.

Black dropped into a crouch, the millions of dollars of combat cybernetics in his body taking over, finding safe cover, looking for an enemy, the targeting systems in his one fake eye kicking in, compensating for the darkness. Wegener had ducked beneath the terminal; the two guards had their weapons raised, while Rose stood, legs akimbo, waiting patiently.

The glass shattered. Not simply shattering, but, exploding, a storm of broken glass and rainwater crashed over them like a flood. One of the guards screamed. He heard Wegener praying. Cold air — the storm, Black realized, it, the living sentient storm — washed over them, pounding at walls, finding an exit, and, with the bending and creaking of metal, making a way out when one couldn't be found. Black, knocked off his feet, tumbled across the broken glass, thankful it was designed to break like safety glass — rounded edges instead of a million skin-tearing points.

Light returned, dim at first, and Black wondered if the emergency lights had kicked on, until he saw the opening in the ceiling. The storm, the girl, tore a gaping hole in the roof. Rain filtered in. He couldn't tell if it came from the creature or from nature.

It didn't seem to much matter.

He looked around. The guard who screamed lay dead on the floor, blood running thin in the puddling water. The other one nursed a broken arm, rifle beside him. The doctor was a soaking mess, hair plastered to his face, one lens of his eyeglasses cracked.

Rose remained standing, gazing up through the hole, appearing for all the world as if nothing had happened.

"Are we supposed to go after her?" Agent Black asked. He had no idea how they could, but it was the only question he could reasonably think of at that moment.

"No," Rose said. "No, this just changes the game a little."

And then she smiled at him again.

The cyborg felt his blood run cold. Professionals, maniacs, and the merciless.

Thinking of a sentient storm in the body of a comatose girl flying across the night sky, Agent Black began to wonder which of the three were the ones he and Rose were working for.

CHAPTER 2:
THE TOWER, THE CITY

Jane loved to fly.

Everything else had begun to feel normal to her a couple of years after Doc took her from the farm. Learning to control the fires she created with her hands had been a challenge, as had mastering the developing power of her own senses — with each passing week, she seemed to hear further, to see further. Discovering that she was nearly invulnerable was much scarier than it was reassuring, and the tests she put herself through to check her own limits still frightened her. But flying, learning to leap off the pavement and into the blue sky, to feel the sun filtering through her skin and giving her strength, never got old, never felt scary.

To fly is to be free, she thought, just above the cloud cover, able to see miles away, skimming the clouds like a seabird skims the surf.

She flew straight up, made a figure eight, and plunged through a cumulus group.

Below, reality set in, but only slightly. The city, the silver and gray urban sprawl she'd come to call home, crept out in every direction. Millions of people going about their daily business, and here Jane was, flying fifteen thousand feet above them. She heard the blare of car horns, the sounds of music and television — even from above. If she listened carefully, she could hear babies crying, lovers fighting, street vendors handing out lunch to businessmen and businesswomen taking a break from the office.

So ordinary, she thought. I wonder if everyone wishes they could fly?

She dropped lower still, racing toward the Tower, the blue-silver building she and Doc called home. According to Doc, the first twenty stories were unoccupied, a façade to hide the nature of the building itself, which had, he told her, been home to three generations of super-powered heroes. It wasn't a building he explained, not really, but they'd always needed a place to hide, a place to look ordinary, a place to seem nonthreatening, and so they built the Tower.

A helicopter landing pad bristled out on one side far above street level. Doc said you could land a real copter there if you wanted to, but it had served for many years as the easiest access for flying heroes to come and go where pedestrians below couldn't see them. Jane landed, the thin soles of her sneakers squeaked on the strange asphalt-but-not-quite substance so much of the building was made of, and headed inside.

She found Doc in the "command center," a wide, sterile room dominated on one side by a monitor so large it felt like a home Imax screen. Several ergonomic, right out of a sci-fi movie chairs were lined up below, in front of computers ranging from so advanced that NASA would be jealous, to incomprehensible, inhuman designs Doc all but assured her did not originate on this planet. Her mentor was leaning back, his feet kicked out in front of him, very still. It took a moment for her to determine that he was, in fact, napping.

"Doc?"

Only the slightest of movements indicated she'd startled him. He smiled, worked his shoulders to stretch out the knots, rubbed his eyes beneath his lenses.

"Have a good flight?"

"Yeah. Have a good nap?"

"Didn't mean to. Got caught up in — well, you're going to see it all anyway. Might as well tell you now."

Jane waited for him to finish. He sat up and tapped out a few commands on the keyboard in front of him, one of the consoles that looked clearly human in origin. Perhaps a time in human history that had not happened yet, but human in origin, certainly.

A series of faces appeared on screen, biographical information

11

glimmered into existence beside each.

"How would you feel about some new folks in the Tower?" Doc asked.

"New folks?"

"You sick of only having me for company around here?"

"Heck yeah, you're crazy boring, Doc," she said.

He laughed.

The truth was, if she were going to be stuck learning how to control her powers with anyone, Doc was a great person to be stuck with — gregarious when she needed the company, quick to give her space when she wanted it, pushing her to try new things when she required encouragement — but, almost preternaturally aware of her limits. He knew when not to keep pushing.

But, if Jane were honest, she would admit she was lonely.

"It's too quiet in here. In the old days if we had fewer than five members at the table this place would feel empty."

Jane plopped down on a chair, one of the strangely curved alien designs Doc told her had germinated as coral on another planet. Not particularly comfortable, but she loved the look of it, how the surface felt beneath her hands, and so it became her favorite in the command center.

"Are they all like me?"

"No," said Doc. "All unique. Only thing they have in common is that they were all worth watching, mostly for their own safety. Most of them are very new to their abilities. They're going to be — "

"Like I was when I got here."

"Actually, you were, whether you knew it or not, already being groomed for this lifestyle. John and Doris couldn't teach you how to fly, but they instilled good things in you."

"Like knowing right and wrong?"

"That, but other things too. Empathy. A sense of responsibility. They just helped you become a good kid, Jane. And from there, a good person."

"So what you're trying to say is, some of these guys might not be good people?"

Doc let out a small huffing laugh.

"They're good people, at heart. We've been watching them long enough to know they're not bad apples, but let's just say some of them are rough around the edges."

"And you think you need to warn me."

"Let's put it this way," he said. "When I was first starting out, I would've appreciated the warning too."

Jane nodded.

"Do I get to come with you on your college recruitment missions to Hero University?"

"Sometimes," Doc said. "But this first one I think I should approach on my own."

CHAPTER 3:
THE DANCER

The girl is seven. She's known as Kathy Miller. She glides across the studio floor in perfect form, a tiny dancer on pencil-thin legs, her frail frame pale and hard.

She spins and spins. Her teacher looks on, impassive, arms folded across her chest. Suddenly, Kathy turns an ankle and falls to the floor, uttering a small cry.

"Ballet is perfection," the instructor says, her accent thick and from some faraway place. "You must be better."

"I am better than this," the little girl, the dancer, says. She rises to her feet, and begins to dance again.

The girl is now eleven and known as *Katie* Miller. Her parents look on from the audience as she performs, partnered with a young boy of surprising grace and strength. During the performance there are flaws — she can sense them, as all dancers can, as they happen, tiny imperfections her parents would not see, but her teachers would — but she powers through, on sheer will, the old ankle injury aching as it always does. It should seem odd for an eleven-year-old to have old injuries, odd that there should be anything old about her, but in her world, children grow old before their time.

The performance ends. She and her partner thank the audience, in the graceful way ballet dancers do. Katie's certain she can see her parents. This makes her heart swell.

Backstage, the teacher is upset.

"You will never be accepted to one of the great dance companies unless you are perfect, Miss Miller," she says. "You must do better."

"I'm better than this," she says, under her breath.

The girl is thirteen. Now calls herself Katherine Miller. She believes this makes her sound older. Her parents are driving her home from an audition for a school in Manhattan. They have high hopes. The instructor she auditioned with took her aside at the end of the audition.

"You have a lot of potential," she said.

"I am better than this," Katherine said, in return.

The car pauses at a red light. One moment, the street is dark and empty in front of them; in another, a moment of heart-stopping silence, before it is filled with men in masks. Three, five, it's difficult to tell in the shadows. They have guns.

"Step out of the car," the leader says. He has blond hair. Katherine will never forget this small fact. The mask muffles his voice.

Katherine's father looks to his wife, then to his daughter.

"Duck," he says.

Her father slams on the gas, plowing through the men in the street. Bodies hammer out of control against the cheap metal walls of the car. Blood, black as pitch, sprays across the windshield. There's gunfire; Katherine covers her head, crawls down to the floor and hides. She looks up once, just once, the very moment a bullet pierces her father's head. She'll never forget the image of her father, alive just moments ago, suddenly nothing more than a husk, an empty shell.

The car stops violently. A moment later, so do Katherine, and her mother.

Now fourteen, she calls herself Kate — doesn't have time for extra syllables. She spends her days in rehab, regaining control of her body. The crash broke her like a vase thrown against a wall; but she lived, her mother did not, and Kate often wonders which was the better fate.

She tires. The physical therapist tells her she can rest.

"You did good today," she says.

"I'm better than this," Kate says, and picks herself up to walk again.

Two days before her sixteenth birthday, she no longer cares what anyone calls her. Her scars have healed well, both because of what doctors call an unconquerable desire to get better, and because her parents left her with their fortune, and there was money enough for plastic surgery to hide the ugliness the accident left on her skin.

She's in a studio. For a different kind of dance these days. In rare moments of peace, she still attempts ballet, but these efforts are far more focused on mixed martial arts. She's thrown herself into combat with an animal ferocity. Her teachers though proud of her, advise she must temper anger.

"Nobody has ever won a fight in a rage," one tells her, an aging instructor who teaches her muay thai. "You've come a long way."

"I'm better than this," she tells him, and launches herself, again, at the red heavy bag.

The girl born Katherine Miller, now eighteen, calls herself the Dancer. She rarely rests. At night, she takes to the streets, behind a mask, claiming to be fighting crime. In truth, she's chasing ghosts.

Tonight, she fights a group of gang members, boys her own age, who play at being older, who act like children. The battered bodies of her adversaries lay splayed on the floor behind her, bones broken, eyes closed. Their leader's still almost a boy himself, the street's made him old before his time. He locks eyes with Katherine and can't see her face. She wears a mask now. It looks like a costume she might have worn on stage.

"You're going to need to do better than that to take me out, little girl," the man says. He flexes his hands. He has blond hair.

"I am better than this," she says. She feels the small, delicate bones in his neck crack when she lands a kick to the side of his head. She stares at his body, watches the small trickle of blood drip from his mouth to the filthy warehouse floor.

Katherine pauses, just a moment, confused that there is no satisfaction in this. She expected something more. Expected to feel complete. Instead, she feels empty.

"I'm better than this," the Dancer says. Suddenly, she's like a child again, like Katie Miller the ballerina, afraid of everything, afraid of nothing.

"You are better than this," a voice says. A man steps from the shadows behind her. He wears rose-tinted glasses and a long black coat. His hair is blue-white. He smiles at her — a smile so very sad that it makes her believe, for a moment that she's not alone.

"Who are you?" the Dancer asks.

The man steps forward, takes his hands out of his pockets.

"Doc Silence," he says. "I'd like to help you be better."

He offers his hand.

She accepts.

CHAPTER 4:
THE PARASITE

Billy Case had a problem.

And not some regular one, either. His friends — rather, the other delinquents he spent most of his time with, all had problems. But, they didn't have an alien living in their body.

If Billy Case — who was, on the exterior, one of the most ordinary teenage boys you might encounter, one part naïve, two parts petulant, a dash of self-absorption thrown in for good measure — were to tell you that he had an alien living inside him, you might laugh at first. He's pulling your chain, after all. And if he persisted, then perhaps you might begin to worry. Maybe he's chemically unbalanced. This must be a cry for help.

But if, by chance, you came across Billy Case in a back alley blowing up tin cans and cardboard boxes with small blasts of blue light flashing out of the palms of his hands like baseballs, then you might begin to wonder.

For Billy Case did indeed have an alien living inside him. And worse yet, the alien talked. A lot.

I don't understand why you insist on being needlessly destructive, the alien said.

It didn't have a name. Or rather, Billy asked the alien its name, and the combination of sounds and empathic thoughts that were returned was something he wasn't able to repeat. So Billy took to calling the alien Dude.

Dude didn't seem to mind.

You goin' to lecture me again, Dude? Really?

What did these inanimate objects ever do to you?

They offend me. The tin can is my nemesis.

You have no idea who your nemesis is.

Oh? I have a nemesis now? Billy asked.

He used to talk out loud when Dude wanted to chat, but Dude told him all he had to do was think the thoughts he wanted to say. Billy found this very disconcerting. Dude said he couldn't read all of Billy's thoughts, but he assumed Dude was lying. Particularly when it came to his ideas about Jennie Furtado at school. If Dude could hear Billy's thoughts, Billy figured his feelings about Jennie Furtado were pretty loud, and they were opinions he'd rather keep silent.

We have a nemesis, Billy Case. You and I, together.

This was news to Billy. After he got past the fact that he wasn't going completely bugnuts and there really was an alien inhabiting his brain — and that the alien had somehow granted Billy some pretty cool powers, like explosive light beams — they'd developed a decent working relationship. Dude could be a bit of a nag, but he was less annoying than most of his friends, and definitely less annoying than his mom, and Billy never asked why Dude had taken up residence in his brain.

I'm not sure I like the idea of a nemesis. Can we give him to someone else? Drop him off at the pound?

We will discuss this later. Your enemies approach.

This was something that Dude did that Billy appreciated. He seemed to have a clairvoyant ability to detect incoming trouble. He wouldn't warn Billy about the small stuff, like if he was running late for class, but things that threatened him with bodily harm were fair game.

Billy stopped blasting tin cans and leaned against the nearest wall. He thought he cut an imposing figure that way.

He didn't.

Three boys came around the corner. The Bender brothers were typical bullies: one too big for his age, the other undersized. One of them had been held back a year, but it happened so long ago everyone assumed they were fraternal twins. Their sidekick, a moon-faced kid named Nick Carney, followed on their heels like a loyal dog.

"Been looking for you, Billy," the smaller Bender brother, Kevin, said.

Billy had learned there are two types of bullies in the world — the ones who are big and mean and who would eventually grow up to be nobody in the world, and the other kind of bullies, who hurt animals and would, eventually, end up on the evening news for committing heinous crimes.

Kevin Bender was the latter type.

Fortunately his older brother, Christopher, was more benign and usually kept his little brother in check. Billy Case had seen some serious beatings dished out by these boys, but when Kevin caught you alone, there would inevitably be scars.

Billy was tired of being pushed around. He smiled and his eyes glowed with the same blue light the blasts were made of.

They're beneath this sort of reaction, Billy Case, Dude said.

Dude sounded alarmed.

They deserve it, Billy said. Have it coming. I should launch them into the harbor.

I will not allow it. I will cut your powers off.

No you won't, Billy said. You need me in one piece just as much as I do. You won't let them hurt me just to prove a —

Christopher Bender's ham-shaped fist clunked into the side of Billy's head. He staggered and stars formed behind his closed eyes.

You're such a jerk, Dude.

Christopher Bender grabbed Billy by the collar of his shirt and lifted him off the ground.

"Neat trick with the eyes," Kevin Bender said. "How'd you do it? You wearing contacts or something?"

"That's just my natural look," Billy said.

Nick Carney stepped up and punched him in the ribs, then looked at Kevin for approval, and the smaller Bender brother nodded. Nick clobbered Billy again.

Ok, Dude. You've made your point.

There was no answer. Christopher Bender slammed Billy against the wall a second time, as if for emphasis.

Dude?

Then Kevin Bender produced a knife from his pocket. It resembled something stolen from an aging kitchen — serrated, dull, cheap, a bit rusty.

All in all, it wasn't an instrument Billy Case wanted anywhere near his person.

I have changed my mind, Dude said.

A surge of electricity pour through Billy's limbs. He examined Christopher Bender's face and saw the light and shadows caused by his now-glowing eyes flicker around Christopher's eyes and nose.

Billy launched a bolt of blue light at Christopher's foot. The big kid cried out in pain and relaxed his grip on Billy, who then tossed a second blast right at Kevin Bender's face. The little sociopath flipped rump over teakettle, nasty knife bouncing away down the alley. Nick Carney watched all of this unfold and, with just a split second's hesitation, ran for the street, never looking back.

Christopher regained his composure and offered Billy a stare of wary threat.

Billy held up his hand.

The fight is over, Billy Case. You do not need to —

Billy tossed a light blast at Christopher's stomach. The air from the bigger boy's lungs rushed out with a heavy woofing noise. Kevin picked himself up and started to run. Billy pulled his arm back like a center fielder preparing to throw a base runner out at home plate.

Billy Case. This is unsportsmanlike.

He chucked a blue bolt of light at Kevin's back. The glowing ball lanced through the air like a comet gaining speed. Then, without warning, it swerved off in the wrong direction, splashing into a pile of garbage at the mouth of the alley. Refuse splattered everywhere.

I didn't know you could do that, Dude.

I did not.

A man strolled around the corner briskly, watching Kevin run away. He had one hand in his pocket; the other hung at his side, a halo of silvery light surrounding it. His hair was bluish white and he wore red-tinted glasses. He pointed directly at Christopher, then motioned over his shoulder with his thumb.

21

"Get lost, kid," the man said.

The bigger Bender brother wasted no time chasing after the little one. Billy wondered, briefly, if Christopher had even noticed Kevin abandoned him.

Dude, should we know this guy?

No.

Should I be worried?

Maybe.

"You Billy Case?" the man asked.

"Possibly," Billy said. He tried to strike a tough pose. Though his knees and hands shook once again.

It ruined the effect.

"I'm Doc Silence," the man said. He stuffed his other hand in his pocket and stared for a moment. "Why don't you tell your friend that I knew Horizon."

Dude, who was Horizon?

The alien did not answer. Billy felt panic, or possibly vomit, rising in his chest.

Dude? Who was Horizon?

. . . Horizon was my friend. We crossed the stars together.

So what should we do?

Again, the alien offered no help.

Billy tried to flash Doc his most charming smile. The act of smiling did not overcome the sensation that he might vomit.

"Um . . ." Billy said. Help me out here, Dude?

Ask him what he wants.

"Dude wants to know what you want."

"Dude wants to know?" Doc said. He smiled. "Okay. Tell Straylight I need his help."

Straylight? Is that your name?

We share it, you and I. It was. One of many. Tell the Doctor we will help him.

"Um, Dude says he'll help you," Billy said.

"Good."

Billy stood there for a very long moment.

"So . . . what about me?"

"What about you?" Doc said.

"Does this mean Dude's going to leave me?" Billy said. Of course he's going to leave me. Everybody always leaves.

I can hear you, Dude said.

Are you going to leave me? he asked Dude.

"He's not going to leave you, Billy Case," Doc said.

"So . . . ?"

"I guess what I should say is I need your help too."

"This is the weirdest day of my life," Billy said.

It will get weirder, Dude said.

CHAPTER 5:
FULL MOON

rowing up, Titus Talbot was afraid of the dark, convinced that around every corner there was something — usually a hungry something — with long, sharp teeth, just waiting to get him. His parents tried to convince him otherwise, but in the end, they were always strangely unconvincing, as if they, too, saw monsters in every alleyway, and that by lying to their son, they were simply delaying the inevitable.

Titus, now a teenager, was no longer afraid of the dark. He didn't grow out of that fear, nor did he find that all his bogeymen were myths and fairy tales. Rather, not long after his sixteenth birthday, Titus turned into a werewolf.

He hated people who complained about acne and body hair. They didn't sprout gray fur, grow long claws, and have their faces elongate uncomfortably into a lupine maw. Anyone who grumbled about their voices changing could simply get lost as far as Titus was concerned.

He hoped, after the first time, that it would be like in the movies — that he'd be able to predict the changes, chain himself to a wall, lock himself in a basement, anything to keep this entity under wraps. But, it turned out the movies were wrong. Two years living on the run had taught him that.

And this was why he could be found sprinting on all fours across a swath of woods on the border of Maine and Canada, tracking a buck by scent. He never quite knew what would set it off. If he got angry, hungry, frustrated . . . if he got lost. If he panicked, got scared, excited or startled. It only took a few accidental transformations before Titus decided his best course of action was to run like hell. He packed a bag and other things, figuring he'd be like that TV show from the '70s with the sad music and the lonely man with anger management issues.

Somewhere in New Hampshire, he lost his bag. He wouldn't say that the guy who caused Titus to wolf out on him didn't deserve it, but, well, Titus started keeping away from cities and towns after that event. He had no desire to have a body count attached to his name.

From a granite outcropping, Titus launched onto the fleeing buck; the creature's hot muscles spasmed when his claws sunk in and his teeth gripped its neck. He often felt like a spectator during these hunts, though he remembered them with more and more clarity each time. With no money and no home, hunting became his only way to eat.

He'd always been a steak well-done kid growing up and was more than a little glad he only barely tasted what he ate as a werewolf. It was like watching someone else eat on television. Strange enough to turn his stomach, but it wasn't scratch and sniff. Not yet.

What worried Titus was that he knew he could — if he wanted to — feel what the wolf felt. It was right there for the taking, if he'd only will himself to reach out and touch it.

Being a spectator was less disturbing, though. And so he let his other half run free. It kept him fed, kept him warm, and his other half seemed far more capable of avoiding human beings than Titus was alone. It was better this way.

Mid-dinner — Titus wished there was a way he could turn away from the corpse of the deer while the wolf ate, but he hadn't mastered that yet — he felt the wolf's body tense. Something was in the air, a scent, a sound, and the beast was suddenly on high alert. He pounced away from his meal, teeth bared, looking, watching.

From the shadow-shrouded woods, a figure approached, a man with pale blue hair, red glasses, a long black coat. He waved.

"Hello, Titus. I'm a friend."

The wolf growled. Titus tried to speak. Nothing happened.

He couldn't tell if the wolf was growling because he had tried to speak, or if the wolf was, of its own accord, threatening the man.

"I know you're in there, Titus. Why don't you come out and chat. I might be able to help."

Come on, furball, Titus thought. Let me out. Relax. Please. I haven't talked to anyone in months.

Instead, the wolf lunged. The man waved a hand; the wolf went sprawling. Titus actually felt it — a spark, like an electric shock. So did the wolf, who yipped and turned to run.

And they were off. Normally this was Titus' favorite part, the running — the whip of passing trees, the blurred world, the strong assurance in every step the wolf took. But now, he simply viewed it as a loss, putting distance between himself and the only person in months who knew his name.

And then, a girl with red-gold hair approached.

Just a girl. Slim, wearing jeans and a wool coat over a bright techwick tee shirt. The wolf charged her. Titus yelled at him to stop. Screamed at him to stop. Then screamed at her to move. He knew the wolf killed people before, but never like this. Titus understood what the wolf could be like when he — when they — were cornered.

The girl reached back and, with perfect timing, punched the wolf right between the eyes.

Everything blurred and went topsy-turvy. Titus felt the cold air of the world, felt the ground rush up to meet him, felt the wolf's body — his body? — slam into the dirt and stone of the forest floor. Oxygen rushed out of his lungs, then back in again. He listened for the wolf's growl, and instead, heard his own ragged breathing.

"I think I fixed him Doc," the girl said.

Titus looked up. A thin trickle of blood ran down his forehead into his left eye.

Doc materialized out of the shadows and smiled.

"There you are," he said. "You okay?"

"Everything hurts," Titus said, surprised at the sound of his own voice. "I'm sorry about that."

The man shook his head.

"No worries. Everybody has trouble controlling their powers at first. Your kind is especially troubled by it. But I can help you if you want."

Titus started shaking. He was cold — he hadn't been cold in longer than he could remember. The wolf must've shed the last of his clothing. He looked at the man, then at the girl. His face grew very hot.

"I — can we talk about this after? . . . Can I have some pants? Please?"

Doc took off his own coat and tossed it to Titus. It was long enough to reach the boy's calves. He stood up sheepishly and wrapped himself in it. The girl had, politely, stared at the ground to her left when he stood up. Titus was strangely relieved to see she looked as embarrassed as he felt.

Doc laughed. "Let's get you real clothes and some people food," he said. "Then we can discuss all the lies people told you about werewolves."

"Lies?" Titus said.

"Yeah, lies. Starting with who's in charge, you or the wolf," said Doc. "If you come with us, I can help you show that hairy bastard who's in charge."

He stuck out his hand.

Titus took it, shaking it like a grown up, man-to-man. He couldn't remember the last time someone talked to him like a human being, let alone like an adult. He couldn't help smiling.

"Can I get a cheeseburger?" Titus said. "I'm dying for something well done."

CHAPTER 6:
ENTROPY

Entropy Emily's super power was her ability to make a smart-mouthed comment. At least, that was what she always said her super power was, until the afternoon she started accidentally throwing cars on Broadway.

It happened that fast, too, the throwing of cars. She was jaywalking — that's what Emily did, because she was young enough to think she was both immortal and morally entitled to cross the street wherever and whenever she wanted to. Of course, the rest of the universe disagreed on both counts, and a small silver sedan driven by a woman in her thirties checking her text messages almost plowed into Emily at forty-five miles an hour.

Emily threw up her hands and thought, how did she not see me? My hair's nuclear blue and I'm wearing a neon tee shirt — oh god don't let that be my last thought on Earth. And then it happened.

She felt an incredible pulse of something, somewhere between adrenaline and nausea, wash through her and out her fingertips then suddenly the silver sedan and its cell phone addicted driver were flying through the air with the greatest of ease. Although the driver didn't seem to agree that this was either great or easy.

Emily waved her hands at the flying car as if to stop it, spouting words and phrases she would have normally avoided saying in front of her mother, and just as suddenly as it all started, the car stopped spinning and came to a stand-still in mid air. But then another car, its driver justifiably showing more concern for the airborne sedan than for the teenager flapping her arms in the middle of the road, nearly crashed into Emily as well. So Emily, being Emily, thought, well it worked last time, and flung her arms at the oncoming car.

This produced a slightly different effect as the car crumpled onto itself, dug into the asphalt, and flipped onto the street.

She remembered dropping the first car, which landed on yet another car — parked and unoccupied — and then she recalled having the wherewithal to run, which she did, because one of the cars exploded. Or something adjacent to one of the cars exploded, but whatever the cause, Emily was pretty sure they were going to blame her for this, so best start moving.

Except she had nuclear blue hair and a neon green shirt on, and everywhere she went people kept pointing at her as the girl who threw those cars.

The news helicopter showed up not long after that. As did the police cruisers. This was unfortunate, because Emily, displaying little knowledge or restraint in her newfound car-throwing ability, had begun using said power to aid in her escape, leaving a swath of destruction behind her that stretched over a mile and a half.

If your only tool is a super-powered hammer, well, then every problem looks like a super-powered nail.

Then, of course, her phone rang.

"That better not be you I'm watching on the news," her mother said.

"Of course not!" Emily said. Act casual, she thought.

"Because not only did I just see someone who looks just like you throw a car at a police helicopter, that same someone also has nuclear blue hair, which my daughter had been expressly forbidden to do to her hair."

"That's totes not me, mom!"

"The girl throwing the car is also wearing a skirt that is so short I'd have told my own daughter to get rid of it immediately. In fact, I'm almost positive my daughter owned that skirt until she allegedly threw it away a few weeks ago."

"Absolutely, positively not me, mom!"

A police cruiser spotted Emily and, with almost unfathomable recklessness, moved toward her at ramming speed. She waved her hand again and the car barrel-rolled sideways until it hit a fire hydrant. Water sprayed everywhere.

"The strangest thing is the girl with the blue hair on the TV is talking on her cell phone right this second, Emily."

"I gotta go. Love you mom mwa!"

Emily hung up. The phone began to ring again immediately, to the tune of the *Jaws* theme song — her mother's ring tone.

Police closed in on multiple sides. Another cruiser sped toward her. She manipulated her hands again, sending the car spinning like a coin through the air.

It came to a dead stop, though, when a flying girl with the red-blonde hair caught it.

"Oh," said Emily.

The girl with the red-blonde hair smiled at the officer in the car, who seemed slightly less terrified at being caught mid-air by a hundred and ten pound girl than he did the moment before, when he was simply in freefall. Emily thought that it was more than a bit ridiculous — she certainly didn't want to see what else a girl who could catch a flying car was capable of.

But, she was denied the opportunity to avoid just that, because, at that moment, a bluish-white bolt of light slammed into her. Someone hooked her under the armpits and lifted her into the air. Suddenly she was moving fast enough that catching her breath became difficult.

"Just trust me," a boy's voice said.

Emily looked up, gasping for air. The boy looked down. "Crap. Hang on, we can slow down in a few seconds. We had to get you out of there."

The flying boy — whom Emily decided looked like one of the dumbest boys she'd ever seen in her entire life, despite the fact that his eyes glowed vibrant white blue — soared upward and deposited them both on a rooftop. Emily glanced around. They landed at least one town away from where they started.

"What the frig was that?" Emily asked.

"Sorry. We needed to get you out of danger so Jane could talk to the press."

"Talk to the press?"

"Yeah," the boy said. "Look, if we left you there we have no idea what they would have done with you."

"Maybe I wanted to be arrested," Emily said, although in fact, her heart wasn't into it. She'd never been a hardened criminal, really.

"Sure," the boy said. "I can take you back if you want."

"Maybe later."

"Right. Anyway, Doc didn't want to have any of us talk to the press yet, but then you decided to start trashing New York, so we had to move the timeline up a bit. I'm Billy, by the way."

"Of course you are," Emily said.

"You going to tell me your name?"

"Emily."

"Welcome to the club," Billy said. The glow of his eyes died down.

Emily noted that underneath, they were a fairly ordinary shade of blue.

"What club is that?"

"The freakshow. I have some bad news for you, kid. You're a superhuman."

CHAPTER 7:
SUITS

Kate Miller sat incredibly still at the giant chrome table Doc asked them all to meet around. So far, she was both terrified and completely unimpressed by the collection of fruitcakes and small gods Doc Silence had been bringing back to the ivory tower his former team of heroes had inhabited. This table was that team's as well, with a giant emblem of a comet circling the Earth emblazoned on it. It supposedly stood for something. Kate pretended not to care. She exercised a blanket policy of pretending not to care about the past.

The first girl, Doc's little prodigy, was okay, Kate thought, looking at Jane with her from-another-planet red-yellow hair. Jane was polite, and humble, and made forays into friendliness which even Kate had to admit hadn't worked only because Kate herself was trying not to like anyone here. She regretted that a little bit. Jane acted a little too nice, a little too perfect, but the one thing she was the just the right amount of was genuine.

But Kate had no time for friends, even if they could fly and melt steel with their bare hands.

The human laser show was another story. Sitting at the head of the table with his feet up on the chrome, hands behind his head, Billy was neither nice, nor perfect — and certainly not genuine. Except for his powers. Kate already watched him in action in the training room. She wondered, not without a little jealousy, why an idiot like him got to walk around with the kind of trippy powers he possessed. He was also enjoying the whole experience entirely too much.

People shouldn't want to be heroes.

But speaking of people who didn't want to be heroes, Titus, coiled up in his chair like an animal, never looked comfortable. His eyes were always scanning for exits, watching body language, staring at you when you weren't paying attention . . . If he didn't seem so damned frightened all the time, she'd swear he was sizing her up to figure out how to tear her apart.

And then the new girl showed up. Younger than anyone else in the room, with more energy than a Chihuahua on a caffeine high, chewing gum and popping bubbles larger than her head in those rare moments when she wasn't talking about something inane, Kate had begun plotting to throw her off the tower roof just to see if she could fly, and hoping she couldn't.

It was Emily who broke the silence.

"So what do you think he's got in store for us? Field trip? We should go on a field trip," Emily said. "Disney. Disney would be rad, wouldn't it? Maybe not. I mean Space Mountain isn't as exciting when you can fly. Right? No offense Katie."

Kate steepled her fingers in front of her and stared.

Emily didn't take the bait.

"No field trip yet," Doc said, entering from the armored elevator that led to street level.

Billy claimed the elevator didn't exist entirely in this world. Everyone else thought he was full of crap, but Emily started floating away on her first trip in the elevator, saying she felt like she "weren't where I'm s'posed to be," and Billy smirked, saying "told you so," and it made Kate wonder all the more what the smiling little arrogant nitwit had inside him whispering in his ear. There was something in there, she knew — she saw him talking to himself all the time, and there was definitely someone answering him back.

"This is where we vote someone off the tower, isn't it?" said Titus.

Kate almost caught herself smiling, even if the joke wasn't anything to evoke a real laugh. The kid was so quiet, so inside himself, that to hear an attempt at humor from him gave the joke more weight than it actually deserved.

"Nope. Technically, this is related to leaving the tower, though," Doc said. "If you're going out in the field, you need to be better equipped. Jeans and Chuck Taylors aren't going to do much for you in a fight. C'mon."

Doc led them to another chamber, a big, airy laboratory dominated by a machine the size of a small car. A strangely normal-looking computer terminal stood at one end, and a tube large enough to hold a person in it stood at the other.

"We're being carbon-frozen," said Billy.

Doc ignored him.

"My friend Annie built this years ago," he said, gesturing to the machine. "Annie had . . . access to technology that nobody else could get their hands on. We called this thing the tailor."

Jane smiled.

"This made your costumes," she said.

"You got it," he said. "I want all of you to spend some time with it. Think about your powers, think about what you need to help keep yourself safe."

He pointed at Kate.

"The fabrics this thing uses haven't been invented yet. Light, durable, but if you add some extra layers they're stronger than Kevlar. Consider using that to your advantage, Kate."

She nodded. Kate had been wondering about what she could do to get herself on more equal footing with the bulletproof girl and the werewolf. A bit of body armor might be a good starting point.

Doc walked out of the room. "Day off from practice. Play with the tailor. We'll have show and tell before dinner."

They all stared at each other.

"I have no use for this," said Titus. "I destroy everything when I change."

Jane was already at the keyboard, looking things over. "Says here the material has a lot of wiggle room to expand with changing masses," she said.

"Sure. Werewolf in a body stocking," said Titus. "It'll be awesome."

"Suit yourself," Billy said, nudging in beside Jane. She swatted him and he backed off, before immediately trying to push his way in front of the keyboard again. "If you want to end every battle buckarse naked, that's your prerogative."

Titus paused, eyes narrowing at Billy. Then, his eyes darted in Kate's direction, and she saw his skin flush.

"I'll try to make some shorts I can wear under my street clothes," he said. "For, y'know. Decorum."

Kate hung back as the others entered the conference room one at a time. Suspended up in the rafters, aware Doc knew she was there. But he ignored her, letting Kate play her game. He hung out in his college tee shirt and jeans, eyes still hidden behind those red glasses he'd never take off. Titus walked in first, still wearing the same baggy jeans and checkered shirt he wore in the tailoring room.

"No luck?" Doc said.

In response, Titus tugged on the waistband of his pants, showing the top of a pair of black pants not unlike yoga shorts.

Doc laughed.

"Figured this was better than a werewolf in a tutu," the kid said.

"Good plan," he said.

Titus nodded, taking up his usual anxious perch at the table.

Jane sauntered in next.

Kate rolled her eyes. Of course she'd do this, Kate thought, looking at the streamlined confection of gold and red Jane created. The girl who could fly had turned herself into an emblem, with a long-sleeved, form-fitting top, the sleeves just a little too long. High red boots, perfectly functional yet somehow looking like something out of a rocket design schematic, on her feet. A cape, a goddamned cape, Kate thought, but diaphanous, red at her shoulders and fading into blue at the hem, slashed through like daylight. She'd added a skirt to the costume as well, which made Kate want to punch her in the mouth. Completely illogical, completely ridiculous, a cheerleader

35

move . . .

"Normally I'd say it's better to put function over form, Jane," Doc said. "But — you grew up around all those photos on the farm, didn't you?"

"Sure did."

"You look like one of the heroes when I was a kid, you know. They all knew the skirts were ridiculous, but they — "

" — knew they were symbols," Jane said. "They wanted to look like something. The form mattered."

"Well, give it a try for a bit. You can always have the tailor make you something different later," Doc said.

Jane nodded and sat down near the head of the table — always near, never at, Kate noted — crossing her legs demurely.

Then Emily entered the room.

Titus covered his eyes.

Jane blanched.

Doc laughed.

"What happened to you? Break the machine?" Jane asked.

"Bite me, twinkle-toes," Emily said. "I like it."

Emily wore a neon green top emblazoned, appropriately, with the nuclear hazard symbol in black and white. She had black pants contrasting almost appropriately with the green of her shirt, but the nuclear symbols, repeating down her legs in neon blue to match her hair, destroyed all subtlety. Massive, knee-high combat boots with too-thick soles that echoed back to bad fashion choices of the late 1990's covered her feet. Fingerless gloves — also black — with her apparent choice of personal symbol on the palms, gripped her hands. And, inexplicably, a scarf wrapped her neck, the most hideous scarf Kate had ever seen, striped in a barrage of bland, washed out colors. It was at least ten feet long.

Nobody said anything until Billy rambled in. And, he spoke for everyone.

"Holy crap, you look like a girl comic books threw up on," Billy said. "Is Eyesore going to be your hero name?"

"I can crush your heart with my brain, Billy Case. Watch your mouth."

36

"What's with the Gryffindor scarf? Hogwarts called, it wants its neck-ware back."

"You're kidding," Emily said.

"I kid not, Harriet Potter. You look like you're being strangled by ugly."

"This is the Doctor's scarf! How do you not know that?"

"A what?" Jane asked.

"The Doctor!"

"Who?" Again, Jane, the walking irony-free zone.

"I have a black hole where my heart should be! I am, in fact, bigger on the inside! Does nobody here watch — oh, forget it," Emily said, playing with a pair of steampunk style goggles resting on her forehead. "Can we make fun of what Billy's wearing instead?"

They all turned to look at Billy's costume and, strangely, there really was very little to make fun of. He created a streamlined suit of white and blue, with a half mask to hide his identity. The white piping was slightly reflective and would catch the light of his glowing blasts perfectly. He truly, bizarrely, looked like an actual comic book personality.

"I thought you were going to walk out here looking like a video-game character," Titus said.

"I've read comic books my entire life and though uniquely unqualified as a hero, I sure know what one looks like," Billy said. He flopped down in his usual chair and threw his feet up on the table again. The lack of comedy in his appearance took the fire out of the room.

No time like the present, Kate thought. She dropped from her hiding spot up in the rafters to the floor below.

"OMG," Billy said.

Kate felt a strange sense of pride that he said nothing else.

"You look like you could murder someone with your pinky," Emily said.

Kate's suit was all clean lines, taking on a slightly sci-fi look where extra padding was added over vital organs and soft tissue. The entire ensemble was made up of blacks and a very dark purple that looked gray in certain lights. Tungsten caps glinted on each knuckle and protected her toes, heels, knees, and elbows — all her striking points. The entire time she'd been playing vigilante she needed to be careful during fights not to chip an elbow or break toes or fingers. It felt good to be able to build in protection for all those breakable bones. She even added a paper-thin metal plate across her forehead under her own half-mask — she'd always liked throwing a good head butt, but it's a move with limited benefits if you knock yourself silly at the same time. Kate also built in a tactical belt and thin gauntlets on her wrists. The rest of the gang didn't need to know what she'd added there, though. She wasn't about to reveal all her tricks yet.

Kate didn't trust any of them enough for that.

"Doesn't look like she'd murder someone," Titus said, quietly. He looked at Kate with something that made her distinctly uncomfortable. Instead of his usual predator's glare, she could have sworn he was gazing at her admiringly — like she was someone to emulate. Kate broke away from his gaze so she wouldn't have to spend much time thinking about that.

"If we're all done staring at the angel of death over there," Billy said, sparing an extra glance at Kate's armored suit again, "Does this mean we're ready for our trip to Disneyland?"

Doc shook his head.

"If you're going to go up against your first supervillain, you should look the part, right?" he asked.

"I have a bad feeling about this," Emily said.

CHAPTER 8: DISTRIBUTION

Doc told them the guy went by the name Distribution because he thought it was funny. When Doc explained the guy's powers, it did actually seem a bit humorous. At least to Billy. He tried to get Jane to understand why he believed so, but, as he stood across the street from Distribution's base of operations in the rundown industrial complex just outside the city, he wasn't having much luck.

"He's got a power suit that uses kinetic energy to create super strength and stuff," Billy said. "And he's a drug dealer! Get it? Distribution? He's all distribution."

"Can you focus? Just for a little while?" Jane's eyes flashed sunset-gold for a split second.

Billy gave up. "Fine."

"Now," Jane said, approaching a black and chrome status symbol of a car parked in front of the building Distribution used as his home base, "We should get his attention."

Jane picked up the car by the front bumper then slapped it down on the pavement like a playing card.

Kate and Titus waited in an alleyway, watching Jane and Billy start trouble.

The plan was for the big guns to deal with Distribution himself, while Kate and Titus took out the goons who'd follow their target out the door. Kate wasn't happy about it, but just this once she'd let Doc's tactics slide. She hadn't kicked anyone in the teeth for some time, anyway.

They watched Jane treat Distribution's car like a beach towel. Titus laughed.

"It's time for me to get angry," he said. He looked at Kate and, for a moment, appeared incredibly young, almost vulnerable. "Sorry if I make a mess."

On cue, a gaggle of thugs, armed with small firearms and the occasional knife, stormed out the main door of the building. Distribution, wearing a full suit and fedora, strolled out behind them.

A fedora, for crying out loud, Kate thought, who does he think he is. She half-expected some big, melodramatic speech from the alleged supervillain. Instead, he kept it simple.

"My car!"

Billy and Jane sidestepped away from each other, waiting for Distribution's first move. The villain took off his suit coat and revealed the glowing wires and silvery armor of a form-fitting bodysuit underneath his street clothes. He reached back and pulled up a hood that protected most of his head in the same glittering material.

Watch this one, Dude said.

Billy nodded. He knew the alien presence would feel the gesture and read it appropriately.

Can we blast him?

We will have to try.

Then Jane leapt full force at the thug and punched him square in the face with a blow that would have shattered the average jaw.

Instead, Distribution laughed.

"You're kidding, right?" Distribution said, and backhanded Jane, sending her sprawling into a nearby wall. Bricks turned to red powder as she landed.

"Crap," Billy said.

Jane dragged herself to her feet and smiled.

"Just wanted to see if you could take a punch," she said.

Then, Distribution's men started shooting.

Kate watched Titus transform, then leap into action. One moment he was a scared kid, the next he was seven feet of gray and black fur with massive jaws. He bounded on all fours toward the gangsters. This was part of the plan, but Kate still felt guilty about it. Titus would approach first because standard bullets couldn't hurt him. She wore plenty of Kevlar, but every shot that connected would stun and bruise, lessening her effectiveness in the fight.

So Kate let the wolf lose some blood first.

She followed close behind, watching Titus struggle to control himself. It was a visible battle — he scooped one thug up in a massive claw and Titus flexed, then relaxed, the talons, so close to slipping them into the gangster's chest and piercing his heart. But, he threw him over a car instead. Jaws nearly latched onto another man's throat, instead they clamped onto his jacket to shake him like a rag doll. Every movement seemed just a hair's breadth away from homicide.

Then, it was her turn.

Kate fought like a dancer. There was no other way to describe it. Spin, leg extended, pointed, armored toes to a throat. Bend, twist, lift up, armored fist into solar plexus. Jump, one leg kicked forward, one back, each foot knocking a man silly with a blow to a temple. She spun and danced to a song only she could hear. Kate lost track of Titus to focus on her own fight. An arm pointed at her to the left; skip, roll, snatch a gun from a gangster's hand. Without pausing to aim, she threw that gun at another thug, not staying to watch when the pistol smashed into the bridge of his nose as if created to be used that way.

She leapt up, graceful as ever, to the roof of a car and surveyed the fight. Titus held a gangster in each hand. He smashed them together. Their bodies sounded like melons dropping onto one another. Kate saw a huge bowie knife sticking out of Titus's shoulder, a half-dozen bullet wounds in his back. If she waited a moment longer, she'd see those holes seal up on their own.

Titus stopped, looked at her, and howled at the moon.

"Me too, kid," she said, and kicked another gangster in the face.

Subduing a single supervillain turned out to be harder than initially expected, Billy thought.

Distribution and Jane went toe-to-toe for a few punches before she tried grappling instead. Billy wished Jane came to that conclusion earlier, however, as, with each pavement-cracking punch she threw at him, Distribution's suit seemed even more capable of throwing them back at her.

Of course, when Jane latched onto Distribution's wrist to try to take him down, she was completely, utterly, and annoyingly in the way of Billy's ability to send light blasts at the bad guy.

"How about a little help here?" Jane said, through gritted teeth. Distribution gripped her cape and attempted to shake her loose.

"Hang on," Billy said.

He pointed his finger like a gun and shot a light blast at Distribution's armor. Unfortunately, the spot he hit turned brighter for a moment, and then Distribution let go of Jane's cape and pointed right back at Billy. He wasn't able to see the concussive blast Distribution kicked back his way which sent him sprawling into a nearby car, denting the door permanently shut.

It appears his suit can absorb the concussive nature of our light beams, Dude said.

"No kidding."

"Are you talking to me?" Jane yelled.

"What?"

Distribution picked Jane up off the ground and tossed her at Billy. Both heroes tumbled. Billy was amazed at her solidity. It felt like getting hit with a marble statue.

"Hey Dude?"

I would not recommend another round of light blasts.

"I wasn't going to suggest that."

"It's really weird when you talk to your alien out loud," Jane said. Her cape flopped over her head and covered her face. She yanked it away.

"Dude, is there a way we can figure out where his power source is?"

"It's us hitting him, Billy," Jane said. She jumped to her feet and flew back at Distribution, striking him with a spear tackle that would have made a professional football player proud.

His power source is incoming kinetic energy. We know this already, Billy.

"Yeah, but it has to be stored somewhere, right? Is there a battery or something? A . . . thingy where the juice flows through?"

A thingy?

"You know what I — "

Without warning, Dude took control of Billy's eyes. Everything took on a sharp, blue-lit tinge, becoming crystal clear. Billy — or Straylight? — saw the energy flowing across the surface of Distribution's armor like trails of light. Up and down his arms, across his back, straight down to his finger tips as he threw another punch at Jane. It took a few moments — and letting Jane block a few more punches — before Billy saw a pattern.

"Got it!"

"Are you talking to me or him?" Jane yelled. She tried to kick Distribution in the groin, but the gangster turned his knee in time, winced a bit, then smiled as the additional kinetic energy surged into the suit.

"You're not good at this, are you," Distribution said.

"Hey Jane, can you hold him still for a minute?"

Jane looked Billy dead in the eyes.

"Are you kidding?"

Distribution threw a haymaker just then which once again sent her crashing into Billy.

"Holy crap, how much do you weigh?"

"Ask me that again, Billy, and see what I do to you."

Jane, relentless, got back up on her feet.

Billy grabbed her wrist.

"'Look," he said, quietly. "He's got a central hub for the energy the suit collects. Did you see that panel on the small of his back?"

"Yeah."

"I can try to blast it or something. If you can help me get a clear shot — "

Jane looked down at him and smirked.

"I got this," she said. "Distract him for a minute."

"Distract him?"

Kate wasn't watching the fight, but she knew Billy and Jane faced more trouble with the head thug than she and Titus were having with his peons. Most of them lay on the ground nursing broken bones. Just a few remained, all of whom had no inclination to save their boss. Titus closed in on one of the lingering gangsters, who extended a beast of a gun out in front of him. Little good it would do him.

"I'm not gonna let you kill me," the gangster said.

Kate wondered if she missed something in the fight, if Titus had gone too far. She hadn't seen any corpses, just a lot of injuries.

The gangster stared at the wolf for a moment, then looked at his gun, then back at Titus. And, quicker than Kate would have given him credit for, the gangster turned the gun on her and fired.

And fired.

And fired again.

The bullets hit her body armor like a kick from a horse. The wind knocked out of her lungs immediately. One bullet struck a hip and her leg went numb — the armor held, she thought, but down she fell, the shock of the impact knocking her over. That might have saved her life, though, as the last bullet — the one that almost hit her head — slammed into a shoulder, sending a flair of pain down her right arm.

And then she rolled on the ground. She couldn't lift herself back up in time to see what Titus did to the gangster for shooting her, but she heard it. It sounded like wet paper being torn to shreds.

Billy launched himself at Distribution in a cloud of white light. Instead of repeating Jane's tackle, though, he threw fistfuls of alien energy at the gangster's face. He wasn't sure if the suit would protect

44

Distribution or not, but it certainly seemed like Distribution himself wasn't convinced it would either, because he kept ducking left and right to avoid the beams. They weren't hard to dodge; Billy didn't really want them to land anyway.

"You know, I always figured it'd be professionals who came after me when this finally happened," Distribution said.

Up close, Billy noticed how young he was — the gangster couldn't be more than mid-twenties, not all that much older than the rest of the team. "Instead I get the teeny bopper brigade. This is disappointing."

And suddenly there was the smell of burning air, and Jane was standing behind Distribution with her hands on fire. She reached for the power core on the back of his suit, grabbed hold of it and didn't let go. The odor of warm air was overwhelmed and replaced by the stench of burning electronics.

"I think we're doing just fine," she said. And then she punched him in the face.

This time, he fell down.

Then Titus howled.

"Crap," Billy said.

Jane grabbed Distribution by the collar of his power suit and flew toward her teammates.

By the time Kate rose to a sitting position — there was no blood, the armor held, but things ached and throbbed under it and she knew they'd be bruises that would hurt for weeks — Titus was gone. She traced the trail of destruction where he'd headed — knocked over street lamps, claw marks across car doors, storefront windows smashed.

Jane landed beside her. She tucked the super-crook under her arm like a football. Billy followed close behind.

"What happened?" he asked.

I wasn't good enough, Kate thought.

"I got shot. And Titus went berserk."

"Berserk?" Billy again.

"The work he's been doing with Doc . . . wasn't enough. I think when he saw one of us get hurt he lost control. He's — "

"I'm on it," said Jane. She dropped Distribution to the pavement and threw back her cape, ready to fly off after the werewolf.

Kate grabbed Jane's boot and then struggled to her feet.

"No," she said.

"But he's a menace like this. I can — "

"I've got this," Kate said.

Jane tried to stare her down. It didn't work.

Kate looked at Billy.

"No argument from me," he said. "If you can soothe the savage beast, go for it."

Kate ran. Or, more accurately, limped aggressively, but she was moving, and each step got easier, as did ignoring the dull hum of pain down her right leg left from the gunshot. Titus howled again and the ensuing adrenaline boost chased away a little more pain. Soon, she was actually running.

You don't need super powers, she said to herself. You just need to be better.

Titus hadn't traveled too far — she found him cornering another of Distribution's goons in a parking lot, slowly advancing on him, jaws slavering, claws skittering across the pavement. Kate heard a deep hiss with each breath.

"Titus," Kate said.

The wolf ignored her.

"Titus, look at me."

A pause. Then the wolf turned. And for the first time, Kate felt truly afraid of him. She'd watched him in action and in the training room back at the tower, but she'd always been able to find the quiet kid behind the wolf mask somewhere. Now, though, the monster was in charge, red-rimmed eyes and huge white teeth. The better to eat you with.

"What's the matter with you," Kate said, trying to keep the fear out of her voice. Stay level. Stay cool. Be better.

The wolf stared at her. Through her.

"I'm okay, y'know," she said. "Look."

She held her arms out at her sides.

"In one piece. Right? . . . You can cut it out now."

The wolf crept toward her. And the gangster behind him took the opportunity to run like hell; in this case, she figured, that was okay.

The wolf reached out to her, slowly, with one massive, clawed hand. He rested one talon on the shoulder where she'd been shot, the touch incongruously gentle, those huge, golden eyes staring, slowly taking in the damaged armor.

The wolf dropped his clawed hand. And, as rapidly as he had changed before, slithered back into another shape, fur and claws disappearing so quickly as if they'd never been there in the first place. Titus stood before her, human again, in his ridiculous bike shorts, and smiled weakly.

"I'm glad you're okay," he said, before falling over.

It was only then that Kate noticed the knife he'd been stabbed with earlier still stuck out of his back.

CHAPTER 9:
INTERLUDE, THE STORM

She remembered her mother.

Tearing across the South Pacific, rain so powerful mortal eyes could not tell the difference between sea and sky. The way the waves rose like colossi across the surface, behemoths to wash away ships and structures. Those same waves crumbling buildings, huts and skyscrapers alike, evaporating all living things in her path.

Her mother had been beautiful.

But storms have short life spans, and soon she was gone, leaving her daughter behind, to find her own way, to raise her own hell.

Until they found her.

Now it was the daughter who tore across the night sky, opening the clouds, hiding the stars. She felt chained, though, prohibited, something held her back. In the center of her being she sensed it, a weight, a tiny voice, a desperate cry.

The voice spoke to her. It asked for help.

It pleaded for her to stop.

CHAPTER 10: LEADERSHIP

I still don't understand why you didn't let me go," Emily said. Jane had her back to the younger girl as she argued with Doc — well, Emily ranted and Doc calmly addressed her concerns, so it couldn't really qualify as an argument, but Emily could argue enough for two people.

Titus lay face down on a bed in the recovery room; Jane watched his skin knit itself back together again.

"Emily, what did I tell you about Distribution's power suit?"

"That it has something something with kinetic whatevers and then it blammo whammo stuffs."

Doc paused for a moment, staring at Emily before speaking. "The suit absorbed kinetic energy. Why would we send someone who has control over gravitational fields, little fine control over her own powers yet, and a tendency to hurl cars at people into a fight against a villain who uses kinetic energy?"

"Jane throws cars too."

"But she throws cars on purpose. If you stop flinging them by accident, I'll let you go on the next mission."

Emily stormed off in a huff, her ridiculously long scarf trailing behind her. When it got caught in the door on the way out, she was forced to attempt her dramatic exit a second time; this took some of the impact away.

"I won't send her out with you until she's ready," Doc said, sitting down next to Jane.

"I'm not sure any of us are really ready," she said.

Doc put a hand on her shoulder.

"Would you believe me if I told you the old team never felt prepared? We saved the day for twenty years and never thought we knew what we were doing."

"I still think we're actually not all set."

"You did fine."

"We almost lost Titus."

Jane kept her eyes on Titus's bare back. It was amazing, the way his body healed itself, even when he wasn't the werewolf.

"He has a long life ahead of him," Doc said.

"Not if we keep almost getting him killed."

"I mean it. Unless someone puts a silver bullet in his heart, that kid will live three hundred years, easy. His species lives for ages."

Jane looked up at Doc.

"Why doesn't he know? Nobody told him?"

He shook his head.

"I will, soon. When he's more used to what he is. In the old days, another one of his kind would have found him and explained things, but they're all gone. The good ones are no longer here. The bad ones are still around, but they're different. A lot different."

Jane stood up, walked to Titus's bedside, and pulled the blankets up higher to cover his back. The werewolf stirred in his sleep. Dog dreams.

"You really expect me to lead these guys?" Jane asked.

She saw her own reflection in Doc's lenses. She looked like a kid in a Halloween costume, not a hero.

"What about Kate? She's better at this. Older. She was doing the whole crime fighter thing before any of us — "

"It's gotta be you, Jane. Kate's very good, and you should listen to her, because she sees the world in a very different way than you do, and you'll need that. But, you're the one they'll admire."

"Billy and Emily and Titus? Billy doesn't look up to anyone, and Emily doesn't even respect you!"

"The world, Jane." Doc smiled at her. "The world will look up to you."

She shrugged and turned back to Titus, sleeping and sedated on the bed. What the world thought of her didn't seem very important at that moment.

CHAPTER 11:
GRAVITY

They hovered twenty miles off the coast, over the Atlantic, and about fifty feet above the water. Jane led the way, flying with one arm forward as always, a mental trick Doc taught her when he first took her from the farm. She hoped to eventually not need it, and certainly understood her powers were not dependent upon pointing a fist in the direction she wanted to fly, but it helped her concentrate and, she had to admit, it did make her appear more heroic.

Jane, while not vain, didn't mind looking heroic when she flew.

Billy performed the usual routine, that effortless drifting flight surrounded by the blue-white light generated by his symbiotic alien companion. Jane was a bit jealous, it came so easily to him, like having a built in copilot with "Dude" coaching him at all times. But she also realized that Billy was more dependent on the alien than he wanted to be, and Jane was already more self-reliant than him, and that provided fine consolation.

Watching Emily "fly" was even greater consolation.

Emily flew only in the sense that she remained airborne; this flight resembled more of a high altitude tumble through the air. She spun and drifted, yet was bizarrely able to keep pace with the others. To say it was a graceless endeavor would be an understatement. Rather, it was like watching someone in a particularly awkward freefall that never ended.

Finally, Jane put on the breaks; all three of them halted in mid-air. Emily stopped moving forward, but it took her a moment or two to cease drifting and spinning in place. Even then, she still moved awkwardly, pin-wheeling her arms when she started to tilt one way and the other. That ridiculous scarf had become entangled around her face during the journey and she yanked it away to reveal her absurd pair of steampunk goggles.

"You're a menace," Billy said.

He laughed, but it wasn't a mean laugh.

Jane had assumed Billy would act more like a bully, but he'd developed a fondness for Emily, and treated her kindly even when they traded verbal barbs. It was the only reason she invited him along on Emily's training flights because, in reality, Billy had little advice to offer.

"I'm not a menace. I'm the least menacing thing out here. I'm like a reject from the Cirque de Moliére," she said.

"Soleil," said Billy.

"Gesundheit," said Emily.

"Emily," Jane said. "How do you fly?"

"Badly."

"No. I mean, what are you doing, internally, to make yourself fly? Do you do anything specific? Focus on anything?"

"Pixie dust. I think about pixie dust."

"Stop it," Jane said. "I'm serious."

"I . . . " Emily said. Then she started listing to the left. Slowly, but distractingly, with that long scarf flowing straight down. "Crap."

"Let me help — "

"No, I got me, I got myself," Emily said.

Using the doggie paddle, Emily nearly corrected her slow descent to the left, but she overcompensated, causing her feet to rise up in the back. She bent at the waist; this did nothing to help, and then she twisted her body into a T shape.

"Downward facing dog. Plank pose . . . Name another."

Billy moved to help her, but Emily pointed at him threateningly.

"Back off, Billy Case. I said I got this."

He waved her off, laughing again.

"And for the record, I think of a bubble," Emily said.

"A bubble?" Jane said.

"Ya. I imagine a bubble of float surrounding me, and that's how I fly."

"A bubble of float. Do you ever listen to yourself?"

"Fight me, Billy Case," Emily said. "A bubble. Okay? I picture it and then I float in that bubble."

Jane reached out to help Emily right herself up, drifting beside her easily and grabbing hold of her shoulder. The moment she got close though, she felt her stomach drop, like on a rollercoaster.

And then suddenly it was Jane who was freefalling.

Spinning, arms flailing, brain not locking onto whatever faculties were required to get herself airborne again. Every rotation showed the Atlantic Ocean rushing up towards her, black and angry. In the back of her mind she knew it wouldn't hurt — I've been punched through a building, this is only water, calm down — but something about her sudden loss of up and down made her heart race. C'mon Jane, she thought, would you "up, up and away" already . . .

Then there was a bright light beside her, a strong grip around her wrist and she was no longer falling. Billy had a hold of her, slowing her descent.

"What are you doing?" he asked. There was, unexpectedly, real concern in his voice. "You're not doing your arm thing! Do your arm thing!"

"My arm thing?" Jane said. Then: "Oh, right."

And she pulled herself from Billy's grasp and started skyward again, toward the still pin wheeling Emily.

"What the hell was that?" Billy asked. He kept pace with her, neither of them at top speed. They wanted a moment to talk before they got within earshot of Emily.

"She thinks of a bubble," Jane said.

"A bubble of float."

"A bubble of anti-gravity," she said. "I've got an idea."

She parked herself mid-air facing Emily. Billy caught up and stopped beside her. Then strayed back a bit, watching. He seemed very glad to let Jane take the lead.

"A bubble?" Jane said.

"That's what I said. Did the fall have an adverse effect on your short term memory?"

"How big is it, Em?"

Emily shrugged.

"Five, six . . . eight-something feet wide. A big bubble. I fit in it."

"Think about a smaller one."

"Like four feet?"

"Little. A little bubble of light that you can hold in your center of gravity." Jane made a shape with her hands, like cupping a baseball. Like cupping a heart. "Think about a little ball of light in the center of you. That's the thing that carries you."

"Wasn't aware we were in yoga class," Emily said.

"You were the one practicing downward facing dog a minute ago."

"Now I'm doing 'really doubtful superhuman,'" said Emily.

"Just do it."

"Or else?"

"Or else I'll set your scarf on fire with my brain."

"Okay. I'll try."

Emily squinted, closed then opened her eyes, then rolled them at Jane, and then squinted again. She dropped a full foot and a half in elevation but stopped immediately, as if catching on a seatbelt. Then she was upright.

"Move around a little," Jane said.

"One thing at a time, Xena Warrior Princess."

But Emily complied, scooting a few feet in either direction, then drifting vertically.

"How does it feel?"

"Well I'm not seasick. Is that a good sign?"

"You're also right-side up," said Jane.

"Depends on your definition of right."

Billy looked at Jane.

She returned his glance.

"Guess there's one last thing to try out," Billy said. "Catch me if I fall?"

"Stop flirting with Thunder Girl and get it over with Billy Case,"

55

Emily said.

"Thunder Girl?" Billy and Jane asked simultaneously.

"Whatever. Do it."

Billy drifted up right next to Emily and put a hand on her shoulder.

"Hey look. No hands!"

Billy gave Emily a playful shove.

She squinted at him.

"Bubble."

Billy dropped out of the sky like a rock.

Jane and Emily exchanged glances.

"I can't make more than one," Emily said. "You probably should save him."

And Jane did.

CHAPTER 12:
THE FAILSAFE

Kate found Doc in the watchtower, a room with an entire wall of windows that looked down onto a gymnasium designated for training exercises. Below them, Titus transformed back and forth repetitively — from wolf to human and then back again. Kate took up a place beside Doc to observe.

It was difficult to watch, and not because the transformation itself was so violent, with the stretching of skin and impossible growth of teeth and claws. More painful was the change back to human. Titus was still learning to control the beast within; sometimes it cooperated and he flowed back to human form like liquid. Other times, he looked like he was engaged in an argument with himself, great wolfish snout snapping at the air as he fought for control.

But then, there were instances when it was an outright brawl, the wolf-man pounding fists into the ground and walls as Titus tried to interject logic and reason on the beast.

Kate examined this inner conflict as long as she possibly could. Her heart ached. Kate's entire life was about control. Witnessing her friend battle for it over and over again was almost unbearable.

Doc observed the process impassively, but as Kate began to understand him more and more, she discerned that he watched Titus not with a scientific curiosity but rather a paternal concern. He clearly favored Jane as he would his own child, but Kate sensed his attachment to Titus and the boy's condition was much closer to empathy than curiosity.

"So I've been wondering," she said.

Doc turned away from Titus and gave Kate his full attention. He always did that. If you asked for his consideration he offered it; this unnerved Kate. She didn't like anyone's complete attention. Especially now, when she planned to ask a difficult question.

"What can I do for you?" he asked.

"Why me?"

Doc studied her for a moment, waiting for more, not responding.

"You've got a sun goddess, a werewolf, a kid with a super-powered alien parasite, and a girl with a baby black hole where her heart should be."

"Quite the party."

"Yeah," Kate said. "And then there's me."

Doc nodded. He walked away and gestured for her to follow.

He led her out of the watchtower and down into a room that Doc's old team had once used as a debriefing area. His old team. They'd all retired, or gotten themselves killed, or flown off to another galaxy to solve some other world's problems. And left him here. Doc never said why. Kate had her suspicions, however. She hoped to run her theories past him directly, but the time never felt right, and it always seemed a little accusatory. Kate wasn't above harsh tones, but everything was too new and she understood she needed him on her side, at least for now. She needed all of them on her side temporarily. Whether that was something she'd always require was still debatable, though.

Doc gestured around the table.

Emblems were affixed on the different chairs in the debriefing room — memories of the costumes and symbols of his old teammates. He lingered longer on the one shaped like an hourglass.

"You're wondering why I chose you?"

"Yeah. I can't fly. Can't lift a car over my head."

"But you were a hero before anyone else here even knew they could be one," Doc said.

"I wasn't a hero. Technically, I was assaulting people without the sanction of law enforcement."

"You put on a mask and went out to try to improve things, Kate. Doesn't matter if you can lift a car over your head. All that matters is you wanted to make the world a better place than it was yesterday."

"That's debatable."

"Debatable or not, how could I ignore that kind of initiative? Self-taught, self-motivated . . . It's the ones who do it on their own who make the biggest difference. They appreciate the work more," Doc said. "Not that there's anything wrong with those who are born into something special, or come into accidental powers. But there you were, playing the hero all alone out there. I knew I could help you, and knew you could help the others here."

"Maybe I was better off on my own," Kate said.

Doc shrugged.

"Maybe you were. Maybe someone would have gotten the drop on you in some liquor store robbery and you'd have been dead by twenty. Who knows? That's not the timeline we're following right now. We're stuck with the one we're in."

"The timeline?"

Doc waved her off.

"Stuff for later. Let's focus on this reality first."

Kate sent him her most intense stare, then shrugged.

He looked at his hands for a moment, self-consciously, then back at Kate.

"There's something else, isn't there?" Kate said.

Doc nodded.

"Back in the old days, when we — my teammates and I — when we were young, something very bad almost happened, and we realized that we needed a plan. A failsafe."

"A failsafe?"

"If we ever lost control. Someone who knew how to shut us down. Who could be trusted with our weaknesses in case — "

"In case you ever had to kill one of your own," Kate said.

He shook his head.

"We hoped it wouldn't come to that. But we knew how to incapacitate each other. One of us always did, in any event."

Kate rubbed her eyes.

"And you want me to be the failsafe."

"Yes," Doc said. "You're the most logical of the group. You assess everyone. Predict their behaviors. Analyze their quirks. You are — whether you know it or not — deeply aware of the human condition. You'd be the first to pick up on it if one of the others went off the rails."

"What if I'm the one to go off the rails."

"You couldn't stand up to the others combined. That's your failsafe."

Kate thought about it for a moment. How do you stop the solar-powered girl? Were those werewolf myths about silver bullets true? Did she really want to know any of this?

Doc sensed her hesitation.

Of course he did. He seemed to know everything, most times.

"You can say no," he said. "The information can be a burden. Wouldn't blame you if you turned it down. But if you think you're up to the task, it's yours."

A soft alarm chirped, alerting them know to activity on the rooftop — Jane and the others returning, most likely. Doc turned to leave.

"Think it over. Plenty of time to decide later," he said.

"Wait," Kate said.

He looked back.

"You were once the failsafe, weren't you?"

He confirmed it with a nod of his head.

"Did you have to kill your friends, Doc?"

And then, he did something Kate had never seen him do before. He took off those rose-tinted glasses — eyes closed, not revealing the reason why he hid behind those lenses, but still, removing them from his face for the first time — and cleaned them with the hem of his tee shirt.

He put them back on and smiled at Kate — a soft, sad smile.

"Nothing like that," he said. "Something much worse."

"Worse than killing your friends?"

Doc palmed the door open in an effort to leave the debriefing room, then glanced back at her.

"Much worse . . . we gave up."

CHAPTER 13:
DISASTER

The first time Doc allowed Emily to leave the tower, it was for a humanitarian mission.

A storm crashed into the coast of South Carolina with virtually no warning. Jane went to bed one evening and woke the next morning to Kate shaking her arm, telling her she had to see the news reports.

The destruction was incredible. Houses uprooted, entire sections of beach and coastline washed away. Even stranger than the ferocity of the storm was the impact of the temperature — it snowed in many places, hailed in others, a bizarre wintery mix on the edge of September.

Jane surveyed the scene from above.

Emily loomed in from her right. An overturned fire truck dispatched on a rescue mission was now in need of rescue itself. A collapsed strip mall lay in the distance. "I got this," she said, unusually quiet, dropping those typical mall rat inflections. Emily extended her hand and lifted the fire truck entirely off the ground. With unexpected care, she lowered it back to the ground. The vehicle bounced on its shocks when the wheels touched down.

Out on the horizon, Jane made out the white streak of Billy's flight pattern. He worked on a nearby apartment building, surgically blasting open walls to free the people trapped inside. Nearby, on the ground, Kate scrambled inside to help victims or lead medical personnel to those she couldn't save herself.

"Jane," Emily said, pointing out over the water. A boat, some kind of trawler, listed to one side and started to sink slowly. Its crew waved at them — their arms a line of X's in orange.

"Got it," she said. Jane aimed her fist toward the ship and arrived there in seconds, trying to determine the best course of action.

"Will it float if I tip you right-side up?" she asked.

The crew didn't know what to make of her, staring blankly until one of them spoke.

"She should stay afloat," he said.

"Hang on," Jane said.

She grabbed hold of the ship and pushed, trying to nudge it back onto its belly. It was a strange process; she'd never attempted to move something of this weight without being able to use her legs to push with. She knew, logically, that she had the strength while in flight to accomplish this, but it took her a moment to figure out the best way. Finally, she got a running — or flying — start and flew at the railing. The impact of her shoulder against the highest point of the ship knocked it right side up again, though she then had to scoop up a few stray sailors who fell into the ocean with the velocity of her push.

"Who are you?" asked one of the sailors when she grabbed his wrist and flew him back onto the deck.

She smiled.

"Call me Solar," she said. It felt good to use the name. Safe. A code name was like a shield and a mask. It made her feel less like an ordinary person.

Rather than risk the ship sinking again, Jane offered them a lift, pushing the craft toward the nearest safe harbor. When they were close enough to dock on their own, she flew away, waving back to the thankful faces onboard.

Then, she heard Emily.

"Uh, help?"

It was unnerving to hear her through one of the small earbuds Doc distributed so that they could coordinate responses with each other. Emily sounded less distressed than confused, but Jane rushed to her side anyway. She found Emily holding two buildings apart, each one tipping slowly toward the other. Jane watched as the faint, heat-mirage-like shimmer of Emily's power encapsulated both buildings. She was having trouble splitting her focus.

"I've got the one on the right," said Jane. She paused before flying too close, afraid Emily's gravity bubbles would knock her out of the air again. Emily let her field drop and Jane leapt in, pushing the building back to a more stable location.

"That's not going to stay," Emily said.

"I know. I just — "

"This is insane," Billy muttered into his headphones. "I know it makes me a bad person, but I'll take fighting a guy in a super-suit over a natural disaster any day."

"Focus, Billy," Kate said. All business. Her voice reverberated. Jane thought she might be underground somewhere.

"He has a point, though," Emily said. "I can move buildings but I'm kinda not qualified to make sure they — "

Jane whipped her head around when she heard Emily cut off only to see the blue-haired teenager lift up a car with the point of a single finger. Underneath, Jane spied the squirming figure of an injured middle-aged man.

"Help!" Emily again, panic rising in her voice. "I don't know what to do!"

Jane rocketed down, landed beside the man, who was now bleary-eyed and unresponsive. She examined him, her solar-powered senses identifying all the injuries assaulting his body, but her very human mind, without any real medical training, at a loss for what to do next.

She launched herself back in the air and gestured towards Emily to remain with the injured man. Jane scanned the horizon searching for flashing red lights. Finally, she discovered an ambulance a few blocks away and raced toward the vehicle.

"I need help," she said, realizing how ridiculous it sounded, standing there in her super-hero costume in front of a team of EMTs. "There's a guy — "

One of the medics, a young man with prematurely receding hair, grabbed a duffel and held out a hand.

"Take me to him," he said.

Jane scooped the EMT up and transported him to the victim's side. She felt the medic's grip on her arm tighten, sensed his pulse rate skyrocket as they took to the air. When they landed, his legs wobbled, but he immediately tried to stabilize the victim. Emily, still there, sat in a childlike crouch, her steampunk goggles pulled down tight over her eyes.

"All kinds of heroes, huh Jane?"

"Yeah," Jane said. "Takes all kinds."

Titus's voice chimed in through their earpieces. They'd left the werewolf back at the tower to monitor news reports. While his strength in werewolf form might have proved helpful, the risks were too great to bring him. Jane imagined Titus sitting in front of the monitor alone. Even Doc had come to help. Earlier, she watched him turn a collapsed stretch of roadway into butterflies with a wave of his hand.

"Guys, you should see this," Titus said.

"Tell me there isn't another disaster area," Billy said.

"Report, Titus," Kate chirped in.

Titus ignored Billy and, as usual, responded to Kate. Jane saw a change in the forlorn werewolf since he'd been partnered with Kate in the field more often. He deferred to her, but Kate also spoke to him like an equal, which she rarely did with anyone else.

"You'll not believe what this," Titus said. "I'm looking at the weather patterns leading right up to the start of the storm. Have you ever seen a hurricane take a ninety degree turn?"

CHAPTER 14:
FOLLOWING THE STORM

o what you're saying is, the storm banged a hard right turn," Emily said.

"I don't know, just don't know," Titus answered.

Jane empathized with his tone because Emily was on still another epic tear of asking intentionally stupid questions. Titus was generally more tolerant of her than most of the others, but even he was approaching his wit's end.

The funny thing though, Emily was right: the storm worked its way up the coast one minute, turned a hard right out to sea and then, before the rest of the team had returned from the disaster zone, turned again, this time heading south and further out to sea.

It wasn't just unnatural, Jane thought, watching the meteorological map reflect this repeated movement over and over again. It seemed deliberate.

"Want me to follow it?" Billy asked.

"You're gonna follow a hurricane? Can we video that and put it online when you get struck by lightning?" Emily said.

Billy flashed an obscene gesture towards Emily.

She stuck her tongue out at him.

"We should track it," Jane said. "But I'm guessing we could do that from here."

Doc leaned against the back wall of the command center and watched them deliberate their actions — letting them make up their own minds. Jane realized, he wasn't so much studying their dynamics as much as allowing them to create their own dynamics. He nodded in assent.

"We have equipment that can track it and alert us to the storm's movement. That's easy," Doc said.

"Can that same equipment retrace where the storm came from?" Kate said.

She'd been standing quietly for so long that Jane almost forgot Kate was there. It was a habit the Dancer practiced that continued to make Jane anxious. Kate behaved like a ghost, until she started talking.

"I like your thinking, Kate," Doc said. "Go ahead and tell the AI to do that."

"How?" Titus asked.

Sitting at the command console, Titus wore a look on his face that made what he thought about a werewolf being the most computer savvy of the group abundantly clear. Jane suspected Kate probably knew more than she was letting on, and Emily spoke ISL (Internet as a Second Language), but Titus seemed the most at home with the futuristic gear Doc had provided access to.

"Talk to it," Doc said. "It's an artificial intelligence. My friend Annie brought it back from . . . elsewhere."

"Are you kidding me?" Emily said. She shoved Titus out of the chair and sat down, fingers wriggling like spiders' legs as she looked over the console. "Does it have a name?"

"*My name is Neal,*" a disembodied voice said.

Everyone except Doc took an involuntary step away from the computer.

"Wait a — you've been able to talk this whole time?" Billy said.

"*I've been online since you arrived, Designation Straylight,*" the voice said.

"Designation Stray — "

"*I am programmed to refer to all members of the institute by their official codenames only as part of security protocol 143.*"

"You're . . . the building?" Emily asked.

"*I am charged with maintaining security and monitoring the safety of all team members,*" the computer said.

Jane looked to Kate, expecting the other girl to flip her lid in anger. Kate had been private to the point of paranoia the entire time, and Jane was curious what her response would be to this invasion of privacy. The quiet girl smiled though — not a happy smile, but a sort of bemused grin, as if storing this information for future reference.

Billy looked at Jane.

"Did you know about this?"

Jane shrugged. She'd been there the longest, and Doc told her there was an artificial intelligence protecting the tower, but she hadn't had a chance to "meet" it yet. She was as surprised as everyone else.

"Do you watch us when we're in the bathroom?" Emily asked.

Of course she'd ask that, Jane thought.

"I do not monitor your mundane biological functions," Neal said. *"You do require access to the bathroom one point eight times as often as any other team member, Designation Entropy Emily. I suspect you have a smaller than average bladder."*

"I pee a lot. Don't judge me," Emily said.

Titus held his head in his hands, rubbed his temples, then finally looked up.

"Neal, would you kindly show us the storm's movement pattern in reverse, all the way back to its origin?"

"Of course, Designation Fury."

"Your super hero name is Furry?" Emily asked.

Titus started rubbing his temples again.

"Fury. We came up with Fury. On account of — "

"On account of you being furry when you turn into the werewolf. I get it," Emily said.

"You're doing this on purpose," Titus said.

"Hey man, if you want to call yourself Furry that's your prerogative. I would have gone something like Super Wolf or Wolf Man or — "

"You call yourself Entropy. Do you even know what that word means?"

"It's the degradation of the matter and energy in the universe to an ultimate state of inert uniformity," Emily said. "I have a black hole where my heart is supposed to be. I thought it fit."

Titus looked at Jane.

And, she shrugged again.

Kate burst out laughing, which startled everyone even more than the discovery of a talking computer.

"And you guys think I'm the crazy one," Kate said, shaking her head.

But Jane looked instead at the monitor, where the storm traced back to a stretch of ocean in reverse and then, very suddenly disappeared into nothing. She watched this happen three or four times.

"Computer? Neal? Can you play that forward again from the beginning?" she asked.

"Of course, Designation Solar."

This time, the storm blossomed like a fireball. The monitor showed clear sky one moment and then, in a blink, a full-strength hurricane setting off for the coastline.

"What the hell is that?" Billy muttered.

Jane, with the benefit of her enhanced vision, was able to see something the others could not — a small, dark mass at the center of the storm. It was easy to overlook against the backdrop of the topographical ocean map.

"Neal, zoom in on that island there."

"Island?" Titus said.

The AI complied, zooming in rapidly until the island filled the screen. It looked no larger than a city block. A single, nondescript building stood on the Eastern half of the island. The roof appeared to have been all but torn off.

"Is this before or after the storm, Neal?" Kate said.

"This image is in real time, Designation Dancer."

"Can you show us the section immediately before the storm, um, blew up?" Jane asked.

"Complying," the computer said.

The same building appeared on screen, with an intact roof.

"Keep going," Kate said. "At . . . a quarter speed?"

And before their eyes, the roof of the structure exploded.

"Great Googly Moogly!" Emily yelled.

"Looks like we're going to check out that place," Jane said.

Doc stood up and picked his black trench coat off a nearby chair.

"I'm coming with you," he said. "Don't want you on your own for this."

Kate stared him down for a moment.

Doc returned the gaze.

Finally, Kate said, "You're probably right."

Jane turned and headed for the roof to fly away. Behind her, she heard Billy muttering to Emily.

"Great Googly Moogly?" he asked.

"I'm workin' on my catch phrase," Emily said.

CHAPTER 15:
BEDLAM

From above, it looked like a giant had punched through the roof with a fist from the inside. Jane spied smoking machinery and broken walls, but when she tried to listen for signs of life with her amplified hearing, she heard nothing but dripping water.

Well, that and Billy talking to himself as he hovered a few yards to her right. No, not to himself, she realized — he was talking to the alien. She heard him muttering like this before, but this was the first time she'd paid attention long enough to realize it was a conversation.

"But I should be able to, right?" Billy asked. "No, not that. Will the shields hold? If I go under. Do I need . . . I know I can leave the atmosphere, so I'm asking, can I?"

"Can you what?" Jane asked

"I'm trying to ask Dude if I can breathe underwater."

Jane raised an eyebrow.

Billy shrugged.

"Why are you asking that?"

"Because I want to know if I can?"

"How come?"

"If you had the option, wouldn't you want to try it?" said Billy. "Can you breathe underwater? You can do everything else."

"I . . . Have no idea if I can breathe underwater."

"Let's try it."

"Or, we can check out this building like we're supposed to," Jane said. In the distance, she saw Emily catching up and Kate and Titus in view. She might be certifiable, but Emily was also a fast learner when it came to her powers — she'd already figured out how to expand or contract her gravity field in order to carry passengers with her. Although, from the look on Titus's face, it wasn't a smooth flight. Kate, as always, seemed impassive.

Jane drifted down into the gaping hole in the roof of the building, avoiding exposed pipes and crumbling mortar. Billy stayed close, raising one hand to light up the cavernous entryway. Doc, already there, sat lotus style on the floor and waited for them.

"I'm going to perform a scan of the building for mystical tampering," Doc said. "Give the place a good look."

"Mystical what?" Emily asked. "Is that like astral projection?"

He raised an eyebrow and then smirked.

"Close enough."

Doc closed his eyes, letting his chin rest on his chest. He appeared to be sleeping, but Jane sensed an alertness that radiated off of him like electricity.

"Come on," she said.

The opening was a living room sized hole punched through three entire landings inside the building. When they flew lower, Jane saw additional floors, doors opening into nothing, broken tiles where there once was a place to stand. She dropped to the first level, the only one left with an actual floor.

It was a lab.

A huge window had been fractured, instruments strewn all around, glass and bricks scattered. Past the now-empty window stood an open space, a large sphere coated in some kind of reflective tile.

"Think they kept something in there?" Titus asked, relieved to be on solid ground once again.

Kate walked the periphery of the room, head cocked, listening.

"Titus, how's your hearing when you're not wolfed out?"

He grinned.

"Not nearly as good as when I am."

She nodded.

"Just wondering."

"Does someone hear . . . banging?" Jane said. Her hearing, after

71

all, was always superhuman.

"Definitely banging," Billy said.

"Machines?" Jane offered.

Kate shook her head.

"It's rhythmic but not consistent enough to be a machine."

Kate took off into the shadows, disappearing from site; her night-colored body armor blended in with the darkness. Titus followed quickly behind her. Jane and Billy exchanged a glance, then shrugged.

"You want to try to tell her what to do?" Billy asked.

"Not even a little bit," Jane said.

Emily, who was scurrying after Kate and Titus already, turned back. "I'm frigging terrified of her," she said, before disappearing into the darkness as well.

Two floors down, they discovered a prison.

Perhaps prison isn't the right word Kate thought as she scanned the hallway. The rooms were reinforced, certainly, and the doors were meant to be locked by the appearance of their massive hinges and latches. A few looked like they belonged on a submarine. But the atmosphere — the colors of the walls, the hospital scent that still superseded the growing musty smell from dampness that pervaded the place — was much more akin to a psych ward.

In any case, the place was clearly abandoned; the doors were open. All but one.

Kate walked up to a metal door, which appeared more like the entrance to a bank vault than a patient room. The hammering definitely came from the other side.

Emily sidled up beside her.

"Bedlam," she said.

"What?" Kate asked.

"Bedlam," Emily repeated, pointing at the sign hanging sideways from a single screw in the wall. "Look."

Kate tried the latch, a circular handle designed to be twisted like a release valve. It wouldn't budge.

"Hey I've got an idea, let's open up the big scary metal door labeled with the word 'bedlam,'" Emily said.

"You don't even know what bedlam means," Kate said.

"A place, scene, or state of uproar and confusion," Emily said. "Also can be used as a synonym for a lunatic asylum."

Kate stared at Emily.

Emily flinched.

"What? You never read the dictionary? It's more fun than Harry Potter."

"I'll try it," Jane said, stepping up to the hatch.

"Uh, I'm with the pipsqueak on this one," Billy said. "The door isn't labeled 'puppies.'"

The hammering grew louder and louder. When she looked closely, Kate saw the door vibrating with each thump.

"Maybe you're right," Kate said.

At that exact moment Jane twisted the handle and they heard the hearty clunk of a massive lock sliding open.

"Got it!" Jane said.

And then the door flew off the hinges, propelling Jane — door and all — through the nearest wall. The entire corridor shook.

"Holy carp!" Emily said beside her, and Kate sensed rather than saw Titus fluidly transform into his werewolf shape. The room filled with the smell of outdoors: forest and mud. His low growl rumbled in Kate's ribcage.

"I'm okay," Jane's muffled voice said from the next room. She sounded stunned but not in pain.

"No you're not," said a new voice, from inside the Bedlam room.

Kate tensed, side-stepping to the right of the newly opened door to prepare to strike from behind.

Moving hydraulics roared, robotic feet clicked and thumped. And out from the debris walked a girl Kate's own age.

"Who the hell are you guys?" the girl asked.

At least she was mostly girl; a lot of her was robot, though, Kate saw instantly. Silver and black cybernetics hung below both her knees — nothing human left at all about them. One entire arm was the

73

same, but unfinished — where there should have been bicep and shoulder, exposed parts moved. The girl wore black shorts and a men's tank top, exposing a metallic ring on her chest that glowed neon green in the center. Her other hand was also cybernetic, but only to the elbow, and revealed a much cleaner architecture than her more robotic arm — it looked almost elegant, and human, with thin black and silver fingers.

It was her face, though, that concerned Kate the most. A very young face ravaged by science, her lower jaw encased — or replaced? — by silvery metal. Her right eye appeared organic, but the other was a glowing green bauble, surrounded by scars running crisscross patterns across her cheek and eye socket. Inexplicably, she wore her hair in a fluorescent orange Mohawk that had seen better days, shaved on both sides. A tattoo marked the left side of her skull.

Titus jumped.

The cyborg girl swung her all-robot arm at him, connecting with his head; the werewolf flipped in the air with the distinctive yelping whine of an injured dog.

"Em, now would be a good time," Kate said.

"To do what?" Emily asked.

Kate wanted to glare at her, but didn't think she could take her eyes off the newcomer.

"I've got her!" Billy said.

And with a streak of light, he football-tackled the cyborg girl and knocked her back into the cell. Or at least that's what Kate thought he was trying to do. Instead, he overshot his mark, and Billy and robo-girl crashed through the hallway, through two sets of walls, and out into the open sky before disappearing.

"Well, to do what?" Emily asked again.

We didn't think this through, Dude, Billy said.

You did not think this through. I had nothing to do with this decision. I would have advised against it.

They hurtled through the open sky, arms wrapped tightly around the very small frame of a surprisingly heavy cyborg. The entire decision making process was doomed from the start, Billy realized. He'd initially been worried for Jane — forgetting, momentarily, that she was invulnerable — but then Crazy Cyborg Girl walked out of her holding cell and Billy found himself at a very strange crossroads.

Wow, he'd thought to himself.

Don't you dare, Dude said.

"I got her!" Billy said.

This will end poorly, Dude said.

And then Billy tried to tackle Crazy Cyborg Girl. He wasn't sure exactly what he'd been planning to do with her when he caught her, but knew he had two goals — get her away from the squishier members of the team, and hopefully get her alone long enough to ask for her phone number.

Combat is not the time to be thinking about flirtation, Billy Case, Dude said.

Billy ignored him.

He carried Crazy Cyborg Girl as far as he could outside the building, wiping out a single tree at the base and crash landing on the very edge of the island. The wet sand almost made the landing bearable. As it was, it was still awkward, with Billy's limbs tangled up with Crazy Cyborg Girl's. They were both out of breath when they stopped falling.

Billy realized he was on top of her, and they were now face to face. So he did the only thing he could think of doing.

"Do you have a boyfriend?" he asked.

Crazy Cyborg Girl headbutted him.

This was not the response he'd been hoping for.

A few minutes later, Jane and Doc found them on the beach standing ankle-deep in seawater. The cyborg girl held Billy by the scruff of his costumed neck.

"I see you met Straylight," Doc said, his tone conversational, light.

Jane wanted to pick the cyborg up and throw her into the ocean. Her ears still rang from being hit with that door.

The girl tossed Billy on the sand in front of them. He groaned; Jane saw a small trickle of blood running from a cut above his eyebrow.

"My name's Doc Silence," he said.

The girl studied him.

Jane noticed the retina of that one robotic eye opening and closing, taking everything in.

"You're not one of them," the girl said.

"No, we're not," Doc said.

The girl glanced out at the water.

Jane's anger abated. The Frankenstein monster in front of her suddenly looked very fragile, and very sad.

"The whole place is empty?" she asked.

"Yeah," Jane said. "Abandoned."

A wrinkled sneer worked its way across the bridge of the girl's nose.

"Was I the only one there?"

"Didn't find anyone else," Jane said.

"They left me," she said. "Those bastards just up and left me."

"Were there others?" Doc said.

"Yeah. Not like me. Different. All kinds of different."

"Different types of cyborgs?" Jane asked.

"No, all kinds of different. Like you people," she said. "Monsters and freaks."

Jane heard footsteps in the sand. Out of the corner of her eye she discovered Kate walking slowly toward them. They'd left Titus under Emily's charge with orders for her to hold him in a gravity field if he regained consciousness in a rage. Jane offered to carry Kate down, but the Dancer refused. She made it sound like she wanted a moment alone, but Jane suspected Kate preferred to do her own search of the building with no one in tow.

"What you gonna do now?" the girl asked. "Lock me up like they did?"

"No," Doc said. "You're free to come with us if you'd like."

The girl studied him, her face hard, the shadows catching in her array of scars.

"Thanks for the offer, Doc. But think I'll pass."

"Where will you go?" Jane said. There was worry in her own voice that she hadn't intended or expected.

"I got by okay before these guys found me," the girl said. "Should be okay on my own after."

"But who were they?" Jane asked.

"Why, you gonna go fight 'em?"

"If we have to."

The girl grinned. It looked almost painful with all the metal attached to her lower jaw.

"In that case I wish I could tell you more, but . . . I don't know nothin'. All I remember before waking up here was the accident."

"Accident?"

The girl gestured at her body.

"I'm not exactly off the shelf here, girlie," the cyborg said.

"Solar. I'm Solar — Jane. My real name is Jane."

The cyborg girl smiled again.

"What was the name on my cell door?" she asked.

"There wasn't a name."

"What did it say?"

"It said 'Bedlam.'"

The cyborg nodded.

"Well that'll do then," she said.

"If you ever need us . . . " Jane said.

The cyborg turned to leave, and looked back. She winked with her one human eye.

"I bet you're pretty easy to find. Good luck out there, Jane."

Bedlam ran along the shoreline. Her robotic feet changed shape to better grip the sand and increase her speed. Then, suddenly, she jumped. As if the ground held no power over her, Bedlam lifted off and flew in a long, high arc over the water. Jane squinted, watching her with superhuman vision, when she splashed down a mile away, then took off again, landing and taking off a second time even further away.

Kate finally arrived.

"This was a research facility," she said. "Most of the records were destroyed, but there's signs all over the place in there, Doc. Bad things were going on here."

"I know," he said. He'd been watching Bedlam leave as well, but crouched down to check on Billy.

"Is he dead?" Kate asked.

"I'm not dead," Billy said. "Can head-butting someone be considered a type of flirting?"

CHAPTER 16:
CONTROL

gent Black guided the helicopter over to the secondary lab location without ever touching the controls. A single cable snaked up out of the control panel and plugged directly into a port behind his left ear. With that in place, he sat back and directed the wasp-like vehicle with his eyes and thoughts. The machine swooped in low over tall trees and found the landing pad tucked away on the western facing side of a mountain that wasn't much more than a glorified rocky hill. The late day sun shattered across the horizon as they swooped up and over the rocks; the dampeners in Black's cybernetic eyes kicked in and compensated for the glare. There were times when he missed the human ability to be effected by daylight. It had been years since he'd needed sunglasses.

They touched down. He looked back over his seat then unplugged himself from the chopper. Wegener, the scientist, appeared much recovered from the incident at the lab, a new pair of glasses on his face and the cuts and scrapes he endured during the escape treated and healing. None of this really mattered, though, as Wegener tried not to look at the looming shadow of Rose sitting across from him in her matte-black jumpsuit covered in assorted knives.

"Relax, Doctor," Black said to him. "We didn't ship any of the pet monsters to this facility."

"Just us," said Rose, smiling like a lunatic. She unbuckled Wegener. "Well, and one more monster, but you'll like her."

She dragged him from the helicopter; one hand dug into his hair to keep him standing upright. Black slid out of the vehicle and followed.

The entrance to the lab had been built right into the side of the mountain — two massive, Cold War era doors hiding all their secrets. Although the doors were open today, a squad of armed guards waited for them. These were Rose's boys, her ninjas, as Black liked to call them. Their employers hired both of them for a reason: one was muscle, the other a scalpel.

"The Lady wants a word," one of Rose's men said.

Of course the Lady wanted a word, Black wanted to say. She was the whole basis for them being called here in the first place.

They led Wegener through a long corridor, hewed rough and unrefined out of existing rock, to a massive freight elevator. Down six stories they rode — Black's internal sensors alerted him to the depth above sea level the entire way — and then they were walked into a strangely extravagant waiting area nearby. Soft couches, expensive rugs, even the art on the walls all felt incredibly out of place here, but they knew it had once been a corporate research and development location, and those mundane forces had left their accoutrements behind.

"I don't understand," Wegener said.

"Just because we're in a cave doesn't mean we have to be savages," Rose said.

"No, not the room . . . who are we working for? Who are we really working for?"

"There's always someone trying to take over the world, Doctor," Black said. "All we're hoping to do is make sure we're being paid by the side with the largest operating budget."

As he spoke, the Lady walked into the room, and, as always, all conversation stopped. Discussion always ceases when the Lady enters a room. She moved like royalty, even while simply clothed as she was today in a white button-down dress shirt and a knee-length black skirt. What she wore mattered very little. Her eyes glowed like lava and exuded a living trail of active flame so it was almost impossible to notice anything else. If you could look past her flaming eyes, she became the most elegant person you'd ever met — confident, regal, sharp-featured, and somehow mutable, as if her face changed slightly each time you stole a glance.

Don't steal too many glances though, Black knew. If you caught her at the wrong moment, sometimes you would see great gleaming horns, fanged teeth, and skin the color of sunburn.

The Lady was not their employer either, although she was much more than a simple hired pawn like Black or Rose. Agent Black didn't believe anyone could really hire the Lady. She traded in a higher currency than cash, which made Black wonder exactly what their employers had offered her to get her on board with this project.

"Natasha," Rose said, and held out a hand.

Both Rose and Black knew the Lady's first name, or at least the name she chose to be called. Neither were aware of any other way to address her.

The Lady took Rose's hand with an easy smile. Not for the first time Black noticed the family resemblance. They could be siblings, or mother and daughter. Rose's ease around the Lady convinced him there was some greater connection than money that joined them.

"Rose, darling. And my favorite professional murderer. Always good to see you, Agent," the Lady said.

Black's stomach performed a little dance; it was nearly impossible to be unaffected by the Lady's presence, and even harder to do so when she turned on the charm. For some reason, she was always complimentary to him, and flirtatious in a completely non-threatening way, and Black was never able to figure out if this was simply her way of being friendly, or if it was a means of manipulation.

For lack of anything better to do, he smiled and nodded an abbreviated hello. Complimentary and beautiful, still, she scared him to death.

Wegener held onto one of the couches to steady his legs. The Lady is something you have to prepare for, Black knew. He gave the doctor credit for staying on his feet. Again, it wasn't her looks — she exuded an air of power, something predatory and infinitely dark.

"You must be Doctor Wegener," she said. He nodded, mute. "You were the one who captured our pet storm."

"I — I was, ma'am."

"And the one who created the control methods that have been failing us?"

Wegener tried to speak, but his mouth emitted only a dry, clicking noise.

"Don't worry, Doctor. I'm not going to eat you. You've been brought here to explain to me how your control measures were intended to function, so I can help you bring them back online."

"You're a . . . scientist?" Wegener asked.

The Lady laughed — the sound of wind chimes.

"Oh no, my friend," she said. "I'm who you call when science no longer works."

The Lady draped an arm across his shoulder and led him out of the room. She turned back to look at Black and Rose.

"We're just going to talk privately for a bit. You'll both be here when we return?"

Black nodded.

"Lovely," the Lady said. She winked at him with one burning eye and left, leading Wegener like a cow to the slaughter.

"Are we going to be disposing of a corpse, or will she really bring him back?" Black asked.

Rose shrugged.

"Depends on whether she can understand what he tells her without opening up his brain. If he can explain his theories well enough, she won't kill him. She's not vindictive. She's just . . . "

"Efficient."

"Right," Rose said. "Did you see the surveillance footage from the old lab?"

Black nodded.

The Bedlam project had become an issue between Black and Rose. Rose wanted to put the girl out of her misery and Black, admittedly out of some sense of fellow cyborg loyalty, argued for keeping her online. The compromise was leaving her behind, but alive, as a kind of booby trap for whoever might come to investigate.

"Interesting group that showed up," Black said.

"They've got a dog boy," Rose said. "He's mine if we have a reason to confront them."

Rose never talked about her issue with shapeshifters, but it wasn't a stretch to posit a few educated guesses. Her missing eye, after all, was surrounded by scar tissue which looked remarkably like claw marks.

"They're kids. It'll be years before any of them is a real problem. The video looked like a bunch of toddlers in a bouncy castle."

"Silence was with them," Rose said.

"Yeah. You going to tell Natasha?"

"If she wanted to know, she knows already," said Rose. "He's always been her favorite problem. It'll be her who deals with him, not us."

"Not if we're caught without her in the field."

Rose sat down on one of the plush couches, kicked her legs up, and leaned back languidly.

Black followed her lead, choosing an armchair across from Rose.

"You worried?" he said.

"About Silence? Not at all. If he got the gang back together again they might be a challenge, but most of them are dead, off planet, or a hundred years into the future. They're not going to be a problem. You worried?"

Black leaned back and closed his eyes, the optics on the false eye mimicking the biology of his real one.

"I just think it's funny."

"What's funny?"

"That we're not the only ones trying to build a better monster."

CHAPTER 17:
A GAME PLAN

Whoever evacuated that base didn't do a great job," Kate said, dumping a broken laptop, a cracked external hard drive, and a pile of thumb drives onto the table in front of her. She was still in costume, although she'd pulled her mask away from her face. Only recently too, because Titus saw red-rimmed lines where the material dug into her skin.

Titus knew he had red lines on his face, also, but they were from the still healing bruises shaped like a cyborg fist. I've got to start fighting smarter, he thought. So far, I'm zero for two — a severe stabbing and a technical knockout.

"Bedlam told us she wasn't alone," Jane said. "Do you think they kept files on the other test subjects?"

"There were like, twenty rooms on that floor," Emily said. She'd wound that ridiculous scarf around her head like a peasant hood and sat in a chair, feet tucked up beneath her.

"I checked them all out before we left," Titus offered. His own voice echoed. Doc let him know that most injuries he sustained as a werewolf would heal quickly, but he sure felt like he was fighting off a concussion right now. "There was evidence of occupancy in only nine of them. "

"D'you think the storm has something to do with one of them?" Emily asked. "I mean like, is the storm actually one of the kids?"

"We don't necessarily know they were all young people," Doc said. "Bedlam left before we could get any more information."

"They were all kids," Billy offered.

The cut across the bridge of his nose looked miserable and raw. It made Titus feel a little bit better that Bedlam had gotten the best of alien-boy too and that he wasn't the only incompetent hero in the bunch today.

"How do you know?" Jane asked. "She didn't say anything about who they were."

"It was her tone," Billy said. "She was talking about her peers when she referred to other test subjects."

"You don't know that," Jane said.

"I don't know it, but I *know* it. Trust me," Billy said.

"Relying on your fellow-hoodlum instincts on this?" Jane said. Titus found her tone fascinating — she was, out of all of them, the least sarcastic, and the most even-keeled. Yet, something about Billy's behavior set her off. Titus wasn't entirely sure he liked it. As out of control as he knew himself to be, Titus appreciated the stability Jane usually brought to the table. The last thing they needed was her losing her cool.

"Forget I said anything. Sorry," Billy said.

Titus took a deep breath, not really ready to say what he had to contribute.

"I can't be a hundred percent sure, but I, uh, can track scents, y'know, when I'm wolfing out? And, um," Titus let himself trail off.

"You could tell by the scents in the room that there were young people locked up in there," Jane said. Calm. Kind. Understanding.

"Either that or they used really young staff," Titus said, his tone apologetic. "For what it's worth."

"You can smell people after they're gone?" Emily said. She'd gone bug-eyed, her nose wrinkled in disgust.

"Yeah, I can."

"That is fricken gross," Emily said. "And I thought my powers sucked. You really are cursed."

"Thanks, Em."

"In any case," Kate said. "I'd like to try to get whatever we can off these drives. I know a guy."

Doc smiled. He always smiled when Kate decided to make a

move on her own.

"Done. Go for it."

"I want to borrow Titus in case I need backup."

"Borrow me?"

"Fine," Kate said, flashing him a rare smile. "I'd like you to watch my back. Better?"

Billy started to talk, but Kate pointed intimidatingly at him. He shut up instantly.

"So what about the rest of us?" Billy asked.

"I suggest everyone else hang back while Kate works her angle," Doc said.

"That's cool, I've got a bunch of Netflix videos in queue anyway," Emily said, standing up.

Jane caught Emily by the scarf before she left.

"I want to see what's inside that storm," Jane said.

"Well I'm not going with you, so let go of my scarf, s'il vous plâit," Emily said.

"No way," Billy said.

"Why not?" Jane shot back.

"Because!"

"What? You worried about me, Billy?" Jane said. "I'm invulnerable, remember?"

"That is hyperbole. And, you can't punch a hurricane."

"Doc?" Jane looked at Silence, who was taking in the entire exchange.

"You want to try it, go for it," he said. "Don't go alone."

"I'm coming with you," Billy said.

"I'm watching TV," Emily said.

"The hell you are," Billy said. "If I'm her back up, you're mine."

CHAPTER 18: CULTIVATING SOURCES

It continued to amaze her how easily light and shadow could be manipulated. Kate did so with some success before she met Doc; but with her new gear and the time to practice, she was getting better and better at being invisible.

She stood in the corner of the small office after hours, waiting. Titus was playing lookout on the rooftop. It occurred to Kate that she didn't need him there — in fact, with his lack of practice on the sneakier side of things, he was almost a liability — but she found herself strangely reassured that he was present if she called. There are worse things than being able to yell for help and having a 250-pound werewolf come knocking down walls to aid you. But this shouldn't be a knocking down walls kind of night, she hoped. Finally, her target walked in. A young man, with the sort of good looks that Kate always thought of as PYT — pretty young thing — features, the kind that make for a good teen idol but would turn soft when he got old. Dark hair in a rumpled bed head. He looked tired, but that wasn't an affectation. She knew this man, and knew he worked too hard.

"Andrew," she said, from the shadows.

He startled in that jangling limbs way people do when they find they're not as alone as they thought they were.

"Holy crap. Kate, that you?"

"Yeah," she said, stepping out of the shadows and into the faint lamplight of the office.

Andrew was officially employed by a tech startup, but ran a

software business of his own in the off hours. Kate knew she'd catch him still there a half hour before midnight. It was working too much that led him to be mugged the night they met, out too late and too alone in the wrong part of town.

"Nice new uniform," he said. "You've upgraded since the last time I saw you."

"I had some help."

"Good," Andrew said. He sat down at his desk, still visibly shaken. "Not that I think you need help. Or just, well, I think everybody could use help sometimes. Even you, Kate."

"Funny you should say that. I need a favor."

"You're the reason I'm still walking around. Anything."

Kate slid the briefcase she carried onto his desk.

"How are you with retrieving data from partially erased and water damaged hard drives?"

"That's it?" he asked. "You know nothing's ever really erased."

"I'm better at kicking people in the head than fixing computers."

"I thought you were going to ask me to do something illegal. I mean I probably can't get everything off the drives for you, but . . ."

"I'm just looking for names. I think there's information about missing people somewhere in this pile of junk."

His face darkened.

"Missing people?"

"I hope. I could be wrong. Might be barking up the wrong tree."

"Why don't I give it a shot? It's worth a try."

"How long do you need?" Kate asked.

Andrew clicked the briefcase open and pulled out the external hard drive.

"Considering you just scared me so badly I almost peed my pants, I'll be up all night now. Want to find me tomorrow afternoon?"

"Done," she said and then stepped back into the shadows. Andrew watched for her, but she could tell by the way his eyes unfocused he couldn't see her.

"Huh," he said, starting to laugh.

"And . . . thank you," she said.

Andrew shook again.

"Holy! I thought you were gone. Now I'm really not going to be able to sleep."

"Just doing my part to help," she said. And this time, she really did disappear into the night.

Kate climbed up to the rooftop with spidery grace and found Titus waiting, the hood of his sweatshirt bracing the night's chill.

"He's a good looking guy."

"Yeah. Why? You interested?"

"That's not what I — I just mean. Is he your? Did you ever?"

"What, him? No. Who has time for a relationship? We're busy saving the world, Titus."

The werewolf nodded.

"Just curious. None of us really know much about each other, y'know?"

"Maybe it's better we don't," Kate said.

"Why?"

"Safer that way. Less chance of something bad happening to anyone's families."

"I guess."

They stood in silence for a moment. Kate couldn't read him, didn't understand what he wanted. She sat down on the lip of the building.

Finally, she said, "My parents are dead." Kate wasn't sure why; it just felt like the right thing to say at that particular moment.

Titus sat down next to her, a respectable distance, but facing the other direction. His feet dangled over the street below.

"Sorry."

"This is all . . ."

"You did this for them," Titus said.

"I did it for me," Kate said. "I wish I did it for them. I really do."

It was the first time she'd said that to anyone. The admission felt like an animal in the pit of her stomach, but she knew it was the truth. You should be better than that, Katie, she thought.

"Mine never looked for me," he said.

"You sure?"

"I checked," he said. "Even double-checked when I came to the Tower. They've filed paperwork for death in absentia."

"Already?"

"They knew."

"Knew what?"

"That I'm, well, this," he said. "I think they just realized that I was never coming home."

They sat on the edge of the building for a while, not saying much, listening to street sounds below. A plane rumbled invisibly overhead.

"I really want to find these kids, Kate."

"Me too," she said, still looking away. "Me too."

CHAPTER 19:
EYE OF THE STORM

They flew fast and low across the water, the waves kicked up a spray of Atlantic Ocean onto their faces. There was a competitiveness to it, Jane pulling ahead for a few seconds, then Billy, back and forth, with Emily hanging a hundred feet behind, not because she was slow, but because she, as always, didn't seem to care.

They noticed the storm on the horizon, blackened clouds laced with lightning. The manner in which the pouring rain churned the surface of the ocean was plainly visible, even in the distance.

"How do you want to do this?" Billy asked.

"Em, you hang at least a half-mile back," Jane said. "You're a good flyer but if anything happens you're completely vulnerable. Stay behind unless either of us needs you to come fish us out of the water."

"No complaints here," Emily said, snapping her bubblegum.

Her scarf hung strangely limp in the breeze, which meant, Jane knew, that the younger girl had already expanded her gravity field beyond the boundaries of her body for safety.

"You fly a perimeter pattern, Billy."

"What?"

"Fly around the edge of the storm. Try to get an idea of its dimensions."

"You're going in alone?"

"That's my plan," Jane said. "I'm the least vulnerable to harm and I don't think we should both be in there in case something happens."

Billy squinted at her — she could tell by the way his glowing eyes dimmed behind half-closed lids — but he didn't argue.

"Anything goes wrong I'm coming to find you."

"Anything goes wrong I won't complain," she said.

They took off, matched rockets, Billy leaving a streak of blue-white light behind him as he started a clockwise circuit around the storm.

And Jane dove straight in.

The wind blew surprisingly strong, not powerful enough to stop her from entering, yet forceful enough that she felt noticeable drag in her flight speed. What she had not anticipated was how bad the visibility would be. The rain was incredible and mixed with hail just past the start of the clouds, but it was the clouds themselves — black and gray and a sickly, smoke-like yellow — that caused the biggest headache. Jane quickly lost her bearings. She allowed her lead hand, the one she held forward as she flew, to become enveloped in flames, that horrible side effect of her powers she so rarely had reason to use. When that didn't help her cut through the morass, she set the other hand to burning as well. The downpour wasn't strong enough to extinguish either hand, but Jane felt the water fighting her, and sensed her own body fighting to keep that light blazing.

Billy believed the storm was messing with him.

He started out nearly at his top speed — or at least the highest speed at which he could convince Dude to let him fly — and followed the edge of the storm, just beyond the tendrils of soupy clouds. He arrived so close to the lightning he smelled sulfur in the air. But it was taking him far too long to run around the edge of the weather pattern.

Where are we, Dude?

The storm is a changing shape, Billy Case, the alien said. *Do not anticipate, just skim the edge like a circle.*

But this is a really big edge, isn't it?

There does appear to be intent. As if the storm knows you are trying to find the end.

It's leading me back to where I started?

Not exactly. It just seems to be creating ridges and patterns to slow you down.

Great. What do you think we should do?

I would push above the cloud cover and fly a direct path back to Entropy Emily. But I know you will not listen to me.

I'm going to fly in and see if I can find Jane.

Why do you never listen to me?

Billy stopped and hovered, watching the storm fluctuate and change shape in front of him. It did indeed appear to be messing with him, trying to delay his flight. He spoke into the tiny earpiece they all wore. "Em? Are you listening?"

"You sound like you're on the moon," Emily said. "What are you doing?"

"I don't know."

"That's not very reassuring."

"Have you heard from Jane? Jane, are you listening?"

There was a crackle of static, a muffled message, something that sounded like Jane, but incoherent.

"Do you need a hand?"

More static and echoing voices.

"That's it. I'm going in."

Jane understood, without a doubt, that she was completely lost. At this point she only knew which way was up because she'd feel her blood rushing to her head if she flew in the wrong direction.

"Jane are you listening?" she heard Billy say.

"I'm really lost, guys," she said. "Any ideas?"

She got a muddled, static-filled response back. She felt worry — not panic, but worry — building in her chest. Worse, she sensed her strength sapping. Jane had overdone it with the firelight and hadn't considered how much strength it took to stay in the air inside the storm, or how much energy she lost with the sun blotted out overhead.

At that moment, the tempest hit her.

It felt like flying into a wall, a head to toe slam against her entire being. Then it happened again, from another direction, and a third time. The gale battered her, turned her around and she had nothing to grab onto . . .

And then there was a girl.

Just for a split second, drifting through the mist, a girl, an ordinary girl in a hospital gown, with skin the color of storm clouds and hair the faintest of blue. She locked eyes on Jane, and reached out with one long, thin hand.

And soon, the storm swallowed her up.

"No! Come back!" Jane yelled, unable to hear her own voice above the storm's din. Another wall of wind hit her; her head grew fuzzy and light. How long had she been in here? An hour? Three hours? Ten minutes?

Finally, she heard Emily's voice on the transmitter.

"Maybe . . . should . . . straight up?"

Jane gathered her strength and aimed, she hoped, for the open sky.

"Maybe she should fly straight up?" Emily said. It just made sense to her. Everyone knew which way was up, right?

"That's brilliant!" Billy said over the transmitter. "Right Dude? Brilliant?"

Emily started flying skyward herself, trying to get above the storm. This was bull, she thought. Who fights the weather? Who considered this a good idea? Now they were down one hero with the other one lost somewhere over the coast of Norway as far as she could tell, talking to his invisible friend.

"Hey Billy and Dude. I'm flying up. Do you hear me? Up! Jane, can you hear anything we're saying?"

Nothing. Fine. Don't listen to me, Emily thought. I won't take it personally if they ignore everything I say, even if I'm always right . . .

"There she is," Billy said, and Emily saw her, except she was weaving like an airplane out of fuel, spinning and drifting on the air currents.

"She's tapped out, Billy," Emily said. "That girl is done-zo."

"What?"

Emily watched as Jane pointed her hand — not her fist like she usually did when she flew, but a grasping, outstretched hand toward the sky.

Not the sky. The sun. The solar-powered girl was reaching for the sun.

"Oh crap Billy she's really out of gas and I can't — "

"I got her."

There was a beat, just a moment, and Jane stopped rising, drifted, and then started to sink.

In the distance, Emily saw a flash of blue light so bright she was forced to shield her eyes.

Steady, Billy Case, Dude said.

Stop talking, Billy said. He aimed his body like a bullet at the red and gold figure in the distance. I totally have this.

Jane began to fall. Not complete freefall, she wasn't running on empty — he would swear later he saw her hand start to sparkle and glow as the sun hit her palm — but if he didn't pick up the pace their fearless leader was definitely going to plop back into the pea soup of the storm.

Billy altered his course just slightly, trying to predict Jane's descent into the clouds. Closer, closer, closer, close enough to make out her facial expression. He reached for her outstretched arm and grabbed her wrist just below the hand. He felt her hand — hot enough to burn his skin — a vice grip on his arm, latch on.

He had hold of her. But something tugged them both.

The storm.

Tendrils of cloud wrapped around Jane's foot and, somehow, took possession.

"Em, I need a little help."

"I gotcha both, Billy Boy. Air Emily is flying non-stop to get us the hell out of here-istan."

And the world let go of its hold on Billy. Not the storm, not some villainous grasping thing, but the Earth itself. He was weightless.

"Holy crap, Emily. Is this how it feels when you fly?"

"Kid, this is how I feel all the time," she said.

And she was there, a few feet away, smiling like a devil, looking like a hero.

"All the time?"

"It's a miracle I don't ever float away and never come back," she said.

"No wonder you're so weird," Billy said.

"Now you're starting to get it," Emily said. "Sh. Don't tell anyone."

Billy glanced down at Jane, still hanging onto his arm. His own wrist was raw; it hurt like a terrible sunburn, but only on the spot where Jane held on tight when she fell. She stared at him, smiling; but her eyes were sunken and hollow. She looked exhausted.

"Hey Em, take us up higher."

"How far ya wanna go?"

"As close to the sun as you can take us."

"This'll be a hoot," she said.

And she carried all three of them higher, above the clouds, above the haze. The stars seemed suddenly and uncomfortably close.

Dude, will we be able to breathe?

You were meant to roam the stars, Billy Case. You have nothing to be afraid of.

What about the girls?

I don't know.

"Em, I don't know if Jane will be able to breathe if we fly much higher. Will you?"

"I've always wondered," Emily said, her voice dreamy. "If I have a black hole for a heart, can I touch a star?"

"Can we not find out today?"

"Okay," she said. "Chicken."

Billy looked at Jane, drifting in the protective bubble of Emily's gravity field. Her skin shimmered like a disco ball, silver and gold glinting across the surface. She held up her free hand and made a peace sign with her index and middle finger.

"That's two," she said.

CHAPTER 20: DEBRIEFING

I'm telling you, there's a girl in there," Jane said.

"Are you sure?" Billy said.

"Why don't you believe me?"

They sat in the conference room with Doc, reviewing the crap show their storm investigation had turned into. Emily milled about, bored, trying to get the chairs to spin around as fast as possible.

"I believe you saw a girl," Doc said. "But there's a hundred things that could mean. There could be someone with inherent, natural powers like your own, able to effect the weather, but not able to control herself. It could be a supernatural being — you said she was colorless?"

"She was . . . she was like the color of storm clouds," Jane said. "Her hair was sky blue."

"That might mean she's something supernatural, if she were showing signs of not looking fully human," Doc said. "If werewolves exist, then you have to understand that there might be lot of entities you once thought were myths and legends. I've seen more than I can remember."

"'There are more things in heaven and earth, Horatio, than are dreamt of in your philosophy,'" Emily said.

Everyone in the room turned to look at her.

"You gotta be kidding me," Billy said.

"Think I don't know Shakespeare?"

"You act like you're semi-literate half the time, and the other half you're some kind of walking encyclopedia," he said.

"Whatever. I'm going to play video games. Call me when you need someone to mess with gravity."

Emily left, and Jane watched her follow through on her threat, plunking down on a sofa in a rec area across the hall.

"What you're saying is it could be anything," Jane said.

"There are a lot of possibilities, and we need to know more before we can do anything about it," Doc said.

"Considering what just happened, I think we can safely assume nobody's punching out the storm," Billy said.

"Maybe she's an alien symbiote. We could deck a symbiote," Jane said.

"Hey."

"I'm just saying."

"Our best bet, for now," Doc said, "is to see what Kate comes back with. Maybe it will help."

"And if not?" Jane asked.

"I suppose you'll get your chance to try to punch out a thunderstorm," Doc said.

CHAPTER 21:
TEST SUBJECTS

ate didn't bring Titus with her when she traveled to pick up the assorted drives from Andrew. Titus couldn't help but have a twinge of jealousy, but she returned quickly and strode directly towards him, bypassing the room where Billy and Jane were dissecting their trip to the storm front. Emily played a video game in one of the entertainment rooms, alone. She waved when Kate dragged Titus down the hall with her bag full of mistreated tech equipment.

They walked into the command center and Kate plopped down onto one of the chairs, clearly inspecting the console for something.

"Tell me this Star Trek nonsense has a USB port," she said.

"To your left, near the bottom."

Kate nodded and slid a new thumb drive into it.

"There wasn't much," she said. "But the funny thing is, Andrew told me, it looked like there was a kill switch on their computer that should have been activated if some specific protocol occurred. He said it was like intentionally putting a virus on your computer."

"They had a failsafe," Titus said.

Kate looked back over her shoulder at Titus, who felt as if he had said something wrong. Not having an idea what he might have done to upset her, he sat down in the chair next to her.

"Yeah, a failsafe," she said. "But remember all the water damage we saw?"

"Probably from the storm."

"Exactly. Well, a few of the machines — the laptop I stole, for example — were damaged by the water almost immediately. They basically became inert objects before the virus could be fired up."

"But if they were inert objects, doesn't that mean they'd be erased?" Titus asked.

"It's like Andrew told me. Nothing is ever really gone," Kate said. "Look, I don't know how he does this stuff. But he was able to salvage a few files. I mean, really, only a few. Not much to go on."

Kate investigated the excessively complex console again.

"Is there a friggin' mouse on here somewhere?"

"Track pad. Right there. It's hard to see."

"Dammit, I need to get better with computers if I'm going to do this detective stuff. I'm way behind."

"You're better than the others," Titus offered.

"Jane knows how to Google and Facebook. Billy can find dirty pictures online without accidentally downloading malware. That's about the extent of his abilities. And Emily, I found out, is some kind of part-time professional Internet troll."

"When does she have time to be an Internet troll?"

"In between sessions of being an antagonistic first person shooter videogame addict, I'm guessing. Did you see what she was doing in there when we walked by? Being a horrible person to people she'll never meet."

"She might need more to do with her time," Titus said.

"I'm not sure if that would make it better or worse. I swear she's posting on Reddit while we're on missions." Kate slumped back in her chair. "Anyway. Andrew found a few leads. Some names. One was a sociopathic teen-aged girl who barely survived a car wreck. Sound like anyone we've met?"

"I can offer a guess."

"And then there was this one," Kate said. She opened up a text file.

PROJECT DESIGNATION: Valkyrie Snow
PROJECT RATING: Partial Success

OVERVIEW: *Subject Valkyrie Snow was an attempt to merge a sentient weather pattern (captured off the coast of Norway [date redacted]) with a human body. Body acquired from Malcolm Height, MD, Miami Central Hospital — body belonged to Caucasian female, age 18, victim of hit and run, vegetative state. Appropriate bribes authorized for transfer of body and necessary paperwork to be filed for subject's legal death.*

Initial merging was a partial success — subject began manifesting post-human temperature/weather control abilities immediately. Storm abandoned body within seconds, however. Process to be examined for flaws in retention. Ideal situation would be a permanent merger. Concerns that the storm's mass, while transient, cannot be limited to single mundane body.

During phase two of the experiment, however, the sentient storm exhibited unexpected intellect and immediately made an escape attempt. Security was increased; several post-human mercenaries have been brought in to supervise.

Tracking implants have been placed in test subject's body, as well as electro-stimulation implants intended to use pain as a control mechanism should the storm remain in-corpus. By the request of management, we have also placed a cortex bomb in test subject's skull. Should all else fail, we can terminate the human component.

"Okay, maybe I'm a little slow, but . . . Sentient storm?" Titus said.

"You know as much as I do," Kate said. "I'm more concerned about the phrase 'cortex bomb' and the fact that it sounds like they bought a girl's still living and breathing body off of a doctor in Miami."

"We have to tell Doc."

"We do," Kate said. "But I was thinking — what if we went to talk with that Miami doctor first? We could see if he remembers anything about these body snatchers."

Titus smiled.

"We could play good cop, bad cop," he said.

"I get to be the bad cop," Kate said.

"But I'm a werewolf. I'm inherently bad cop by definition."

Kate flashed her most vicious smile.

"Okay," He said. "You're bad cop. But how are we going to get to Florida on our own? We're a little . . . sedentary."

"Weren't we just saying there is someone living in the tower who could use more responsibility?"

"Emily," Titus said. "But do you think she'll have a problem if we play the bad cop card?"

"You haven't seen what she posts online," Kate said. "She might be more evil than either of us."

CHAPTER 22:
VALKYRIE

Her name was Valerie.

She was born in a suburb of Chicago to a pair of pleasant if slightly boring parents; her mother was a realtor, her father an engineer, and they met later in life, and married later in life, and retired young, when they were tired of the harsh Illinois winters. They moved to Florida with their daughter, who was a teenager at the time, too young to stay behind, but old enough to resent them for taking her so far away from the life she built.

She acted up. She misbehaved. Nothing criminal, but often enough and recklessly enough that when she lost control of her car and drove headlong into a truck on I-95, there was more resignation than shock.

Her best friend, another reckless rebel, died instantly. Valerie ended up in a coma.

The oncoming truck and the flashes of pain and confusion during those first few minutes were the last things she remembered until this other being took control of her body.

She sensed the other presence, knew it was alive, but it never spoke. All Valerie felt was this creature's raw emotions: rage, confusion, loneliness. When she opened her eyes she saw only the black and yellow clouds of a ferocious storm, and sometimes the ocean beneath her, or flashes of destruction she knew the storm — that she — was causing.

But when she closed her eyes, she could see everything.

She was the eye of the storm.

And it was thrilling.

After the first few hours, she felt an agonizing electric jolt beneath her skin, inside her. It tore through her, all the way to her bones. It seemed to try to push her in one direction or another, the right side would hum with electric pain, causing her to jerk away. The storm never left her behind; if she pulled away, the clouds and rain went with her.

But the third time this happened, the other thing, the presence, took notice. She felt it turn its attention to the pain, and the next time the shocks began, she watched as the electricity was diverted from her body, out into the clouds like lightning.

And she heard a voice. Not with her ears. She heard it from within, some stranger inhabiting her own brain.

"No," the storm said.

"Who are you?" Valerie asked. "Will you let me go? What's happening?"

And again, the voice spoke.

"No," the storm said.

Days went by without another word. Valerie watched like a passenger in an airplane as the world flowed by.

And then someone was there in the storm. An intruder. Valerie called out to her, yelling for help, but she felt the storm fighting her, hammering her with rain and hail, trying to push her back.

"Let me talk to her!" Valerie yelled. "Please let me talk to her!"

But the storm pressed on, growing more violent; Valerie could feel the rage at this intrusion like it was in her own heart. She experienced something else also though, a thrill, a living strength as the storm built in her limbs, in her veins. She felt stronger than she ever had in her entire life.

And she was terrified.

Then the other girl appeared, dressed so strangely in a red and gold costume, cape flapping violently in the wind, her hands on fire, like torches held in front of her to light the way. They locked eyes. Valerie reached a desperate hand out to her.

But the other girl was swept away.

CHAPTER 23:
THE HOSPITAL

Kate performed a bit of research before their surreptitious flight from the Tower, and found that this Dr. Height had an office on the fifth floor of Miami Central Hospital. Emily flew them in with surprising ease and brought them to a soft landing on top of the building because Kate was positive they would have an easier time avoiding security if they broke in from the roof. With the hospital clocking in at six stories high, it also meant fewer floors to bypass while hunting for Height's office.

They landed. Titus dropped to his knees and all but kissed the ground.

"It wasn't that bad," Kate said.

"I rocked this trip," Emily said.

"I was convinced every time you got distracted you'd forget about us and let us fall," Titus said.

Kate refuted him. "Look, I only almost did that once and you barely noticed."

"You did forget about us!"

"I said almost!"

Kate ignored them and found the access door on the rooftop. Locked from the inside, she gave it a solid tug, then put her booted foot against the frame and tried to use her lower body strength to pull.

A familiar outdoorsy smell drifted from behind her. She turned to see Titus in werewolf form, those giant white teeth gleaming in the ambient light of the city. He looked ridiculous, the loose-fitting size-morphing pants Titus had taken to wearing (yoga pants, Emily called them) now stretched tight across the wolf's massive legs. He still wore an oversized hooded sweatshirt, but big enough that it simply appeared one size too small instead of ripping along his back.

"Teenage mutant ninja werewolf," Emily said, laughing.

The werewolf — Titus, Kate reminded herself, for she could see him looking back at her through those luminous wolf eyes — reached past her, grabbed hold of the door, then firmly gave it a yank. Kate half expected him to over-do it and alert the whole building, but he exhibited surprising restraint. There was a clank when some part of the lock snapped, and the werewolf pulled the door open the rest of the way.

"Um," Kate said. "If you can, maybe you should change back to human. You're a little conspicuous."

"You're dressed like Assassin Barbie," Emily said. "And you're picking on him for being conspicuous? I'm the normal one here."

"Titus, if you can't change back, it's okay — you can wait here. We'll come back," Kate said.

The wolf shook his head vigorously. Then, almost comically, one huge, clawed hand reached out and pulled up the hood fastened to his sweatshirt. It did hide his massive ears, but the grayish snout still jutted out into the open.

Emily started giggling.

"The better to eat you with, my dear!"

"That isn't even a little bit funny," Kate said. She reached up and gently adjusted the hood so it wasn't crushing his ears awkwardly, and draped it a little better to mask his jaws.

"That'll almost do. Just don't look directly at any security cameras."

Not that it really mattered, she thought. She was already convinced security knew they were there, and if they didn't now, they would within seconds. Emily did have a point. Showing up in costume wasn't their best idea, though it provided the fringe benefit of hiding their identities if they were caught. Emily's ridiculous steampunk goggles hid her eyes and, because of their size, half her face, and Kate's own mask was intentionally designed for anonymity.

They rushed in, sticking to the fire access stairwell until they reached the fifth floor. Kate stepped out into the hallway first, checking room numbers. Great, she thought. We came in at the wrong end of the building.

"Quickly," she said. She changed to her most confident walk and started following door numbers in the direction of Height's office. Behind her, Emily mimicked Kate in such a way that Kate began wondering if her confident saunter actually made her look like she was nursing a hamstring injury. Poor Titus shuffled along last, arms so long they almost reached the ground, his weirdly jointed werewolf legs bowlegged and awkward under the harsh hospital lights.

They reached Height's office door without incident. Apparently this area of the building was mostly administrative, with no wandering patient families to spot them.

"Follow my lead. We're going to rifle his office, see if he has any documentation we can use to prove his connection to the test subject. If we get lucky, he'll show up and we can ask him ourselves," she said.

"Keen, yo," Emily said.

Titus nodded.

Kate opened the door.

Dr. Height sat at his desk eating a sandwich, which he dropped onto his desk instantly — mayonnaise, oil and bits of lettuce dripped out onto paperwork below.

He reached for the phone.

Kate launched herself across the room, stepped onto his desk on the point of one foot, and punted the phone across the room with enough force to disconnect it from the wall. She then used that same foot to pin Dr. Height in his seat.

"Who the hell are you?" he asked.

Kate decided to try full-on vigilante mode. Her voice grew husky and she moved her kicking foot to his throat.

"You've been a bad man, Dr. Height."

"You can't do this."

Kate let the tungsten tip of her boot dig into his neck a little.

"You're going to tell us about the girl whose death you faked," Kate said.

"I don't know anything about — "

Emily started pulling binders off shelves along the wall with her mind. They spilled out onto the floor sloppily; more than once she left a dirty footprint on pristine white pages.

"Which files are for illegal dealings? Those in the red binders or the blue?"

"Stop it! Those are patient records!"

"There was a girl in a coma. You were paid to fake her death. Who paid you?"

"You're not the police. You've got nothing on me."

This wasn't working, Kate thought. A boot to the throat didn't seem intimidating enough. She'd need to figure out better ways to increase the fear factor in the future — maybe dangling him from the roof? For now, though, she thought of an easier solution.

"I may have nothing on you, but I do have a werewolf. Titus, come along and say hi."

After a deep, rumbling growl, the werewolf's weight — his physical presence — filled the entire room. Titus leaned in so close his saliva dripped onto the doctor's shirt.

"What the hell is that!"

"My friend," Kate said. "He doesn't play nearly as nice as I do. Entropy, close the door so Titus can introduce himself properly to Dr. Height."

Emily flicked a finger at the door and it slammed shut.

Kate grimaced at the noise, but had to admit it projected the right effect.

"Stop! Okay. It was a woman. Don't know who she worked for. They got me out of . . . I was in big trouble for something else."

"What else?" Kate said.

The doctor hesitated, but Titus growled again and he loosened up.

"Okay okay. I was about to get caught diverting drugs. Would have ruined me. They said they took care of it, but would take it all back if I didn't do one favor for them."

"So you sold them a teenager for a clean record." Kate jumped off the desk and grabbed the doctor by the collar, letting the fabric of his shirt dig into his neck.

"She was a vegetable! The family was having trouble letting go. I would never have done this to someone who had a chance of recovering."

Kate pulled harder, memories creeping in of her own hospital stay, of that moment of despair when she knew she'd never dance again. She might have sold herself at that moment if she could.

"What were they going to do with her?" Kate said.

"I never asked," Height said. "Just did what I was told."

"That is so messed up, dude," Emily said. "Can we throw him out the window?"

Titus made a huffing noise in agreement.

Kate hauled the doctor out of his chair.

"Give me something. A phone number. Name. An address. What do you know!"

"I don't have anything!" Height said. He was sweating through his shirt. "She had an eye patch! Like a something out of a movie!"

"What else!"

"She said — when I turned over the girl, she said they just might give her . . . an interesting life! That's all she said! I was convinced they were going to kill me too!"

A knock came at the office door. Kate shook her head at Height.

"Doctor? Security. You okay in there? We heard yelling."

"Don't," said Kate.

"Help! Help me!" Height said.

The door opened, and Kate threw the doctor over his desk and at the security guards when they walked in.

"You've gotta be kidding me," one of the guards said. He looked at his fellow guard, who stared, frozen, at Titus.

Titus moved.

Kate yelled, a barking "No!" thinking he was moving to attack the guards. But instead, the werewolf looped one arm around her waist and bound across the room, scooping Emily up with the other. He roared a challenge at the guard, a horrific, primal scream, and then ran for the office windows.

"Em, close your eyes!" yelled Kate.

Titus's massive body shattered the windows easily, sending all three of them soaring into the night air.

"Fly us, Em! Fly!"

"I can't I'm too busy peeing my pants. What the hell is he trying to do? Get us killed? Oh my gawd!"

"Shut up and fly!"

But instead of flying, she felt Titus's supernaturally strong legs hit the ground far earlier than expected, and opened her eyes to see they had landed on the roof of an ancillary building, only two stories below. *Only* two stories, she thought, werewolf boy can fall two stories and land on his feet carrying a couple of people. Not bad.

And then he jumped again, onto the side of a neighboring taller building. She heard his claws digging into the brick, finding or creating purchase in the masonry. Without using his hands, Titus hauled them quickly up the side of the structure. He ran towards the edge.

"Can you fly now, Emily?"

"No! Yes! Yes I got us!"

"You sure?" Kate asked.

"Ya!"

"Good, because — "

And Titus launched them off the side of the building as if he himself could fly.

Kate felt her body go weightless when Emily's powers took over. They stayed level for a few hundred feet, and then Emily regained her confidence and flew them higher and faster, both girls still cradled in his vast, furry arms.

"You can let us go now, sport," Kate said.

"No," Emily said, scooting herself up higher so she was almost sitting on Titus's shoulder. "I kind of like it here."

She wanted to argue, but instead, Kate settled in, letting their monstrous friend hold them tight while Emily carried them across the night sky and home.

CHAPTER 24:
WHAT WE KNOW

So let me get this straight," Jane said, as the entire team sat around the conference table. "You broke into a hospital and assaulted a doctor."

"Kate barely hit the guy!" Emily said. "Mostly just poked him with her boot."

Jane turned to Doc.

"We can do this? Is it cool? The assault thing? I didn't think we could attack people who didn't have it coming."

"Back in the old days, we all had methods," he said. "One of my best friends was fond of dangling informants off the roof of buildings to get them to talk."

"Did he ever drop anyone?" Emily asked.

"On purpose? No. But, he slipped, once."

"No way," said Billy.

"Accidents happen. In any case, I've seen worse. Scaring people into talking can be effective, but you have to be judicious about it. Your reputation will make or break you. Some people, like my friend, used that fear to his advantage, but he was never loved by the public, and that caused him a lot of problems down the line."

"What was *your* tactic?" Jane said. "When you needed to make someone talk?"

"Magic," Doc said. "And if I'm being completely honest, I think magic is a lot less ethical than using fear to make people talk. It's a slippery slope. I only did it when nobody else's methods worked."

"So, ignoring the fact that Kate is now officially our biggest bad-ass on the team — "

"I was there! I intimidated!" Titus said. "Growled, drooled and everything."

"That's practically cheating. Kate scared him with her voice and she doesn't have fangs," said Billy.

"Some might call it cheating. I call it using your basic assets," Titus said.

"Anyway — what kind of leads did you get?" Billy said.

"Well," said Kate. "Based on the information the doctor gave us and some medical records I stole — "

"You stole medical records?" said Jane.

"Are you worried about HIPAA? Jeez. I was going to put them back, but we got interrupted. Anyway, based on those, I think I know where her parents are. The girl in the storm."

"What's our next move?" Billy said.

"Someone should talk to them," Emily said.

Doc nodded.

"What's the point?" Kate asked. "They won't know anything about the storm."

"But they should know their daughter didn't die," Jane said. "They deserve to know that."

Kate stared at her, but Jane didn't flinch, the two locked eyes while everyone waited for their momentary power struggle to work itself out.

"Kate's right. They won't know anything, but they do deserve to be told what happened," Doc said.

"Who goes?" Jane said.

"I do," Doc said.

Everyone leaned back into their chairs. No one was interested in visiting with grieving parents, even Jane who had so strongly wanted them to know what had occurred. "I'll go. Emily, you'll come with me."

'Why me?" she said.

"Just a hunch. Don't argue."

Emily crossed her arms, anxiety flashed across her face.

"Someone should find Bedlam," Doc said. "If controls were put in place on the girl in the storm, she may be walking around with an explosive device in her head. Even if she doesn't want our help, she deserves to be warned, and the fact is, Bedlam's a walking weapon. If she's been armed in that way they could use her at any time as a living bomb."

"I'll go," said Billy.

Jane rolled her eyes.

Billy shot her a look.

"I was going to suggest that," said Doc. "Bring Titus."

"She punched me in the face," Titus said.

"She head-butted me and I'm not afraid of her," Billy said.

"That is due to all manner of reasons I have no intention of getting into right now," Titus said. "Why send me?"

"I got the impression Miss Bedlam related better to boys," Doc said. "She'll be less defensive around you two than around the others, which is what we need. We don't want to fight her — we hope to offer our help."

"We supposed to bring her in by force if we have to?"

Doc shook his head.

"Let her decide. Tell her we have the equipment here to scan for implants and the ability to help her if they're there, but don't force her."

"Got it," Billy said.

"What about us?" Jane asked.

"You and Kate should review the files Kate's contact was able to salvage. See if there's anyone else we ought to be looking for. Maybe we'll get lucky," he said.

Kate and Jane stared each other down once again.

"This going to be a problem?" Doc asked.

"Nah," Kate said. "We'll get along just fine."

CHAPTER 25: MOURNING

Their house was a small ranch in a small city twenty minutes outside Miami. The hard Florida sun bleached the streets silvery white and the walls were the color of a clear sky. The sun shone so bright overhead the entire world appeared whitewashed and dreamlike with distorted waves of heat.

Their surname was Snow. At another time, Emily might have thought that funny: the "Snows of Florida." But when she saw the dog in their window, a yellow lab searching outside for the girl who would never return home, the "Snows of Florida" didn't seem that humorous anymore.

The poignancy of that scene gripped Entropy Emily's heart like a fist. She bit her lower lip and thought about flying. It almost helped.

Doc asked her to dress down for this visit, so she dressed as normal as she was capable of, a tee shirt without a weird cartoon on it, cargo pants that hadn't ripped yet, a pair of Chuck Taylors that didn't glow in the sun. She wore her goggles while they flew, but even these she took off, looping them around her wrist, hoping they didn't appear conspicuous.

Doc looked like Doc. He still wore his long, dark coat, but he didn't seem to mind the heat. Emily wondered what it was like to have the kind of magic at hand to make the sun's warmth feel like a light breeze.

"Are you ready?" he said.

Emily attempted to say yes, but she had an odd sensation in the back of her throat, and her tongue felt slow and confused, so, without thinking, she grabbed Doc's hand. He smiled, that sad, kind smile Doc always seemed to revert to when he had nothing else to say. Emily half expected his smile to push her over the edge, but instead it made her feel safe. Doc sensed what she was feeling. He had no desire to knock on that door any more than she did.

But they walked up the flagstone path anyway, passed a neglected palm tree, an abandoned garden hose, and knocked.

Mrs. Snow was very blonde, with the fading tan of someone who had stopped spending much time in the sun. She answered the door with a haunted look, her eyes appearing older than the rest of her face. Mr. Snow wore that same haunted gaze, and Emily wondered if that was simply the look of someone who had outlived his or her child. Both seemed tired, unhealthy. Emily wanted somehow to touch them, to hold their hands or hug them. Instead, she stared at the floor.

"Can I help you?" Mrs. Snow asked.

She spoke with a light accent, something northern European that Emily couldn't quite place. Maybe Swedish, maybe Norwegian. Somewhere Emily had never visited, that much was for certain.

"Mr. and Mrs. Snow? We have information about your daughter. We need to speak with you," Doc said.

"My daughter's dead," Mrs. Snow said.

Her husband moved to close the door on Doc's face, and Emily watched Doc's fingers twitch, just a little, and the door stayed open.

"Your daughter was taken," Doc said. "I make no promises that she ever woke up from her coma, but I swear to you she was still alive when she left that hospital."

"But her ashes," Mr. Snow began.

Doc shook his head.

Emily watched the father's eyes dart around. Unsure of what to do, what to say, she grabbed Mrs. Snow by the hand.

"I'm Emily," she said and then looked into the woman's eyes. "May we come in?"

The couple sat on a cream colored sofa, hand in hand. Emily took up residence on a loveseat, alone. Doc remained standing.

"Who are you?" Mrs. Snow asked.

"Doc Silence," he said.

"Not the — " began Mr. Snow.

Doc nodded solemnly.

"I thought you were all dead," the father said.

"Most of us are," he said.

"But why you? What does this have to do with us?" Mr. Snow said.

"We're investigating missing children," Doc said.

Emily listened closely and heard Doc twist the truth just a little, to make it simpler, less frightening. He didn't say, "we think someone turned your daughter into something else." But instead, "We're just looking for missing kids."

"Some of what we've uncovered proves that your daughter was taken. She wasn't the only one," Doc said.

"But why our Valerie?" Mrs. Snow asked. "What possible purpose could taking her from us have?"

"I don't know," he said, softly. "The few we've found out about were all in terrible accidents. I'm not sure what that means. It might mean nothing."

"Do you think she's still out there?" Mr. Snow said. "What are you going to do?"

Doc pulled an ottoman away from a sofa chair so that he could sit directly in front of both parents.

"I can't say for certain what we'll find. Can't promise you that the people who took her haven't changed her, somehow, or if she'll still be in a coma if we find her. But I came here today because no one should have to live thinking their daughter is gone when there's a chance she's not. And I came to promise you that we'll do everything we can to find the truth for you."

The Snows looked at Doc, then turned to each other in unison. Mrs. Snow put a hand on her husband's shoulder.

"What can we do to help?" she said.

"An item of hers might help us find her," Doc said. "Anything. A favorite piece of clothing, a childhood toy. Perhaps a hairbrush?"

Neither Doc nor Emily glanced back as they left the house and took to the air together. They flew no more than a few blocks before Doc motioned for her to land. When they touched down in a small park, Doc sat on a bench. He looked more tired than Emily had ever seen him.

"You okay?" she asked.

"Damn it. I wish I could look people in the eyes," he said. "I'm tired of never being able to look anyone in the eyes."

Emily sat next to him. She knew she should do something, so she lifted a hand and hovered over his shoulder awkwardly for a few moments before touching him.

"Will the brush really help us find her?" Emily asked.

"If she's the storm, we're not going to have any trouble finding her," Doc said. "I can cast a very simple spell that should tell us if the girl in the storm is really Valerie Snow."

"Will it help us save her?"

"Probably not," he said. "Science and magic are funny. Sometimes they play together like it was meant to be, and sometimes it's like they work in two different realities. Hard to predict."

"Why did you take the hairbrush?" Emily said.

Doc rubbed the bridge of his nose, looked up at the sky and let out a heavy sign.

"If all else fails and she keeps destroying whole cities, we might be able to stop her with a lock of her hair."

"By stop her, you mean kill her."

"Yes," he said.

"We can't do that to those people," she said.

"When I say when all else fails, Emily, I mean when we have absolutely no other option. I want her to go home as much as you do."

"Have you ever done it before?" Emily asked. "Killed someone with their own hair?"

"I still wake up at night dreaming about it," Doc said. "Come on. Let's bring this girl home."

CHAPTER 26:
BEDLAM (AGAIN)

They found her on a beach not far from the town hit by the storm, a lone figure sitting on an outcropping of rock, debris from the hurricane still rocking in the soft ocean tide. Bedlam had wrapped herself in a parka three sizes too big to hide her mechanical arms. The entire effect caused her to look like a lost urchin.

Billy, still nursing a pair of fading black eyes from Bedlam's head butt, had no plans to let her fool him. Or so he hoped. He continued to formulate ways of asking for her number.

"There's your hot robot girl," Titus said.

They'd landed a quarter mile away in order to approach on foot, boots squelching in the wet, gray sand, both of them in their street clothes. Advance in silence, proceed in a low-key fashion, hopefully don't get head-butted again: this was Billy's plan.

"Hey! Bedlam!" Billy yelled.

"Hey! Sparkles!"

"I don't think Sparkles is a nickname that inspires a lot of fear," Titus said.

"Shut up," Billy said, and started climbing up the rocks. "Been looking for you."

"Here I am. Do I need to kick your ass again?"

Titus laughed.

"Titus, she knocked you out with one punch. Shut it."

"You're the wolf, then?" Bedlam said. "You're better looking the other way."

"I get that a lot," Titus said.

Billy pointed at a rock near Bedlam.

"Mind if I sit?"

"We're not going to fight again?"

"No."

"What if I head-butt you right now. Can we fight then?" Bedlam said. "Because I really want to punch something. A lot. I need to break things."

"Your anger management issues rival wolf-boy's over there," said Billy.

"I have a condition!" Titus said, slipping on sea slime while climbing up to meet them.

"Look," Billy said. "We come in peace. Just wanna talk."

"I'll give you three minutes. Less if you annoy me."

"You might have a bomb in your head," Billy said.

"What?"

"And so obviously, since you insist on slamming your head into things — namely my own face, I thought you might appreciate being warned," Billy said.

Bedlam turned her full attention to him. Billy heard motors whine and sigh when she shifted on the rocks.

"How do you know this?"

"We recovered some of the files from the lab," Titus said, finally reaching the top. He casually brushed the sand off his palms and sat down. "They installed cortex bombs in at least one other person as a failsafe in case they got out of control. Which, it could be then postulated, they did for everyone."

"You could be lying."

"Trust me, if there's one thing I don't lie about, it's brain bombs," Billy said. "If the bomb was in your liver I'd be making pâté jokes."

"I should punch you just for making that joke," Bedlam said.

"Don't fight him," Titus said. "He thinks you're cute and he won't try hard enough. You can fight me though. It's been way too long since I've really let loose."

"Really, Chewie?"

119

Billy threw up his hands.

"Don't! Fight! Dammit!" Billy sighed. "Look, we came to say we can try to help."

"You gonna perform brain surgery on me, Sparkles?"

"Doc says we've got technology back at the base that could remove the bomb. Or deactivate it. Or something," Billy said.

"Oh good," Bedlam said. "More lab rat stuff. I'll take my chances with the brain bomb, thanks."

Titus stood up and started to leave.

"Hey, don't say we never offered," he said. "You want to leave an explosive device in your head someone else can detonate at any time, that's your thing. I don't care. Billy's the one that thought we should warn you."

"I am!" Billy said.

You are not, Dude chimed in. The alien had been so quiet for the entire conversation that his voice visibly startled Billy.

"Having seizures there, cowboy?" Bedlam said.

Dude, Billy said, silently, don't embarrass me in front of my friends.

It was Silence's idea to warn her. It is dishonorable to take credit when it is not deserved.

I'm telling you Dude, we're just playing good cop, bad cop. I'm not being dishonorable, Billy thought.

I am inside your mind, Billy Case. I know exactly what you are doing, all the time.

And can we talk about how creepy that is, Dude? Can we? Because we should talk about how creepy that is.

"Seriously," Bedlam said. "Is he tweaking out? What's happening over there."

"He has an alien living in his brain," Titus said. "Sometimes they have disagreements."

"I'm fine!" Billy said, as Dude continued to snipe at him over what Billy considered a very minor lie. "But seriously. We came to warn you. And to offer help. We're not going to drag you back to the base and operate on you. But if you change your mind . . . "

"Yeah, we went through this once before," Bedlam said. "I know how to find you."

"Right," Billy said. "Well then. I guess. I guess we'll be going."

"Bye, Sparkles," Bedlam said.

Billy followed Titus down the rock formation slowly, looking back up at the cyborg girl as if expecting her to change her mind. She didn't speak again until they both reached the sand.

"She did all this? The storm girl?" Bedlam yelled.

"Yeah," Titus yelled back.

"She doing it on purpose?" Bedlam said.

"No idea," Billy said. "If I were to guess, I think she's just lashing out."

Bedlam laughed. It wasn't a pleasant sound.

"Yeah," she said. "There's a lot of that going around."

Billy and Titus walked back the way they came, Titus a full ten steps ahead of Billy.

Bedlam called out again.

"Hey. Thanks for the warning. Would've sucked if my head blew up and I didn't know why."

"Any time," Billy said.

But by then Bedlam had already turned her back on both of them, looking out at the water like a flesh and metal gargoyle.

CHAPTER 27:
HACKERS

Jane was shocked, or possibly appalled, when Kate suggested they bring the files back to Kate's apartment to give them another look.

"I'm sick of the tower, Jane," Kate said, packing up as if their departure was a foregone conclusion. "I can't think here right now."

"I can. In fact, I prefer to think here."

"I need to get out. You can come with me or I can go alone. Your call, Sunbeam."

"Sunbeam?"

"Let's go."

A half hour later they were sitting on the floor of Kate's little flat, reviewing notes, and tossing theories at each other. For a brief moment, Jane thought they might even be getting along.

"What if it's some evil version of Doc, building his own super-villain team?" Kate said.

"An evil Doc? Like, his evil twin?"

"That's the stupidest thing I've ever heard," she said.

"We hang out with alien-boy, werewolf boy, and gravity girl, and you're going to tell me 'evil twin' is a stupid idea?"

"Good point," said Kate. "But I meant that this might be someone like him, a relic from a bygone era before the super-powered folks went off the radar, someone who's trying to bring back the good old days. Or the bad old days, if we're talking about a villain."

"That . . . makes a lot of sense," said Jane. "Do you think Doc had an idea something like that would happen? Maybe that's why he decided to bring us all together now?"

Kate shook her head.

"I think Doc always thought something bad could happen. But really, I think he picked now to bring us together because we're the right age. Old enough to go out there — "

"But young enough to make sure we don't go bad," Jane said. "That's why he took Emily so young you know."

"Because she's a menace to society if left to her own devices?"

"Because he was afraid someone else might try to turn her into a weapon."

"Thanks for the nightmare material, Jane."

"You're welcome."

They paused, shuffled some printouts around, and Kate pulled a laptop they had liberated from the tower's office in front of her.

"Let's review some of the files on here that weren't personnel documents," Kate said. "Maybe there's something we missed."

They spent a while opening up different files of exotic types, finding indecipherable pages of code. Eventually they discovered an .exe or exec file.

"Wonder what happens when we click that?" Jane said.

"In the history of computers, nothing good ever comes from clicking on executable files," Kate said.

"Maybe we should."

"Oh yes, let's click an executable file discovered on a super-villain's hard drive. It's probably a virus that will destroy the Internet for the entire planet."

"Or, it's something that could lead us back to the people we're searching for."

"How?"

"What's the worst that could happen? The tower has a hundred of these laptops. If it's a virus it ruins the laptop. It's probably just a version of the same virus that destroyed all the computers at the lab site," Jane said. "Might be interesting to see what it does to this super mojo futuristic laptop, right?"

Kate squinted at her.

"I know this is a terrible idea, but you're piquing my curiosity, and I haven't seen you play the devil's advocate before," Kate said. "This might be an opportunity we shouldn't miss."

"Want to do it?"

"Of course."

"What are we waiting for?" Jane asked.

"Wait just a — hang on."

Kate tapped out a message on her phone quickly then set it aside.

"What did you do?" Jane said.

"Sent a text message to Titus saying we were about to do something really stupid and if he doesn't hear from me in ten minutes to send a lot of help."

Jane nodded.

"Good plan. On three?"

"One, two, three."

Kate double-clicked the executable file.

They both sat back and watched. Kate held up her phone, aimed it at the computer screen, and Jane saw that she was recording video.

"Just in case — oh crap," Kate said.

A symbol appeared on screen, a cross between a skull and an octopus, in a deep, royal purple. It started to blink.

"Knew this was a bad idea," Kate said.

She stood up and began to unbutton her shirt, revealing the armor underneath. She empted the contents of a knapsack onto the floor; out spilled gloves, boots, and a utility belt. Kate started pulling each item on with rapid precision. "Did you bring your suit?"

"I'm wearing it under — where we going?" Jane said.

"We're not going anywhere," Kate said. "They're coming to us." She pulled her mask up over her face and flexed her fingers.

Jane took her sweatshirt off, uncovering her own costume, minus the cape.

"You hear that?" Jane asked.

"What?" Kate said.

And then they both looked up when they heard the sound of several metallic thumps overhead.

"They're on the roof," Jane said.

They ran from Kate's apartment, leaving the laptop behind. Kate pointed down one end of the corridor, then to herself. Jane nodded and headed in the other direction. Both ends of the hallway ended in sets of stairs leading up and down.

Turns out it didn't much matter who went where, as heavily armored men with the most ridiculous sci-fi rifles Jane had ever seen stepped through the doors on each end. She let her hands burst into flames.

"Let's try something new," she said, pointing two fingers at the first enemy's rifle. Flames burst from her fingertips and into the barrel of the gun. The metal warped and bent.

At the other end of the corridor, Kate charged her target, jumping up onto the wall and then pushing off to land a hearty punch into the first armored man's head. The titanium caps on her gloves clanged against the man's metal helmet.

Then the man's neck began to spark. Kate threw a spinning kick at his head and it popped off. Exposed wires flashed, hissed, popped and smoked.

"Robots! Jane! They're robots! Don't hold back!"

Jane launched herself, airborne, down the hallway, driving a blazing fist into the chest of the first robot. The smell of burnt electronics filled the corridor. Not slowing down, she threw an uppercut at a robot that followed her, knocking its head clear and bouncing it off the ceiling. Behind her, Kate beat a second robot into malfunction with the butt of its own rifle.

They heard metallic stomping coming from both stairwells.

"Too many people in this building, Jane," Kate yelled.

"I know!"

Kate pointed at her.

"Make me a hole in the wall!"

"A — wait, what?"

Kate ran back to her apartment and disappeared inside. Another robot arrived at the foot of the staircase. Jane yanked a mechanical arm off and used it to decapitate the robot. Kate reappeared, carrying the laptop.

"A hole! Make me a hole in the wall!"

"How big!"

Kate shook the laptop at her. Behind her, more robots arrived and took aim with their rifles. "This big!" she said.

With both of her arms, Jane picked up what remained of the last robot. "Duck!" she yelled.

Kate dove to the floor.

Jane tossed the robot's body into its two cohorts at the end of the hall, toppling them like bowling pins. She turned, walked into the staircase, casually put her fist through the chest of another robot, and then went to kick a laptop-sized hole in the exterior wall of the building.

She underestimated her own strength, and most of the wall exploded out the side of the building. The remaining hole was more than slightly bigger than a laptop.

"I, ah, made extra room!" she said.

Behind her, Kate pounded away at one of the robots with a barrage of kicks and punches, her tungsten knuckles sparking off their metal hides. Another walked around with its head on backwards clearly confused by the entire situation.

As if part of a choreographed routine, Kate kicked the laptop with a free foot, sending it skittering down the hall to land right at Jane's feet. She picked it up and tossed it out the hole in the building.

Instantly, a half dozen more robots leapt from above in pursuit of the laptop. Their rifles fired green lasers, not bullets. They hissed in the night air.

Kate sprinted down the hallway, a pile of broken robot bodies in her wake.

"Come on!" she said.

She ran past Jane and then, without stopping, jumped out the opening into the air.

"Wait!" Jane yelled and lifted off as well, attempting to catch her falling teammate. Then Kate reappeared outside the window, arm around one robot's neck in a death grip, both of them held aloft by what appeared to be rocket boosters in the robot's feet.

Jane blasted out the window, picking the nearest robot and grabbing its head with both hands; she turned up the heat until the head

126

began to melt. She threw the body at another passing robot, sending it spinning into a nearby building. Despite scanning the area outside Kate's apartment building, she couldn't get an accurate count of how many enemies they faced. Jane caught Kate trying to force the robot she was riding to blast his comrades. Her efforts were only successful in one instance.

"This is really inefficient!" Jane heard Kate yelling. She flew four stories from street level and climbed further, but Jane was beginning to think this wasn't part of Kate's overall plan.

Jane aimed for efficiency as well, zipping around, knocking heads off a few airborne robots, before getting clipped several times by their laser rifles. The pain wasn't enough to knock her out of the air, but with each zap her energy started to flag.

"There's too many of them!" Jane said.

Then one near her crumpled like tinfoil. Jane looked up and saw Doc and Emily hovering a floor above them; Emily reached out a hand and clenched her fingers into a fist. Another robot crumbled into a ball.

"Gravity sucks, huh Optimus?" Emily said, crushing a third just as easily.

Jane smashed the head off another robot and saw Doc, with the casual wave of his hand, force yet another to deviate from its flight path and explode against a building. Then Jane spotted one, thrusters blasting, retreat into the night sky. It had abandoned its rifle in favor of cradling the laptop in its arms.

"Let that one go — oops!" Kate yelled, losing her grip on her own robot. It turned to blast her with its rifle when she fell, but Jane threw a ball of flame like a baseball at its head and Emily scooped up the plummeting Kate with a simple hand gesture. Kate spun loosely all the way to the ground, and Jane saw Emily smirking the entire time, weaving her fingers as if she were spinning Kate like a top.

Jane watched Kate try to stand up, then, like someone getting off a particularly bad roller coaster ride, bob and weave until she fell to one knee.

All around them, smoking husks of broken robots lay inert. Aside from the one that got away, it appeared as though they had destroyed them all, at least twenty. Doc drifted down to hover next to Jane.

"Glad to see you two getting along so well," he said, smirking.

CHAPTER 28:
SHARED SPACES

nce the fear and shock began to subside, Valerie decided it would be worthwhile to try to reason with the entity.

She wasn't sure if the other being could understand English, but it was the only tool Valerie had, and so she simply started speaking to it. At first asking for it to pay attention to her, asking if it could hear her, asking it if it could understand. When she got no response — aside from a swell of annoyance here and there, like a horse batting a fly with its tail — Valerie commenced a one-sided conversation, hoping the other creature would join in.

"Are you technically a hurricane?" she asked.

No answer.

"If we traveled inland, would you become something else? A blizzard, a tornado? Or do we have to stay along the coast?"

Again, no response.

They edged slowly out to sea, away from the Atlantic coastline, but Valerie felt them change directions sharply many times. There was no way to know if the storm would reverse course again and hit the mainland if that was its whim.

"We had lots of hurricanes in Miami. Obviously. The gulf and all," she said. "But I grew up in Chicago. No hurricanes there, but we confronted all kinds of weather. It's the Windy City. Did you know that?"

No reply. The only sound: simply the whistle of a strong breeze.

"It's not really the windiest city in America though. I remember reading that somewhere. It's just a nickname. Our winters are pretty unbelievable though. Really frigid."

Valerie thought back to the snow-swept streets where she grew up, the piles of graying snow standing as high as she was tall, the way she didn't miss the winter until she moved to a place where snowflakes never arrived.

"Can you make snow? Or are you only tropical? Is rain your thing?" Valerie said. "My last name is Snow. Pretty funny, named Snow and living in Miami. Maybe we could drop snow on Florida. They'd hate it, but it might be kind of cool. Give the kids something to remember when they're grown."

She felt the storm changing directions, but she couldn't quite tell to where. A breathy intake of air from one side, pulling her here and there.

"Look, I don't know if you're understanding any of this," said Valerie. "But if you are . . . I just want to go home. Haven't you ever just wanted to go home? Haven't you ever been a little frightened? Or lonely? Maybe this wouldn't be so bad if we could talk, but we can't. I don't remember the last time I said anything to anyone. I think I'm going crazy."

The silence felt like a wet blanket on her shoulders, a thick weight tightening around her chest.

"You ignoring me?" she said, finally, feeling an ugly combination of anger and self-pity rising up in her belly. "Are you? You can understand me, can't you! You know what I'm saying! I'm going crazy in here! Let me go!"

The winds around her began to pick up, swirling and dragging the cloud cover into a vortex around her. The air temperature plummeted dramatically.

"I hate you! Hate being here! I want to go home!"

Purple and blue lightning lanced across the sky. The clouds grew darker, violet and black — massive, muscular thunderheads.

"Why won't you speak?" Valerie screamed.

And then the storm began to move in earnest.

CHAPTER 29:
FOLLOW UP

So I have to ask," Doc said. "What exactly did you do?"

Somehow, despite the table being a perfect circle, his presence gave it a distinct head. Jane couldn't help but feel like she was in trouble, even more so when the boys walked in a few minutes later to find everyone sitting around covered in scorch marks from the robots' laser rifles.

"What did you do, Ray?" Billy asked, before sitting down heavily and putting his feet up.

"Manage not to get head-butted again, Billy?" Jane asked.

"Yes," he said.

"But you didn't bring her back with you."

"Had a very pleasant conversation and she's going to consider our offer. Why you wearing jeans with your uniform? And what's that smell? It's like someone set a tire on fire in here."

"We fought the droid army and won. Pretty awesome," said Emily. "I can crush things with my thoughts and it's really fun."

"I'll keep that in mind," Billy said. "What happened?"

"We found an executable file among the stuff my contact salvaged," Kate said.

She'd pulled her mask down and held a cold compress on her leg where she'd been nicked by a laser, something she hadn't noticed until the fight was over.

"You clicked on a super-villain executable file?" Titus asked.

"That was my initial reaction," Kate said.

"But fortune favors the bold," Jane said.

"Oh great, they're finishing each others' sentences now," Billy said. "This can't end well."

"Are you angry, Doc? We could have thought it through a bit more I guess," Jane said.

"Honestly," Doc said, pulling off his overcoat and tossing it onto the back of his chair, "I'm more curious about what you discovered when you did it. Other than the robots."

"A symbol," Kate said. "An elongated human skull, but the mouth had tentacles, like a squid."

Doc rubbed his forehead, remaining silent for a few seconds.

Jane sensed everyone around her growing nervous.

"What is it?" Titus said.

Doc picked up one of the computer tablets that were scattered around the room. He tapped the screen a few times and then slid it onto the table. The exact symbol Kate and Jane saw earlier filled the screen.

"What does it mean?"

"Ai, ai! Cthulhu f'taghn?" Emily said.

Doc stared at her, eyebrows rising slowly.

"You are so consistently weird in so many inconsistent ways, it's remarkable," he said.

"Thank you," said Emily.

"Anyway," Doc said. "They were a group who called themselves the Children of the Elder Star."

"I was right? They're an end of the world cult like in a Lovecraft story? We're screwed, guys," Emily said. "I was joking with the Cthulhu thing. This isn't good. We're definitely screwed."

"No," Doc said. "The world thought they were these crazy cultists — blood sacrifices, supernatural plots, and some of them did tinker with black magic, certainly. But they hid behind this cult backstory, pretending to want to raise dead gods to destroy the universe. It was all propaganda. What they were really interested in is the manipulation of world events. Finances, wars, governments, political leaders. They wanted to work the angles of chaos and order to their advantage. It was about money and power. The world was a big chess board to them."

"So they might want to control something like, say, a pet hurricane," Jane said.

Doc pointed at her.

"Got it in one," he said. "Now, we have no concrete evidence that the people running that lab were the Children of the Elder Star. Could be someone new using their old technology. My teammates and I tried very hard to put the Elders out of business, but they were like roaches. Every time we picked up a rock we'd find more of them."

"It could be them," said Kate.

"I wouldn't rule it out," he said. "What we do know is that they don't want anyone getting a look at their information. Those robots were simple hunter-killers. They've probably been sitting dormant somewhere waiting for someone to try to open that file, perhaps for years. They certainly weren't state of the art."

"They were flying robots," Emily said. "What do state of the art robots do? Sing and dance while they fly and shoot at you?"

"Wait," Kate said. "So those robots might have come after anyone who tried to launch that file?"

"If that was how they were programmed, yes," Doc said.

Kate jumped to her feet and ran out of the room, pulling her mask up as she went. Doc rushed to the door but couldn't stop her in time.

"Where's she going?" Emily asked.

"Oh, no," Titus said. "I know exactly where she's heading."

CHAPTER 30:
BURNING BRIDGES

itus found Kate across the street from Andrew's office building, an entire city block ablaze. She stood on the rooftop watching, a pure black silhouette against the red and gold glow of flames. Below, fire trucks blasted the structure with water and police cordoned off the street.

"I killed him," Kate said.

Titus walked up to the ledge and stood beside her.

She made no eye contact. "This is my fault. I killed my friend."

"No you didn't," Titus said. "You didn't know."

"This is why we can't get close to people, Titus," she said. "Every time we let someone in, we put them in the way of all the bad things in the world we're supposed to be standing up against. We're supposed to protect them from things like this."

"How were you supposed to know?"

"Doesn't matter. I put a regular person in harm's way. I have to be better than this."

Titus crouched down beside her, opened himself up to letting a bit of the wolf through. He heard the voices in the street, smelled everything burning — brick and carpet, wood and books . . . and people. The wolf's reaction to the latter sent a chill down his spine, so Titus reined him in, held him back. Not now, big guy. Not here.

"Maybe he wasn't there," Titus said.

"No, they came for us so fast, Titus. Andrew was there. He wouldn't have known he should try to make a break for it. He'd probably have attempted to stop it from launching, but Andrew never would have thought to run," she said. "Who would? What normal person thinks killer robots are going to come flying through their window and burn their lives to the ground?"

Titus shook his head.

"I can scout around, see if I can find anything," Titus said. "Maybe I can — "

"Don't," Kate said. "I'll get the autopsy report."

"Anything I can do?" Titus said.

"Stay here with me and watch," she said. "I want to see if anyone shows up to make sure the robots did their job . . . And then, you can help me find these people and make sure they never do this to anyone ever again."

CHAPTER 31: MOM

Billy woke up the next morning to the sounds of an arrhythmic banging on his bedroom door. Staggering out of bed, he opened the door and found Emily, standing there with a backpack strapped to her shoulders, dressed as much like a normal person as Billy had ever seen her.

"Hey," she said.

"Everything okay?" he asked.

"I've gotta see my mom. Was wondering if you would come with me."

Why do I think this is a terrible idea, Billy thought.

You should go, Dude said.

I want to go as much as I'd like to be kicked in the head by an angry cyborg, Billy thought.

Your friend needs you, Dude said. *If you do not help her, I will not be responsible for if and when you lose your access to our powers at a most inopportune time.*

You're such a bully, Dude, Billy thought.

"You're talking to your alien right now, aren't you," Emily said.

"No. Maybe. Yes. Yes I am," Billy said. "Why?"

"Your eyes glaze over when you talk to him and you look kind of stupid," Emily said. "You should try to work on that."

"Noted," Billy said.

I really glaze over? He asked.

You do take on a dazed expression, Dude said. *My last partner was able to multitask more easily than you can.*

It's way too early to have you guys busting on me in tandem, Billy thought. Also much too soon to be managing multiple conversations.

"Everything okay with your mom?" Billy asked. "Why the visit?"

"I — look, I saw some stuff yesterday. None of it was even like remotely okay and I want to see my mom and let her know I'm fine," Emily said.

"That makes sense. I think," Billy said. "But why ask me?"

"None of the others have . . . well, parents," Emily said. "So it seemed a little insensitive to ask them."

They took the train out of the city. When Billy asked why they didn't just fly, Emily laughed.

"You never take the train?"

"Public transportation was the bane of my existence before I learned to fly," Billy said. "Why would I go back?"

"It's one of the few things that make me feel like a normal person," Emily said.

Billy caught himself nodding, and then leaned back in his seat, letting the rhythm of the train rock him back and forth.

"What does your mom think about you being a superhuman?" she asked.

"I don't know," he said.

"She hasn't said?" Emily asked. "Mine wants me to check in twice a day to let her know I haven't left the planet."

"We haven't talked much since I left home," Billy said. "I didn't leave much of a goodbye."

Emily gave him the stink eye.

"What d'you mean?"

"I left a note."

"A note?" Emily's voice cracked.

Several other passengers looked them both over. One got up, took his newspaper and moved further away.

"Yeah. 'Off to save the world. I'll call when I can. Love Billy.'"

"You just . . . bailed on your mom and dad?"

"Yeah. I bailed."

"Why would you do that?"

"Trust me, Em. Better than saying goodbye. Even better than staying. I . . . I'm a nicer son when I'm not there I think."

Emily stared at him hard for a moment, then looked down, studying her shoes.

"I saw a lot of things that were not okay yesterday, Billy Case," Emily said. "Why do you have to keep piling on the depressing stuff?"

"Sorry."

"We should go see your folks next," Emily said.

Now it was Billy who studied his shoes.

"I'll think about it."

Emily's mom lived in a suburb, one of those towns that was still too close to the city itself to have a big back yard or much by way of trees, but with enough space to have a few bedrooms and a place to call your own. Painted brown and white, the house had a chain link fence that stretched across the front and gated the driveway. Emily opened the gate confidently and hopped up the front stairs, pausing at the door.

"It's weird," she said. "I feel like I should ring the doorbell, but know I don't have to."

"Want me to ring it for you?" Billy offered.

"I can hear you out there," Emily's mother called through the open front window. "Door's unlocked."

Emily scuttled in, looking even younger than she usually did. Billy followed slowly. After overhearing a dozen conversations between them, Billy expected her to be much older, but it turned out she just looked like an older Emily. Sure, she probably dyed her hair to stay blonde as often as Emily dyed her own blue, but otherwise they were so much alike Billy almost laughed.

"Who's this one?" her mother asked.

"Billy," Emily said. "My favorite teammate."

"I'm your favorite?" Billy asked.

"Well, you're the only one who treats me like I belong at the big kids' table, so yeah," Emily said. "You get the favorite label. That okay?"

"I can live with it."

"I'm Melinda."

"Um. Shouldn't I call you missus . . . "

"Melinda's fine," she said, laughing. "As long as you don't refer to me as 'Emily's mom' it's fine. I like to think I still have an actual name."

They sat in the living room a while, and Emily unloaded, talking of the meeting with the Snow girl's parents, which Billy hadn't heard about, and then about the rescue of Kate and Jane, which Billy only caught bits and pieces of after everyone had returned to the Tower.

Kate's gonna be okay, right Dude? Billy asked. I mean, I'd lose it if I got my friend killed, but I don't really have any friends to get killed. Will she be okay?

Everyone grieves differently, Billy, Dude said. *Especially when someone dies violently, and particularly when you feel they died because of you.*

Have you ever lost anyone like that, Dude?

I have been partnered with heroes like you for hundreds of years, Billy Case. It always feels like my fault when one of them is killed in action.

So you've lost a lot of partners, huh? Wait — when they get killed in action? Does this happen often?

You should listen to the conversation, Billy Case.

We are talking about this later, Dude. I'm not dropping it.

"Everything okay, Billy?" Melinda asked.

Her voice possessed the unmistakable tone of motherly concern. Billy hadn't realized how long it had been since he heard that.

"He's talking to his alien," Emily said. "You can tell because he goes all slack jawed and it looks like he's going to sneeze."

"Thanks, Emily. But, um, yeah. I was asking Dude a question."

"Your alien's name is Dude," Melinda said.

"His name is Straylight too, but he didn't tell me that until I'd been calling him Dude for like, a year, so he's stuck with it. I'm not entirely sure he's happy about it." Billy paused and took a deep breath. "I have to ask you something."

"Go ahead," Melinda said.

"You don't seem even a little bit freaked out that your daughter's a superhuman hero who can control gravity with her mind. And, I'm sitting on your couch talking to an alien in my brain. You're totally unfazed. I don't get it."

"What's not to get?"

"No disrespect, missus . . . Melinda, but the average person would be a little freaked out right now."

She started laughing, then looked at her daughter.

"I suppose now's as good a time as any," she said.

Emily's mother stood up and crossed the living room to a book-shelf lined with photo albums.

Of course they have pictures all lined up on bookshelves, Billy thought. They're normal people. Normal people have photo albums.

Melinda returned, opened to a specific page, then handed it to Emily. Billy looked over her shoulder.

"You were in the circus?" Emily asked.

In the photo, a much younger Melinda was dressed in a leotard and cape, a half-mask hid her eyes. She was smiling and leaned on the shoulder of another caped woman. Behind them, a bruiser of a guy in body armor and a mask stood grinning, a hand on each of the women's shoulders.

"Sixteen years of this and I still can't tell when you're playing dumb," Melinda said. "Em, I was one of you."

"What?" Emily said.

She bolted up out of her chair so fast Billy scrambled to catch the album so it wouldn't spill onto the floor.

"I mean I wasn't one of you, up in the Tower. Wasn't nearly as strong as you are. But I had my fun."

"You're teasing me," Emily said. "You're doing this to get back at me for all the times I dyed my hair when you told me not to."

"Nope," Melinda said. She tapped the photo. "That's me. I was Sparrow."

"Does Doc know?" Billy asked, studying the picture intently, trying to recognize faces. He flipped to the next page and saw a few others, their costumes a bit out of date, a bit too colorful despite the fading quality of the photos. Heroes from another era.

"Doctor Silence?" Melinda said. "Of course. Doc knows a bit of everything. I always thought that's why he looked so sad all the time. He's privy to too many secrets."

"But . . . what did you do?" Emily asked. "I've never seen you do anything more super than make awesome brownies."

Melinda smiled. Her smile was one of the most joyful things Billy had ever witnessed.

I remember her, Dude said. I know her face now.

"I could fly, baby," she said. "That's why they called me Sparrow. All I could do was fly."

"No offense, ma'am — I mean, Melinda, but flying is the best thing any of us can do."

"I know, Billy."

"But," Emily said, still standing, seemingly trying to pace and stand still at the same time, "Why'd you stop?"

"I had you, Emily," she said. "Didn't quit right away, of course, but it's really hard to risk your life every day when the most important thing in your whole universe is back home. And then your father passed away and, well, it was just me and you against the world. So, I stayed home."

Billy watched as Emily attempted to process all of this. It was as if the hamster had fallen off the proverbial wheel; she could barely form sentences. Her oversized steampunk goggles were askew on her head, practically falling off.

"Can you still fly?" she asked.

"I can."

"And you don't?"

"Oh no, I still do," she said, her smile absolutely radiant. "I didn't, not for a long time. But when you were a little older I'd wait for you to fall asleep, and then I'd go for short trips. Just to remember what it was like."

"Do you think Emily's powers came from you?" Billy asked.

"I don't know," Melinda said. "It's hard to say for sure one way or the other. Those of us with special powers tended to have special kids more often than those without powers, but it was never anything we could count on."

"If you can fly, and I can control gravity, what does that mean my kid'll be able to do?"

"Maybe your daughter will get to see the stars," Melinda said. "But somehow I think you'll do that yourself."

"That's what I keep telling these guys," Emily said. "I want to touch the stars."

CHAPTER 32:
GUARDIAN ANGEL

For twenty-four hours, the city became the worst place on earth to commit a crime.

The Dancer moved like bird of prey from rooftop to rooftop, prowling, waiting. She prevented a car theft, a purse snatching, and a pick pocketing during the morning rush hour; witnesses were so confused by a vigilante thwarting small crimes in the daylight they never stopped to think about who their rescuer might have been.

Three men were left badly beaten after an attempted robbery of a convenience store at eleven in the morning. She beat one of the men senseless with a bottle of soda then apologized for the mess. The owner said the costumed vigilante was a girl who wore a mask, but never spoke. He called the police and mopped up, glad to have his business still intact.

At lunch, a domestic dispute ended with an abusive boyfriend tied to a streetlamp, a fat lip and black eye not given to him by his girlfriend the only traces that remained of the hero who broke up the fight.

A masked woman, who witnesses spotted dropping on the car from above, foiled a carjacking in the afternoon. The vehicle needed a new bumper; the two men who stole it needed hospitalization.

A road rage incident nearly turned ugly during rush hour when one driver pulled a gun on the other. The armed man was left unconscious with a deep bruise on his forehead that mirrored the exact shape of the butt of his own pistol. The second man involved wouldn't say anything about the woman who broke up the fight other than the fact that she uttered one single word: "Behave."

That night, at eight o'clock, police received an anonymous tip about a dog-fighting ring in an unoccupied warehouse downtown. Later, they found twenty-seven men suffering from concussions, broken bones, and worse. Several had been stuffed forcibly into undersized dog crates while awaiting arrest.

An hour later, a dog crate filled with crumpled wads of cash was left on the doorstep of a local no-kill animal shelter. Many of the bills were blood-stained.

At nine thirty, a female jogger was attacked on her way home. Her assailant was injured so severely doctors stated he would never walk without a limp again.

Still later that night, police received another anonymous tip about a truck full of stolen rifles and handguns abandoned in an alley uptown. Two known local gangsters were discovered zip-tied to their seats inside. Both men refused to speak with the police. One would require extensive dental work.

At midnight, associates of those gangsters planned retaliation against the masked vigilante who cost them two reliable gunrunners and a significant sum of money. Three hundred pounds of werewolf that had been following the Dancer all day — secretly watching over her during the rampage — kicked in their door and altered their plans.

Finally, at one in the morning, the Dancer returned to the Tower, spoke to no one, closed the door to her room and bolted it behind her.

Titus, wearing a new shirt and freshly scrubbed of gangster blood, did consider knocking. Instead, he went to bed. If it was Kate's intention to continue crime fighting the next day as part of her emotional therapy, he would need his sleep.

Guardian angel duty was exhausting.

CHAPTER 33: MAGIC

Curiosity and caution overlapped uncomfortably in Agent Black's head ever since they'd handed Wegener over to the Lady. He came out of the meeting in one piece, but the scientist hadn't been the same since — barely making eye contact with anyone, disappearing into thought, often nervously chewing his nails or tugging on that awkward hippie ponytail.

"What do you think she did to him in there?" he asked Rose eventually.

They stood together on a catwalk overlooking the main hall of the underground base. Wegener sat in the makeshift commissary, drinking black coffee and talking to himself.

"Why don't you ask her?" Rose said.

"You've worked with her more often," Black said. "You don't have any idea?"

She shook her head.

"It's not torture, exactly," Rose said. "If they wanted him tortured they would have had me do it. All I know is nobody ever leaves an interview with the Lady in quite the same way."

"Speak of the devil," Black said.

The Lady walked across the atrium towards them. She appeared to be dressed in pajamas. A red, voluminous robe was intricately wrapped around her and her feet were bare. Several of Black's mercenaries and even a few of Rose's assassins watched as she drifted by.

The Lady beckoned Black and Rose.

145

"Think she heard us?" Rose said.

"Come along, my friends," she said. "Our clients have selected the city they want to test their pet storm on."

The Lady brought them to a small room several levels below the main amphitheater. The space had been carved directly into the cave wall — as most of the rooms were — and she shut off all the electric lights, instead choosing to bathe the room with dozens of small candles. Black's cyborg eye kicked up the light compensation. He wished he hadn't.

The floor was covered in bare stone, but someone — the Lady herself, he assumed — painted strange images all around the room, including a circle of alien symbols surrounded by a ring of candles.

"Doctor Wegener's control mechanisms have failed, but his theories were sound," she said. "There was no way to know that the storm wouldn't process pain the same way a living creature would."

As she spoke, the Lady finished her preparations, scribbling an additional symbol here, lighting incense there. The room smelled like the palm reader's establishment Black visited once when he was young.

"Fortunately, they can still be useful as anchors for my own work," she said. "I can channel commands through them into the human girl's body, which the storm is now dependent upon to stay alive. A little malignant guidance is all we need."

"All due respect, ma'am, but why are you telling us this?" Agent Black said. "We're just the hired guns."

The Lady favored him with one of her heart-rending smiles. He immediately regretted speaking.

"Just assumed you'd be curious, darling," she said. "I like you both and thought you might want to share in our next maneuver."

"That's . . . generous of you, Lady," Rose said.

Under ordinary circumstances, it should have entertained him to see Rose a bit off her game, yet it only made Black more nervous to see his partner's confidence waning.

The Lady smiled again, knelt down in front of the circle of symbols and began to sing.

Slowly, the emblems positioned throughout the room started to glow. At first, Black thought it was a trick of the light, but he saw them warming in the dark, a light red, like heating metal. The place grew warmer. A trickle of sweat slipped down his forehead, becoming trapped in his eyebrow.

The Lady's voice changed, sounding less like singing, more like a conversation, a call and answer in some language Black, couldn't decipher, had never heard before.

Inside the circle, something . . . congealed. A shape. Almost human, but most definitely not human, a strange form with thin, brittle wings.

Black slowly, cautiously, took a step forward and to his left. Rose shook her head at him, her one good eye wide. The candles played with his night vision, but the Lady's face was clear and bright.

She had horns. Long, black, polished horns rising like elegant weapons from above her brow. Open flame engulfed her eyes. For a moment, Agent Black was convinced he would run — fight or flight kicked in again, but this time there was no fight to be garnered. He struggled for control and took a deep, incense-addled breath.

And then the lights went out.

Every candle extinguished simultaneously, leaving the room in complete darkness. After images of the glowing runes remained, but they faded into pale red burns in his vision.

Something crossed incredibly close to him. A warm body. He started to draw his weapon, but then light spilled in from the open door. Framed in the doorway, the Lady leaned to one side. There was an attempt at confidence in her stance, but Black sensed tiredness, too, a body weariness that told him the magic he just witnessed cost her something.

"Well then," she said, her voice upbeat, but slightly strained. "Shall we see what happens when our baby storm meets a major metropolitan area?"

Elsewhere, Valerie Snow was seeing things.

Shadow creatures. Skinny men made of smoke, with wings like burnt bone, flying around her, there one moment, gone the next. They'd reach out to her, prodding new scars, and her insides would burn, like hot metal pressing against her skin from the inside.

If it were not for the pain, she'd have thought she was hallucinating. But the pain was too much, and whenever she tried to push one of the shadow men away, another would reach out for her from the other direction. They teased and taunted. She tried to make out their mouths — smirking things — too wide and too thin to be human mouths, filled with splinters of sharp, sharp teeth.

She yelled for them to stop. And cried out to the storm for help. Valerie knew the other entity was distressed; the rain and wind around her growing more and more violent with each attack by the shadow men. Particularly vicious attacks provoked shards of lightning.

With nothing else to do, Valerie willed herself to move.

And she did. She began to fly — slowly at first, but faster the more she willed it — away from the attackers. The storm moved with her like a cape, wrapped around her, billowing out as they gained speed together. Valerie and the tempest, black and violent thunderclouds traveling across the Atlantic.

Later, she would realize the shadow men were driving her in a specific direction, but that didn't matter now. For the first time in weeks, Valerie Snow was in control of her own body, and moving by her own will. And even when chased by monsters, even when surrounded by a resentful alien sentience, to find herself moving, the wind in her hair, had her laughing like a child in a playground.

CHAPTER 34:
HURRICANE

People forget Providence is a port city, Jane thought, standing on a half-shredded brick warehouse. Smoke mixed with rain and dense fog for miles; she passed an area where a gas main exploded, taking out half a city block with it. The storm hammered into the coast like a charging bull, faster than they'd seen it move thus far, flooding entire streets, knocking cars over with winds of unheard of proportions.

Doc and Emily landed beside her. Billy scouted on the edge of the horizon, his blue-white signature glow nearly eaten up by the density of the fog.

"How do we fight a force of nature?" Jane asked.

Doc watched the sky, hands thrust in his pockets, lips pursed in a hard, pale line.

"I'll be damned," he said. "What are those doing in there?" He sounded wistful as he spoke.

"What are what doing where?" Emily asked.

He ignored her.

"Here's what I want you to do, Emily," Doc said. "Try to push the storm away with one of your gravity fields."

"Sounds like a terrible idea," she said.

Jane thought the exact same thing.

"Just try," he said. "If you feel the least bit out of control, simply let go."

"Oh sure. Push the dragon, Emily. Poke the tiger! What if it chases after me?"

"We're already standing in the worst of it," Doc said, his blue-white hair fluttering in the wind, long coat snapping and swaying.

"Bubble of float," Jane said.

"What?" Emily and Doc said, together.

"Keep your bubble of float above the buildings, Em," she said. "So you don't float away any of the buildings."

"I still think this is a terrible idea," Emily said.

But she closed her eyes and held a hand out in front of her and flexed her fingers. Jane discovered that Em had updated her gloves and now a nuclear fallout symbol decorated both palms.

The storm noticed.

As if a living thing, the clouds pushed back, pounding away like an angry animal against the unseen wall Emily created. Lightning crackled and flashed, splintering the gray sky with pale light.

"Is the storm actually attacking us?" Jane asked.

"Sure looks that way," Doc said.

He knelt down on the rooftop and pulled out a hunk of plain white chalk from his coat pocket. Doc sketched symbols on the ground, circling some, connecting others. Then he drew a perfect ring large enough to hold a person.

"Don't stand inside that circle," he said.

Doc sat lotus style in front of the circle. Jane could barely hear him, but she could tell he was talking to himself, chattering under his breath. The longer he spoke, though, the louder he got. His words sounded like Latin, but dirtier, more feral. They sounded, Jane thought, like things human beings were not supposed to hear.

She watched the circle grow darker, as if filling up with shadows. The shadows moved, with limbs and long fingers and wings. Eyes stared at her with malice and hunger. Several creatures — maybe three, maybe more, it was hard to tell the way they seemed to glom together — writhed inside the circle like eels.

"Hello, gentlemen," Doc said.

The creatures reached for him, but couldn't pass through the circle he'd drawn. Jane heard their shadow nails squeal across the unseen surface.

He pulled something from his pocket and looked at Jane.

"When I throw this, I want you to set it on fire, and then I want you to close your eyes," Doc said.

She nodded.

He tossed the object — some sort of oversized capsule — in the air directly at the creatures. Jane projected a blast of fire from her fingertips. Even as she closed her eyes, she witnessed the blinding flash it created, a phosphorus explosion of hot white light. She heard the screams of the shadow creatures dying, and the sounds of Emily swearing.

Then, Jane opened her eyes.

The storm started to drift away from the city. Jane couldn't tell if it was moving because of what Doc did or if it was reacting to Emily's gravitational push, but it was clearly headed back out to sea again, gathering up its dark clouds like a shawl.

Doc touched the tiny radio receiver he wore in his ear.

"Straylight, can you hear me?"

"I'm here, boss," Billy's voice said through all of their receivers.

"Do not pursue," he said. "See what you can do to help rescue personnel, and then head back to the tower."

"Sure thing."

They watched Billy's aura arc back toward the city, disappearing between downtown buildings.

"What were those things, Doc?" Jane said.

"A complication," he said, watching the storm recede.

CHAPTER 35: ACTIVATION

The expression on Rose's face was all the information Black needed. She was speaking to their employers. Her conversation took place over a phone in the windowed conference room off the main atrium of the underground headquarters. Rose's guise projected the right combination of self-righteousness and terror for the call to have been from the top.

She nodded several times, then hung up.

"They're curious," the Lady said.

Black nearly climbed out of his skin; he hadn't noticed Natasha standing next to him. The audio sensors contained within his cybernetics should have warned him that someone was approaching, but he remained convinced that she simply materialized beside him. She'd done stranger things in the past.

"Word from upstairs," Rose said, joining them on the catwalk outside the office. "They'd like us to throw a few of the rejects into the field."

"What for?" Black said. "Most of them are useless."

"Not useless," Rose said. "Uncontrollable. Doesn't mean they don't have their uses."

"Will it be up to me to implement some controls, then?" asked the Lady.

Rose shook her head.

"Not this time. They want us to cast them out to stir things up. The bosses are curious about our new opposition," she said.

The Lady nodded.

"Good. I'd like some time to look into who it was that banished my little pets yesterday," she said.

"The folks upstairs might have some information for you," Rose said. "They wouldn't be averse to a phone call."

The Lady unleashed one of her disarming smiles. Rose understood the smile wasn't meant for her; yet, she smiled back.

"I'm sure they wouldn't. But, I'll do my own research, if it's just the same," the Lady said. "I prefer to look into these things first hand. No need to tell them that, though."

"Of course," Rose said.

Agent Black scanned the atrium below them, looking for Wegener. The scientist had grown more and more withdrawn since his meeting with the Lady. Black was certain the man would never be the same.

"Which ones are we using?" he said. "I'm guessing they want expendable ones."

"Tinder and Hyde," Rose said.

"Really," Black said. "Interesting choices. I won't mind seeing the back of Hyde, but did they mention why they chose those two?"

"The right combination of inherent destructiveness, and they both failed the psych tests with flying colors," Rose said. "They're much more useful as improvised weapons than long term projects."

Black frowned. The Hyde project — or rather, the test subject himself, not the overall concept — disgusted him, but Tinder was one he had hoped would work out. He fought back the twinge of pity that wriggled in his gut.

"Where are we deploying them," he asked, instead.

"You're sure to get a kick out of this," Rose said, smirking.

CHAPTER 36: ATTENTION

What did you mean yesterday?" Jane said, interrupting Doc in the observation room, where she found him chatting with Titus. "When you said a 'complication'?"

He waived Titus off.

The werewolf settled down in front of the monitors and began a circuitous scan of the globe. The Tower's computer regularly made use of satellites planted long ago to detect anomalies and occurrences on the surface, and were able to indentify large-scale events like explosions or violent weather patterns. The computer — *Neal,* Jane reminded herself, forgetting that the mainframe seemed to have more personality than a lot of humans she knew — also tapped into news feeds and Internet chatter for the strange and violent, ready to alert them if anything unusual appeared. Neal would break into the Tower's loudspeakers if needed, but it — he? — sometimes seemed to work best when a human was helping him organize what was being seen. No matter how powerful the AI, a human touch always appeared to make things work smoother. Oddly, the werewolf got along better with the artificial intelligence than anyone else on the team.

"What I meant was that the constructs — the creatures you saw — were familiar to me," Doc said. "And that might mean we're dealing with a bigger threat than I originally anticipated. Have to do some digging to make sure though. I could use your help later."

"How can I help?"

"I need someone to — "

"Doc," Titus said. "You've got to see this."

Titus had launched on screen an enormous red spot that appeared on a heat-register map of the US. He zoomed in and converted it to real time video.

Fire. A massive one in California.

"Not again," Doc said.

"Worse, Doctor," Neal added. *"Zooming in."*

Neal took control of the monitor from Titus and brought them in quite close to the epicenter of the fire. A human shape stood there, walking slowly. Rather than engulf her, the fire appeared to emanate from her, spilling from her body like water. The girl's skin glowed like heated metal, and her hair flickered and waved like a candlewick.

"Is that what I think it is?" Jane said.

"Looks like a pyrokinetic," Doc said. "Where did she come from?"

Neal intercut surveillance footage from an hour earlier and maximized its size to fill the screen. It showed a black helicopter, military grade, flying low over the forest canopy. The door opened, and a body was throw from the copter. Before the body hit the tree line, however, she burst into flames, the ensuing fire caused hair and clothes — green hospital scrubs, of all things — to burn to ash in a heartbeat.

"Someone just dumped her there?" Titus asked.

"Looks like," Doc said. "Jane. Find Billy."

"Right here," he said, walking into the room and already half-suited up for action. He struggled to pull the left sleeve of his costume on. Emily followed and angrily helped him force an arm into his uniform.

"Great," Doc said. "You and Jane are the only two who can fly fast enough to get there while there's still time to do some good. Billy, I assume your force field is fire proof?"

"And laser proof and heartbreakingly beautiful to look at," Billy said. "Is Jane — "

"I'm solar powered," she said, cutting him off. "Fire doesn't burn me."

"We bringing her back here?" Billy said.

"See if you're able to subdue her. I'm leaving the call up to you. Ping us if you need advice on scene."

"Got it," Jane said. She turned to Billy. "Race you to California."

"You're on."

"Crap! Doc?" Titus said.

"What've we got?" he answered.

Again, Neal took control of the screen. Minimizing the scene of burning trees in California to a quarter of the screen, the computer retrieved an image from downtown, just a few miles from the Tower.

"This happened ten minutes ago," Titus said.

The screen showed a teenage boy walk into the center of a major intersection downtown. Cars in both directions spun out to avoid crashing into him. When all traffic came to a stop, the boy opened his jacket to reveal a contraption embedded in his chest, a circular emblem dead center with wires and tubes jutting out of it and into his skin. The boy pounded the symbol on his chest once with his fist. His whole body spasmed. Muscles began to pop and grow, veins ravaged the surface of his skin. He took on a grayish tone, and when he stretched out his hands, his fingers elongated, arms grew apelike, legs hunched and thickened. Even his face changed, mouth now a wide rictus of pain, filled with huge white teeth — a parody of a human face.

"No way," Emily said.

Then the boy, the monster, picked up an entire car and hurled it into the closest building.

The car exploded in a fireball, leaving a crater where the wall once was.

"I should — " Jane said.

"Let me take this one," Titus said.

"You sure?" Jane asked.

"He's just a bully," Titus said. "I know how to handle them. Go stop the firestarter."

He winked at Jane.

She was so surprised by the smile on his face her jaw dropped.

"What?" Titus said. "I've been looking for someone my size to tangle with for weeks. Good luck, guys."

"What about me? Should I help?" Emily said.

"I want to hold you back in reserve. This looks intentional," Doc said. "If there's a third incident, you'll need to jump in."

"Got it," Emily said.

"Where's Kate?" Billy asked, adjusting his mask.

"On patrol again," Titus said. "She's running out of people to punch."

"Emily, try to get her on the radio," Doc said. "Everyone else, off you go."

"Tell her I'm fighting a he-man monster downtown but I've got it completely under control and don't need backup," Titus said, walking out of the command center.

"How's that supposed to help find her?" Emily asked.

"Trust me, that's pretty much guaranteed to bring her running downtown," he said, then loped down the hallway and out of sight.

CHAPTER 37: THE GIRL OF FIRE

Jane and Billy rocketed cross-country faster than any aircraft could have taken them. They flew above the cloud cover to let Jane soak up more solar energy; the altitude made her feel immortal and super-powered, and when she saw the streak of blue-white light Billy left in his wake, she produced fire from her hands and left her own red-gold trail beside his.

"I feel like a hero," Billy said, grinning at Jane, who smiled back.

"Race you," she said, and burst ahead like a shuttle launch.

They're smiles disappeared when they dropped closer to the surface and learned how far the fire had spread. Miles of devastation, trees like burning skeletons stretching for the sky, smoke black and gray darkening the air.

"What a nightmare," Jane said.

"We've got to find her," Billy said.

She motioned toward a single point on the horizon; it burned brighter and more out of control than the others. The forest fire looked natural, but in this one place, it boiled over into something fluid, an elemental nightmare of fire.

Dude, will I choke on all this smoke? Billy asked.

Our shields will clean the air for you. The same way I explained how they would protect you underwater, the alien said.

You promise? Billy said.

If one of us should have trust issues about the other, should not it be the other way around? Dude said.

Point taken, Billy said, and swooped in to ground level.

Beside him, Jane swatted a few dead trees out of the air, sending up swarms of ash and embers. At the top of a ridge in front of them, the burning figure of the girl of fire walked, her back facing them.

"Hey!" Jane yelled.

The figure turned. Even at this distance, Billy could see the pain that registered on her face. She looked confused, terrified and raised her hands as if to say stop, but gouts of fire poured from her palms and rolled down her arms. A serpentine swath of flame rushed down the sloping hill towards them. Billy and Jane leaped in opposite directions to get out of the way.

Can't help it, can she? Billy thought.

She does not appear to be in control of her abilities, Dude said.

Billy watched Jane charge the girl of fire, letting the snakelike river of flames wash over her like water. He looked on with alarm when he saw her cape catch fire in a few spots, but the futuristic material of their uniforms seemed to retard the flames and they sputtered out quickly.

Jane reached the crest of the hill and tried to grab the girl, but a massive tree, burning hot enough Billy saw its glowing red insides, toppled, knocking Jane to the ground and sending her rolling back down the hill.

Billy took off, flying over the broken and burning trees littering the path to the top of the hill. The girl focused her attention on him, the tendrils of fire lashed upward and washed over Billy.

"Hot! Dude this is hot! You promised!"

I said you would be able to breath, Dude said. *I did not say you were in an air-conditioned force field.*

"It hurts!"

Then you should try moving out of her line of fire, Billy Case, the alien said.

I can't see, Dude!

Stay calm and fly up.

Billy, in a rare moment of humility, listened. Or, tried to listen. Up, however, was more difficult to figure out when he was half-blinded by the blast of flames, and so he took off fast at more of a forty-five degree angle, smashed into a tree trunk and knocked himself silly. He fell, crash landing only a few feet away from the girl.

She peered into his eyes. Her face contorted with pain. When she spoke, her mouth was more the absence of fire than anything real or alive.

"I can't stop it," she said. "Help me. Can't stop this from happening."

"I'm — I'm here to help," Billy said.

"Please," the girl said. "Everything burns . . . "

Dude, what am I supposed to do, Billy asked.

The alien was quiet. Billy could almost hear him thinking.

Dude? I need help. I can't — how do I extinguish her?

Lethal force.

What? No. No way, Dude. I can't. You won't let me.

I have stopped you from using excessive force when it was inappropriate and childish, Billy Case, the alien said. *This might be the only way to stop her. I see no way to help her shut down her powers.*

I don't want to.

I am open to suggestions, Billy.

Jane, covered head to toe in soot and char marks, clambered up the hill to crouch beside Billy.

"I feel like I'm inhaling mud," she said.

"Do you have a plan?" Please have a plan, he thought.

"I'm fire proof. I could grab her and try to bring her up into the atmosphere. Maybe if we get her off the ground . . . "

"What if she needs to breathe like a regular human, Jane? Won't that suffocate her?"

"I don't know," she said.

"It will. If flames can't survive up there, neither can a person," he said.

"Billy," Jane said. "We're miles from a town. The way this inferno is spreading we could be looking at hundreds of lives at risk. We have to do something."

Dude?

You have my support, whatever you decide, Billy Case.

"Yeah, we have to do something," Billy said.

He felt a swell of energy in his left hand as he prepared a blast of light to strike at the girl. He looked her directly in the eyes.

"I'm so very sorry," he said.

"You're going to — no you're not!" Jane said.

She whacked Billy's arm and the blast he'd prepared went skittering off through the burning forest, leaving ash and embers scattering like fireflies.

"I don't know what else to do!" he said.

"Let me try — " Jane started, but the girl of fire interrupted her.

"I know what I have to do," she said.

Her voice had a hollowness, an echo, a sadness that stabbed Billy in the chest.

"No! Wait! Let us try to help!" he said.

The air grew hotter, suffocating. The hot ground burned the soles of his feet.

The girl shook her head.

"There's only one way this ends," she said. "Step back."

"What are you doing?" yelled Jane.

She shook her hands in helpless frustration.

What are we going to do, Dude? Billy asked.

I think we should do as she says, Billy Case.

"I don't want to do as she says, I want to help her!" Billy yelled.

Jane looked at him, unsure if he was talking to her or to the voices in his own head.

The girl stared from Billy to Jane and then back again.

"I'm sorry. Tell everyone hurt by me that I'm so sorry."

And then she started to get brighter. From orange to pale yellow, from yellow to white. She transformed to an inverted silhouette, a being of pure light.

"Jane! I can't see you! We have to get back!"

He felt Jane's small and impossibly strong hand grip his arm. Together they took flight. Billy tried to fly east, away and toward home, but Jane flew straight up, above the flames above the intensity of the growing heat.

Below them, an explosion erupted so powerful it interrupted their flight, propelling them higher up into the air, a wave of superheated pressure sent them sprawling. Jane relinquished her death grip on Billy's arm. He watched as she regained control of her flight and let himself tumble a minute until the air itself felt more stable and he was able to circle around.

The ground deteriorated into a blackened dead zone. Trees here and there still flickered with loose flames, but for the most part, the explosion seemed to have knocked out the fire itself, whether through the force of the blast or simply by devouring all available oxygen.

"It's all gone, Dude," Billy said. "Everything once living down there is gone."

I'm sorry, Billy Case.

"Yeah," Billy said. "Hey Jane?"

But when he looked up, Jane had disappeared, her fiery wake a long streak in the distance. She left him there alone.

CHAPTER 38:
RUMBLE

Once Titus left the Tower, following the rampaging villain was easy. The kid, who Titus had begun thinking of as "the bully," had smashed, thrown, or flipped over every vehicle in his path for three city blocks. Fires broke out in several places, and, cartoonishly, one hydrant had been smashed off its moorings, sending water spraying thirty feet in the air. Fortunately, the civilians along his path seemed to have taken the hint and ran away. The streets were all but deserted.

Titus spotted the bully a block away, and slipped out of his shoes. He stuffed his hands into the oversized hooded sweatshirt he'd taken to wearing and walked up behind him, careful to avoid stepping on the broken glass that seemed to be scattered everywhere.

The bully picked up two smaller cars and smashed them together like a pair of cymbals.

Then Titus cleared his throat. "I bet you were the kid who destroyed other kids' toys at recess, too," he said.

He dropped both cars onto their wheels, shocks squeaking in unison as they bounced back into place.

"I haven't thrown a human yet," the bully said. "Wonder how far I can fling you?"

His voice was thick, stupid, as if vocal cords and tongue worked too hard to form words. The contraption on the bully's chest continued to pump some sort of chemical into his body.

"Like to see you try," Titus said.

The wolf snarled in the back of his mind. Hang on, old boy, Titus thought. One more minute and we get to have our fun.

"Who are you? The Karate Kid?"

"Nah. Name's Titus."

"Titus?"

"Yeah. And I'm really looking forward to tearing you apart."

The bully flexed his hands, his massive, deformed fingers looking like a set of vice grips. He took one step forward.

Then Titus let the wolf come out to play.

The rippling tore through him, a screaming pain of bones thickening and stretching. Muscles expanded and howled into new, alien shapes. His fingers screeched when claws grew and hardened. The tendons and bones in his face clicked and snapped as his jaws extended, and massive canines sunk into place.

And then he roared.

"What the f — " the bully started to exclaim.

But Titus was already in motion.

He speared the bully across the middle, pushing him into a telephone pole, the post snapped under their combined weight. Titus howled when the bully grabbed a fistful of fur. He clamped his jaws down onto the bully's shoulder, but released when he received a return punch in the gut. Those vice-like hands grabbed hold of the werewolf and tossed him down the street. Titus was able to right himself mid-air and land on all fours; the claws on his toes tore canyons in the blacktop. He roared another challenge, and the bully ran at him, twice the size of a professional football linebacker. Titus prepared for the impact and rolled with it; his ribs cracked, and he used the opportunity to dig his claws into the bully's back.

Together, they slammed into a storefront, glass shards ripped their skin to shreds. Titus backhanded the bully across the face with one hand and steadied himself with the other. The bully landed a solid punch to the werewolf's face and the skin above Titus's eye split. Blood began to pour. They circled each other like old wrestlers.

Titus felt more in control of the wolf than he ever had before, relying on the monster's instincts but holding him back from making impulsive decisions. He couldn't fight every movement, though, and the werewolf lashed out with a clawed hand at the bully's face. The bully countered by grabbing Titus's wrist and holding it tight; he slammed his free hand into the werewolf's elbow. Titus felt bones snap brutally. Just as quickly, though, he felt the cool, strange sensation of those same bones mending instantly, knitting back together, realigning with tendon and muscle.

Titus reached out with his oversized free hand and wrapped his long, clawed fingers around the bully's head as if palming a basketball. He dug his claws in and dragged the bully out into the street again, feeling skin tear under the points of his fingertips. Once in the street, the grip on his wrist loosened. He squeezed tighter around the bully's head.

Then, the world went white and filled with a high-pitched ringing sound. The bully had pounded both fists into the sides of the werewolf's head. Titus released the grip on his opponent's head and yipped in pain when the bully threw a hard punch into his solar plexus.

Never looking up, Titus grabbed him by both legs and dug his claws in, planting into the oversized muscles there. The bully headbutted him, but they both reeled from that blow; like a drunken boxer, he landed a few feeble punches on wolf's muzzled face, and Titus lashed out with equally weak attacks across his enemy's face and chest. The bully tried another combination of punches, but Titus latched onto his forearm with his jaws; his attempts to yank his arm free were hurting more than helping, and when he punched the werewolf in the face to try to force him to let go, the bully only did more harm to himself, pushing the wolf's teeth in deeper and causing him to pull away again reflexively. He raised one foot and kicked Titus square in the chest. The blow forced Titus to loosen his bite, but when they separated, the bully's arm hung weak and loose with pain.

The bully pounded the palm of his good hand into the disc on his chest. The gadget came alive, pumping more of the mystery fluid into his body. Cuts and tears across his body were visibly healing, not unlike Titus's own.

"You got this one, kid," a voice said above them.

Titus rolled his weary yellow eyes up to see Kate in full battle gear standing on a second story ledge above them. She grinned demonically. "You know what to do."

Titus charged.

The bully, reinvigorated, pounded away at the werewolf's body with fists like stone. Titus felt more bones breaking, an entire tooth chipped in half in his jaw and grew back instantly. The rain of punches to his face left him half blind, but with a horrible, feral energy he pushed forward, leaving a railroad of lacerations across the bully's arms and upper body.

Then, the werewolf's claws clenched around the device on the bully's chest. Titus pulled.

The mystery substance sprayed in the air like arterial blood, a bizarre, blue-black fluid thick enough to be syrup. Where the contraption once rested lay a set of surgical scars, ports for plugs and tubes, the burn marks of a fresh injury. The bully writhed not in pain but in frustration and visibly began to lessen in size, muscles fluidly shrinking; his face became less apelike, more human. He collapsed to his knees. Panting, he stared up at Titus.

"You bastard," the bully said. "You took my toy away."

Titus, still in full werewolf shape, sniffed the contraption once and then threw it aside like a piece of rotting fruit.

Kate quietly snatched up the discarded machine and looped it awkwardly on her belt.

"You better kill me," the boy said.

Even with his power source gone, his injuries were healing, slower but steady, sealing up as if they never happened.

"What do you say, big guy?" Kate said.

She stood shoulder to shoulder with Titus, looking delicate beside the massive werewolf. The wolf's lips pulled back from his teeth as if to growl, but then those teeth began to recede, the fur disappeared, ears shrunk down to human shape. A moment later Titus — still in his strange yoga pants and a bloody but mostly whole hooded sweatshirt — stood there instead, breathing heavily, his own cuts and bruises fading as if in time lapsed photography.

"That was a lot of fun," Titus said. "We should do it again some time."

CHAPTER 39:
WORKING OUT DIFFERENCES

Titus found Doc and Emily on the observation deck of the training room. Below them, what appeared to be a continuation of Titus's brawl was taking place between Jane and Billy.

He limped over to the window and watched Jane hit Billy hard enough to send him flying into, and nearly through, one of the walls. They both looked like they'd been left on an outdoor charcoal grill much too long, their costumes charred black, faces covered in greasy gray soot.

"What's happening down there?"

"Fight!" Emily said. "Isn't it awesome?"

Titus raised an eyebrow at Doc, who observed the brawl passively, the combatants reflected in his red glasses.

"We're fighting each other now?" Titus said.

"They're working out a difference of opinion," Doc said.

"Should we stop them?" he asked.

"No way," Emily said. "How else we gonna know who's stronger?"

Doc shook his head. "It's a long standing tradition among heroes. Fight first, work out the aggression, talk about it afterward," he said.

"You gonna let them destroy the training room?" Titus said.

A bolt of Billy's concussive light blasts bounced off the observation deck window and scattered like broken glass.

Titus jumped.

167

Emily pressed her nose to the window.

"The room was built for this sort of thing," Doc said. "They'll be fine."

"Fine?" Titus asked.

Another loud bang echoed when Jane bounced Billy off the ceiling. Rather than falling, he flew straight back down, fist cocked and ready to throw a punch.

"They'll also be easier to talk down after they've worked out some aggression. Let it pass. How did *your* fight go by the way?" Doc said.

"You look like someone worked your face over with a tennis racket," Emily said.

"I'll get better," Titus said. "We have a . . . We have a prisoner? I guess? We brought him in, didn't know what else to do with him."

"Good," Doc said. "We'll call someone in to help us. The Tower isn't the place for keeping super-powered beings who've been captured."

Billy and Jane, now tangled up, and throwing weak punches at each other, crashed into the window again, and fell arm in arm to the floor.

"We could just lock him in there," Emily said.

Doc pointed at Emily as if to say something, shook his head, and turned to leave. "Don't let them kill each other," he said, over his shoulder. "Titus, come with me. There's someone you should meet."

"You were going to kill her!" Jane said, punctuating her lines with her fists.

She struck him in the face, sending him sprawling across the training room and leaving a Billy-shaped dent in the wall. Billy-shaped dents littered the room now; although his force fields kept her punches from really doing much damage, he could not, in any way, stop himself from being tossed around like a kitten.

"I didn't know she was going to do that!" Billy said.

Jane moved in to thump him again and he shoved her back with a double-handed light blast.

Why won't you tell her? Dude said.

Billy dodged another punch from Jane which left a fist-sized hole in the wall.

Tell her what?

That the blast you had built up would not have been enough to kill her.

Billy caught Jane's next blow with his hand, but while his protective field could keep her from breaking his fingers, he didn't match her strength, physically, and the shock thrust him flat on his back.

Because I didn't know it wasn't strong enough to kill her, Billy said. He wiggled his way out from a swinging kick from Jane.

Yes you did.

I swear. Thought I'd kill her with it.

Billy, I am inside your mind. You know you could not do it. It is admirable. Tell her.

"Jane," Billy said, interrupted by another smack to the mouth.

"We don't do stuff like that. We can't go around . . . killing people because we don't think we can help them!" she said.

He tried to lean back against the nearest wall, missing entirely, and flopped down on his backside. Billy scooted back so he could rest his shoulder against one of the dented areas his own body had damaged.

"You're right," Billy said.

"What?"

"You're right. She thought I was going to kill her, and that's why she did what she did," Billy said. "And I . . . didn't want to, but how else were we going to save the people in that neighborhood she was heading for?"

"We would have figured something out."

"Then talk to me, Jane," Billy said.

"About what?"

"What should we have done?"

Jane's nose wrinkled and her eyebrows drew together; Billy couldn't tell if she was furious or about to cry. Instead, she sat down across from him and anxiously pulled her hair back and away from her face.

"I have no idea," she said.

"Me either."

"She was like us. Just one of us without anyone to help her though."

"I know."

"And someone used her. Those people in the helicopter. Used her like a weapon. That could have been any of us. Could have been Emily or me or you — just as easily as that poor girl."

"We'll get them, Jane," Billy said.

She looked at her feet for a few seconds, lost in thought.

"We never even knew her name," she said.

They stared at each other a long moment, the weight of what happened sinking in.

Guilt gnawed in Billy's stomach.

"You're a mess," he said, trying to break the mood.

"So are you."

"Let's not fight anymore," Billy said.

Jane laughed, the sad, choking, self-conscious type of laugh that you hear at funerals. A pair of exhausted tears left lean streaks in the soot on her face.

"But punching you was the only thing making me feel better," she said.

Billy dragged himself to his feet and almost tipped over when he stretched to full height. He offered a hand to Jane to help her up. She stood with less trouble than he had.

"Let's talk to Doc," Billy said. "We can find out if there's someone else you can knock around instead."

CHAPTER 40:
TESTED

The mountainside base rumbled with movement as personnel began clearing equipment for transport. Agent Black observed the activity from a window in the conference room above the main atrium. He marveled at how much work had gone into making this underground base habitable, to make it almost corporate, only to be abandoned because of paranoia. They received orders that morning to move on to a secondary location and to leave no trace of their activities.

Meanwhile, Rose retrieved the surveillance results of their two-pronged provocation of these new metahumans. She seemed appalled at how poorly events had gone; Black was relieved they hadn't thrown a full-fledged attack at them before testing their behaviors in the field.

"Project Tinder was a complete loss," Rose began, projecting footage on screen of the raging forest fire the test subject had started. "Her potential as a superweapon was enormous. I'm not pleased we weren't able to salvage anything from her."

"There's no shortage of pyrokinetics out there," the Lady said.

She wore high heels, was dressed in an elegant tuxedo-styled shirt and skirt, and her hair was pinned back away from her face. If not for the streams of fire drifting out of her eyes, she'd have looked like she was perfectly suited to sit in a boardroom and conduct a project deconstruction. Black wondered if the Lady was mocking them.

"If we'd been able to use Tinder, she could have been another option for controlling natural disasters," Rose said.

"Trust me, there's firestarters everywhere, darling," the Lady said.

"You'll find another one."

"She destroyed herself, right? Am I reading these scans correctly?" Black said.

The death reflected on the screen bothered him. Not softhearted by any stretch, but he would feel better about the whole experiment if they were using older test subjects. Something about these throwaway kids troubled him. Admit it, Black, you were a throwaway test subject once upon a time yourself. Stop empathizing.

"She overloaded herself. Went supernova," Rose said. "What I'm curious about is this though." She tapped a few keys and cut to footage of the kid in blue and white — the one with the laser-like blast powers — who seemed to be prepping for a massive strike only to be stopped by his partner, the girl dressed in red and gold.

"Looks like a killing strike to me," Black said.

"Possibly," said Rose. "Which tells me either he's one to look out for in the future because he's not afraid to pull that trigger, or . . . "

"Or you might bring him in yourselves," the Lady said. "Don't bother."

Rose quirked an eyebrow at her.

"Why not?"

"Petal, I've made a career out of reading bluffs," the Lady said. "That boy could have killed our girl at any point. He was procrastinating. Waiting for someone or something else to take the decision out of his hands. That's what you want to know about him, not if he's a killer."

"So he's a weak link?" Rose said. "Funny, from what we've seen he's second only to the girl next to him in terms of power scale."

"I wouldn't call him weak. I'd say he lacks confidence," the Lady said. "The girl does too, but she deals with it better. Watch her movements. She's cautious but doesn't hesitate to take act."

"Didn't really work for her here," Black said.

Rose allowed the video footage to play out. "And I wouldn't want to pose as junior psychologist, but she left her boy here behind after they failed to stop Tinder. Perhaps some infighting?"

"They're kids," the Lady said. "Adults have infighting. Kids have spats."

"Don't you think you're underestimating them?" Black said.

The Lady smiled broadly.

"I wouldn't undervalue what they're capable of. Just saying their brains aren't fully formed yet. Don't let them fool you into thinking they're more experienced at this sort of thing than they really are."

Rose switched over to the footage from the Hyde experiment. The showdown in the street between Hyde and the werewolf played out on screen in silence. Rose's body language altered completely; she was now tense and attentive.

"Relax, Rose. This one is yours," Black said. "Nobody's going to take your werewolf away from you."

"It's not that," she said. "It's that he's evolving. At the lab he acted completely out of control. Here he's more rational. Still fighting like a berserker, but you can see it from the way he moves, even the transition from human to werewolf — he's getting better at it."

"What does that mean?" Black said.

"I don't know."

"What about the footage from the drones that pursued our lost tech?" he said.

"That's interesting," Rose said, tension easing slightly from her voice.

Lighter topic. Get her away from her beef with werewolves, Black thought. "They were older models, cheap hunter killers never meant to take out metahumans, but we've got something."

Rose called up the grainy eye-camera footage from their robotic drones as they fought the two girls in the apartment hallway. The drones were defeated easily, but as Rose noted, they were really meant to eliminate civilians, not legitimate threats, and anyway, they'd been sitting dormant for so long they were significantly outdated models.

"This girl," Rose said, tapping the screen as the masked fighter appeared. "She's good."

"Any indication of what she's got up her sleeves in terms of augmentations?" Black said.

"Nothing so far," Rose said. "But watch these moves. The other girl has some level of invulnerability so she over-relies on it. She has no reason to develop into a skilled fighter because she's stronger and more indestructible than pretty much anything that comes her way."

Black watched the footage again and paused the screen.

"This girl on the other hand, has been training in legitimate fighting styles for years," he said. "I recognize at least a half-dozen schools of martial arts in just these few minutes of footage, and she fights mean. Look at her."

"You sound as if you like her," Rose said.

"So do you. We're able to appreciate a cutthroat fighter when we see one, I guess."

"Maybe she's a mundane," the Lady said. "Every so often a mundane puts on a mask and holds his or her own with the monsters and aliens."

"You might be right," Rose said. "But what makes me more curious is why all of the drones' surveillance cameras shut off simultaneously when the fight moved outside the building."

"Some elements of that response were magic-based," the Lady said. "Someone on site employed a very simple spellcasting technique to tinker with the footage. But there's another thing entirely at work, too."

"You mean technological?" Black asked.

"Not my field. I'm the magical consultant, you're the cyborg."

"Well, this is all we have," Rose said.

"No it's not," the Lady said.

"How so?" Rose said.

"They took your Hyde project captive."

"He's a little jerk anyway," Black said. "We should have dumped him at the start of the experiment."

"Not what I meant," the Lady said. "Haven't you placed trackers in all of the test subjects?"

"We have," Rose said.

"And cortex bombs?"

A grin crawled across Rose's face.

"Then darlings," the Lady said. "What you have now are options."

CHAPTER 41:
DIVISION OF WHAT

The Tower, for better or worse, housed an area that amounted to a set of holding cells. When Jane and Billy followed Doc, Emily, and a worse for wear Titus, down into a deeper section none of them had visited before, they found their captive, the kid Titus had fought, in one of the cells.

Kate stood guard outside, cutting a sort of nightmare figure. She selected a place between the overhead lighting to stand in maximum shadows and altered her mask to white out her eyes.

"What's your deal," the kid in the cell said. "Don't talk?"

Kate remained perfectly still, arms crossed.

"The werewolf your boyfriend? I bet he is. Bet you go for the weirdos," the kid said.

Jane waited for Kate to knock his teeth out, but she just stood there, expressionless. Then, when Doc and the crew arrived, she took a few steps away from everyone else, to watch from a distance.

"It's the freak brigade," the kid said. "What happened to you two? Someone set off a bomb in your pants?"

Jane forgot that she and Billy were covered in soot with burns and tears littering their uniforms.

"Can I squish his brain?" Emily asked. "I think I know how to do that now."

She made a fist with her right hand.

"Little bubble. Squish."

"We're waiting for someone," Doc said. "Got a name, kid?"

"I'm Hyde," he said.

"Of course you are," Titus said. "I figured it was either that or Kong."

Doc waved Titus off.

"Who you working with?"

"Don't work for nobody," the kid said.

"Right," Doc said.

At that moment, the door at the end of the cellblock opened, and the skinniest old man Jane had ever seen walked in. He sported an impressive gray moustache, wore a fedora, and the sleeves of his light blue dress shirt were rolled up. His tie was knotted perfectly, but loose around his thin neck. He carried an old military style rucksack over one shoulder.

"Gang, this is Sam Barren. An old friend."

"Pleasure," Sam said. He took off his hat respectfully, revealing a mostly bald head, any hair that remained was predominantly gray.

"Hello, sir," Jane said. "I'm — "

"Just code names, please," Sam said. "It's safer that way."

Doc laughed.

"Sam is the head of the Division," he said. "He's worked with superhumans and heroes for decades. He's got rules."

"Former head," Sam said. "You know they shut us down after all that bad business happened. We weren't needed nearly as much as we were in the beginning, anyway."

"The Division of what?" Billy asked

Sam roared with laughter.

"Did I make a joke?"

"You did, actually," Doc said.

"We were just called the Division, capital D," Sam said. "But everyone always wanted to know what we were the division of, and so it became an in-joke with law enforcement. 'Call in the Division of What, we have a super-powered problem.'"

"I think the Division of What is an awesome name. We should steal it," Emily said.

Sam extended his hand to her.

"And you are?"

176

"Entropy Emily," she said.

"I'm almost afraid to ask what you do," he said.

"I make things weird," she said, nodding in a self-satisfied way.

The rest of the group introduced themselves easily. When Kate identified herself, Sam pointed at her.

"You, I know about," he said.

"You do?" she asked.

"When you first started up I was still keeping tabs on what was going on out there. Heard we had ourselves a do-gooder in town. I was hoping you'd turn out okay."

Kate nodded, but said nothing.

"And what do we have here," Sam said, walking up to the cell.

"Bite me, old man," Hyde said.

"Heard someone already did that today," he said.

The old man rummaged around his rucksack, then pulled out a blocky device like an oversized remote control.

"What's that?" Hyde asked.

"A neat little contraption I boosted from the Division before they shut us down," Sam said. He winked at Jane. "Always figured I'd need this stuff again. Heard they sold a lot of our gear once we were gone."

Sam held the device in Hyde's direction and tapped a few buttons.

"What. What are you doing? What's happening?"

"Relax, twinkle toes, I'm just scanning you," Sam said.

"How are we looking?" Doc said.

"Without that device strapped to his chest, he's just an ordinary kid," he said. "You probably didn't need to bring me in."

"Why not?" Jane asked.

"The Division was the group that locked up all the super-powered folks when they were caught," Sam said. "Doc here thought he might have one for transport."

"Transport where?" Hyde said.

Jane heard the bravado he'd possessed earlier fading.

"Were thinking we'd throw you in with the other metahumans," Sam said.

"Not crazy about that idea," Doc said. "You're giving the amateur access to the professionals. He goes in, makes a few connections, next thing you know he's in the latest league of evil somewhere."

"Send me there! You can send me there. I'll be fine," the kid said.

"Nah," Sam said. "You're just a regular little guy without your machine. We can hand you over to a standard prison."

"What?" Hyde's voice leapt two octaves.

Billy burst out laughing.

"Did you attack us just to get yourself locked up with other supervillains?" Billy said.

"No, I . . . no," Hyde said.

"So why did you attack?" Kate said, still half-shrouded in the corner. "You were obviously calling us out."

"I didn't. I wasn't . . . regular prison?"

"Talk," Kate said.

"No. No. You know what? I want a lawyer. You can't keep me here."

Sam pulled a another device out of his rucksack and ran a second scan. The machine beeped twice, loud.

"That's not the happy fun sound, is it?" Emily said.

"Doc," Sam said. "I think you've got two problems right now."

"Why are there always two problems?" he said. "Can't we just once have one problem instead?"

Sam wasn't smiling, though. He showed Doc the scan.

"It's okay. They're all fine, everyone can hear this," Doc said.

"Well, for one thing, he's been tagged," Sam said.

"Tagged?" Hyde said.

"You've got a tracking device in you," he said.

"A tracking what? Where?"

Titus hopped up on his toes to peer at the screen over Doc's shoulder.

"Oh man, you don't want to know," he said.

"Not — not there!" Hyde said.

"Worse," Titus said. He flashed a very strange grin at Hyde, Jane noticed. Cruel and predatory.

"That's not the worst of it. This kid has a cortex bomb in his head," Sam said.

"A what?" Hyde said.

"We should've known," Billy said.

"I'm so glad I didn't crush his brain," Emily said.

"What's a cortex bomb?"

"A bomb in your brain," Titus said. "Were you one of the lab rats?"

"I was a supervillain," he said. "I wasn't an experiment. People were afraid of me."

"Trust me kid," Billy said. "We've seen scarier than you."

"You were one of their pet projects, weren't you?" Jane said. She leaned in toward the futuristic glass that served as bars on the cell. "You've got to be honest. Tell us."

"I don't have to tell you anything," Hyde said.

"Not to alarm everyone, but I'd recommend evacuating the room, pronto," Sam said. "For all we know they sent him as a Trojan Horse. Get him in the building and then blow his brain bomb."

"Blow my brain bomb?" he said, voice cracking.

"Doc, I was serious," Sam said.

Doc pointed at Kate and Titus. "You two, out now."

"I can handle — " Titus started.

"Not everything, you can't," he said. "Humor me. Head up to the control center. Have Neal initiate a blast door lockdown on this zone."

Titus nodded.

Kate stared Doc down a moment, then left wordlessly.

"Billy?" Doc said.

"Shields up, boss, you got it."

"Sam, you should go with the others," Doc said.

"Doc, I don't have the gear to disarm a head bomb," Sam said. "This kid is — "

"I'm working on it," he said.

"Working on what? Working on what?" Hyde said.

"Calm down," Doc said. "Were you one of the lab experiments?"

"I — yeah, there was a bunch of us, a girl in a coma, a girl who

179

set everything on fire, some guy with scales . . . "

"How many were there," Sam said.

"Nine, ten. Maybe twelve," Hyde said. "I don't know, they didn't let us talk. I'd see them walking the others around — get this bomb out of my head? I'm sorry! I didn't mean anything. Just trying to be a badass — "

Jane walked up to the glass and put her hand on the surface. She was deliberately putting herself between Hyde and the others, hoping if he did blow up her invulnerability would protect Doc and Emily and Sam.

"Stay calm. You don't know what might trigger it," Jane said. "Just take a deep breath."

"I just didn't want to go to jail!" the kid said. "They bought off my parole officer! Said they could hook me up with these great powers — this stuff wasn't even fun, it hurt like hell every time I used them!"

"Where did they keep you?" Jane said.

"I don't know. We were on an island for a while," Hyde said. His eyes were welling up. "Then they moved us — am I going to die? Can you help me?"

"We're going to try," she said.

"I don't want to blow up."

Jane turned back to Doc.

"I can't have this happen twice in one day," she said.

"Does anyone else hear beeping?" Hyde asked.

"Oh no," Billy said.

"Nobody else hears it?"

"Sam, Emily, get moving," Doc said.

"Not just them, Doc," Jane said.

"What are you doing?" Billy said. "Is there anything we can do?"

"If we had twelve hours," Doc said, rubbing his eyes. "Dammit. These things. Annie left us a machine but . . . "

Sam walked up to the glass.

"I'm sorry, son," he said. "These things aren't designed to be taken out."

"Can we try to rush Annie's machine?" Emily asked.

Doc shook his head.

"It's embedded in his brain. The machine works very slowly to remove it, bit by bit . . . One misstep and it goes off."

"Help me," Hyde said. "I'm begging you . . . it's getting faster. The beeping is getting faster!"

"Out!" Jane said. "Everyone out."

Doc eyed her. She shook her head. Then, leaned in to whisper in his ear. "I can survive the blast, Doc. And I'm not leaving him here to die alone."

Doc nodded once, slowly.

"Can I do anything?" Emily said. "Can I help? Doc? What can I — "

He took her by the arm and grasped Sam on the shoulder with his free hand.

"You might protect us with one of your bubbles, but you couldn't . . . I'm sorry, Em. We've got to get you out of here."

Emily turned back to Hyde.

"I'm really sorry I made those jokes," she said.

Jane waited until the door closed. She could hear thumps and hydraulic sounds as the hallway was sealed tight. Then she noticed Billy had stayed behind.

"Get out, Billy."

He walked up to the cell door and tapped the release button. Hyde ran out, ran for the corridor door, pounded on it.

"I know what you're doing, Jane, and you're not doing it alone," Billy said. "Kid. Hyde. Come here."

"Screw you. I'm not going to die in here. I'm not!"

Jane approached him, held her arms out. She saw that, despite his attitude, despite his anger, he was young, younger even than her, not much older than Emily.

"Come here," she said again.

Hyde walked into her arms.

Jane hugged him. This close, she could hear the beeping timer of the bomb. Faster. Faster. Faster.

The corridor filled with flames. Lights flickered. Then, Billy's body slammed against the wall with a thump. The concussive blast rattled Jane, knocked her off her feet, but didn't break her skin. Hyde didn't utter a whimper. He was there, and then Jane's arms were empty.

She heard limping footsteps behind her, and felt Billy's hand on her shoulder.

"Jane," he said.

She stayed seated on the floor, shaking her head.

"This has to stop."

"Come here."

"I can't let this keep happening."

"Jane."

"What?"

Billy was one big bruise with lips split and an eye swollen shut — as if he'd spent the afternoon in the boxing ring. He spoke in a tiny voice, almost a whisper. "I really could use a hug right now."

She climbed to her feet and wrapped her arms around him.

Jane felt the raised bruises and lacerations on his back from the second blast. And there they stayed until Doc opened the doors and the others returned for them, two blackened, shadowed figures who had witnessed more death in one day than either had seen their entire, brief, lives.

CHAPTER 42:
CONTROL ISSUES

Somewhere over the Atlantic, Valerie Snow was angry.

The other entity, the storm, was angry too — Valerie could decipher its mood by the hail and lightning thrashing up the ocean surface. She'd given up trying to reason with it, yet that didn't stop her from spending hours talking out loud to the other thing. The chatter was meant to keep herself sane. She no longer hoped for a response.

For no immediately apparent reason, the storm tugged itself quickly in a different direction. They fought over where they wanted to go sometimes; now, the storm seemed to resent that Valerie could push for control when she wanted to, but it exhausted her to try to maintain that much influence over the weather's movement, so she usually abandoned her efforts.

She wondered what caught the storm's attention. Weary, she closed her eyes, wishing she could rest. The drifting fogginess of sleep started to cast itself over Valerie.

And then she could see what the storm saw.

Overwhelming, at first; she had no idea what had happened or why she was able to view something she shouldn't be seeing with her eyes closed. In the beginning, she thought it was a dream, but then she knew — she was envisioning a wide, panoramic vista of the ocean just outside the clouds. She could see for miles.

"Is this what you see?" she asked. "Is this your vision of the world?"

Then, on the horizon, she spied what caught the storm's attention. Like a rabid animal, the entity latched onto anything it could strike out at, and Valerie knew what the storm wanted: a massive shipping vessel, like a floating brick, chugged along in the distance.

The storm moved incredibly fast, too fast for Valerie to try to wrestle control from it again. They pounced, predatorily, onto the watercraft, swarming it with fog, hammering it with rain and wind.

"Stop it!" she yelled. "Why are you doing this?"

She heard the boat creaking and straining against the tempest. When she closed her eyes, she could zoom in on the decks to see the crew rushing around, hear their panicked voices in the wind.

"They weren't doing anything!" Valerie screamed. "Leave them alone!"

The vessel rocked on powerful waves generated by the storm. Huge swells threatened to tip it onto its side. Foam roared over the decks like avalanches.

Valerie gritted her teeth and wrestled for control. She tried pulling the storm with her, but the entity fought back. For every few feet she dragged them away from the ship, the entity pulled it back with equal force.

She watched in horror as the ship began to tip. Valerie held out her hand, a pathetic attempt to will the boat not to capsize. To her surprise, an intense gust of wind followed her gesture, shoving the boat in the opposite direction. The ship rocked back into an upright position.

This caused the tempest to roar in frustration at her actions. Valerie smiled, thinking she'd finally taken back more control from the creature. Then she saw the lighting. One, two, three lightning strikes in quick succession lacerated the ship, then more, blue lances of light and sulfur bursting onto the vessel's frame.

Desperate to stop the destruction, Valerie tried to force the storm to move, hoping, if nothing else, she could provide the ship with enough time to recover from the strikes. But she was worn-out, too weakened by the fight already, to be the victor in this test of wills. Exhausted, horrified, and furiously angry, all she could do was watch as the-container ship began to sink.

"This has to stop," she said.

And the storm drifted away to find some other victim to unleash its anger on.

CHAPTER 48:
THE PLEA

illy found Bedlam walking down a deserted stretch of highway, still wrapped in an oversized coat that hid her cyborg features. She wasn't hard to find; one of Dude's alien powers, apparently, was the ability to identify and track unique energy signatures, which, Dude told Billy, was exactly what Bedlam's cyborg nature gave off.

Billy landed twenty feet away; he kept his hands away from his body.

"Hey," he said.

"You've got to stop following me. I'm gonna get a restraining order."

"You going to hit me?"

"Looks like someone beat me to it," Bedlam said. "What happened?"

Billy still had trouble seeing out of his right eye because of the swelling. Dude's powers allowed him to heal at a faster rate than regular humans could, but it'd be a few days before he didn't look like he'd just lost a boxing match.

"This is why I'm here, actually."

"You think this has enhanced your appearance and you're hoping I'll say yes this time if you ask for my number again?"

"No," Billy said.

His stomach fluttered a bit when she made the joke. Half of him was strangely curious about her and not the least bit put off by the chrome glinting on her face and hands; the other half had this terrible guilt about Jane, who had, one hug aside, mostly treated him like he was a dolt.

Bedlam threw her arms out to her sides, frustrated.

"You gonna stand there and stare at me all day? Or, do you wanna tell me why you're here?"

"This happened when one of your fellow, um, experiments, ah. Um."

"What!"

"Hyde's cortex bomb blew up. Pretty much in my face."

"Hyde?" Bedlam said.

"You didn't know each other's code names, did you?"

"No," she said. "I'm guessing he was one of the experiments with super strength they were playing with," Bedlam said. "Was he . . . a good guy?"

"Kind of a jerk actually," Billy said, shrugging. "But mostly he was just scared and, I don't know, trying to figure out where he fit in with all this stupid business. He thought he was a super villain and then they blew him up by remote control."

"Crap."

"Yeah," he said. "We think he was sent to try to test us out. They released a firestarter too, at the same time."

"Not the little blonde girl."

"I don't know," Billy said. "When we found her she was like, lava, like walking lava, y'know? But . . . "

"She's dead too?"

"Yeah," he said.

Bedlam flexed her fingers a few times.

Billy heard the soft whine of motors, the clicking of artificial joints.

"They just threw them away to see what you guys would do?"

"I think so," he said. "I don't know. Maybe they were . . . "

"Making room in their new lab," she said.

"Look," Billy said. "We've got this machine, I guess it's from the future or something, it can take the bomb out of your head. It takes hours, so you'd have to stay for a little while, we can't just pop it out like a car tire, but, y'know, if you wanted to get rid of it just in case."

"Why not just blow me up yourselves and get me out of the way?"

"We're trying to develop a no-blowing-up policy. It's been a little hard to implement but it's become part of our strategic plan."

"You make no sense, you know that?" Bedlam said. "Be honest. You're just doing this so I don't demolish a McDonalds somewhere and become the next news story."

"I know you think I'm a jackass. Pretty much everybody does, it's okay, that's cool. I'm used to it. But . . . When you're not headbutting me, I like you, and I think it'd suck if you blew up. So I'm just saying."

"You don't like me. Nobody does," she said.

"From one fellow misfit to another, Bedlam. We've got to stick together. If we don't like each other, who will?"

She laughed, a short, barking chuckle.

"Fine," she said. "I've got to take care of something first. Where can I text you when I'm done?"

"Did you just ask for my cell?" Billy asked.

"Don't push your luck, alien boy," Bedlam said. "Just tell me how to find you, and if I haven't blown up by then, I'll let your magical machine fix my brain."

CHAPTER 44:
ON THE DEFENSIVE

The first thing Kate noticed was Billy's absence.

She'd been curious to see how well he'd recovered from the explosion; after he walked out of the holding area, it was pretty clear his alien force field was far from invulnerable. She also wanted to know what had transpired with the firestarter girl. Kate believed she could get the whole story out of Billy because of his tendency to run his mouth off. Jane hadn't said a word, she'd taken on a miserable, quiet air since the events of that day.

And, Kate couldn't hold it against her. They'd both experienced things they hadn't wanted to lately. Though she would never admit it out loud, she empathized with Jane.

Doc sat at the head of the debriefing room's table and tapped a few keys on a console embedded in the tabletop. A screen lit up behind him. The faces of the known experimental teenagers — two deceased, one crazy, and one a hypothetical living storm — appeared.

"Where's B — Straylight?" Emily asked, eyeballing the old man across the table.

After Hyde's death, Sam Barren decided to hang out — much to Doc's visible relief. Kate figured the responsibility of keeping five inexperienced heroes alive all by himself had begun to fray on his nerves.

"Went searching for Bedlam," Doc said. "He won't be back for a bit."

"He what?" Jane said, her voice sharp.

"Wants to try to bring her in again," Doc said. "She's in danger. If the Children of the Elder Star, or whoever is working for them, decide she's worth throwing at us, we should know where she is. And even if they don't, she's in jeopardy. They may decide to terminate her the same way they killed Hyde."

"More civilian deaths, too, if that happens," Titus said.

"But — did he volunteer?" Jane said.

"She'll talk to him," Doc said. "It's our best bet. He's in no shape to do much more than that anyway right now."

"If she attacks him he won't stand a chance, Doc," Jane said. "You should have sent someone with him."

"He'll be fine, Jane," Titus said. "Don't worry. She can't catch him if he decides to fly away."

Doc cleared his throat.

"Here's what we know," he said. "The Children have commissioned the creation of their own set of metahumans. Some have worked out better than others. All seem to be designed for maximum environmental destruction. Fire, weather, urban mayhem."

"Why kids, though?" Emily said. "I don't get it. Why kids?"

"Back in the old days," Sam began, "the Children would work with whatever they could get their hands on. Maybe they just thought these young test subjects would be more available. Or controllable. Perhaps they were less expensive."

Emily raised her hand.

Sam smirked.

"Yes, dear."

"Do you think they were trying to make a bad version of us?" Emily said.

"It's not a weak theory, but I doubt it," Doc said. "They're not the type to mirror their enemies just for the sake of doing the same thing. It's always about getting the best end result. I think we should be more worried about why they're planning large-scale destruction than the age of their lab victims."

"I still believe they tried to make an evil version of us," Emily said.

"Noted," Doc said.

Sam chuckled in spite of himself.

"What about the homing device?" Titus asked.

"Probably safest to assume they know where you are, and will eventually plan something using that information," Sam said.

"That's reassuring," Titus said.

"Would you rather I lie?"

"Alarmingly brutal honesty is fine," Titus said.

Doc sat back in his chair, creaking against the leather of the seat cushions. "We need more information about what's happening on their end," he said. "I'm going to launch a little scouting expedition."

"I could do it," Kate offered. "Tell me where you need to go."

"This isn't the type of reconnaissance mission any of you will be able to perform," he said.

"You're gonna use astral projection," Emily said.

Everyone at the table turned to stare at her.

"What?" she said.

"You astound me," Doc said. "Yes. Close enough. I'm going to trace back those creatures that attacked our girl in the clouds and see who's controlling them. Solar, I'll need your help."

"I'm not projecting my astral anywhere," Jane said.

"Oh my gawd, Solar made a funny," Emily said. "Didn't think you had it in you!"

Even Doc laughed a little.

Kate watched his eyes. Although the glasses obscured his face, she knew he was exhausted.

"I need someone to watch over me in case anything tries to follow me back," he said. "You'll be safest if that happens."

Jane nodded. "Is it dangerous?"

"You'll be fine."

"I meant for you, Doc," she said. "Will you be in danger?"

He shrugged.

"Everything's a little dangerous," he said. "Nothing can go wrong if you're there to watch out for me, right?"

Jane offered a blank stare.

"Solar, come with me. Sam, you've got the run of the place, make yourself at home. The rest of you, keep an eye on the monitors — I

191

have a feeling that the homing beacon situation is going to come back to bite us much faster than we're expecting."

Doc got up, started to leave, and let Jane fall in beside him. They strolled out, chatting softly. Titus and Emily left the room arguing about whether Billy would be in fighting shape by tomorrow morning.

"Give me a moment," Sam said to Kate.

"This code name stuff is garbage," she said. "If you're staying here, you should let us use our first names in front of you. You're being ridiculous."

"Probably right. Old habits die hard," he said. "But we have something else to talk about."

Sam lifted his rucksack off the floor and thumped it on the table. He unzipped it slowly and began rummaging around.

"You don't have any superpowers, do you. You're a regular person," he said.

"Thought you didn't want to know anything about us," she said.

"You don't have to tell me. I'm going to say what I have to say anyway," Sam said.

"I'm not a metahuman," Kate said. "Does that disqualify me or something?"

"Nope," Sam said. "It just means you're the best person to give these things to."

Sam began pulling out a set of gadgets from the rucksack. A duplicate of the scanner he'd used on Hyde, a slate gray utility harness, a pair of goggles, a small computer clearly built to be mounted on a wrist. The items kept coming. All small, portable, and not easily identifiable in function.

"What is all this?" she asked.

"When I raided the Division's equipment the day I got wind we were being shut down, I stole multiples of everything. Figured I might not have a second chance to get my hands on this tech again. I've been sitting on spare gear for a while now."

"Congratulations?"

"You're almost as unfriendly as the last guy I gave Division equipment to," Sam said. "With a little work you can be a complete misanthrope. You've almost nailed it."

"So now we're critiquing my heroic persona," she said.

"Yup. Do you want the spares, or not?"

"For what?"

"To make your own ice cream with," Sam said. "For crying out loud. I have a bioscanner, a voice identifier, a portable crime scene analysis kit . . . this thing, whatever this does . . . "

He picked up a device that looked like a squat pistol or taser. When Sam pulled the trigger, a small, hooked claw shot out and embedded into the wall opposite him, a thin cable led from claw to gun. He clicked the trigger again; the gadget was yanked from his hand and the cable withdrew, leaving the device stuck to the wall.

"Wow, I never tried that before," he said. "You want it? I can probably give you both of those, I'm not going to need them at my age."

Kate inspected the bag of tricks, seeing dozens of little devices that could be of use to her immediately, others that she could find a use for eventually, and still others that she couldn't even fathom their original purpose.

"Why are you doing this?" she asked.

The old man smiled at her.

"Because we're not all born with laser beams shooting out of our hands, or with magical healing abilities or invulnerabilities," he said. "Some of us just have guts to venture out into the world and try to make it a better place. And those folks need a leg up when they can get it."

"That's it?"

"That's it," Sam said. "I think you're brave as hell. It's the least I can do to lend you a hand."

Kate smiled in spite of herself.

"Okay, I'm sold," she said. "What does that circular thing do."

"I have no idea," Sam said, smirking. "What do you say we find out?"

CHAPTER 45:
ASTRAL PROJECTION

Jane followed Doc into a room in the Tower she'd never seen before, a large, and mostly empty, circular chamber. He waved his hand and a globe of light drifted off his fingertips. She watched the globe split into two, and then those globes split; suddenly the room was lit by a cool, blue light.

Doc knelt down and drew strange symbols on the floor. They looked like letters from an alphabet Jane had never been introduced to.

"Is this dangerous?" she asked, watching him take vials of powder out of his coat and make patterns on the floor with them.

"You'll be fine, I promise," he said.

"No," she asked again. "I mean, is it dangerous for you. Could you get hurt?"

He paused for a moment, studying her; then, smiled.

"I'll be fine. Done this more times than I can count."

"I can't handle it if anyone else dies on my watch today."

"I'm not going to die, Jane."

"Promise?"

"It's the best way to find out what we're dealing with," Doc said.

"I'm not done learning from you. So if you die, I'm gonna hold you personally accountable."

Jane folded her arms across her chest and watched him finish these preparations. He lit murky incense on fire, talked to things she couldn't see, made symbols in the air with his hands.

"Do you know where I came from?"

"What do you mean? We found you."

"No, I mean . . . what am I? An alien like Billy? A lab experiment?"

"Why you asking this now?"

"In case you don't come back," she said. "You're the only one who might know where I came from, and. . . "

"I'm gonna be fine," Doc said. Then he smiled. "You want to know where I think your powers come from, though?"

"Of course."

"You have the Gawain Gene."

"The what?" Jane asked.

"The Gawain Gene," he said. "You remember the story of Gawain?"

"King Arthur stuff? Knights of the Round Table?"

"Got it in one," Doc said. "Some of the stories say that Gawain's strength came from the sun. That he was stronger as the day went on, and weaker under the evening sky. He lost his duel with Lancelot because it went on too long and they fought into the night."

"You're saying I'm like Gawain?"

"Gawain was real, Jane," he said. "A lot of myths were real. Think about all the historical figures — heroes, gods — who derived their strength from the sun. Greek, Egyptian, Norse — every mythology has a sun god. Some of them weren't authentic, and actually were just a way to explain the movement of the sun in the sky. But others were just like you."

"So, I'm an accident?"

"You were born special, Jane," Doc said. "What's the one thing all those solar powered characters have in common."

"They're dead?"

"They're heroes," he said. "Every so often humanity gets lucky and a hero is born. And they shine in the sun."

Jane looked at her feet, waved her hands around awkwardly.

"Don't put pressure on me, Doc."

"None at all," he said. Then his expression darkened. "Jane, this thing I'm about to do — it might look scarier than it is. Don't panic."

"How am I supposed to know if I have to jump in and save you?"

"You'll absolutely know if something goes wrong."

"Okay."

Doc slipped out of his long black coat and tossed it aside, careful to not hit any of the symbols he'd drawn on the floor. He pulled his tee shirt over his head and sat down in the center of the room lotus style. Blue-black tattoos from neck to belt and down along both arms covered him. This shocked Jane. Some were identifiable, abstract images of animals or creatures. But most were strings of sigils and symbols, whirling patterns of alien letters, geometric shapes that bent and changed when stared at.

Then he took off his glasses.

The smallest of gasps escaped Jane's lips.

Doc's eyes burned, swirling pools of purplish-red flames, the trails of which drifted out of the corners like an open fire.

He closed his eyes. And then, he was gone.

Jane didn't know how she knew; his body remained perfectly still on the floor, but she could tell his consciousness, the part of him that mattered, had disappeared.

She found an empty bit of floor to sit on and waited, patiently, for his return.

CHAPTER 46:
THE PLATFORM

Agent Black preferred the last helicopter landing pad to this one.

The new location, much to his displeasure, was a base made to mimic an oilrig in international waters. The sky and ocean were very nearly the same color, a slick midnight blue, broken by stars above and whitecaps below. The chopper's lights gleamed off the water and the rain-slicked landing pad.

"So we're moving from an underground fortress to a tree house in the middle of the sea," Black said to Rose.

She was not happy. Spacious and solid, this castle on the ocean's surface, yet the rig still seemed fragile compared to their last base.

"A tree house in international waters," Rose said. "Boss's orders. They're ready to make their next step and don't want their operatives on American soil, or anyone else's for that matter."

"That's not alarming at all," he said sarcastically.

"How many left?"

It was Wegener who spoke.

Black and Rose exchanged looks of shock at the sound of the scientist's voice.

He'd muttered to himself on occasion since his meeting with the Lady, but hadn't spoken to anyone, outright avoiding both of them. But the Lady had chosen to travel by her own means to the oil rig, "riding a giant bat," Black suggested, and Rose shook her head and warned him he was closer to the truth than he even knew. Perhaps her absence had loosened Wegener's tongue.

"What's that, Doctor?" Black said, cordially.

It was his job to put a bullet in Wegener's head if he went too far off the edge, but he felt a kind of pity for what was left of the man after his meeting with the Lady.

"How many experimental children remain? They all gone?"

Black started to answer, but Rose shook her head.

"A few," he said, instead. "You remember. A few were killed when Project Valkyrie escaped."

"I do," Wegener said. "A waste."

"We saved who we could," Rose said.

"Some were better than others," the scientist said.

They touched down in a listless rain, the mercenaries sent ahead to secure the platform waited, armed but unfazed, more worried about the weather than any actual danger. Two men escorted Wegener away and into the complex. One of the escorts handed Rose an umbrella. When Black raised an eyebrow, the man shrugged in response, embarrassed.

"What, I don't rate an umbrella?" he asked. The merc started to stutter, but Black jabbed him on the shoulder and told him to get out of the rain.

"Dammit," Rose said.

Black followed her gaze and spied another incoming helicopter, bigger and quieter than their own, moving intently, an owl across the night sky.

"That the Lady's private copter?"

"I didn't know they were sending someone," Rose said. "Come on."

Rose shared her umbrella with him and they moved to meet the incoming helicopter on a secondary landing pad. Black was impressed by the machine — dead silent, slick maneuverability, the best money could buy.

A group of guards in expensive suits who moved like professional killers slithered out of the copter, securing the area. One of them signaled to the aircraft and out stepped another suit, a male, wearing a cloth mask over his face. The emblem of the Children of the Elder

Star was etched onto the mask; the eyeholes lining up with those of the squidlike creature the symbol portrayed. The man walked briskly over to Rose and Black, a guard on each side, one held an umbrella for him.

"I wasn't aware the Children were sending someone," Rose said. "I would have prepared a nicer welcome."

"No need," the man in the mask said, his voice pleasant, unaccented, American. "In fact, my colleagues think you're doing a hell of a job."

"I know there've been missteps, but —" Rose began.

"Please, Rose. Excuses don't become your reputation. If you thought I came here to have you done away with you would've put a knife to my throat already and killed half my men. Even the missteps have worked in our favor, all part of our calculated risks. We harbored no expectations that the Tinder or Hyde projects would survive those tests."

"And the destroyed lab?" Black said.

The man waved his hand dismissively.

"Expensive equipment but cheap property. We got what we wanted, didn't we? A working storm."

"It works when the Lady tells it to," Black said.

"You must be Black," the man said.

"Did my winning personality give it away, or was it the fake eye?"

"You have a reputation for being blunt," he said. "It's why you were hired for this job. We needed someone to counterbalance the eggheads and . . . where's the Lady? Is she here?"

"She's making her own way here," Rose said.

"Giant bat."

Black couldn't see his face, but knew the man frowned behind his mask.

"That woman is playing her own game," the man said. "Be wary of her."

"Every minute she's around, I can assure you," Rose said. "Would I be too bold if I asked what brought you here, sir?"

"You wouldn't," the man said. "But if you don't mind, I'd like to get out of the rain. These are nine hundred dollar shoes."

"I'm the designated Voice of the Children of the Elder Star," the masked man said. "It's my job to deliver our premiere message to the world."

"Which we'll be doing . . . here?" Rose asked.

They sat in yet another conference room inside the rig, a huge, polished table between them, the walls right out of a corporate suite. If I thought I'd spend this much time in conference rooms, Agent Black mused, I'd have skipped mercenary work and gone into plumbing like my father wanted.

"Yes. You've given us a series of natural disasters to lay claim to. We have the opportunity to use the storm on the American East Coast and possibly further. It's time to scare the hell out of the world."

"Another storm assault?" Rose asked.

"Could I make a suggestion?" the Lady said, walking in unannounced.

Black never even heard the door open — as usual — convinced she simply appeared in the room out of thin air.

The man in the mask, visibly thrown off by her presence, maintained a cordial tone.

"I'm willing to listen to your ideas, Lady Natasha."

"Please, no need for formalities," the Lady said. "I'd suggest you need something different as a show of strength."

"Throwing a hurricane at Boston isn't sufficient?" Rose asked.

"Show them you have your fingers in everything," the Lady said. "Make an earthquake."

"None of the test subjects had any seismic abilities or — "

"No, they didn't," the Lady said. "But John, you left something in the city, didn't you? A decade ago. You left a toy behind that would be just perfect for this."

The masked man rose to his feet.

"How do you know my name?"

"Am I wrong?" the Lady said. "On any account?"

"If you've been spying on me I'll have you — "

The Lady pointed a dainty finger and it silenced him.

"You'll never threaten me. Ever. You will maintain a civil tone or you'll incur my deep, deep enmity, and I can assure you that no one has ever benefited from losing my favor. Right now I'm working with you and your people, John, but if you speak to me in that tone again I'll make sure they want to kill you slowly themselves just to get back into my good graces. Am I understood?"

The man nodded.

"Now," the Lady said, sitting down gently in a chair at the head of the table as if nothing had just happened, "let's talk about what you left sleeping under the city, shall we?"

CHAPTER 47:
CAN'T GO BACK

I thought you didn't trust the old guy," Titus said, watching Kate test out some sort of mobile taser weapon Sam gave her. She had a set of these tasers, which were somewhere between throwing stars and stun darts. Kate practiced on a human-shaped target dummy, experimenting awkwardly with overhand, underhand, and side-arm tosses. In spite of all the completely terrifying things Kate was capable of, Titus thought, she really couldn't throw very well.

But as with everything Kate did, she was trying to perfect her technique. He already witnessed her improvement with the taser discs and she'd only been practicing for a few hours.

"So?" she said.

"He gives you a bunch of gifts now you're cool with him? He's like a creepy uncle buying his niece off with presents."

"First, I can't be bought off," Kate said. She hurled the disc again and it landed with a disconcerting noise on the forehead of the dummy. "Second, he's not creepy, he's completely bugnuts crazy."

"Well, that's reassuring," Titus said.

"No, I mean, he's one of us. Crazy and wants to make a better world. I don't entirely trust him but he's on our side," she said. "I have a feeling about these things."

"Took you at least three weeks to trust me."

"You didn't give me presents," Kate said. "And, Sam doesn't lose control and change into a murderous werewolf when he gets in a bad mood."

"Touché," Titus said. "Kate?"

"What?" she said.

This time the disc nailed the dummy above the heart. She walked to retrieve it, returned, and then threw again, repeating the heart-shot. Kate nodded to herself approvingly.

"You ever wonder what'll happen when this is all over? When, y'know. We stop the bad guys. What happens to us then?"

"We find more bad guys, Titus," Kate said. Ambitiously, she now took two discs in hand and flung them together. They spun out of control, missing the dummy entirely. Titus retrieved one, Kate the other. "There are always more bad guys . . ."

"I know," he said. "But does all this mean we totally forfeit, like, any sense of normalcy?"

"You're a werewolf. Normalcy? I'd say that shipped sailed."

"I don't know. It'd be nice to go to college or something," Titus said. "Although the application process would be a trip."

"Like to see the essay."

"How I spent my summer saving the world, by Titus Talbot," he said. "Billy and Em have families. Jane talks about the people who raised her all the time. Bet she misses them like hell."

"And then there's us," Kate said.

"Yeah," he said. "Seems like a really lonely life, y'know? I mean — I bet there haven't been three dates total in the lives of anyone in this building."

"I bet Sam was a player in his youth," she said.

"You know who I mean. Us. The gang. The team. Wouldn't it be nice to, y'know . . . have a life?"

"It's overrated," Kate said.

"Have you tried it?"

She narrowed her eyes.

Titus put his head in his hands. "You know what I mean."

She exhaled harshly, then threw her hands up in the air.

"I don't know if I could."

"What?"

"Have a life," Kate said. "What's it like when you wolf out? How does it feel?"

"Lately, not so bad, but for a long time it was completely out of control. Felt like I couldn't stop moving no matter how much I wanted to."

"That's me all the time. I don't sleep. If I sit still, I worry. I've got to be on the go. Can't have a life."

Titus stopped rubbing his forehead and looked at her in silence for a few seconds.

"I know," he said.

"You can't keep following me when I go patrolling, Titus," she said. "When you transform, you're a two hundred and fifty pound werewolf. It's like being followed by a dump truck with fangs."

"Just wanna watch your back."

Kate smiled — a rare treat.

"I know," she said. "I appreciate it. But you don't have to."

"I'm sorry."

"It's okay," Kate said.

They stood in silence a while, Kate whipping the taser discs at the dummy repeatedly, developing a good rhythm.

"One of those three dates yours?" she asked, finally.

"What?"

"You said we had three dates between the lot of us. You ever been on a date, or did the wolfing get in the way?"

"Maybe once."

Another long pause, more flinging of discs.

"I've never been on a date. The training seemed more imperative. Always something more important to do," Kate said.

"It was really difficult to see someone when I was on the run and howling at the moon," he said.

"We should go . . . When this is all over."

"You'd go out with me?"

"I'm not asking you to marry me. Just saying. It could be fun — the blind leading the blind."

"You'd date a werewolf?"

"Why not? I think I'd rather date a literal werewolf than a figurative one."

Titus smiled broadly.

"Now all we have to do is save the world," he said. "Guys have had to do worse things to convince a girl to go to the movies with them."

CHAPTER 48:
THE OTHER SIDE

On the other side of the looking glass, everything was luminous. Doc never ceased to be amazed at the beauty of it all, the shimmering glow of the new reality layered over the mundane — everything lined in light and dusted with silver. He waved his fingers and a blue path rolled out in front of him like a carpet. When he walked, his tattoos glowed, leaving trails of light in his wake.

Eventually he found the place where he'd left the bodies of the demons that had been sent to attack the girl in the storm. Still dead, but unchanged, without signs of decay or rot. Death's got a different meaning on the other side.

Carefully, he examined wings and teeth, eyes and skin. These weren't constructs, nor magical illusions dredged up from another sorcerer's mind. They were real, flesh and blood and bone, creatures from dark and terrible places that existed only in myth to the average person.

If their enemy could control real demons, then this was indeed a true threat. They had access to dangerous tools.

Doc lay one of the demons on its stomach, spread the wings out, and drew a symbol between the creature's shoulder blades. He did the same to another, and then a third. As he completed tracing the rune with his fingertip, a thin trail of light spilled from it, running off into the distance, a tiny trail of breadcrumbs back to where the creature had come from. Unsurprisingly, the lines converged, became brighter, racing off into the sky.

Doc took a step back and saw his own shadow. He reached down and tugged, lifting the shadow from the ground with his fingertips. It separated easily. Doc stood the shadow on its feet — on *his* feet — and breathed into it. This shadow, now a full-fledged man shape, featureless and dark, stood awaiting orders. He placed a hand on either of the shadow man's shoulders and pulled. Shadow man split in two, creating an identical, faceless version of himself. Doc split this mirror image in two also, pointed at the glowing trail, and the shadow golems flew off into the strange night sky.

With his shadow men acting as bloodhounds, Doc began dissecting the demons, peeling them apart, looking for sigils of control. Most often, creatures like this were controlled with a brand, a binding that enslaved them to the magician who etched it into their skin. All three were scarred, but all demons of this sort were scarred, skin covered in keloid bumps and old lash marks. Yet Doc discovered nothing — no marks, no symbols. He checked between fingers and toes, inside their mouths, on the insides of their eyelids.

If they were not bound by traditional means, that meant any of several other possibilities. They could have been acting out of general malignance, which, for little gremlins like this, was not unheard of. But the situation — driving a storm, the science involved — it all felt too organized and deliberate, and when left to their own devices, small demons were always poorly disciplined. They might terrorize a fishing vessel but they would never bother with something on this grand a scale.

Alternately, they could be under the influence of a like-minded creature. Something similar to them, yet more powerful, more malicious, more organized. Doc and his friends had fought several demon lords over the years, immortal, malignant, pitiless things. But again, the technology. The lab. Creatures from the other side don't have time for science, they never do. They work in bargains and night terrors . . .

Still, there are those who work exclusively in bargains, Doc thought with a twinge of panic. Please don't let it be her. Don't let her be involved.

He felt his shadow men as they were destroyed, a twinge of pain

in his fingertips and between his shoulders. The men were construct-
ed from his willpower and when they were gone that power came
flooding back, but so did the pain that wiped them out of existence,
an incredibly swift negation of the spells Doc utilized to build them
from his own shadow.

He discovered the incoming attack just in time, an arcing ball of
red flames racing along the threads he weaved from the backs of the
dead demons. Doc projected his most powerful protective spell in
front of him and the fireball crashed into it, changing the blue and
silver world to purple and gold. The tattoos all over his torso swam
and spun, forming new, alien words, building spells faster than his
own mind could formulate them. They surrounded him with armor,
erased his footsteps, and masked his face from probing eyes in the
distance.

Doc pulled a small, hooked knife from his pocket. Spying another attack heading his way, he stabbed the knife deep into his own
palm. He gasped at the pain, but the astral world began to fade, to
reduce back down into the mundane . . .

Jane hovered over him as he came to, his strange purple eyes
flaring brighter than ever. Doc's tattoos burned under the palms of
her hands but his skin was ice cold, hair tarnished with sweat.

"What happened!" she yelled, helping him lay down on his back.
Doc was shivering. She grabbed his long coat and draped it over him.
He smelled different — a bizarre blend of charcoal and freezer burn.
"Are you okay?"

"I have . . . had better ideas," Doc said. "Please start kicking
those patterns in the sand. Break them up so they're not readable."

"I wasn't able to read them," Jane said, but did as she was told.

"I just want to make sure I can't be traced back," he said.

"What happened?"

"I think I know who's working their magic angle for them," Doc
said, pushing himself up onto one elbow.

"Someone like you?"

"Lady Natasha Gray," he said. "Don't know why she'd be caught up in something like this though. Experimenting on kids seems beneath her. She must have an angle."

"Sounds like you know her," Jane said.

"Taught me everything I know."

CHAPTER 49:
THE VOICE

All Emily knew was she missed some weird stuff today.

It was partially her own fault because she'd spent the day harassing her nemeses online, but it wasn't as though anyone had invited her along to help with whatever they were doing. Now Titus and Kate sat next to each other at the meeting table — Kate never sits next to anyone, she barely ever sits, Emily thought — and then Doc walked in looking like he caught a bad case of the flu, seeming so worn out that Jane's death grip on his arm was likely the only thing that kept him standing.

He grunted like an old man when he sat down, also with Jane's assistance, and Emily didn't like that one bit.

"I've done some digging," he said, his voice exhausted. "I wanted — why are you smiling?"

His question was directed at Titus who was, in fact, grinning like an idiot.

"I'm not smiling."

"Been smiling since you walked in here," Emily said.

"Everything okay?" Doc asked.

Titus looked at Kate.

Kate glanced back at Titus.

He stopped smiling.

"Everything's perfectly normal — not different at all," Titus said. "Morose werewolf boy at your service."

Doc shook his head.

"I want to warn you that it looks like we've got a big player in the game now, a world-class sorceress. Let me tell you one thing, and one thing only: don't engage her. Don't even talk to her. If she tries to talk, run."

"What if — " Kate started.

"Run," Doc said. It was the hardest he'd ever spoken to any of them, and Emily picked up on real worry in his voice. "Leave her to me. Magic is . . . Magic has its own rules. I haven't prepared you well enough to fight someone like her."

"Or like you," Kate said.

"Nor someone like me," he said. "Until I do, just promise you won't try to fight her."

"You gonna to tell us anything about her?" Jane said. "You said — "

"Let me figure out how we're going to deal with her first. Then, I will. Where's Sam?"

"Out," Kate said. "Do we get to know this woman's name at least?"

"Out?"

"Said the food in this place still 'tastes like 1980's space food' and wanted to get a deli sandwich," Kate said. "Name?"

"That picky old man," Doc said.

"Her name is Lady Natasha Gray," Jane said.

"That's historically inaccurate," Emily said.

Everyone turned to look at her as if she'd said something strange. "What?"

Meanwhile, Kate engaged in a stare down with Doc.

"She's dangerous, Kate," he said. "Even more dangerous if you let her speak with you. She makes deals. Makes promises. It's worse than it sounds. We need to plan ahead before we engage her."

"That's all I'm asking for, Doc," Kate said. "Thanks."

He stood up wearily. "That process took the life out of me. I need to sleep it off and try to develop some methods to deal with this latest threat," he said. "Stay out of trouble for a while?"

"Sure thing," Emily said.

"Especially you," Doc said. "Someone please wake me up if Sam gets back."

Neal, the Tower's computer, chimed in with a gentle warning bell. It was so unexpected, yet so polite, nearly everyone in the room jumped out of their skins. Everyone but Kate of course. It startled Titus so much he cursed under his breath.

"Designation: Silence," Neal said, courteous as always. *"There is a broadcast occurring right now you should be aware of."*

"Where?" Doc said.

". . . everywhere, sir," Neal said. *"I have not confirmed its worldwide distribution but it appears to be cutting into all cable and satellite television, as well as streaming video from all major providers."*

"So play it, Neal. From the beginning."

"Yes sir."

The wall-sized screen behind Doc lit up. It revealed a simple image of what appeared to be a bank branch manager with a deep purple sock over his head. A squid design was etched on the front of it.

"Oh my gawd it's the Cthulhu people!" Emily yelled.

Doc waved his hand and shushed her.

"I'm the designated Voice for the Children of the Elder Star," the man said. He had a good voice, Emily thought. He could record audiobooks. "We've been silent for too long. The world has forgotten us."

"The demands," Kate said.

"I speak for us, but I don't command us — we're many, and all around you. You're in our world. You simply don't realize it yet."

"What could they want?" Jane asked.

"You've seen a series of unnatural hurricanes strike the Atlantic coast. A raging forest fire in the American west. Acts of destruction perpetrated by children. I'm here to tell you that those are the least of what we can rain down upon you.

"We control the weather, and have an army of human bombs and walking weapons at our disposal. You'll do as we say, or be taught to understand that this is no longer your world, but ours."

Titus suddenly stood up and cocked his head, listening to something outside the room. He walked softly around the table, his eyebrows drawn tight in concentration.

"We know you'll find this difficult to believe, and so, to prove our threats are real, we'll launch one final attack. You'll see that we not only control the weather, and are able to burn your forests to the ground, but can initiate earthquakes at will. As such, there'll be an earthquake in the city momentarily."

"Do you guys hear that?" Titus asked.

Jane was on her feet, heading for the landing platform. "Emily, come on," she said.

"Nations of the world, our demands will follow shortly. We sincerely hope you choose to cooperate and not force us to deliver another demonstration."

The screen blipped blank.

Then, the entire Tower shook.

CHAPTER 50: EARTHQUAKE

From above, it looked like a giant anthill, a dirt mound rising up out of the street, with a gaping hole at its top. Jane flew down to investigate and discovered something had blasted or burrowed its way up from the city's subsystems. She peered all the way down past the subway and into the deeper earth.

Jane turned to see Emily pointing at an equally large hole torn into the side of the Tower itself. Glass shards and concrete blocks littered the street, the interior of the building left gutted and unrecognizable.

And then the culprit of this destruction emerged.

"You've got to be kidding me," Jane said.

A monster the size of a city bus crawled out of the building. Its body, sloping and shambling like a grizzly bear's, was covered in short, shiny, mottled fur. Instead of paws, the two front limbs terminated in tarnished, chrome-plated lobster claws. Jane caught sight of an extra set of limbs set halfway back on its torso which allowed it to creep on four legs while snapping away with those massive sickle-shaped claws.

As for its head, she found no eyes to speak of, and its muzzle consisted of a drill half the size of a car. When the creature noticed her, the drill began to spin.

"I think he likes you," Emily said. "Can we keep it?"

Instead of attacking, though, the creature reentered the hole in the Tower. It started to dismantle the tower at its roots and the building shook.

"Do something!"

"What should I do? Pull its tail?" Jane said.

And then the creature roared in pain.

The building rocked, the monster struggled, lashing out with all limbs. Its cries, and the whines of the drill, deafened.

Titus, twice as big in werewolf form as he'd been upstairs and still wearing that ridiculous hooded sweatshirt, bounded out of the building's side; his muzzle covered in blood.

The creature pursued him. Those huge claws snapped, but the werewolf remained one step ahead, digging his own claws into sensitive flesh on the monster's arms with each missed swing. Titus scurried underneath and raked the creature's underbelly. It rolled over, swatted the werewolf away and scampered into the hollowed out side of the building. Windows seven stories up shattered and fell under the pressure.

"It's like the thing is chopping down a tree," Jane said, gesturing towards the building.

One whole corner began to buckle, most of its supports torn away. Jane pictured the entire structure toppling like a cherry tree.

"Emily, catch the building if it falls."

"You kidding me?"

"You control gravity!"

"I can barely control myself!" Emily said.

Meanwhile, Kate dashed from the building, scurried up the back of the creature and planted something at the base of its skull. She leapt off gracefully and thumbed a trigger. The monster howled in pain again and Kate hit the ground, rolling like a gymnast.

"We gotta get that thing out of there," Jane said.

"Can Titus bait it?"

"He's not very rational at the moment," Kate said. "You got anything else?"

Jane flew in fast, leaving Kate standing there waiting for an answer. She punched the monster in the spot she hoped was between its eyes. The skull felt like concrete.

"Hey, beautiful," Jane said, flying just out of reach of the huge metal claws.

With surprising speed, the creature scaled the edifice, its back legs breaking through glass and metal to locate footholds. Jane flew higher, leading the monster up a distance from street level — not her best idea, but at least she'd lead him away from civilians.

The Tower creaked and groaned. Jane sensed Emily's bubble of anti-gravity wash over her, and suddenly she was no longer in charge of her own flight, spinning loosely in the air.

The monster grabbed hold of her in one of its massive claws, its grip impossibly strong.

"Oops!" was all she had time to say before the monster slammed the claw, with her in it, into the side of the building. The beast moved slow, obviously impacted by Emily's bubble as well, but it held the upper hand over Jane with its clutch of the structure. It smashed her into the exterior walls a second time and climbed higher, one claw at a time.

Then Titus flew into sight.

In other circumstances, Jane might have laughed at the sight of a flying werewolf, but she could barely breathe clamped down by the monster's crush. Titus must have deliberately jumped into the gravity bubble, letting his momentum carry him like a bullet to the monster. The werewolf landed and sunk his teeth and claws into the creature's skin to keep from floating away. The beast roared again. Globs of its own blood drifted in the gravity field, flesh torn by Titus. With its free lobster-like arm, it swatted the werewolf away, sending him earthward. Jane witnessed the exact moment Titus went from drift to freefall, exiting Emily's gravity field and dumping unceremoniously to the pavement.

Finally, Doc appeared from the base of the Tower, waving his hands left and right, turning hunks of concrete blocks and building bricks into dust or butterflies. Then he focused on Jane trapped by the monster.

She pushed at the claw with both arms, trying to pry herself free, but its grip was still too tight. Jane allowed heat to generate in her hands, which turned the metal claws red hot, but all that did was cause her own costume to start smoking in a low-level burn.

The monster remained unfazed.

Then, the top of the building began to give way.

Not fall, though; rather, the upper level floors of the Tower separated and floated up into the sky like a zeppelin.

"Emily, whatever you're doing you need to stop!"

"I'm not doing that!" she yelled back. "My bubble doesn't go up that high!"

"Then what's — " Jane began.

Doc flew up beside Emily and fired off spell after spell to obliterate the falling debris before it could land on any of the spectators or rescue workers who had begun to arrive.

"I should have told you," Doc said. "The Tower isn't really a tower."

The top of the building peeled away; Jane noticed machinery, like jet thrusters, affixed to the bottom of the detached floors. The upper levels then tore free completely and flew away from the structure.

"Dude, we were living in a space ship?" Emily said.

"I'll explain later — can we get you out of there, Jane?"

"Can you turn this thing into a pumpkin?"

"Not with you in it," Doc said. "We need to give you some distance. Where's Billy?"

Of course, at that moment Jane caught sight of Billy's signature light trail streaking across the sky. Zeroing in at top speed, his aim was directed right at the drill monster like a bullet.

"Oh no," Jane said. "Billy, tell me you're wearing your radio . . . "

He wasn't, obviously.

She filed it away in the back of her mind to scold him later about maintaining proper communication, if they all survived, then watched Billy's elegant arc of attack turn into an awkward, gravity-free tumble the second he contacted Emily's bubble. He gurgled a stream of obscenities and spun, pathetically, toward the monster and to Jane.

When Billy ground to a sad little stop within earshot of her, he shrugged apologetically. "Oops," he said.

Then the monster swatted him and drove him tumbling back up into the air.

"Enough," Jane said.

She lifted both fists above her head and started pounding on the claw holding her in place, over and over again, with all of her strength. It's metal began to dent and the creature roared; still, she was trapped. The monster continued to thrash the side of the building to pieces. That drill snout made several petulant passes across the surface of the structure, tearing it apart.

"Emily, drop your gravity field for a few seconds," Jane said.

"That's a terrible idea. You should probably reconsider," Emily said.

"I can't get free, so I'm gonna fly straight up. Take this guy with me."

"You're insane," Kate chimed in. "Good luck."

"Jane, I can let go of the building but if it falls, I'm almost positive that I'll not be able to grab it fast enough to catch it again before it crashes."

"I've got it," Doc said.

"You sure? You don't look so good," Emily said.

"I got it, Em. Let go."

Jane's stomach swam as gravity returned in full force. She felt the building lurching, teetering toward complete collapse. The monster slammed her down against the tower again, but this time she caught the blow with her feet and kicked off the building for leverage, pulling herself, and the creature, into the air.

The monster flailed about. Jane's flight sputtered weakly, bobbing and weaving she tried to pull them higher. Its drill and claws tore chunks from nearby buildings when they swung in too close.

Above her, the tower fell.

She watched Doc's magic at work.

Instead of stopping the fall, his supernatural powers converted the edifice — or what was left of it — into something else, a fine, silvery powder. The spell erased the building, transforming it into white dust — a taste in the air led Jane to think Doc had turned the building to salt — which drifted to the street below. Not fast enough though, as the last few stories tumbled to the earth unchanged. At the last minute, these solid pieces stopped falling and floated slowly to the ground when Emily caught hold of them.

"He's too heavy," Jane said, still holding the bus-sized monster aloft but making little headway getting it further into the sky.

"Would it help if I pushed?" Billy said, nearby.

The air grew bright then, and the weight of the creature lightened when Billy flew up from below.

He was not nearly as strong as Jane, but between the two of them they thrust the creature up above the skyline and out of reach of other buildings. The monster howled in frustration, yanking its arm as if trying to pull Jane back to Earth.

Kate's voice chimed in Jane's ear.

"Has anyone seen Titus?" she asked.

Jane heard Titus's distinctive roar, but it was definitely not through her earpiece.

The werewolf clung to the side of the monster, his claws leaving a bloody trail as he held on. Titus continued to make his way toward Jane, stopping at the monster's shoulder, before sinking his teeth deep into muscle.

The creature emitted a horrible howl of pain, but the claw opened, sending Jane rocketing in the air, unburdened by the weight of the beast. Titus was shaken free and sent plummeting back to the ground, snarling and waving his claws. Billy cursed again as he tried to take on the full weight of the creature and failed, barely able to slow their descent.

"Leggo, Billy!" Emily said, grabbing the flailing Titus with one hand and picking up the monster with the other. Billy's flight sputtered — nearly caught in Emily's gravitational anomaly — but instead he was able to swoop in to snag Titus and carry him back to the ground.

Jane and Emily hovered near each other, staring at the huge, pitiful creature that destroyed their home. High above the ground with nothing to break, it seemed more tragic than threatening, a miserable hybrid of animal and machine.

"How you doing?" Emily asked.

"Feel like I'm gonna throw up. You?"

"I'm cool," she said. "Can you ask Doc where the wild things are discarded? I don't want to float around with this giant centipede mole bear forever."

CHAPTER 51: THE CHILDREN

Black watched their pet storm on the horizon, moving against all nature and heading out to sea. He wondered if she knew they were here, or if it was just a coincidence. Their personal hurricane had been moving at will up and down the eastern seaboard for weeks. It was difficult to tell what movements were deliberate and which were just confusion and rage.

"I've never met one of them in person," Rose said.

She took a sip from her coffee and placed her feet up on a conference table. They hadn't seen the Voice since he presented his speech. Or, was that manifesto? Instead, the masked man remained holed up in the inner chambers of the oilrig, conversing with his betters.

"All these years, all these gigs, never met one of them face-to-face," Rose continued. "Always through an intermediary. Lawyers or soldiers."

"You really think he's one of them?" Black said. "I've never met one either. What's to say he's not just another peon like us, a hired actor to be the face of their organization so they can remain in the shadows?"

"The Lady knew him," she said.

"But that doesn't make him one of the Children," Natasha said, entering the room without a sound. "He's a cog. The Children never come out to play. They know where they belong. Cutting checks and winning wars."

"But you recognized him," Black said.

"He's been working for the Children for years, much as you two have."

"What, you don't work for them too?" Black said. "I figured we were all their hired agents provocateur."

"I'm working on their behalf, but not working for pay, darling," she said. "One doesn't simply hire someone like me. You have to offer something much more significant than money to me."

Black watched her for a moment then returned his gaze to the storm.

"What do we think of the attack on the city?" he asked.

"Not as much collateral damage as we would have liked, but knocking over an old super team's home base was pretty thrilling," Rose said.

"Didn't exactly knock it down," Black said. "One part flew away . . ."

"And the other turned into a pillar of salt," the Lady said. "There aren't too many magicians who know that trick. One of them used to live in that tower. I'm guessing he probably still does."

"How does that work, anyway?" Rose said. "You point at a building, say *abracadabra,* and it turns into dust?"

"Why, pet, you have to *ask* the building to change to dust. And you must ask it to do so using its real name," the Lady said.

"What?"

Black turned around and leaned against a heavy glass window making up the wall to the outside world.

"Did we realize they had some kind of massive hovercraft that comprised the top floors of the building?" he asked.

"We had to know they didn't just have a bakery and a shoe repair shop on the top floors," Rose said.

"What next, then?" he said.

"We wait," said the Lady.

Black looked at Rose.

"She's right," Rose said. "I suspect they'll want to use the storm again."

"Which we don't fully have under our control," Black said.

"Where's that damned scientist?"

Rose looked at Black like he'd said something horribly offensive.

"What?" he said.

"Don't remember seeing him since we got here," she said.

"I spoke to him on the helicopter. He has to be here," Black said.

"Did he get off the helicopter?"

"Had to," he said. "Right?"

"We . . . did we lose our scientist?" Rose said. "I'll kill him."

She hopped out of her chair and stormed to the door.

"Well, Mega Man? Come help?" she said.

With little choice in the matter, Agent Black followed.

CHAPTER 52: DINER

Jane, Billy, Titus, and Kate sat in a pizza parlor a block from where the Tower once stood, waiting for Doc and Emily to deposit the drill monster on the island where their ruined lab now sat empty.

Emily had castigated Doc about the deplorable conditions they left the creature in. Upon their return, they were still engaged in an animated conversation

"What's it gonna eat?"

"Those things were designed to hibernate," Doc said. "When it discovers there's no food, it will dig a hole and go to sleep for ten years. We can return for it later."

"How would you like to be abandoned and left alone on a desert island?" Emily said.

"It'll go right back to sleep, Em."

"I should visit. Keep it company."

"No, you shouldn't," he said.

Doc pulled a chair up to the booth where everyone else sat, taking a small piece of sad, droopy pizza covered in powdered concrete and salt.

"What was it, anyway?" Kate said.

Her tone was flippant, but she slid a paper plate across the table with another full slice on it — this time, cement free — for Doc, who appeared more and more lethargic every time they saw him.

"I thought we dealt with all of those creatures," he said. "When I was around your age, a group of aliens unleashed a swarm of them on earth as a precursor to a terraforming expedition. It took us months to hunt them all down. Looks like we missed at least one."

"So Bubba has been sleeping for fifty years?" Emily said.

"Fifty — what?" Doc said.

"Bubba?" Titus said.

"How old do you think I am?" Doc said.

"Like seventy, right? Seventy five?"

"Forty. I'm forty years old. Do I look that bad?"

"You really want an answer?"

"No he doesn't," Jane said, throwing sugar packets at Emily from across the table. "So, do you think it was left there on purpose?"

"Maybe," Doc said. "Probably not for us. I bet somebody knew one was buried under the city and was just waiting for the best time to activate it and get the most terror for their buck."

"We're missing a bigger problem here," Titus said. "Our base . . . flew . . . away."

"No it didn't," Doc said.

"I'm a werewolf. That means I have anger management problems, not eyesight problems. Our roof flew away like a space ship," he said.

"It really didn't fly off. It's a few miles away, waiting for us."

"Flying?" Titus said.

"More like hovering," Doc said.

"You see what my problem is here, regardless," Titus said. "How do Kate and I come and go? Rope ladder?"

Kate made a shushing gesture at Titus. The two proffered a strange little silent exchange that Jane thought was almost cute, and then Kate directed her attention back towards Doc.

"Is it one of your friend Annie's inventions? A flying base?"

Doc shook his head.

"That ship was here long before Annie came along. Before I came along."

"Did you just say ship?" Kate said.

"I did."

Billy, who had somehow managed to get even more bruised and

battered than he had from the explosion, put his head down on the table, his face landed in the pizza, a little bit of sauce dripped from his cheek. "It's a space ship," he said.

"No way," Emily said.

"Dude just confirmed it for me. He wants to know how many of the others are still active."

"Others?" Doc said.

"Yeah. Dude says . . . let me use his exact words: nobody actually knows how many starships are currently masquerading as buildings on planet Earth," Billy said.

"The Gherkin in London better be a rocket ship or I'm gonna be super disappointed," Emily said.

"You've been to London?" Jane said, raising an eyebrow at her.

"Why is everyone so surprised when I know anything!" Emily said.

"Were they trying to attack us to send a message? Was it to make us look bad on TV? What was the reason behind it?" Kate said.

"It could have been to keep us busy while they get something worse planned," Jane said.

"All plausible," Doc said.

"Can we go back to discussing how we're living in a space ship all this time and never knew it?" Emily asked.

"Or how there are apparently countless spaceships disguised as buildings all over the world?" said Billy.

Just then, Sam walked in, his coat slung over his shoulder and fedora tipped back on his head.

"I leave for a few hours and your entire building blows up?"

"Didn't blow up," Emily said. "It crumbled."

Kate turned back to Doc again.

"Why salt? Why not just make it evaporate?"

Doc threw up his hands.

"It's magic. Movement of energy back and forth," he said. "I couldn't just displace it, and didn't want to turn it into something awful, and I wanted to transform it into something that could dissolve in the rain. It was the first thing I thought of. Next time I'll try baking soda."

"Caught the whole thing on the news," Sam said, sidling over. "Considering an entire building is now gone — including the part of it that flew off into the sunset — you guys did a great job containing the problem."

"Sure did," Emily said.

"Except I think we did too good a job," Kate said. "If their goal was to maximize destruction, why attack our home base? They knew we were there. They placed that homing beacon in Hyde. This wasn't coincidence."

"So, we're back to asking what they get out of distracting us," Jane said.

A phone rang, an awkward, muffled, deep in someone's pocket ringing. Everyone looked around the table, then to Emily — the only one who ever got a call on her cell — and then back to each other until Billy scrambled to pull one from his pocket.

"Uh, hello? Oh. Wow. No — yes. I'm okay. No. Really. I'm — you don't have to . . . But . . . Okay. Okay. Yes. I'll try."

He hung up, put the phone away, and leaned back in his chair. Everyone looked at him, waiting.

"What?" Billy asked.

"Who was that?" Titus asked.

"Nobody. I'm cool."

"I'm cool? Nobody? Are you serious?" Jane asked.

"It was — it was my mom," Billy said.

"Holy crap. Your mom?" Titus said.

"I, like, she saw us on the news. I wasn't wearing my costume. She recognized me."

"Saw you on the news?" Jane said.

She tried to picture the horror of a parent watching their child fighting a giant monster on TV. But then thought of her own adoptive parents and wondered how often they saw her and worried. Doc said they raised more than one hero, but could it be something that got easier over time?

"Just wanted to make sure I was okay."

"That's . . . " Titus said.

"Really nice," Kate said.

"I guess," Billy said.

"Do you check in with her much?" Titus asked.

"No," he said. "I don't want her to have to, well, do this. To worry."

"You don't call your mom?" Kate asked, incredulous.

"Emily calls her mom during missions!" Titus said.

"I just . . . whatever," Billy said.

"You should go visit her," Emily said, finally.

Billy raised an eyebrow.

"I'll go with you," Emily said. "She should know you're all right."

"Looks like he got hit by a bus," Titus said. "Wouldn't call that all right."

"Maybe another time," Billy said.

"Doc?" Emily said.

"It's up to you, Billy. How you conduct your private lives is entirely up to you. It'll always be up to you."

Billy rested his hands on the table and stared at his fingers, refusing to make eye contact with anyone.

"Billy," Kate said, as always free of irony or sarcasm. "If I had the opportunity, I would."

He looked at her, eyebrows raised in puppy-like guilt.

"Okay," he said.

Doc stood up, adjusted his coat, exchanged a long glance with Sam.

"Why don't you do that right now, Billy," Doc said. "I have a feeling things are going to get worse soon. Take advantage of the time while you have it."

"I'm going with him," Emily said.

"Okay," Doc said. "We'll get the rest of you back up to our — "

"Starship!" Emily said.

"Our base," he said.

"If this involves a teleporter I quit immediately," Titus said.

"No teleporters," Doc said. "I promise."

Sam roamed up to the counter to pay their bill, and everyone else shuffled outside. Billy stayed behind, still sitting in his chair. Emily debated with Doc about whether their base could really fly deep into outer space or not. Jane lingered at the door, watching Billy mope. She opened her mouth to speak, but, knowing he probably wouldn't pay attention, turned and left.

Billy watched her leave out of the corner of his eye, and said nothing.

Emily came running back in, almost knocking Sam over as he passed through the door. She sat down opposite Billy.

"Let's go, Sugar Bear."

"Why you doing this?"

"Because you're like my big brother."

Billy laughed.

"Big brothers are supposed to be the ones who do the looking after, Em."

"That's one of life's great falsehoods, Billy Case," Emily said. "Big brothers always need the most looking after. Because nobody ever knows how much they need it."

CHAPTER 53:
THE DEFECTOR

hat's infinitely worse than a teleporter," Titus said, examining the best option for Kate and him to commute to and from the now airborne Tower base.

"Trust me," Doc said. "This is much better."

"I'm not E.T. riding a bicycle across the moon."

Kate saw the bikes before — that's what they were calling them, one- and two-seat flying contraptions which could be retrieved by remote from a storage bay in a room none of them had visited much before. She understood Titus's concerns, truth be told — they were like oversized motorcycles, but instead of wheels, some futuristic repulsor system jutted out from the bottom and rear, allowing them to fly well into the atmosphere.

And they weren't equipped with seatbelts.

"What if I fall off? It's windy up here!"

"You won't," Doc said.

Jane, who tagged along out of morbid curiosity rather than need, laughed. "You fall off of everything," she said.

"See?" Titus said. "I'll die on these things."

"I wasn't going to tell you, but there *is* a teleporter on this ship," Doc said. "Hasn't been used in a while, but . . . "

"How about no," Titus said.

"We'll figure something out," Kate said, pulling Titus away from the bikes. She wanted nothing to do with them either, but the first rule of being Kate was to not show fear. The idea of riding thousands of feet above sea level made her vaguely nauseous.

"Where we going?" Titus said.

"I want to check where storm girl is," Kate said.

Sam, another tagalong back to the ship, chuckled as they left.

"Should I tell them about the time . . . "

"Save that story for another day," Doc said.

Kate and Titus walked briskly down the corridor toward the communications suite. Strange, everything on the ship gave the impression of being moved around since it uncoupled itself from its earthbound moorings. Now Kate took wrong turns and needed to ask Neal to help her find things.

When they located the suite, both plopped down in chairs to search for the storm.

"We're getting the short end of the stick on this one, Kate," Titus said.

"Historically, heroes who couldn't fly suffered a lot of indignities," she said. "It's the way of the world."

Kate tapped a few keys and connected to a satellite view of the Atlantic. The storm stalled northeast of Puerto Rico, a huge, swirling mass of clouds far enough off shore that none of the runoff appeared to be reaching land.

"What's she doing out there?" Kate said.

"Waiting? She'll raise hell whenever they get around to sending her back to the mainland."

She tapped the keyboard a few times.

"Something's happening out there."

A sound neither of them had ever heard suddenly squeaked from the control console. They glanced at each other in surprise.

"What did you touch?" Kate asked.

"I'm just sitting here. You're the one tapping things."

"Designation: Dancer," Neal said. *"There is an incoming call from an unknown source. How would you like to proceed?"*

"Answer it," Kate said. "And . . . trace it? Can you trace it?"

"I trace all incoming calls. Patching the call through now."

Kate placed her mask on.

Titus pulled his hood up.

She looked at him incredulously.

He shrugged and mouthed — "what else should I do?"

The screen illuminated and the saddest sack of humanity either of them had ever seen appeared on screen, three times the size of life. He wore a hippie's ponytail, thick glasses, and a hangdog look smeared in week-old stubble.

"Who are you?" Kate asked sharply.

"I'm — have I reached . . . " the man started laughing, a wet, almost drunken laugh. "Have I reached the good guys? I'm sorry. Don't know what else to call you. I'm just . . . I'm trying to reach the good guys."

"I suppose you have," she said. "What do you want?"

"I'm — my name is Hans Wegener. Doctor Hans Wegener," the man said. "These disasters, these . . . these bad things, they're my fault. Sort of my fault. I know where they came from. I'm — I'm sorry, your costume is a hooded sweatshirt?" Wegener asked staring at Titus.

"Focus, doctor," Kate said. "Why are you contacting us?"

Wegener rubbed his eyes. They were red, raw, bloodshot. The eyes of someone who hasn't slept in days.

"I want to set her free," he said. "Want to let the storm escape before they use her for something terrible again."

"How?" Kate said. "We saw a girl in the storm — is that who you mean?"

She gestured with her hand for Titus to get the others.

He shot back a look of confusion.

Kate repeated the motion.

Titus shrugged — "what?"

"No, the girl is . . . The storm required a body. The life span of a sentient storm is less than a year. We thought if we bound it to a human, we could control it, or control her. Rationalize with it. Or . . . use pain to direct her actions."

"Like the others. Like the cortex bombs," Titus said.

"Yes," Wegener said. He looked over his shoulder. "I don't have much time. I — there are controls here. I'm transmitting my passwords to you now. If you destroy the controls here, they won't be able to hurt her anymore. She'll be free."

"The girl and the storm will be free of each other?" Titus asked. "We'll set her loose?"

Wegener shook his head.

"Without the storm, the girl is a vegetable. The storm breathed life back into her. But without the girl the storm has weeks to live. Maybe less. They're bound to each other. That can't be fixed. Not without killing them both."

"But we can take her away from your people," Kate said.

"You have to," he said.

"Neal?" Kate said.

"Source located, Designation: Dancer."

"Where are you, doctor?" Kate said. "Do they know what you're doing?"

"They'll find out," Wegener said. "They always do. I haven't been . . . "

"You need to stay safe," she said. "Don't do anything stupid. We'll come get you as well."

"No," Wegener said. "I — I can hear them now. They're looking for me. I don't deserve your help anyway. I'm Doctor Frankenstein. Made nothing but monsters."

"Then why call us?" Titus said.

"You've seen the storm," he said. "She deserves to be free."

"Everybody does, sir," Kate said.

Wegener smiled at her, a sad, tiny smile.

They heard a hissing noise, and then the smile faded, his eyes blurred, his shoulders slumped.

A woman's hand slid onto the screen. It reached behind Wegener's back and pulled out a blood-covered throwing knife. She pushed him over, and the scientist dropped to the floor. The woman crossed into the camera; a refined face marred by an eye patch surrounded with scars.

"Oh, hello," she said. "Sad little man, wasn't he? Was he looking for a rescue?"

"Maybe," Kate lied.

"I suppose we all want to be rescued sometimes." She looked at the body on the floor off camera. "But we can't have everything. Can we?"

"We're going to find you," Titus said.

"Which one are you? I don't recognize your face," the woman said. "Ah, you must be the werewolf."

"How — "

"It's funny, I rarely see one of your kind with their human face on," Rose said. "Do you want to know which body you keep when you die? I've killed enough of your people to be an expert on it."

"What's it like having no peripheral vision?" Titus said.

"I'm going to kill you as well, you know."

"Do you trip a lot?" he said. "Sometimes, do you miss your chair when you try to sit down?"

"Slowly. I'm going to exterminate you slowly."

Kate disconnected the line. The screen went blank.

"I refuse to be murdered by a chick with one eye."

"And taunting her seemed to work so really well," Kate said. "Titus, she just stabbed a man on camera."

"I'm having trouble processing that part," he said. "I blame that on too much TV — it really happened, right? Wasn't a show produced to try to deceive us?"

They glanced around the room, then towards each other, unsure of what their next move should be. Finally, Kate spoke.

"Neal, can you please pinpoint their location for us?"

"Already done."

"Good," she said. "Now you and I tell Doc what we found."

CHAPTER 54:
DOC

Twenty years, Doc thought, and I'm still not sure how to beat her.

Once upon a time — and shouldn't all stories about magicians begin this way — Doc Silence was a punk kid in baggy pants and combat boots, a street magician who knew a few spells and how to coax minor creatures out from the shadows. He played with fire. He played with blood.

And then he went down into the sewers to save a little girl who had been stolen away, and Doc thought he was a big old hero. But there are still nightmares lurking in the sewers, he learned, and there are still monsters living in closets and under beds, and there are so very many things that go bump in the night.

He ventured into the bilge of the city's underground plumbing, brought the little girl out, and left a piece of himself behind.

Doc abandoned the city then; got on a train, and then he walked, and then he flew to one country, and another, conjuring money like doves from a top hat. He conversed with mediums and shaman, with old stage magicians who'd learned more than they should. He spoke with men of God and men of other things. He tried to master his craft.

In a cave deep in the Australian Outback, he fought a nightmare that had wandered out of someone else's dreams by accident, with a dozen legs and a dark and malicious intelligence. In London he set fire to a building with Molotov cocktails so that no one would have to see what he found inside. He exorcised a house in Louisiana with wall paintings that moved when you walked by. And then Doc nearly died in Moscow at the hands of a witch older than time.

In an abandoned Paris opera house, a demon with too many faces offered him a bargain. Doc refused, and when he next looked in the mirror, his hair was bluish white. He was twenty-five years old.

A year passed and another malevolent creature challenged him to a duel. Doc won, but his eyes were forever changed, some small piece of that demon latched onto him, leaving each eye its own tiny inferno.

The Lady approached him a month later, on Christmas Eve. She was as beautiful, as she was kind. And Doc was tired of losing pieces of himself in every battle with the darkness.

She offered to teach him.

"You don't have to fight them, darling," she said.

She removed her movie star sunglasses and showed him her eyes, pits of fire like his, but brighter, more like real flame. "Most everything that goes bump in the night can be reasoned with. Can be bought. You just need to know how to make the right deal."

He accepted.

Doc assumed she'd be angry when he left a few years later. She taught him a new kind of magic, darker, more utilitarian, with more to gain, but with much higher stakes. He could envision where this path would lead, and he saw what the Lady had become as a broker of dark things. He understood that the world needed creatures like her, but he knew also that he couldn't be one of them.

They parted friends.

Doc Silence and the Lady Natasha Gray would cross paths again many times over the years. Never as allies, because he returned to the business of saving little kids from sewers and battling and the evil things that lurk under beds and in closets. Doc and his friends would interfere with the Lady's games sometimes, and she'd defeat them, or they would defeat her, and she would always come out on top, and Doc wondered for many years if he wasn't somehow part of her long con, her big scam. She trained Doc just enough to make him useful for her and her eternal game.

Doc knew one thing: he possessed no means to destroy her. And he was not sure he wanted to — even if he were able. But if there were a way to strike a bargain, cast a spell, or cajole her out of the game . . .

Doc poured over old books, found ancient scrolls he thought might help, uncovered diagrams for hexes the Lady would shrug off like the wind.

He thought of the storm, the destruction that would lay waste to whatever coastal city the enemy chose to target, the number of lives that could be lost. He thought about things he could bargain away. About their friendship, their fallout, the things they shared, the things that kept them apart. He thought about what she held most dear to her, her immutable rules. And then . . . about a storm without a sorceress behind it, pulling its strings. If only there was a way he could convince her to stay out of it . . .

There was indeed one option. He didn't like it.

"But I enjoy this world," he said to himself. "Like being in it."

"I like it too," Jane said, walking into Doc's study without warning. "Who you talking to?"

"Old ghosts," he said.

He looked at this girl, the one who would make a finer world if given the chance, who he'd picked up from the wreckage of that aircraft and held in his arms, feeling the warmth of the mid-day sun radiating off her little body. The one he handed over to John and Doris Hawkins, because he didn't know what else to do with her, because he knew he was no man to raise a child, because he knew someone else could keep her safe and help her grow up to be a better person than she would in his care. Annie, for all the good she was capable of, could never understand why he was so upset, why he had been so heartbroken, to give Jane away.

He'd done the best he could with the time he had, he thought. And this was the only way to keep her safe and give these inadvertent heroes a fighting chance to save lives.

If he did this . . . well, it's not as though he would be gone forever. That was the problem, though: the not knowing.

"You okay?" Jane asked. Earnestness in her voice. She — more

235

than all the others — was so earnest. That was John and Doris speaking. They did a fine job helping her grow.

"Jane," he said, and he could hear the tone in his voice, could see her pick up on it. She'd never seen him upset before. There'd never really been a reason.

"You're not okay."

"There's a way I can take the Lady out of the fight. When we make our big move," Doc said. "She's too much for anyone else to handle. Too much for all of you to handle. But I can . . . I can just remove her from the fight."

"That's a good thing, right?" Jane said.

"Yeah," Doc said. "Except I have to take myself out of it as well. And it . . . it might be a while Before I get back."

"What do you mean? Where you going?"

"Jane, there are worlds upon worlds," he said. "Layers and layers of reality, all piled on top of each other. I'd really hoped I'd get to show you a few of the good ones some day."

"You still can, right?"

"I think so," he said. "I just. Just don't know how long I'll be gone. It may be a long time."

"We have other options, right? There's got to be other options."

"There isn't time," Doc said.

Jane tried to speak a few times, the words not forming. Then she latched onto him, a bear hug too big for her small frame. She still radiated heat like a warm day.

"You can trust Sam," Doc said. "He knows things. He can help you."

"What are we going to do without you? We barely know how to do anything on our own. You can't — "

"If you only knew how great you are already," he said.

"Stop talking like you're gone already," Jane said.

"And look out for the others while I'm away," he said. "They'll follow you. You set the tone; they'll follow you."

She looked up.

"I'll leave Emily in charge if you go," she said, sniffing back tears. "I will. You can't leave."

Doc smiled. She'll be fine, he thought. She just needed someone to show her how to fly.

"When?" Jane asked.

He didn't answer.

Then Neal's voice chattered over the intercom.

"Designation: Doctor Silence," Neal said. *"Designation: Dancer is looking for you. We have pinpointed the enemy's base of operations. Shall I recall Designations: Straylight and Entropy?"*

Doc kissed the top of Jane's head and wiped his eyes.

"Now's as good a time as any," he said.

CHAPTER 55:
HOME

Billy's family lived, Emily was surprised to discover, in one of those suburban towns large enough to feel like a real city but small enough to not have the name recognition of a genuine metropolis, an outlier stuck with all the big city problems without the big city fame.

His mother waited on the porch of their house: a two family located on a side street off a busy main drag. She paced until they touched down. Her eyes widened when her son and his goggle-wearing friend dropped out of the sky and landed.

"You," she said, and then ran down the front steps and clenched him in a huge hug.

Emily smiled.

"Told you it was a good idea," she said.

"We saw you on the news," his mother said, fussing over his face, which was, Emily thought, still pretty well busted up. Billy looked like he crash-landed into a tree trunk. "What happened to you?"

"Last week, I got punched in the face by a giant bear crab mole and was exploded on yesterday — or the day before. I forget."

"Billy Case," his mother said, adjusting and dusting off his beat up street-clothes jacket. "We thought you were dead."

"I didn't think you'd worry," he said.

"That's the dumbest thing I've ever heard," she said. "Your father's been beside himself."

"Dad?"

"Yes."

"He here?"

"Waiting inside," she said.

Billy looked at Emily in a plea for help.

She simply smirked.

"Go on!" Emily said.

Billy's mom looked her over, squinting at her hair and clothes.

"This your girlfriend?" she asked.

"No way, " Emily said, laughing. "Billy's like my big brother. But he totally has a crush on one of the other super girls and doesn't know it yet."

Billy scowled.

Emily shrugged her shoulders.

"I'm just glad you're here," his mother said.

I shouldn't have come home, Dude, Billy said.

His father sat in the living room, looking as big as he always had — all shoulders and dark hair and that long, exhausted face that said so much about how he labored too hard at his dying hardware store.

Billy knew that face. He'd seen it as the face of disappointment, because his son was, admittedly, lazy, and, also admittedly, inept at almost everything he applied himself to. His father wanted him to take over the family business, but Billy had little aptitude with his hands and even less with money, and then there was that unspoken truth between them that the store would probably not survive another bad turn in the economy.

More than once, Billy suggested they adopt another son who might be better suited to save the business. He gave his father credit for never taking the bait, even if they both knew it would have probably been for the best.

So there the old man sat, staring at him like he was a stranger, and all Billy could think of was, who was working at the store right now?

I really screwed up, Dude. Should have stayed away.

Give them time, Billy Case, Dude said.

"That was you all the while, flying around the city?" his father asked.

"We never recognized you, until the news covered that . . . thing attacking a building," his mother said. "We'd seen you hovering around but you all wear masks and . . . "

"I was . . . on an errand when that happened," Billy said. "Didn't have time to put my costume on."

"My boy's running round the city in tights," the old man said.

"They're more of a space age polymer, chemically manufactured, under sterile — uh, never mind," Billy said.

"Who would have thought . . . You up and leave us and we imagined you'd taken off to become homeless or do drugs and you're a goddamn superhuman," his father said.

"Something like that."

"Same people, down south helping out with the hurricane cleanup?"

"That was us," Emily said. "Billy's not quite as useful at cleaning up as he is at fighting monsters, but he tries."

"You should see his room," his mother said.

"Why didn't you tell us what you were running off to do?" his father asked. "Wouldn't it have been better if you told us the truth? You scared your mother worse than I've ever seen her. We've been nailing posters to telephone poles thirty miles in every direction looking for you."

"You looked for me?"

"You thought we wouldn't?" his mother said.

They looked for me, Dude. I didn't think they'd . . .

We are all wrong sometimes, Billy Case.

I can't even run away from home the right way, Billy said. I even screwed this up.

"But . . . would you have believed me if I told you?" Billy asked.

His father nodded yes.

"Fair enough. Actually, you would have locked me up in the loony bin."

"Perhaps we would have had you see a psychologist, yes," his mother said. "You can fly? I saw you fly, and what was that stuff? Shooting lasers out of your hands?"

"That's. . . way cooler than how I usually describe it."

"But how did it happen?"

"I . . . " Billy said. And then: how did it happen, Dude?

I picked you.

Why? Why pick someone like me?

Does it matter?

Maybe?

I am a very good judge of character, Billy Case.

I wouldn't have been anyone's first pick.

My other choices were already inhabited by aliens.

Did you just make a joke?

And then he heard something he had never, not once in all his time with him, heard before: Dude laughing.

"Why are you smiling?" his father asked.

"Because I have an alien living inside me," Billy said. "Which sounds, like, completely insane, and also really creepy. But one day I'm walking home from school, and this bolt of light hits me, just, pow, out of the sky, right? And I felt awful for a few days, and you wouldn't let me skip school — "

"— Because we thought you were faking," his mother said. "You have to admit you faked it a lot."

"Yeah," Billy said. "But after a few days I start hearing this voice, and begin to think I'm losing my mind, except this voice starts telling me all these amazing things I can do, and they turn out to be true. So I thought, well now I'm a freak."

"Well, you are," Emily said. "We all are. That's why we get to do what we do."

Billy's father directed his attention to her for the first time.

"Who are you, anyway?"

"Billy's teammate, and also his Jiminy Cricket."

Billy's dad stood up and paced back and forth across the small living room.

"So you're not crazy, and you have all these powers, and, what, now you . . . you save people? That's your job?"

"It doesn't pay much," he said. "But the benefits are pretty rad."

His father stopped pacing and looked Billy right in the eyes.

"You know, we saw you on the news, and I thought, that can't be my kid," his father said. "And then I saw how bad it was, and how much destruction was happening right there in front of me, and I thought, I hope that isn't my kid. Then I realized what you were all doing, and how you're all out there together like a bunch of, I don't know, miracles, and I said to myself — no, I wish that's my kid."

"And there you were," his mother said.

"Why did you wish it was me?" Billy said.

His father laughed, that scratchy, ex-smoker's laugh that no friend or family member ever heard enough of. The man never had a lot of reasons to laugh.

"Because I was so damn proud of you, Billy," his father said. "You were doing things the rest of us could only dream of. And you were out there without a single consideration for yourself."

"I, uh, think about myself a lot during these expeditions. Mostly how to keep from getting blown up. Again," he said. "The again part is important."

"Keep doing that," his mother said. "I'd prefer my son not get blown up all the time."

"You're really proud of me? Not mad?"

"I'm still mad about the note," his mother said. "I expect the best mother's day present ever to make up for that."

"There's a lot of things people would do if they had your gifts, your power. And you've decided to do the noblest thing you could with it," his father said.

Did he just call me noble, Dude?

You are not noble yet, Billy Case. Give it time. You might get there.

Thanks for keeping me humble.

It is not easy. You are particularly prone to moments of self-aggrandizement.

Emily's transmitter beeped. A second later, Billy's did as well.

"What's that mean?" his mother asked.

"Em?"

Emily popped into dining room to answer the call.

"You get paged these days?" his father asked.

"I tried to talk them into using a spotlight as a signal, but it didn't work well during the day."

His father laughed again.

It wouldn't take much convincing to get used to that sound, Billy thought.

Emily rushed in and pulled her goggles down over her eyes.

"We gotta head back," she said. "Kate found something important. Gotta move quick."

"Off to save the day again?" his mother asked.

"People are in constant need of saving, you know that? I never knew," Billy said.

"Do you really have to go?" his mother said. "Can't they do this one without you?"

Billy looked at Emily.

She frowned.

"Jane sounded really worried," Emily said.

"I think they need me," he said.

Billy's father stuck his hand out.

They shook hands, like adults, like grown men do. It made Billy feel taller, somehow.

"Go get 'em, kid."

"Sure you're not mad?"

"Just come back in one piece," his father said. "Maybe bring your mom flowers when you visit."

Billy responded with a smile so wide it hurt his cheeks.

"You got it, dad."

His parents followed them out onto the porch, looking on with a mixture of disbelief and excitement when Billy and Emily took flight.

"Roses!" his mother yelled as they increased altitude. "My favorite are yellow!"

"I'll be back soon," Billy yelled.

But as they cranked up their speed and headed home, Billy wondered if they could ever really promise anyone they would return at all.

CHAPTER 56:
A NEW BALLGAME

The entire gang sat around the conference table, in full costume — a sports team before the big game. The monitor displayed the Atlantic Ocean, the swirl of the living hurricane, and a small blip where Neal had traced the call Kate and Titus received. Everyone sat in near silence; a fretful weight overtook the room.

Finally, Emily broke the quiet.

"I know I'm gonna regret this, but are we really making our big move based off of a prank call?"

"The information looks legitimate," Kate said. "I think the scientist was trying to help us."

"I've seen a lot of movies," Emily said. "And this is usually where the ambush happens."

"We have to go with what we know," Kate said.

"It's a trap!"

Kate stared Emily down with her worst glare.

"What we do know is that thing," Titus said, pointing at the monitor, "is going to strike the east coast very soon and hurt a whole lot of people. So if we have a chance to stop it . . . "

"Her," Jane said. "That's a her, not an it. And we have to help her, not stop her."

Titus frowned and nodded.

"So here's the plan," Doc said.

It was the first time he'd spoken since they all sat down. He deferred to Kate instead, letting her take the lead, watching closely from the sidelines the entire time. "Jane, you, Billy, and Emily will try to distract or contain the storm temporarily. Kate and Titus, you'll mount an assault on the base they've established. When arrive, you'll disable the technological controls they have over her. Hopefully, the information your informant gave you is legitimate, because that not only will eliminate their method of harming her remotely, it'll also take the trigger off the cortex bomb if they have one implanted in her head."

"And those things we saw last time?" Billy said. "The creatures attacking her? They were definitely not technological anything."

"I'll take care of those," Doc said. He exchanged a long look with Jane. She averted his eyes and turned her gaze down towards the desk. "They're my job."

"And after we've disconnected her from all these controls?" Billy said. "Won't that just mean she's . . . cut loose to do whatever she wants?"

"That's when the three of you have to talk her into managing her own powers," Doc said.

"The three of us what?" Emily said.

"You, Entropy Emily, are going to contain her. Make sure she can't go anywhere," he said.

"That's a faboo idea," Emily said.

"A big bubble of float, Em," Jane said. "You can do it."

"Right. Big bubble of float, big enough to hold an entire hurricane. You realize I can barely do long division."

"You have a genius level IQ, Emily," Doc said. "Stop pretending you don't."

She folded her arms across her chest and glared at Doc, furious he let her secret out of the bag.

"Reason with her," he said. "Billy, you're living with a symbiote. You might be able to help her. Jane, try to convince her she can do it. According to this scientist, they are sharing the same body. Someone has to take control."

"*My* symbiote actually doesn't do anything I tell him to do," Billy said. "Mostly he just tolerates my behavior and cuts me off from my powers when I'm a jerk."

"What are our other alternatives?" Jane said.

"The other alternative is the one we don't want," Doc said.

"We kill her," Kate said. "Destroy the human body, the sentient storm dies. That's what the scientist says."

"I'm not gonna kill her," Jane said. She turned to Billy.

He shook his head.

"Not going down that road again," he said. "Jane, we can do this. We'll be able to help her. I know it."

"You don't know anything," Emily said. "But I like your optimism."

"I have a question," Titus said. "If you're going to be here, Doc, and they're going to be chasing the storm, how are Kate and I getting to this base in the middle of the ocean."

"I was thinking we'd take one of the flying bikes," Kate said.

"We'd what?"

"You don't have to ride alone. We can ride doubles. I'll drive."

"Can't we have Emily drop us off?"

"I'm going to be too busy trying to make the biggest bubble of float the world has ever seen," Emily said. "I think you should take the bike. It'll be fun."

"We're not taking a flying bike," Titus said.

"You could swim," Kate said.

"Maybe you're part Labrador?" Billy said.

Titus growled at him.

Billy laughed.

"So this is it," Jane said. "We just go charging off into the middle of the ocean and hope we can stop them."

"That's the plan," Kate said. "This is their big splash. They need this storm to work, otherwise all these threats they've been making seem ridiculous."

Jane nodded. She kept looking at Doc out of the corner of her eye.

Kate viewed the exchange, but said nothing.

"I have something for you, before we go," Doc said.

He pulled a small pouch from his coat pocket and dumped its contents onto the table. A set of flat metal objects toppled out with a clang. He tossed the first to Titus, who caught it easily.

"No joke," Titus said.

"What, we get presents?" Emily said.

Titus held the object up. It was an emblem in the shape of an abstract wolf's head. Doc tossed the next one to Emily, who caught it with her gravity powers and drew it to her hand. It was the same nuclear fallout warning symbol she'd adorned her entire costume with.

"Wicked," she said.

The third went to Billy, a silver-blue comet. Doc handed Jane hers, an idealized, artistic version of the sun done up in gold.

"I don't have a symbol," Kate said.

Doc slid a final emblem across the table to her. She stopped it with the tip of her finger.

"I took my best guess," he said. "I hope it works."

Kate held it up between her forefinger and thumb. It was a woman in silhouette, a dancer, spinning in a pirouette. She examined it with a lost and longing look, and then set it back down on the table.

"Close enough, Doc. Thank you."

"You're welcome," he said. "Back in the old days, we kept our personal symbols on the backs of our chairs. Don't know why, it's not like we wanted to stake a claim to a particular seat. It just . . . felt like the appropriate thing to do. To make it official. Whenever someone new joined the team, they got one of these for their chair."

"So we're official?" Titus said, smirking.

"You've been official for a long time," he said. "Consider this your graduation gift."

"No turning back now, is there?" Billy said.

"Like there ever was," Emily said. "We were in it the minute the big guy showed up."

Everyone stood, brushed invisible dust off their costumes, checked buckles, exchanged worried glances.

"Here goes nothing," Billy said.

Emily followed him out into the hall, taunting Titus about his pending bike ride. Jane stared at Doc a moment longer before joining them. Doc caught Kate by the arm as she walked by.

"One minute, Kate," he said.

"I knew you had something on your mind," Kate said. "What's wrong?"

"There's someone you should contact if anything happens to me today," Doc said.

"What do you mean?"

"I'm going to do something particularly stupid and there's a chance I might . . . be gone for a while," he said.

"Is particularly stupid a technical term in the magical vernacular?" she said.

"I'm going to set a trap for the woman controlling the girl in the storm," Doc said. "If she tries to hit back at me, we might . . . get kicked out of this world for a little while. I don't know how long."

"Kicked out of this world?" Kate asked

"I'm gonna lead her on a merry chase," he said, a sad smile across his face suddenly tugged on a part of Kate's guts she spent most of her time trying to surpress. "And it might take me quite a while to get back."

"You're going to die, aren't you?"

"I'm not," Doc said. "There's rules to what I do, Kate. She and I can't murder each other. It's just not done. It's not allowed."

"But you're going to lead her away. From us."

"I'm going to lead her away from you."

Kate shook her head at him, musing.

"You're the old man in that parable."

"What parable?" Doc said.

"I remember a story once. Maybe it was a Buddhist story. Maybe it was in the Bible. I don't know," Kate said. "But an old man helps a snake, or maybe it was a scorpion, cross a desert, or a river, or . . . somewhere. And at the end, the snake bites the man, and asks, why did you help me all this time, when you knew in the end I'd bite you? And the man tells the snake he was leading him away from his village the whole time, and he'd led him too far away to ever do any harm."

"I wish I could remember that story," Doc said.

"Is she really that bad? That dangerous?"

"The most dangerous person I've ever met," he said.

Kate rubbed her eyes. She studied Doc's face again, saw the worry, saw how thin he'd become since they first met. He wasn't an old man, but he was older now than he was just a short while ago, and it seemed terribly unfair to her.

"You'll come back," she said.

"Fast as I can."

"I wish I was kinder to you, Doc Silence," Kate said. "I could have been easier to get along with."

"You've been exactly the way you had to be," he said.

She nodded. In a lot of ways, he was precisely right.

"So this person I should meet. Who is he?"

"Neal will help you find him. Just ask him. He'll be able to tell you where he is."

"Why me?" Kate said. "Why not Jane?"

"Because you remind me of him," Doc said. "He was like you. An ordinary person who willed himself to be extraordinary. He always distrusted those of us with great power for that reason. He'll like you, respond to you. And you might need someone to turn to while I'm gone."

"Is he as good a teacher as you've been?" she said.

"No," Doc said. "He was always afraid to teach. But he never refused to help when we asked."

Kate pursed her lips, nodded again, held out her hand.

Doc shook it.

"I hope you're wrong. Hope you're here when I get back."

"Believe me, Kate, so do I."

She released his hand.

"The others know?"

"Only Jane."

"Great. Always her and I, isn't it."

"Get used to it," he said.

Kate smiled a crooked grin.

"Safe travels, Doc."

"Be careful out there."

CHAPTER 57:
TO STRIKE FEAR

Agent Black found the Lady and Rose talking on the deck. The storm was closer than ever and out here on the open ocean the enormity of the thing — of her, he reminded himself — became clearer. She stretched on for miles in every direction, clouds so dark they were nearly purple, rain so heavy you could see foam forming on the ocean surface with the human eye.

"She's angry," Black said.

"Your men ready?" Rose asked.

Black had watched Rose's agents, her ninjas, setting up their positions throughout the rig. In a way, this structure was easier to defend than a land-based location. The perimeter was the edge of the rig, and with guards at the proper points, they could set up a three hundred and sixty degree lookout.

But there was also nowhere to go if things went bad, and it was a large rig — a lot could go wrong very quickly.

"They're ready," Black said. "You think they'll come?"

"Yes," Rose said. "Wegener revealed enough to pique their interest."

"He spoke longer than that," the Lady said. "Do you know what he told them, exactly?"

"No," Rose said. "And he was smart enough to encrypt his outgoing message. We could crack it, given a little time, but . . . "

"We have things to do," the Lady said.

The Lady raised her face to the sky, feeling the mist of the ocean gathering on her skin. Black found himself wondering, as always, why she did what she did. It all seemed beneath her, working with the Children. Maybe it was just a game to her. Maybe they were simply bugs to pull wings off of.

"You won't let your problem with werewolves get the better of you, will you Rose?" the Lady asked.

"I don't have a werewolf problem," Rose said.

"We both know that's not true," the Lady said. "But I do hope you have fun killing the pup. It must be so much less satisfying killing one that isn't fully grown."

"A pelt's a pelt," she said.

"And what about you, Agent," the Lady said. "Any special vendettas you're hoping to feed today?"

"Yeah," he said. "I'd like to stay afloat long enough to get paid."

"We all have our motivations," she said. "Would either of you care to join me during the ritual? I love having an audience for these things."

Black shook his head.

Rose's face was blank.

"I won't be of much use if the little things do try to attack us," the Lady said. "I imagine they'll do something to try to stop my pets from corralling the storm toward land, so I'll be adding a bit more complexity to my spells. Some additional security, so to speak."

"We'll have guards posted at your door," Black said.

"No," the Lady said. "If I can't have the two of you, I'd rather work alone."

"Done," Rose said.

The Lady flashed them her radiant, seductive smile.

"Well then. Enjoy your party," she said, and walked off toward her chamber.

"You see their list of demands?" Black asked.

"Yeah," Rose said.

He spit into the ocean.

"So what happens if they don't get everything they asked for," Black said. "They send a hurricane against the East Coast every day 'til they do?"

"Maybe," she said. "We'll be pushing her across to Europe too, you know. They want to hit England next."

Black spit again.

"Lotta work."

"Yeah."

"It's not really about the demands, is it?" he said.

"Is it ever?" Rose said. "It's about creating fear. It's about making everything unstable. The Children always did best in times of chaos."

"So their goal is really just . . . to make a mess?"

"Yep," she said. "And then, be there to pick up all the pieces. It's an old game."

"Huh."

"You having cold feet, Agent?"

"Nah," Black said. "I'd rather be on the side picking up the pieces than on the side losing them."

"So long as the check clears."

"Exactly," he said.

Black scanned the horizon again, his cyborg eye looking for signs of an impending attack and coming up empty. He felt tired, just then.

"Oh, c'mon," Rose said. "Have a little fun. You didn't get into this to have a normal life."

"That's for damned sure," he said. Black checked his stubby rifle one more time and started to leave.

"Have fun slaying your werewolf," he said.

"Don't fall into the ocean."

CHAPTER 58:
INTO THE EYE

Three figures raced across the surface of the ocean, each with their own unique wake: a trail of golden fire, a blue white light, and a faint signature like heat distortion. Jane, in the lead, kicked up mist below her as the warmth of her flight path changed the water to steam; Emily created tiny realities, turning choppy water still and still water into waves with whitecaps. Billy passed in near silence, his bright energy signature transforming to silvery highlights on the sea's surface.

The storm grew ever closer, becoming more threatening, more ominous, and vaster with every meter traveled.

They pulled up short, less than a mile from the wall of blue-black clouds terminating the horizon, and watched as lightning flickered like pale veins beneath the storm's skin.

"Oh yeah, I can totally just put this in a bubble," Emily said. "Totes easy."

"This is turning out to be such a bad idea," Billy said.

"It's our only choice," Jane said. "Would you like that thing hitting Florida?"

"Is this a multiple choice question?" he asked.

Jane surveyed the storm from left to right, marveling at how alive it appeared, how organic. Every time she looked, it seemed as though the storm were taking on a more definitive shape, an amorphous animal.

"Emily, fly up a bit. Maybe if you can get an idea of its dimensions you'll be in a better spot to contain it."

"Are you watching the same storm I am?" Emily said. "I'm gonna need to be like, satellite height to get a good look at it."

"So go atmospheric," Jane said. "You know you want to."

"What about us?" Billy said.

"I'm going to head in. Maybe I can find and then reason with her one more time. Talk to her like a person," Jane said.

"That went really well last time," Emily said.

"We didn't know as much about her last time," she said.

"And what am I going to do?" Billy said.

"You're going to deal with them," Jane said, pointing to the south, where dozens of targets were suddenly flying their way.

"What are they?"

"Robots, I think," Jane said. "Same as the ones that attacked Kate and me at her apartment."

"I'm going to be in a dog fight with flying robots."

"You have a problem with that?"

"No," Billy said. "Been hoping to fight flying robots my whole life."

Kate and Titus raced across the water's surface as well, trying to stay low and underneath whatever sensors the rig might have searching for them. Kate drove, hunkered down on the hoverbike like a professional racer. Titus, in his lean human form, clung to her waist.

"Why didn't I drive!" he yelled.

"Because you're chicken!" she hollered back. "Don't fall off!"

"Would you save me if I did?"

"No!"

She could distinguish figures on the deck: men in fatigues, clearly carrying firearms. She pointed.

"Don't take your hand off the controls!" Titus said.

"Stop being a wimp!" Kate snarled. "We're going to have to come in hot!"

"What does that even mean?"

"It means we're going to have to hit them as soon as we get off the bike!"

Titus was silent.

Kate looked back.

"You okay?"

"I've got an idea!" he yelled. "Fly up there and pull a U-ee!"

"A what?"

"Make a u-turn!"

Kate squinted at him then turned back to the rig. She gunned the controls of the bike and kicked up speed, narrowing the gap between them and surface of the deck. At the last second, she pulled up and above the deck and then slammed the controls to the right, banking a hard turn.

Titus let go of her and jumped off.

The werewolf could be a graceful critter when he wanted to be. Titus transformed smoothly mid-air, doubling in size, the silvery fur of his werewolf form sprung into existence, huge jaws projected where once there was a boyish face.

Kate floated mid-air long enough to see the looks of the two guards closest to Titus as two hundred and fifty pounds of wolf-man crashed to the deck. Titus wrapped one massive paw around the first guard and tossed him overboard as if he didn't weigh a thing; he swatted the gun from the other man's hand, sending stray bullets skittering across the deck, and then grabbed him by his fatigues and hurled him into the water.

More men rushed in to assist, setting up a firing squad and taking aim at Titus. Kate jumped from the bike, leaving it hovering fifteen feet off the deck, and landed a kick to the face of the closest mercenary on her way to the ground. His partner tried to turn his gun from Titus to Kate, but she punched him in the throat and kicked his inner knee, dropping him to the floor, yowling in pain. She picked up the man's rifle and clubbed him with it, knocking him unconscious. Then, she jogged over to catch up to Titus, who just made a mess of two more mercenaries. They lay bloody, but alive.

"You gonna be okay?" Kate said.

Titus stared at her with those enormous yellow eyes and opened his jaws.

"Behind me," he said, barely human, a deep, rumbling, monstrous voice Kate hadn't heard before.

She smirked.

"You got it, big guy. Let's find us that lab."

Billy was having the time of his life.

He wanted to send a thank you note to whoever decided to send inanimate objects to try to kill him. Without fear of injuring anyone, he was able to fly like a lunatic, blasting through heads and chassis with blinding white light, tearing the robots apart. He got into an aerial dogfight with two of them; they attempted to catch him through pirouettes and loop-de-loops.

Dude, this is the most fun I've ever had in my life.

You need to be more careful, the alien said.

Why? I'm not hurting anyone.

Billy heard a mechanical whine; the robots opened up a pair of hatches on their backs. Now, small rockets bristled there, and with a harsh whistle, they launched, trailing smoke and fire. Billy kicked up his speed, trying to outrace the missiles, but they followed, heat seekers like those in blockbuster films, so he figured he'd try something he saw in the movies a few hundred times. Spinning with stomach-lurching speed, he turned back on the robot attackers and sped between them. One exploded at the receiving end of its own rocket, the other got torn apart by two of its own, but Billy was still being chased by a remaining missile.

What if I blast the rocket? Billy asked.

Try to be responsible, Dude said.

Billy fired a hand-blast at the missile, which detonated on contact. The force of the blast knocked him out of his flight path momentarily and he skipped along the surface of the ocean, salt water kicking into his eyes.

Well that burns!

I told you to put goggles on your mask, Dude said.

They keep fogging up.

Two of the robots closed in, trying to hit Billy with some sort of laser weapon strapped to their metallic forearms. Too close for a proper blast, Billy clenched both fists, causing them to glow bright white with built up energy.

Rock 'em, sock 'em . . . he thought.

Some day you will learn you are not meant for comedy, Dude said.

Billy punched the head off of each robot with wild haymakers. "I love this!" he yelled.

His victory was cut short, however, by a barrage of laser blasts. More robots headed his way, including one that looked like the bigger, nastier sibling to the others, a winged monstrosity ten feet tall.

How does it even stay in the air? Billy asked.

Physics, Dude said.

Right, Billy said.

He charged the oncoming robots, blasting through the smaller ones easily. His energy beams staggered a larger model, but it seemed to be shielded against his attacks. Each blast knocked the robot off its flight path but otherwise it remained unharmed.

Dude?

He appears to be a later version than the others.

No kidding. Any suggestions?

Try harder?

You want to get me killed?

I am hoping to make you learn.

You really pick the worst times to —

The robot opened up its palm and fired a concussive blast, not unlike Billy's own, right back at him. He spun mid air, his vision becoming a nauseating blend of sky and ocean. When Billy righted himself, the robot was nearly on him, swinging a huge, rust-colored fist. He dodged the punch and countered with two more of his own to the robot's face. With the strength of Dude's energy powers behind him, he'd dented the surface, but the robot was relentless.

I have an idea.

I am not going to like it, am I?

You can read my thoughts, you already know what my idea is.

I was hoping you had something else in reserve.

Billy cut away at top speed, giving himself a bit of distance from the massive robot. He started generating his light blasts, first in his hands, and then letting the power spill down onto his head and shoulders. Billy aimed himself like a bullet at the robot.

This did not work in the city, and it is a terrible idea now.

Ramming speed, Dude. Ramming speed!

Billy poured everything he could into his forward propulsion, all but disappearing in his blue-white energy signature. The robot waited for him, preparing to deflect more of his blasts — its palm outstretched, ready to fire.

Why hasn't he hit me yet?

He appears to be recharging.

Oh good. In that case, this should actually work . . .

Billy plowed into the robot's torso at full speed. His entire body shuddered with the impact, leaving him jarred to the bone, his ears rung, but his shields held. All around him, the robot's mechanical body was torn to shreds, a violent, squealing mess of metal plates and ripped wiring. The smell of burnt electronics filled the air.

Billy, however, kept going, slamming into the surface of the water and kicking up a spray fifty feet into the air. He drifted a moment underwater, the cold shock of the landing kept him from losing himself in the dizziness of the impact.

That was a terrible idea.

All of your ideas are terrible, Billy Case.

He started choking on seawater before he realized he'd let his shields drop. Quickly, effortlessly, he brought them back up and half-swam, half-flew into the air.

He breached the surface and started laughing.

Another ten foot tall robot was flying his way.

"I'm having so much fun," he said.

Miles above, Emily surveyed the size of the storm and began a conversation with herself. More often than not, she answered back.

"Oh, oh, just contain the storm, Emily," she said, in her best imitation of Jane's voice. "Just use your powers nobody understands, it'll be easy!"

To her right, she saw the flashes of white light indicating that Billy was in a pickle. She could go help him, she thought, but while that would be entertaining, it really wouldn't solve her problem with the storm.

"Question, self," she said. "You have, so far, never tried to move something you couldn't see all of. Giant bear mole was easy. You could see his top and tail. This storm has neither top nor tail."

She reached out with her mind, trying to imagine the boundaries of the storm, but without some visual queue to latch onto, she couldn't create the parameters she needed to put a bubble around the whole thing. Happily, she sensed that she really could make a bubble that extended miles across. . . but she would need to know where it ended. Which she didn't.

"Come on, Entropy Emily, think about this," she said. "Think about what? Bubble of float. This should be super easy. Big bubble. It's just a big bubble."

As she muttered, the storm began to move. She looked through the clouds for Jane's fiery heat signature but they were too thick, too murky to see anything below them.

A tendril of cloud lurched out, separate from the rest of the body of the storm. On a whim, Emily prepared a bubble outside the storm, like a wall. The tendril struggled for a moment against it, sputtering out into a fine mist, before splitting in two and working its way around the bubble. She expanded the bubble, and the tendrils did much the same, evaporating before her eyes but then working with alien intelligence to find its way around the wall she created.

"Big bubble. I could put a big bubble around Florida," she thought. Then she imagined all the cars and tourists and people in mouse costumes and Princess Ariel's kingdom floating away when she suspended their normal field of gravity so, thought better of the idea.

"Big bubbles, little bubbles," Emily said. "Think different sizes. Lots of bubbles?"

She waved a hand and scattered little gravitational fields like marbles in front of the storm. Again, the living clouds wrestled with the possibility of going through them but quickly realized it was impossible and weaved their way around the pockets of antigravity. Emily let those pockets disappear, and the storm, like water, filled in the empty space.

"I need to put it in a fishbowl is what I need to do," she said.

That same tendril snaked forward, moving more aggressively toward the coast. Irritated, Emily made a fist with her hand and snapped a medium-sized bubble around the tendril, trapping it.

The cloud within the bubble simply disappeared. There one moment, gone in a flicker of condensation the next.

"Well that was tricksy," she said.

She repeated the gesture, this time wrapping her mind around a chunk of the storm still part of the main body of the clouds. A sphere-shaped emptiness appeared, like someone had taken a giant bite out of the storm. She released that sphere and did it again, twice, taking two more huge sections out of the storm. Each time she let go, the clouds filled back in, rushing to replace what had been destroyed. But so long as she maintained that bubble, nothing happened inside.

"Well wouldn't that be funny," she said.

In a darkened room, Doc Silence found her.

It was the only time he could catch the Lady unawares; she had to be deep in a ritual spell so that she tuned out her environment enough to not notice him right away. And there she was, sitting cross-legged in front of a demon-trap, communing with creatures from another plane. He spied them through the trap. Scaled, winged things, angry with her for commanding them, desperate for her attention, loving her, hating her.

This is the way of all who come in contact with the Lady. All monsters want to serve her, and then they hate her for it.

She'd been busy for a while before he got there. Doc saw the smoking burn marks where her pets had touched the floor, smelled the sulfur of their passing, heard the strange way their echoes lingered in rooms long after they were gone.

He caught himself hesitating. Was he frightened of her? He'd never been afraid before, even at the beginning, when she took him under her wing. He was too young and too cocky to know he should have been terrified, and too clever by far for her to trap him like she did everyone else. That was why she was willing to teach him so much. The Lady once said that a hundred years had passed since she met someone she couldn't trick.

No, he wasn't frightened. Was he worried? They were friends, once upon a time; and they weren't truly enemies now, though they had, for years, been on opposing sides of the same fights. He knew in a way she admired his willingness to do the unselfish thing. It drove her insane, sometimes, and it frustrated her at other times, but she always enjoyed knowing that one of her students had volunteered to do the right thing instead. He could have been a world-class dark sorcerer, she told him once, and instead he was a do-gooder with a pocket full of parlor tricks. There seemed to be something stupidly noble in that.

Perhaps Doc was just worried he would finally cross the line. To say that she played the game fairly with him over the years was an outright lie, the Lady always played the game unfairly. Yet she played it unfairly always. In this, at least, she was consistent, and there was a sort of honor in that as well. Honor among thieves. Among cheats. Among magicians and liars.

But later he watched her conjure her last pet, the hulking red thing with skin like cracked stone and eyes full of the sort of malice you only see on the other side of the Pit, and Doc knew he really had no choice. That was no gremlin to torment the girl in the storm. That was a whip-cracking demon, a herder of souls. He wondered why she chose to use such a creature for this — like bringing a canon to a knife fight. Overkill. And, irresponsibly so.

She dismissed the creature, all craggy muscles and calcium deposits, off to do something at her command. Doc wondered if it would confront Jane out there over the ocean. Did her invulnerability extend to things not of this world?

He stepped from the shadows.

"Natasha," he said.

He saw her mouth quirk into a smile even before she turned to face him. Slowly — so as not to lose the threads she was holding to control the storm — she stood up, like a dancer, graceful and strange.

"My Doctor Silence," she said. "I had hoped you weren't among the ones who ran away. I thought you loved this place too much to quit."

"Someone had to stay behind," he said. "Might as well have been me."

"What are you doing here?" she said. "Have you come to challenge me to a duel? You know you can't win."

"I know," he said.

"Then shouldn't you be out there with your little pawns? They're out of their league, you know."

"Why are *you* here, Natasha?" he asked, taking a step closer. "This whole game is beneath you. The Children? They're simply businessmen in funny masks. You're so much more than any of them."

"They offered me things I wanted," the Lady said. "They offered me things they didn't know they were giving away. Darling, this was my retirement plan."

"Money? You're doing all this petty nonsense for cash?"

"You know I don't trade in earthly currency," she said.

"What were they giving you?"

"Enough to close my account ledgers with the beyond," she said. Doc squinted.

"You made a bad deal," he said.

"Brokering with the beyond always has its risks," she said. "I would have caught up eventually. This just simplified things."

"Who did you owe? What could possibly scare you into settling a debt early?"

"I deal with the high rollers," she said. "But it's over now. I'm free and clear. I finish this petty nonsense, I destroy a piece of America, and I go home. You should come with me."

"Why did you send that last demon out there," Doc said. "That was a slaver demon, wasn't it?"

"I mean it," she said, ignoring his question. "You should come with me."

"Why did you send a slaver demon, Natasha? I saw you."

"You were here for that?" she said, musing. "Funny. You're sneakier than I remember, Doc."

"Why — "

"He's not in the bargain for the Children," the Lady said. "That was my own sidebar. He's cleaning up loose ends for me."

Doc felt a wave of relief pour over him. He wouldn't want to fight that red monster himself, let alone allow Jane and the others to have to face him.

He could see distraction in her eyes, though. I got lucky, didn't I, Doc thought. She's not just controlling the storm. Her mind is in three places right now. Thoughts upon thoughts upon thoughts.

"You mean it, don't you? That I should go with you."

"Doctor, I'd enjoy spending two hundred years trying to convince you to go back to dark magic," she said. "You'd be a wonderful conversation piece in my retirement."

He took another step closer. When he was younger, before he knew who she was, he possessed such feelings for her. Young man's love, a youthful crush, admiration and adoration all wrapped up in one confusing package. But, he'd seen her other side, he watched the fire in her eyes until his head began to spin, he witnessed her traverse the night sky on wings the color of the absence of all light.

Doc pushed those other reflections away. He let the whispers of a young man's infatuation bring a smile to his face. Not because he wanted to go with her, but because he needed her to believe him, for just a moment longer.

He found himself standing in front of her. She reached her arms out. Doc let her wrap them around him.

"Come along, my little doctor of silence. Leave all this petty nonsense behind. There are worlds we've never seen."

The knife he'd strapped to his left forearm hours before, slipped into the palm of his hand.

"I know there are," he said.

He kissed her, just a little kiss, like something between old friends. With his left hand he slashed upward at the empty air behind the Lady, the knife, a timeless dagger with a handle of bone from a creature who never existed in this world and a blade like a reflecting pool, sliced a thin gash into the very fabric of reality. A tear, an opening just big enough for a person to fall through.

A person, or perhaps two.

He pushed the Lady into the gap, and as he did he opened his eyes. Doc saw a million realities through that gap, an endless array of worlds, some new, some old. He didn't let go of her. Instead, he followed her through, one arm wrapped tightly around her waist.

He let the knife fall from his hand. It clattered to the ground.

Doc Silence and Lady Natasha Gray fell through reality. And reality sealed itself back up again quickly, like air rushing into a vacuum.

All that remained was an empty room, the scattered remnants of the Lady's spells now dormant and useless, the glimmering blade a forgotten relic resting on the floor.

CHAPTER 59:
CONTROL

The ninjas were proving to be problematic.

On the other hand, the mercenaries — thugs with firearms and body armor — had become easier pickings than expected, mostly because they hadn't anticipated a werewolf who shrugged off gunshot wounds and a girl who moved without a sound and punched with a titanium-protected fist. They made up for lack of competence with sheer numbers, yes, but between Kate's moves and Titus's utter menace, they weren't presenting much of a problem.

The bigger hurdle, until the ninjas showed up, was the complete lack of a floor plan. Finding the laboratory where they could shut down the controls on the girl in the storm posed a more substantial obstacle than previously anticipated. The rig was bizarrely large with a multi-tiered leveling system and a frustrating lack of OSHA-compliant signage.

It was then that the guys and girls in the skin-tight body armor showed up. They looked like ninjas from an old movie and that's certainly how Kate dubbed them in her mind, though she had no idea who or what they really were, other than people in need of a good, swift kick to the solar plexus.

Kate almost lost the plot when she encountered her first two because she mistook them for regular mercs and approached them as such, thinking a few quick spin kicks would suffice. Instead, in a shadowy rig corridor, surrounded by steel bars and exposed framework, she confronted two legitimate martial artists. Their training was similar to hers, and as they traded blows — kicks, jumps, spins, elbows, punches, blocks, kicks again — Kate worried that she finally found herself out of her league.

Then, she remembered the tricks Sam gave her.

Rather than throwing it, she palmed a taser disc and it stuck into the armpit of one of the ninjas. He yelped and fell down, struggling to figure out where the pain came from. The shock of his reaction caused his partner to lose her focus, and that's when Kate bashed her across the nose, knocking her silly. She finished her off with a taser zap and looked for Titus.

Four more ninjas slowly picked him apart. It was embarrassing. They had a variety of weapons on hand: two with paired short knives, one with a staff, one with — and Kate found herself oddly jealous — a literal set of nunchaku.

She reared back with a throwing disc but couldn't get a bead on any member of the enemy force, and didn't know what kind of effect an electric shock would have on an already enraged werewolf. As it was, he looked terrible; his eyes lost the rational element that had been developing behind the feral exterior, and his swipes at the ninja became more and more erratic. One stabbed Titus cleanly in the shoulder, but the werewolf rewarded him with a horrific blow, sending the black-clad fighter into the darkness, where he stopped moving.

Kate thought about the other items from Sam, then pulled out the weird, squat, gun-like apparatus they'd tinkered with in the training room. She fired it above Titus's head, wondering if the clawed end of it would latch onto the metal wall behind him or clatter off. She hoped it would be able to penetrate the metal.

It didn't.

The clawed projectile, and the thin but strong cord attached to it, became an additional party in Titus's fight, flapping around out of control, a hindrance as much to him as it was to the other fighters. At one point, it bonked off Titus's forehead, sending the werewolf into a pained howl; then, it kicked back in the other direction and, unexpectedly, wrapped around one of the ninjas' necks. Kate took advantage of this, hit the recoil button on the device and dragged the claw, the rope, and the ninja back to her. She used the butt of the grappling device to knock the fighter unconscious, tapped another button to cut the cord off at the barrel, and then jumped in to help Titus with the last two ninjas.

Before she got any closer, though, Titus, obviously in a rage, pinned one ninja down with a massive, clawed foot, and sent the other flying into the shadows of the exposed framework, clattering like a dropped penny. Titus ground his claw into the chest of the ninja he'd pinned. The man whimpered in the darkness.

"Titus!" Kate said.

The wolf turned on her. She didn't recognize anyone looking back, only yellow eyes, white teeth, red rage.

"Titus. Enough."

He stared her down, fangs bared, but soon relented, removing his foot from the fighter's chest. The man glanced up at Kate, grateful. She kicked him in the head.

"We've been all over this damned rig," she said, keeping an eye on Titus.

He huffed, his huge shoulders rhythmically rolling in the dark. This was the most feral she'd seen him in a quite a while. It worried her. She needed him in control.

Someone moaned in the darkness. Kate followed the noise until she found the source, one of the ninjas Titus had thrown. The man was in horrific shape, but alive, clearly nursing two broken legs.

"Where is Wegener's lab," Kate said.

"You don't scare me, kid," the man said.

She took a step closer.

"Tell me where his lab is, or you will be frightened."

"You think I haven't seen worse than you?" his voice was strained, but hard.

Kate put her heel on the man's shin and pressed down.

He screamed.

"That bone is fractured. I can break it the rest of the way if you want," Kate said. "Scared of me now?"

"You wouldn't — "

She pushed harder. He screamed louder.

"Okay! Stop! . . . One flight down, it hangs off the bottom of the rig. There's nothing else there. We left him to die anyway."

"Left him?"

"It's too late. You can't save him," he said. "Rose killed him. Shark bait. We didn't even bother weighing the body down."

Kate took out one of her taser discs and zapped the man with it until he began to drool. She put it back into the pouch on her belt and turned to Titus.

"You ready, big guy?"

He wasn't listening to her, though. Instead, Titus surveyed the iron steps that led back up to the surface platform. Someone was coming.

She drifted into their view like a shadow. Dressed in the same tight armor as the other ninjas, her face was exposed, revealing red hair framing a hard, angry face; one good eye smiled at them, the other hid behind a black eye patch and scars. The woman who killed Wegener.

"Look at you," she said.

She held a knife in each hand, dangling lazily from her fingers. The blades shone incredibly bright in the darkness. "You're just a baby. I've never killed a puppy before."

Titus watched her like a hunting dog, stock still, unblinking.

"This is hardly going to be a challenge. Bet nobody's even showed you what silver feels like," the woman said. "It's been so long. I would have believed your people were all extinct by now. Haven't had an opportunity to hunt one of you in years."

She edged her way closer, moving like a killer, light on her feet, trying to distract them both.

Kate moved to join Titus on the walkway. He held an arm up, keeping her a few paces behind.

"I bet I killed your mother," the woman said. "You're the right age. Right coloring. Then again it's so hard to tell. With so few of you left, you all kind of look alike these days."

Titus growled, the slow, rumbling growl of a guard dog.

"Poor lost pup," the woman continued her taunting.

"Titus, allow me," Kate said.

He turned her gaze back to her, all trace of humanity drained from his face. She knew, without a doubt, he'd gone completely feral.

Then he spoke.

"Go," he ordered.

Kate nodded. Then turned and ran. Finish the mission, she thought. Remember what's important.

She heard the crash of combat behind her, howls of rage and pain. But Kate rushed on. There were more lives than one at stake.

CHAPTER 60:
JANE VERSUS THE SKY

Jane stared down the storm like she would another fighter, tensed and ready to move. She knew she didn't want to use the same method she employed the last time — charging blindly into the blackening clouds; but somewhere in there, Jane also understood, was a girl, not unlike her, trapped with strange powers and feeling very much alone.

Instead, Jane shot straight up into the sky.

Breaking free of the cloud cover, those ambient rainclouds that rode the storm's energy like lampreys, the gold light of day bathed her. Sun soaked into her skin, creeping into her veins, from eyes to fingertips. Jane felt warmer, stronger. She paused, hanging in mid air, so close to the skin of the earth's atmosphere she could see the stars.

And then she turned around and headed right for the eye of the storm.

Letting gravity do most of the work, Jane saw her opening, the spinning, empty eye, the calm heart of a storm bigger than entire states. She wondered, momentarily, where Emily was, and if she could see her approach, but then Jane was in the thick of it, the storm sensing her presence and launching fast tentacles of clouds at her. She battered her way through these claws, fighting against a wind that seemed to turn an inhuman will toward preventing her from entering the storm.

In an instant, there she was.

The tempest swirled around her, an epic turbine of clouds and rain and hail, but Jane drifted on the soft winds in its eye. The silence was painful, an eerie emptiness with only the whispering song of the storm itself humming in the distance. Her cape yanked and danced on the light breeze.

"Where are you?" she said. "Please come out. I'm not here to hurt you."

A hand emerged from the swirling clouds, gray-skinned, mottled like dark marble. Then another, and then an entire person, a girl, small, elfin, with hair the color of a summer sky and lightning flickering all around her like fireflies at play. She examined Jane curiously and, with a movement that would fit just right on a mermaid, she swam to her across the empty air.

"I can't stop her," the girl said.

"You can," Jane said. "The storm is you now. And you're the storm. You're linked."

"I don't want this," the girl said. "I need to go home."

"You can't," Jane said. "They . . . it's impossible to live without her. And she can't live without you. I'm sorry."

The girl turned her lightning blue eyes away, taking in the vast storm all around her.

"So, if I die, the storm dies?"

"Yes," Jane said.

She turned her strange, alien gaze back to Jane.

"You have to kill me, don't you?"

"I will not," Jane said. "I'm here to help. You can control the storm. This is you."

"I've tried," she said. "Tried so many times."

"You have to fight her," Jane said. "I don't want you to — "

"Oh no," the girl said.

"What?"

"They're back."

More of the winged creatures Jane had seen attack the girl before came burrowing out of the cloud cover. Burnt red skin, green eyes glowing, horns made of scar tissue jutting from their faces, they flew directly toward the girl, gleeful malice on their faces.

Jane launched towards them.

The first seemed genuinely surprised when Jane's fist, engulfed in orange flames, slammed into his nose. He chattered in pain, speaking some language she hadn't heard before, something that sounded old and filthy at the same time. A second creature attempted to fly past, but Jane grabbed him by his skinny neck and held on. He clawed at her hand and arm, trying to wrestle free, but his yellowed nails couldn't break her skin. Then a third and a fourth headed for the girl, and Jane tossed her captive toward the ocean and caught the others by their tails; scaly and lizard-like, they felt like hard muscle beneath her fingers.

The demons all turned on Jane as one, punching, biting. Not strong enough to hurt, they tangled and distracted her. One flipped her cape over her eyes and cackled as the others continued to attack. Jane ripped it off at the seams and flung it away. More of the little demons emerged, laughing scratching, seemingly forgetting their original target.

The girl yelled.

"Leave her alone!" Valerie said. "Look at me!"

Their attacks subsided as the creatures — all these skinny, mis-shapen little monsters — turned their attention to the gray-skinned girl a few meters away.

The girl pointed at them.

"Leave her alone," she said.

And a web of lightning lanced from her fingertips and splashed into the closest demon. The creature screamed, illuminated from the inside. The lightning arced to the next creature, then split in two and electrocuted two more. The little monsters fell away, pinwheeling on the breeze and plummeting to the ocean below.

"How did I do that?" the girl asked.

Jane gazed at the clouds and saw another monster, bigger, with horns curling out of its forehead, climb out of the mists.

"I don't know, but can you do it again?"

The girl extended both hands, lashed out with more lightning, and the bright blasts skittered across the monster's skin. The large demon screamed, yet still clamored forward on huge wings the color of burnt meat.

Jane soared to meet him.

She grabbed a horn in each hand and yanked. The creature howled in pain, its bone-like material of horns flexed and strained. Jane kicked her knee straight up, clicking the monster's jaw shut and then pulled again, pushing with both feet planted against the monster's collarbone.

"Hit him again!" Jane yelled.

More lightning flashed, this time from above, a pure strike. Electricity illuminated the monster from the inside, the current tingled up Jane's arms, and caused her heart to skip a beat. She released his horns and punched him once, twice, three times between the eyes. The monster blinked, bared his teeth, then went blank before he too fell from the sky toward the ocean below.

The wall of clouds grew near, the eye of the storm closed in.

"Any time now, guys," Jane said.

CHAPTER 61:
WEGENER'S LEGACY

Kate discovered the office at the bottom of a flight of sea-rusted stairs, some sort of forgotten storage room converted into a lab. She pushed the door open, surprised, but not completely, to find it unlocked. Inside, neglected computers illuminated the room, their screens emitted an unhealthy glow of monitor blue. Sheets of paper with scribbled notes were scattered all around. Kate picked up an open book and inspected a sketch of a type of mutant: half-man and half-reptile, the caption 'Cretaceous Man' was scrawled above it.

She cocked her head, listening for Titus, but heard nothing except the lapping of the water below her. Kate sat down in front of the computers, typed the password Wegener gave her onto the keyboard and launched a program labeled "controls."

When it opened, she found a set of virtual monitors that tracked the vital signs of a dozen beings. Some were clearly deceased, including two labeled Tinder and Hyde. She read Bedlam's vitals — they appeared healthy — and noticed the spiking adrenaline of another subject labeled Valkyrie.

There were others, as well — Cretaceous, Megalodon, Harpy, Tremble, Plague. Still more, whose names simply consisted of a random string of numbers and letters. According to the program, most were still alive.

Where are they? Kate wondered. Out there, on the run like Bedlam? Or, still in captivity?

With a few keystrokes, she could terminate all of them right now. Put them out of their misery. Remove the threat. She wasn't interested in finding out what havoc a lab experiment named Megalodon or Plague could cause.

But so far, every single one of them had been a victim. Hyde was a little jerk, yes, but in the end, even he'd been sincerely repentant, just another pawn caught up in these experiments. There was no guarantee they'd ever find any of them. They might never know the threat they posed.

Kate inspected each control panel again. The terminate button was easy enough to identify. Red, with a multi-tiered command set. No accidents.

But there existed another command. Release. Could that mean she'd unleash them on the world? In the case of Plague; would there be a person roaming the countryside spreading some unknown pestilence?

Might be easier to destroy them all, she thought. Click a few buttons, put them all down. Save the world. Nobody would have to know if she killed them. Not even Titus. He would believe her, that she had no choice. It was the right thing to do. Titus wouldn't — couldn't — do it if he were here. But he was upstairs. Possibly dying. Possibly dead.

Then she found the third command. Deactivate. Terminate, release, deactivate. Murder, set free, and . . . disarm?

She browsed around, found various dropdown menus for each experiment. It had to be more complicated than that. Had to be clearer. Had to be something else.

Kate wished Wegener had survived just a few minutes longer. Then, she could have asked for better instructions.

She scrolled up and down at random and stumbled across a command simply called "the red wire." Of course it's the red wire, she thought. Wegener must have possessed a sense of humor, once upon a time. Snip the red wire.

And so, one at a time, beginning with Valkyrie and working her way up the list, she cut every red wire. Even Bedlam's. When nothing around her exploded — she suspected at least a few of the lab experiments were housed here on the rig, like Bedlam had been — Kate slumped back in her chair, exhausted.

This room housed everything, she thought. Information on all the experiments. Where they were, what they were. She could try to steal it, take it with her. Find these other kids. Help set them free. But there didn't appear to be a way she could save everything. And here also was the method for making monsters. If this ever got in the wrong hands, someone could build an army. A fleet of ogres.

The door creaked open. Kate leapt to her feet, ready to attack. She paused, though as the figure in the doorway leveled a squat, angry-looking gun at her.

He seemed ordinary in a lot of ways. Almost. Neither tall, nor big — nor handsome, or ugly. Stubble-headed, with a lined face, a weary but strong gait. Just a man, despite the glowing red of a cyborg eye, the silver glint of cybernetics on his face, the gleam of an entire arm rebuilt by science. That arm held the gun, which seemed to flow into the man's hand as if it were integrated, a part of him.

"I wondered which one of you would find Wegener's stash," he said.

Kate waited. She inched her hand toward the taser discs on her belt.

The man shook his head. "Come on now, I could empty my gun into you before you reach your belt," he said. "What did you do in here?"

"I deactivated the cortex bombs," Kate said.

The man nodded, almost imperceptibly.

"Never liked that, myself," he said. "Seemed wasteful to me. Cruel."

"Everything you people have done is cruel," she said.

"No point arguing that, I suppose," he said.

"Are you sure you could shoot me before I take you out?" Kate said.

The man shrugged.

"Probably. I'm not going to shoot you, though."

"What?"

The man gestured around the room with his free hand.

"To be honest, I was never comfortable with all of this," he said. "I mean, look at me. Once upon a time, I was one of these kids."

"You're not going to try to kill me?"

"I'm done with this business of killing children," the man said. "Besides, the check cleared. I'm only sticking around as a professional courtesy."

"You're not going to fight me?"

"You were hoping for that?" the man said. "Listen, I've seen you on video. You're good. But I've been killing people for twenty years. Professionally. And you're no killer."

Kate huffed out a sharp laugh.

"So you're just . . . going to leave?"

"I saw her, you know," the man said. "The girl in the storm. Before they made her into this. She was just a kid. Like you, I imagine. But the money was good and the job seemed easy and . . . Ah, hell, you don't need to know all that. I'm just done with their game is all. Time to move on to the next one."

Kate stared, half-expecting him to change his mind, to pull the trigger. Instead, he unclipped something from his belt and left it on the closest counter.

"Do me a favor, kid."

"I don't owe you any favors."

"No, you don't," he said. "But you might want to begrudge me this one."

He backed out of the door, the gun never wavering from Kate's body. He stopped.

"When you're done in here, pull the pin on that thing and run like hell. Sink Wegener's garbage into the ocean. Let it float away like he did."

He left, and the door clanked shut behind him.

Kate raced after him, tearing the door nearly off its hinges when she opened it. But, he was gone.

"Not bad for an old man," she said.

She stepped back into the office and looked at the egg-shaped device he'd left behind. Just as she suspected. A grenade. A simple, ordinary, military-grade grenade.

Kate tapped her earpiece.

"Solar from Dancer," she said. "Valkyrie is free."

Kate picked up the grenade, pulled the pin, and flung it into the office, where it clattered beneath Wegener's computers.

And, just like the man instructed, she turned and ran like hell.

CHAPTER 62:
WOLF AND ROSE

Titus was on the prowl, hunting.

And being pursued in turn, hunted as well, among the cargo crates and helicopters and crumpled bodies of the mercenaries on the surface of the rig. For every step he took to track his enemy, she proffered a counter-move, both of them hunkered in shadows, trailing the other by instinct.

The initial fight hadn't gone well for him. Covered in cuts and gashes, his wounds burned where the woman's silver-coated knives pierced his hide. But these injuries weren't healing as fast as the others had and they continued to weep blood as he fled deeper into the rig's top level.

For a while he knew Rose was tracking him by his bloody paw prints, but he became wise to that, and began doubling back, leaving false prints, climbing up onto shed-like buildings or slithering down between crates.

He smelled her. She bled as well, Titus's claws left gashes in her body armor. He wondered if Rose trailed him by scent also. Slowing his breathing, hiding his rasping gasps, he sensed her approaching and scurried up onto a gangplank above.

Now injured, she hid it well with a swaggering walk, but Titus knew that one of his attacks damaged her leg; Rose masked a limp on her right side.

Or was she? Something in his predator's mind, the animal brain he always fought against, told him she might be faking it. Rose was

Matthew Phillion

used to fighting his kind. She understood they could hardly resist attacking a lame target.

"What pack are you from?" she said.

Did she know he was watching her? Was Rose losing her resolve? Or was she calling him out? "The Winter Walkers up in the north? The Dust Howlers? You might be a Dust. I thought you were all dead. Can't be one of the Whisperings. You're too American to be from the Whispering pack."

Titus shifted his weight and prepared to pounce from above. Without even looking at him, she turned and flung one of her silver knives. He almost dodge it, but the blade sang against his left thigh, a burning flash tore into him and boiled up more rage behind his eyes.

Stay in control, Titus, stay in control . . .

He dropped down, slamming his jaw against the metal floor of the rig as his injured leg gave out from beneath him. The woman confronted him in a second, slashing with her other knife. She aimed for his eye, but missed, instead leaving a bloody line below his cheekbone.

Titus swatted. Rose danced back. She'd been faking her leg injury. Light on her feet, she continued to taunt him.

"I wonder if you're the last one," she said. "Wouldn't that be nice? To be the one who killed the last werewolf on earth. I think I've earned it."

Titus struggled to reach her, but his left leg buckled under again. She edged in closer, holding her dagger like a fencing blade.

Titus lunged forward, ignoring the pain. He caught her wrist.

Rose gazed at him with complete and utter shock.

"No," she said.

Titus pulled, ready to slam her against the nearest wall. She kicked him in the leg, a perfect shot to his wound. He howled and almost lost his grip on her wrist. Then, she lacerated his palm, not deeply, just enough to burn and bleed. Rose used his blood to wiggle free.

"Now we're simply playing games," she said.

She hopped up onto one of the nearby cargo crates, lighter than air, laughing when he limped and tried to scramble up to grab her.

Titus felt like King Kong, pathetically trying to scale the Empire State building.

"What's the matter?" she said. "Can't reach?"

He shoved the cargo crate instead. The entire structure toppled, taking the woman with it. Titus leaped over the fallen crate, but Rose was gone. Her footsteps clanked against the surface of the rig. Limping, he circled around and down another row of boxes, on all fours, not caring if she could hear him. He pushed the crates over, battering them around like toys, creating chaos and destroying any cover she might find. Finally, he heard Rose let out a winded yelp when one of the crates landed on top of her. Titus tried to pounce, but couldn't find her among the spilled rations, supplies and broken cases.

Another knife whistled toward him, landing perfectly in his right shoulder. He howled, reached back, yanked the blade out his own back. He'd never felt this kind of pain before. Blood spilled hot and dark down his flanks, staining fur.

Titus hobbled toward the edge of the rig. He spied the storm in the distance, lightning continued to create pale veins in the surface of the clouds. The ocean smelled strong. Clean. Like the forest. A natural place. He peered all around, but couldn't see his attacker anywhere.

He jumped overboard.

"No you don't!" he heard Rose yell.

With his good arm, he caught the metal framework of the rigging below and, monkeylike, swung along the underbelly of the rig. Titus's injured arm screamed in pain, but he forced it to work, climbing along like a spider. Through the cracks in the walkway, he could see the huntress reach the edge of the platform and look down into the water.

"This isn't how it ends!" she yelled. "I'm not going to let you drown! You're mine!"

She paced back and forth above him, looking for the wolf to resurface in the water. His whole body shaking with pain, he climbed along the bottom of the rig's platform. Rose left her perch on the top level and he listened as she headed for one of the iron stairwells.

It was darker here, the lights more sporadic, the shadows deeper.

He held on with every ounce of strength. She reached the bottom of the stairwell and began patrolling the edge of the second level, looking out into the ocean, still convinced he'd landed in the sea. The waves swelled. Great, monstrous things built up by the churning storm.

Slowly, Titus crept along the ceiling, handhold to handhold; his long back claws helped maintain balance and grip. Blood dripped onto the floor beneath him; he hoped she couldn't hear the splattering sounds.

Nearly above her, Titus took a deep breath. He prepared to drop down onto her, a predator landing the killing blow on its prey . . .

His maimed arm finally gave out and Titus fell from his hiding place, landing flat on his back onto the floor below.

The woman spun, pulled another knife from her belt — how many could she have? he wondered — and leapt on top of him. He batted her knife away from his face with his good hand but Rose still held the better position, and tried to deliver the fatal strike again.

"Why won't you just die!" she said, and raised her knife with both hands above her head.

Titus coiled both legs in front of her and kicked. His injured left leg roared with so much pain he saw blue and white dots; but both feet connected with her midsection and sent the woman flying. He wriggled to a sitting position fast enough to see her soar backward, almost land on her feet, but then hit the railing of the rig hard enough to make a ringing noise. She locked eyes with him for just a split second before toppling over.

Adrenaline kicking in, Titus staggered to his feet and raced to the rail. He hesitated, his one good arm ready to strike, and looked down, fully expecting to see the woman flip back onto the deck and stab him again.

Instead, he spied a shock of red hair drifting in the swelling waves below, struggling against the tide.

For one brief moment, he thought about jumping in to help her. She knew about his kind. Perhaps she knew more than anyone. Maybe he should save her.

But then the waves of pain began, the fiery screams of all the cuts and punctures she'd inflicted on him building up, their full impact finally hitting him as his adrenaline rush began to wane. The wolf's anger started to take over, and then something else, a pride of winning, the joy of living to fight another day.

He howled again. Only this time, it was not in pain.

CHAPTER 63:
CONTAINMENT

They all heard it. Kate's voice on the transmitter. The bomb was deactivated. Now was the time.

"Crap," Emily said. "Right now?"

"Emily," Jane's voice came through the receiver next. "Are you ready?"

Emily scanned the storm once again: bigger, horrifyingly immense, nightmare big.

"This is bad," Emily said.

"Now would be good, Em," Jane said. She sounded tired. "What do you need me to do."

"Um," Emily said. "I have a bad idea."

"Any ideas are good right now."

"Can you see the girl?" Emily said.

"I'm right near her," she said. "And we're not going to hurt her."

"I wasn't going to suggest that," Emily said. "You're the one who punches everything! I'm the pacifist on this team!"

"Emily from Kate," Kate said.

She sounded exhausted. Everyone sounded exhausted.

They're going to be very angry if this doesn't work, Emily thought.

"Kate from Emily, what's up?"

"What the hell are you doing up there?"

"Thinking!"

"We're doomed," Billy said.

He didn't sound exhausted. Rather, he sounded like he was smiling. "C'mon, Em. We have faith in you. Do what you gotta do. We'll be here to catch you."

Emily blinked. That was not a bad idea at all. "I need two things!"

"Hurry up," Jane said.

"Jane, can you send me a signal so I can see where you are, with the girl? Like a flare?"

"Just say when."

"And Billy, ah, just, like, be ready."

"For what?" all three of them said at the same time.

Emily started laughing.

"You'll know it when you see it. Now would be good, Jane!"

Below her, Emily saw a burst of flame like a tiny sun flickering within the storm.

Emily dove, in as much as her airy flight could really dive, and prepared her most important bubble of float ever.

Kate's message caused Jane's stomach to curl into a knot.

The bomb was gone. The girl was free. And, the storm clearly understood somehow. The whirling winds in the eye of the storm churned up, violently, darkening, now almost black as smoke, hardly resembling clouds at all.

They looked like rage.

"Doc?" Jane said, quietly, triggering a private channel to Doc's receiver. "Are you out there?"

Silence.

Jane waited, anticipating further attacks by the winged creatures she'd fought, but they never returned. Doc had stopped the attacks somehow. She had to have faith in that.

But he hadn't sent a message, hadn't let them know. Hadn't said goodbye.

"Doc? You okay?"

Nothing.

Then she heard Emily's nervous chatter over the general line,

285

and she tried to regain her focus. She could worry about Doc later; right now, there was everyone else to take care of. She gazed at the girl in the storm, the gray, almost featureless face, the huge, luminous eyes, the alien way the lightning danced across her frame.

You'd better be worth it, Jane thought.

Emily asked for a flare.

Jane, still buzzed with the energy she'd soaked up from the sun earlier, obliged her. The flash of light illuminated the eye of the storm, creating strange shadows in the clouds. For a moment, she almost thought she saw a face there, the face of a furious girl, of elemental rage.

"Emily? Now would be good!"

She felt Emily's approach before she saw it, the thrum of the world going sideways, the way reality stopped working properly in her presence. Then she saw it, Emily's antigravity field, like the bow of a ship, parting the black clouds, pushing them away and out of existence. There was Emily, in her ridiculous costume, goggles down, that bizarre scarf fluttering in the wrong direction in the wind.

Emily's bubble crashed over them, engulfing Jane and the girl like a soap bubble.

The second, the very split second, Emily encased the girl in her antigravity field, the world changed. It was as if the storm collapsed upon itself, the clouds expanding and lashing out like hands with too many fingers, then sputtering into a mist. The rain stopped in the bat of an eye. The rumbling of distant thunder silenced.

The sun splashed on Jane's face.

Emily reached for the girl and grabbed her by the hand.

She smiled.

Then, Jane began to fall.

Billy watched Jane in freefall, a half mile away. Her cape was gone. She plummeted backward, not even attempting to fly, arms and legs loose as she dropped toward the ocean.

She got caught in Emily's weirdness field, Dude, he said.

She did.

I gotta catch her.

Go!

Billy held both arms out in front of him, trying to streamline his body, to become a rocket in flight. A few seconds later, he realized he wasn't planning this right, that he was aiming not for where she would be but where she was. He tried to course correct, to aim himself lower to match her trajectory.

I've never been good at math, Dude!

You can catch her.

I have to.

You will. Don't worry.

A swell of power hit Billy, a dizzying strength he hadn't felt before. No longer just flying, he broke the sound barrier.

You've been holding out on me, Dude.

I was waiting, Billy Case.

For what?

For you to act like a hero. Now save your friend.

Billy poured on the speed, no longer worried about predicting where she would fall but knowing, just knowing, he would be there. Closer and closer, he saw things more clearly than he ever had before, the alien energy let him feel like he could see molecules move. He fixated on her right hand, those nails painted with a faint gold polish.

I never noticed her nails before.

Another time, Billy Case.

I know.

Billy reached out. He caught her wrist. Her small, strong hand snap shut around his own. The tug of her weight against his shoulder. He grabbed her other arm. Without thinking, he pulled her into his arms.

"That's three," she said.

"Told you," he said.

Jane laughed.

"You're glowing, Billy."

"I'm what?"

"Literally glowing," she said. "You can let me go now."

Billy released her, and Jane took flight on her own again. He glanced down at his hands. He really was glowing, and not just the usual signature of blue-white light he projected when his protective shields were active. He glowed from the inside.

Dude?

It will pass.

Pass?

It is a side effect.

Side effect? I have side effects?

It will pass.

We need to discuss this later, Billy said.

"Are you coming?" Jane said.

"Where?"

"To find out what our Emily is doing with a storm in a jar."

CHAPTER 64:
SILENCING THE VOICE

ate scrambled back to the top of the rig, running into but not needing to fight what was left of the remaining mercenaries. A few stopped and lifted their guns, but then backed away cautiously. She wondered if the cyborg she met in Wegener's office had issued some kind of evacuation order.

At one point, she witnessed a pair of the ninjas carrying on a whispered conversation. Kate jumped to grab hold of a bar above her and pull herself into the rafters as they passed. They spoke a mixture of several languages, English, French — a Slavic language Kate couldn't identify, and Mandarin, but she caught "gone" and "escape" among the English, and knew enough French to decipher the word for wolf.

She wondered if Titus had survived. She wondered, more darkly, what she would do if he hadn't.

Up on the main deck, several helicopters took off, ignoring everything occurring on the surface. The storm still raged out across the water; rain and lightning peppered the sky. The copters paid her no mind. Things were finished here, it appeared.

Then, she saw the man in the squid-marked mask being escorted by a set of guards toward the biggest helicopter.

"Well, why not," she said.

Kate ran at him, tossing taser discs at the two lead bodyguards, watching them jitter and stagger when the electricity hit their skin. Before the others could get a shot off, she kicked a third in the mouth, elbowed a fourth in the eye, and prepared to keep going when someone cracked her head with the butt of his rifle.

She fell to the ground, stunned.

"Should I shoot her, Sir?"

The man in the mask spoke. Kate remembered his voice from the television. It was pretty, for a man. A television announcer's voice. Someone who could narrate film trailers.

"None of this matters," he said. "We've failed. We're all going to die. They'll have us killed when they find out."

"So where we going?"

The Voice turned to his bodyguard. "Wouldn't you like to know?"

"Huh?" one of the guards said.

Kate watched the exchange; two other bodyguards continued to train their weapons on her. She stayed low, feigning to be in worse shape than she really was. The blow to her head made her see stars, but she could move if forced to. At least that was what she hoped.

"You're going to kill me, aren't you," the Voice said. "You're on their payroll. I'm to be the sacrificial victim for this failure. What did they promise you?"

"I swear, I'm not — "

"Give me your gun," the Voice said.

"What?"

"Your sidearm. Give me your pistol."

The bodyguard, confused, handed the pistol on his belt to the Voice with his free hand. The other man accepted it and pointed it at Kate's head.

"Why did you do this?" he said. He sounded scared, the smooth richness of his voice giving way to panic. "What did you hope to gain?"

Kate smiled.

She wondered if she was fast enough to get her head out of the way if he pulled the trigger. Even if the bullet hit her body armor it would be better — it would hurt like hell, but she hadn't armored her head enough for this sort of thing.

"Bring her," he said.

"Bring her?"

"I'm not going back empty handed," the Voice said.

"You're not bringing me," Kate said.

The Voice fired. Not at her head — the bullet clipped off her armored hip, sending a shockwave of bruising pain up and down her leg.

"Bring her," he said again.

The bodyguard tried to pick her up but she bashed him across the nose with her forehead, the man staggered backward in pain. His cohorts opened fire, but Kate was already on the move, five feet from where they were aiming.

The Voice fired also, wildly, all self-control lost.

Kate felt another bullet slam into her protective covering, mid-back and to the left, knocking the wind out of her.

"Forget her!" the Voice said.

He stormed off for the waiting helicopter; his guards followed. The blades of the helicopter's rotor began to spin and the Voice climbed in through a side door. Kate noted that the one who'd been speaking to him, the commander of the bodyguards, had been left behind, still on the ground holding his nose together from Kate's head butt.

She pulled out the grappling gun again and fired it, puncturing the helicopter's tail.

"This is a terrible idea," she said. But she prepared to hold on, looking for a way to clip the firing mechanism to her belt. They can't get away, she thought. Someone has to be held accountable for all of this.

The helicopter started to pull away. Kate ran across the deck of the rig, wondering if the winch in the grappling gun was strong enough to carry her high up to the landing gear.

And then, two hundred and fifty pounds of werewolf launched into the air and slammed into the tail of the helicopter.

The copter spun like a top, Titus's bulk sending it out of control. Kate saw the pilot struggling to right the vehicle, to no avail. Sparks flew as the landing gear scraped across the deck.

The cable connecting the gun to the grapple held true. Kate

found herself dragged violently across the deck. Bouncing and bumping her way to the edge of the rig, she tried to get a handle on the grappler, to hit the release button, but she was rolling, wrapped in the cord, the centrifugal force of the copter's spin growing faster and stronger. The helicopter gained altitude and pulled off the deck. Just in time, she found the release button and fell back, landed and started to roll. Out of the corner of her eye, she saw Titus ejected from the tail of the aircraft, a frightening and comical sight as the werewolf fell with all the grace of a belly-flopping diver to the deck.

The ground opened up beneath her when she rolled to the periphery of the deck, and toppled over.

Somehow, she grabbed hold of the edge on her way down. Kate's full weight tugged at her grip. She felt the bruised pain of the second gunshot blare, a thrumming ache that took the breath from her lungs. Broken ribs, she thought, I can't hold on . . .

The entire structure shuddered with a vast metallic bang. Heat washed over her and the helicopter exploded in a ball of flame. Kate's hand burned as if she'd held it under hot water too long. She tried to reach up with her other, her breath hitching and catching in her throat. The water below churned hungry and dark.

Pale, thin fingers grabbed hold of her wrist. Those fingers jutted out of a familiar, if ripped and bloody, hooded sweatshirt.

Titus's face, his human face, appeared over the edge. He clasped her arm with both hands. Slowly, she hauled herself back onto the deck.

The helicopter lay crashed and nearly dead center on the rig. Boxes and small buildings burned hot. No one moved inside.

Kate glanced over at Titus, who half-lay, half-sat against the guardrail of the deck. Covered in cuts and bruises, one arm lay limp against his side, and she could see that his pants, those silly yoga pants Emily made fun of him for, had been sliced open across a leg, an angry wound visible through the gash in the fabric.

He smiled.

"Had an interesting afternoon," he said. "And you?'

Kate punched him on his good shoulder and tried to stand up. Her legs went watery, so she sat back down. She put an arm around

Titus protectively, and pulled his hood up over his head.

"I can't believe this stupid sweatshirt survived," she said.

"I'm thinking of getting a new one."

"Don't you dare!"

And then, almost without warning, the sun came out. Dark clouds on the horizon slowly disappeared.

Funny what a little daylight can do, Kate thought. She rested her head against the top of Titus's shoulders and closed her eyes, the heat of the sun warmed her cheeks.

CHAPTER 65:
THERE ARE SO MANY WORLDS

Doc woke to find the Lady standing over him, arms crossed, legs akimbo, a look that would turn an ordinary man's hair white on his face.

"What did you do, Silence?"

"Used a planar knife," he said, pushing himself up onto one elbow, struggling to get to his feet. They were in the middle of a desert, the sand almost snow-white, the sky above them an unnatural shade of blue. The air was strangely temperate. It felt more like beach than desert. Water was in the air.

"You didn't," she said.

"I couldn't come up with any other way to stop you, so thought I'd just remove us both from the equation and let the mere mortals sort things out," Doc said.

He stood up, dusted off his clothes, and shook sand out of his jacket. His rose-tinted glasses jutted out of the sand like a lost toy. Doc picked them up and cleaned them with the hem of his shirt.

"Where are we?" she said.

"I don't know. I didn't tell the knife where to go."

"A planar knife can open a door to anywhere!" she said. "Where is it?"

"I dropped it."

"You . . . dropped it?"

"I did," he said. "Didn't want to risk you getting home before me."

294

"You threw us through a dimensional window and didn't bring the key with you?"

"I didn't."

"Why didn't — I have seven of those knives," she said. "If I'd known — "

"You have six," Doc said, then smiled.

He smiled.

The Lady glared, paused, and then laughed her silver bell laugh.

"Clever boy," she said.

They looked around, scanning the distance. On a ridge, silhouetted against the sun, a group of travelers riding animals with too many legs made their way across the salt-colored sands.

"Never been here before," she said.

"Me either."

The Lady sighed, rubbing the bridge of her nose between her thumb and forefinger.

"Do you have any idea how long it will take for us to get home again?" she said.

"Nope," he said. "But I was thinking we'd get home a lot faster if we worked together to find it. I'd like to get back sooner rather than later, myself."

She stared at him, the fires in her eyes glowed hotter and brighter than usual. Then she laughed again.

"Very clever boy," she said. "Fine."

The Lady waved a hand up and down her frame and her clothes twirled into a new shape, a loose fitting robe, vibrant gold and orange. She pulled a hood up over her head.

"Well? Straighten yourself out, Doctor Silence. You've put a serious damper in my retirement plans, and I want to get a move on back to them."

"But I always look like this," he said.

"You would," she said.

"Come on. Let's ask those folks on that hill what world we're in."

She pointed at him.

"You owe me for not killing you, Doctor," she said.

"Well, we have some time to negotiate a repayment, don't we?"

he said.

"Beginning with you getting my planar knife back," she said.

"Done."

"Not done, Doc," she said. "This bargain's not done by a long shot."

They bickered as they walked, the Lady in her golden robes and he in his long black coat. Doc wondered, and hoped, that his charges were okay.

CHAPTER 66:
THE CALM AFTER

They watched her, the trio of heroes, floating there outside her cage. The golden girl, the silver boy, and the strange one with her goggles and scarf. She felt the storm inside her now, because it had nowhere else to go, no way to escape. It wailed and cried in her head, but every time it tried to extend its reach, to lash out at their mutual captors, this sphere of emptiness stopped it from attacking.

She knew how strange she must look to them, twitching and squirming as the storm tried to take control of her body. But now it couldn't; the storm remained inside her, it could not take her body from her. She felt the storm's rage spill off her like waves.

"You must take control," the golden girl said.

"What if I can't?" she said.

Even her voice — colored with hints of pouring rain, of howling wind — no longer sounded like her own; it sounded elemental.

"I saw you," the golden girl said. "Saw you control the lightning to help me. You saved me."

"I don't know how I did it," Valerie said. "It just happened."

"You willed it to happen," she said. "You took control."

"Does she speak?" the silver boy said.

He lacked pupils. His eyes glowed white, from the inside.

"What?" Valerie said.

"Does the storm speak to you."

"She doesn't talk," Valerie said. "Only feels."

"But can she communicate?" he said.

"I've tried; tried so many times," she said.

"Try again," the younger girl said. "Maybe she was too big to listen. Or just didn't want to."

Valerie closed her eyes.

At first she spoke in English, in words, phrases — then in pleading sentences: please stop fighting, please work with me, please be one with me. But, later she gave way to feelings, sadness, loneliness, fear. She wanted to go home. She wanted to be free. She wanted to live. She wanted to fly.

And she felt those feelings returned to her. Childlike, more raw, unfiltered. The enormous sentiments of a child, not the controlled emotions of an adult. Such rage, such fear, such joy. They caused her heart to pound in her chest, her eyes to ache with tears.

"She's listening," Valerie said.

The storm's passions crept in, making her feel more, more of everything. She'd never been so afraid, so angry, so alone in her entire life. Valerie wasn't sure that any human being could sense these things as desperately as she did now.

"Can you control her?" the golden girl said.

Valerie closed her eyes again. She reflected on a vision of her mother, the storm's mother, smaller, but still strong, still destructive, still impossibly vast; she remembered being born, breaking free, a rain cloud left behind after the death of a hurricane, just a bit of condensation and sky, growing into a downpour, into a thunderstorm, into a tropical storm, into a vortex.

She was majestic. And she knew how to do only one thing.

Valerie hoped to show her how to be so much more. She wanted to be something to this juvenile storm, this alien intelligence. She had incredible things to learn, and without Valerie, very little time to do it. Without Valerie she'd vanish like a summer shower come morning.

Stay with me, she said. We need each other. We can learn so much.

Waves of rage, waves of sadness, a spike of fear . . . and then, clarity — cool water in her veins. She looked at her hands, at her arms. No longer harsh, dark gray, instead, they swirled marble white,

298

cumulous ivory. The calm after a storm.

"She's gonna be fine," the younger girl said. "Look at that. She's gonna be totally fine."

"What should we do?" the older girl said. She was looking to Valerie. Asking her.

Valerie smiled. It had been so long since she smiled, it hurt. Her cheeks ached, tiny facial muscles in atrophy — unused for months — now creaking with effort.

"We'll be okay," she said. "Do what you have to do."

The older girl looked to the boy, whose own smile, a cocky grin, glowed with inner light.

He nodded to her. "She's going to be fine, Jane," the boy said.

The older girl put a hand on the younger one's shoulder.

"No more bubble of float, Em," she said.

"Finally," the younger one said. "This isn't easy, you know."

"Yes it is," the older girl said. "For you it's always easy."

"Well, yeah," the younger girl said.

She opened both hands in front of her like a magician releasing a dove, and Valerie felt the world tug at her again, gravity and air and wind and sky — all the things that made her real. Clouds moved across her skin like thoughts.

"I'm sorry for everything we've done," she told them.

"It was never your fault," the older girl said. "You just wanted to go home."

"Isn't that what we all want?" Valerie said.

And she let the storm inside her take flight. Sleek clouds followed her like dolphins along the bow of a ship. The sky opened up. The sky was hers. And she was home.

CHAPTER 67: GENERATIONS

Bedlam often thought about hitchhiking. Not because she was exhausted. Her cyborg legs and whatever engine they'd given her to keep her heart pumping ensured she was never tired. But a constant plod north, particularly in the rain like today, got old fast.

And as much as she hated to admit it, she missed talking to people. She pretended to dislike everyone, but even the world's worst curmudgeon wants someone to have a conversation with once in a while.

Maybe that's why she was heading for the city. That idiot boy she beat up seemed nice enough. It was fun taunting the werewolf. Teasing counted as conversation, right? And the alien boy had been almost interesting. Not actually interesting mind you, but close.

So fine. She was going north because she was lonely. She could admit that. But would they really let her feel like one of them? Of course not. Why would they? They'd never trust her, not with where she came from and where she got her powers. And she hadn't exactly made a great first impression. She needed to stop punching first and asking questions later.

That was becoming a really bad habit.

And as for hitchhiking, well, yeah, who was going to pick her up? They might slow down, since she looked practically like a normal girl in a poncho from behind, but when they saw her face, or noticed that the thumb sticking out looking for a ride was dull chrome, would they call the cops, or just gun it and run? Either way, she wasn't interested in that particular kind of human interaction.

People suck, she thought. That's pretty much the sum of it.

Because of all this, she looked at the truck pulled over on the side of the road ahead of her with some trepidation. She couldn't really help, unless they were stuck in a ditch or something. Not like she could give them a jump-start if their battery was dead. And she really didn't want police attention, or some trigger-happy road warrior thinking she was a threat.

The driver slid out of the car and looked right at her. Fight or flight kicked in when she saw his face, one side bristling with cybernetics that ran down his neck, an entire arm replaced with a robotic one, like hers had been. He looked familiar.

And then Bedlam realized he might be from the lab. There were other modified people there. Would they bother sending someone like him after her? Was she worth pursuing?

She tensed, ready to attack. So much for not punching first and asking questions later, she thought.

Then he waved and smiled, almost sheepishly.

"You have got to be kidding me," she said.

"You Bedlam?" the man said.

His voice was definitely familiar. She wondered if he'd been in the room during some of the early experiments, when she wasn't fully conscious yet after the surgeries.

"You're from the lab," Bedlam said. "You're not bringing me back alive."

He waved a hand dismissively.

"Lab's gone," he said. "I'm not here to bring you back."

She flexed the fingers of her robotic hands. He didn't look as powerful as she was, nor nearly as modified, but she knew there were a million ways to build a six million dollar man.

"Then what do you want?" she said.

"Can I come over there?"

"No."

He laughed.

"Fair enough," he said.

"Are you gonna to tell me what you want, or am I gonna have to punch you in the face?" she said.

"I'd rather you didn't," he said. "Have you thought about your future?"

My future? She thought. Sure. Mall job. Working at Build-A-Bear. I'd be great at it, my arms never get tired. What a stupid question.

"I was thinking about going to veterinary school," she said. "People suck, dogs don't."

"If that's what you want, good luck to you," he said. "Look, I was at the lab. Never really liked what was going on there. You in particular, because, well . . . "

He gestured at his own face.

"Because I could relate. I'm not working for them anymore."

"Oh really?"

"Yeah. I'm done," he said. "And I knew you were out here on your own, and, well, like I said, I could relate."

"You're here out of the goodness of your heart?" she said.

"I'm here because once upon a time I was like you, and someone gave me a leg up," he said. "Granted it was a leg up into a pretty violent career, but it was better than what I could've been doing."

"What do you want from me?"

"I'm thinking of starting a new business," the man said. "I need a partner."

"You gotta be pretty desperate if you're offering homeless girls on the highway a partnership."

The man laughed again.

"I'm not desperate. I'm just figuring . . . I got some karma I'd like to balance off. I can help you get that bomb out of your head. Show you how to get around this world looking like we do without needing to put a trash bag over your head."

"I think my poncho is quite fashionable."

He shrugged.

"Up to you, kid," he said. "I'm not forcing you. Your choice."

She offered him a long dose of stink-eye.

The man shrugged again and turned to get back in his truck.

302

She called out. "What's your name, anyway?"

"Name's Black," he said. "You got a name you prefer to Bedlam?"

"Nah," she said. "Bedlam's what I am now. It stays."

"What do you say, Bedlam? Want to join cyborgs for hire?"

She raised an eyebrow.

"Do I have to sign a contract or anything?"

The man shook his head.

"I'm sick of the paperwork. You leave any time you want to. At least let's get that thing out of your brain. If you want to work at a fast food joint after that, I'll pay for your train ticket to wherever you'd like to go."

"That's a crap offer," she said. "Nobody's letting me on a train looking like this."

"Lesson number one, Bedlam," the man said. "When you look like this, you can do almost anything you want."

She pulled her makeshift poncho over her head and then threw it onto the side of the road.

"I'm in," she said. "Was sick of wearing a trash bag over my head anyway."

CHAPTER 68:
THE OLD FRIEND

Neal's directions sent Kate to an old industrial building on the edge of town. The exterior looked as if it hadn't been touched in a decade, the brick walls crumbling and slathered with moss and vines, the parking lot more rubble than pavement. She vaulted the fence — not a simple task with the barbed wire skirting the top — and walked up to the front door.

Before she could knock, the door unlocked with a heavy thump and creaked open.

"Huh," she said and walked inside.

The interior was an abstract painting of shadows and cobwebs. Things moved in the dark, small rodents, a night bird squawked at her interrupting presence. Kate took a few steps inside and paused in the light of one of the large, cracked windows.

"Hello?" she said.

Sam had gifted her a pair of infrared goggles, which she now slid down over her eyes. But all she saw was more of the same: cobwebs, small mammals. Nothing human, not yet anyway.

"You have a recurring pain in your left ankle, an old injury that never healed right," a voice in the dark said. "You've recently been wounded in the shoulder. You're moving sluggishly on your left side. You're what, eighteen? Start seeing a chiropractor now. It'll do you a world of good if you hope to have a career after thirty."

"Where are you?"

"You haven't given me a reason to show my face yet."

"Doc Silence sent me."

The voice stopped.

She could almost hear him formulating his response.

"He's not dead," the voice said.

"We don't think so," Kate said.

"We?"

"My friends and me. Doc's students. He's gone, but said he didn't know how long it would take him to get back," she said.

"Magic," the voice said. "Most dangerous thing in the world. Stay away from it. Another tip for having a long career."

"Doc said you might help us."

The voice went quiet again.

"You were the Alley Hawk, right?" she said. "One of the heroes who stayed. Doc's friend."

"He used that word liberally," the voice said.

"You weren't friends?"

"I didn't say that," the voice said. "Just don't believe everyone who says they were once his friend. Doc trusted too many people. Never wore a mask. Never hid his identity."

"Wait. His real name was Doc Silence?"

The voice laughed, sounding like car tires on a gravel road.

"I don't think Doc even remembered his real name. It's a magician thing. Stay away from magic."

"I'll keep that in mind," Kate said.

She lifted the goggles off her eyes and blinked as her pupils adjusted. When she opened them again, a man stood in front of her. Shorter than she expected, and powerfully wide. He wore a khaki jacket with a hooded sweatshirt underneath, the hood pulled up to hide his face.

"You're the Dancer," he said.

"Why did you quit?" Kate said.

"Didn't quit," he said. "But things got too hot. I was getting older. Slower. Figured there was a better way to do things. Tried to set up a legacy. Failed on that count."

"And now you hide here."

"Not hiding," he said. "Waiting."

"For what?" she said.

The man pulled back his hood. His face was carved out of a cinder block — hard lines with tired eyes. Small scars marked his skin; a large one cut from above his right eye and into his hairline. His hair had been shaved down to stubble, but more because of that scar than for vanity. The man resembled a gargoyle.

"I've been waiting for a world worth throwing my life away for again," he said.

"Well, it's not, really," she said.

The Alley Hawk laughed his car-on-gravel laugh again.

"At least you're honest," he said. "Doc said you needed help."

"He just said you'd help us."

The Alley Hawk shook his head.

"With what?"

"We . . . we don't know what to do next," Kate said. "Without Doc."

The man sighed. He sounded tired, but not angry.

"You're doing fine, you know," he said. "I've been observing. Just keep doing what you believe is right. It's the only way to stay sane in this job."

"But what if we screw up?" she said. "What if we make the wrong decision? We're a bunch of kids. We don't know anything."

"That's a lie," he said.

He turned and began to walk away.

"That's it? That's all you have for me?"

The Alley Hawk stopped and turned around.

"It's what we all did, kid," he said. "But I'll be watching. If you need a hand . . . I'll do what I can."

Kate's eyes followed him as limped into the dark, the pain of each step evident in his every movement. And she wondered, was this the future she had to look forward to?

CHAPTER 69:
THOSE LEFT BEHIND

Jane sat in her same chair, next to Doc's empty one, as the others shuffled in. With everyone dressed in their dusty and disheveled street clothes, costumes now abandoned, they seemed weary and more than a little haunted. Kate, in particular, looked like she'd seen a ghost.

Jane wished she knew how to communicate with Kate. She understood it was something she must learn. They were going to need each other from now on, more than ever.

Titus relayed his battle with the werewolf hunter and her silver-plated knives, which had more than slowed down his normally miraculous healing. He still patched himself back together better than a normal human could, but these cuts would leave scars. They all worried about the shoulder wound, in particular, but he assured them that he was healthier and stronger every day.

Yet watching him fiddle with his sweatshirt, Jane could see he was still struggling. He flexed his fingers often, to keep them from tightening up with pain.

Billy stopped glowing. Mostly. His eyes weren't the same, though. His irises, now closer to silver than their former blue, shined faintly in the dark when his eyes opened. Nothing like Doc's fiery gaze, yet still unearthly and strange.

Emily was just Emily, texting on her phone when she stumbled in and barely looking up when Jane opened the meeting. "Do we know where Valkyrie went?" she asked.

"We tracked her for a bit over Europe," Titus said. "But she seems to have the storm under control — there was an unseasonable snow squall in London a few days ago, but nothing terrible. We lost her yesterday, no strange weather patterns have been reported . . . "

"Can we leave her alone for a bit?" Emily said.

"We've got to at least keep an eye on her," Kate said. "If she loses control of the storm, we're back to square one."

"I'm just sayin', she has some crap to work through."

"Noted," Kate said.

"We'll try," Jane said. "What about the others?"

"Bedlam's dropped off the map entirely," Billy said.

"You must be heartbroken," Titus said.

"I *was* hoping she'd come in and at least let us help with the bomb," Billy said.

"She'll show up if she wants to," Jane said. "Sorry your charm wasn't enough to woo her back to the Tower."

He shrugged, a scowl lined his face.

"And the other names on the list Kate found are . . . nowhere," Billy said. "I guess we'll just keep hoping they show up."

"No," Emily said. "One of them was called Megalodon. I think we have a pretty fair idea what he's going to look like. I'm not wishing he'll show up."

Everyone stared blankly. And, she threw her hands up into the air.

"Megalodon? Prehistoric shark? Ate dinosaurs? Come on, am I the only one who reads around here?"

Jane sat back and sighed, allowing Emily her minor meltdown. They'd become endearing. Everything was becoming so. Emily's nonsense, Kate's practicality, Billy's cockiness, Titus's sarcasm. She didn't want it to end.

"So I guess the only thing to talk about is: what happens next?" she said.

"What huh?" Emily said.

"For us? Do we go home? Stick together? What are we, without Doc around?" Jane said.

"We're talking about splitting up? I didn't know this was on the

308

agenda!" Billy said.

"You and Emily have homes to go to," Jane said. "You don't have to stay."

"I'm not going home," Billy said. "Finally found something I'm good at. I'm staying."

"I've stopped annoying my mom," Emily said. "I'm not goin' anywhere."

"We just keep doing what we're doing," Kate said, her tone flat and authoritative. "I'm in."

"That leaves you, Titus," Jane said. "What about you?"

He sighed.

"I, ah, need to leave for a bit," Titus said.

Kate sent him a death look that made Jane's heart skip a beat. Titus wilted under the glare.

"Just need to go home for a little while. The woman I fought on the rig said a lot of things. I want to find some answers. Where I came from. What I am," he said. "I'm not quitting. Just want to check things out. See if I can get a better handle on who I am."

Jane nodded. "Makes sense. You want any help?" she said. "I bet we could lend a hand."

Titus looked at Kate and her alone. She shook her head once, almost imperceptibly. He acknowledged it with a tiny tilt of his head. Then, he looked back to Jane.

"No, I'll be okay," Titus said. "I won't be gone long. Promise."

"Well, you need us, you call, furball," Billy said. "We'll be there faster than a speeding — "

"If you finish that sentence Billy Case I will punch you in the mouth," Jane said.

"Why is everyone so violent around here?" Billy said.

"It's how we show affection, I guess," Emily said.

They dispersed, Billy and Emily both intent on checking in with their families, Jane saying she wanted to look through Doc's notes to see if he left any clues to where he went.

Titus watched them go, a cold fist in his stomach. He'd been alone a long time before Doc found him. He wasn't looking forward to repeating the experience.

Kate grabbed him and shoved him against the wall.

"You skinny little jerk, you're leaving?"

"Why won't you come with me?" he said. "I want you to come. We could — maybe we'd have fun."

Kate's face darkened, her mouth twisted in a hard frown.

"I can't just leave, Titus," she said. "There are parts of this city that I'm the only one looking out for."

"You could take a few weeks off," Titus said. "Just a few weeks?"

Kate exhaled sharply.

"It — I don't want to meet your family, Titus. Don't like what they did to you. And, don't want to know what I'd be like if I met them. Not sure I want to see that part of myself."

He smiled.

Kate's eyes flared open. She almost hit him.

"What are you smiling about?"

"You care about that stuff?"

"Of course I care about that stuff you idiot," she said.

"Will you wait for me, at least?"

"What?"

"I mean, will you not go looking for a boyfriend or anything while I'm — "

"Oh, I don't know, I meet scrawny little superhumans who turn into monstrous creatures all the time, I may find a new one while you're gone."

"Now I'm jealous."

"I'm going to punch you."

"No you're not."

"Yes I — "

Titus kissed her. Just a quick kiss, light on the lips. She pulled back and really did look like she wanted to punch him.

Then, she kissed him back.

He bit his own lip at the force of it.

"You're taking me to a movie before you go."

"Okay," he said.

"I get to pick the movie. . . . And we're seeing something funny," she said. "I'm sick of everything sucking."

"Me too," he said.

For once, she smiled at him, and for just a split second, Titus thought she looked her age, without the world resting on her shoulders.

Out of a hot Florida sky, a single cloud fell. It moved faster than any cloud should, and with far too much purpose; it had a place to go, and nothing would stop its momentum.

The cloud took shape. It became a girl. Her eyes glowed like distant lightning, her hair the color of the summer sky, her skin mottled white and gray, ever changing.

She paused outside a small ranch, a modest home; peered through a window. She saw a man and a woman sitting together on the couch, watching television, but not watching television, the blank-eyed stare of those who are searching for anything, anything at all to distract them from the things that are breaking their hearts.

She wanted to call out their names. But she knew she was not the daughter they lost, and never would be again, and she was afraid, so very afraid, that she would startle them. She didn't want her mother to be frightened of her. Didn't want to break her father's heart.

But she wanted very much to say she was sorry for letting them down.

The sky clouded over. It was subtle, at first, then faster, and later a light mist began to fall. The sky wept, because the girl made of clouds was weeping, and the sky was her body as much as this form she wore to help her feel human.

Inside, she felt the other presence, the sentient storm, grieve with her. They had talked, the past few days, about their losses. Not spoken in words, but in feelings and memories. The little storm had lost her mother.

They'd come to understand each other, if only in the most raw and saddest of ways.

The rain tapped against the window panes. Valerie's mother

stood up and closed the window closest to her, and then turned to look at the one Valerie was staring through.

Her mother's eyes grew wide. She called her father's name. He jumped up quickly, as if to defend his wife, but then he saw the face in the window, the face Valerie realized was not the one they remembered. But they knew. She could see it in their expressions, in the tears welling up in her father's eyes.

Together, they walked to the window, hand in hand. Her mother pressed a palm against the glass. Valerie put her own on top of it. Their hands stayed there for awhile.

Nothing would be the same.

Perhaps some things would be okay.

Saturday morning. Quiet. Three figures flew above the cloud line, surveying the world.

"How are we supposed to look after all this," Jane said, in awe.

She'd flown hundreds and hundreds of times, but she never stopped to look at the enormity of it all. This world went on forever.

"One day at a time," Billy said.

"When did you get Zen, Billy Case," Emily said. Her goggles were down, and the pink clouds around them reflected in her lenses.

"I'm not Zen. Dude's Zen," Billy said. "Just trying to listen to him more."

Jane breathed in sharply. She looked away from both of her friends. "I miss him," she said. "I never realized how much he was doing for us."

"We're gonna be fine," Emily said. "You're in charge. What can go wrong?"

"Everything," Jane said.

"No," Billy said. "That's what would happen if I were in charge."

"Or me," Emily said.

"You always do the right thing," Billy said. "We trust you."

"That's really comforting coming from two of the craziest people I've ever met in my life."

"Did she just say we're crazier than a werewolf?" Billy said.

312

"And Assassin Barbie," Emily said.

"I'm okay with that," Billy said.

"I'll take it as a compliment," Emily said.

"Great," Jane said, starting to laugh. "Titus leaves and now I'm stuck with the Comedic Duo."

"Is that our new nickname?" Billy said.

"I vote yes," Emily said.

They high-fived.

Jane laughed.

"You know, we have no name," Jane said. "We need a name."

"Team Emily," Emily said.

"The Unbeatables," said Billy.

"Invulnerables," said Emily.

"The Rock Stars."

"The Indestructibles," Emily said.

Billy and Jane both looked at her in shock.

"What was that last one?" Jane asked.

"The Indestructibles," Emily said. "It's what the ancient Egyptians called the two stars they could always see around the North Pole. One star is in the Little Dipper and the other is in the Big Dipper. They believed the area the stars circled and protected was heaven."

Billy's mouth hung open.

"Every once in a while I'm convinced you're the smartest person on Earth," he said.

"I'm a genius, yo," Emily said.

"And then you say something like that."

"It works," Jane said. "It really works."

"We're not indestructible," Billy said. "Maybe you are, but the rest of us officially don't qualify as indestructible."

"No, but we do circle the world and keep it safe. We're like those stars."

"For this one I vote yes," Emily said.

"That's because you came up with it," Billy said.

"We'll wait 'til Titus gets back and take a real vote," Jane said. "But I like it."

They hovered there for a moment, the world going about its everyday business a mile below them. Everything felt very quiet, and easy.

"I hope he gets back soon," Jane said.

"He will," Emily said. "Let's return to the Tower and call Titus. I don't want to wait 'til he's completed his walkabout to be able to tell people our name."

"You go on," Jane said. "I'll catch up."

Billy looked at her with a level of concern that always surprised Jane when she discovered it, those times when his cockiness fell away and she saw real worry in its place.

"You okay?" he asked.

"Fine."

Billy raised an eyebrow, but nodded.

"C'mon, Em, I'll race you."

"No fair, you fly, I float."

"We'll teach you to break the sound barrier yet," he said.

Billy put a hand lightly on Jane's arm, just for a moment, and winked at her. He took off like a shot, leaving Emily cursing and following in his wake.

Jane closed her eyes, and let the sunlight's warmth sink into her. She felt her heart beat, and her strength swell. She felt indestructible, brave . . . and yet, very much alone.

She opened her eyes, took a deep breath, and headed west.

There was a farm she yearned to visit, and two people she loved above all else that she needed to see.

Jane landed in their cornfield like a falling star, touching down in the same spot Doc Silence chose all that time ago.

Her parents were waiting on the front porch. They smiled as if she'd never left.

"We are the stars," Jane said.

THE END

The Indestructibles

Reading Group and Discussion Question Guide

1. While the characters possess special powers, many of the problems they confront are those faced by young people ever day. What are some of the challenges the heroes experienced that you relate to?

2. How does the theme of family relate to all of the heroes and even some of the villains in the story? How might it impact the characters' actions?

3. The story arc / journey for each character is unique. Who did you relate the most to during the story? Was there anyone you had trouble relating to?

4. Which character do you feel had developed the most by the end of the story? How has he or she changed?

5. Some of the characters need to make difficult decisions along the way to do what they think is right. Did you agree with the choices they made? Is there anything you would have done differently if you were in their place?

6. If you could change one event in the story, what would it be and why?

7. Some of the characters hide things about themselves in order to fit in with others. What were a few examples of these actions? How did they impact the character's story?

8. What story revelation surprised you the most? What reactions or emotions did that revelation elicit in you?

9. Some of the villains turn out to not be completely evil in the end. Why do you believe they changed? Do you think their actions in the end make up for their conduct earlier in the story?

10. Throughout the story, references and hints are offered about the previous generation of heroes and why they are no longer around. Why do you think they are gone? What do you think might have happened to them?

Some Other Books By PFP / AJAR Contemporaries

Blind Tongues - Sterling Watson

the Book of Dreams - Craig Nova

A Russian Requiem - Roland Merullo

Ambassador of the Dead - Askold Melnyczuk

Demons of the Blank Page - Roland Merullo

Celebrities in Disgrace - Elizabeth Searle
(eBook version only)

"Last Call" - Roland Merullo
(eBook "single")

Fighting Gravity - Peggy Rambach

Leaving Losapas - Roland Merullo

Girl to Girl: The Real Deal on Being A Girl Today - Anne Driscoll

Revere Beach Elegy - Roland Merullo

a four-sided bed - Elizabeth Searle

Revere Beach Boulevard - Roland Merullo

Tornado Alley - Craig Nova

"The Young and the Rest of Us" - Elizabeth Searle
(eBook "single")

Lunch with Buddha - Roland Merullo

Temporary Sojourner - Tony Eprile

Passion for Golf: In Pursuit of the Innermost Game - Roland Merullo

My Ground Trilogy - Joseph Torra

What Is Told - Askold Melnyczuk

This is Paradise: An Irish Mother's Grief, an African Village's Plight and the Medical Clinic That Brought Fresh Hope to Both. - Suzanne Strempek Shea

Talk Show - Jaime Clarke

"What A Father Leaves" - Roland Merullo
(eBook "single" & audio book)

Music In and On the Air - Lloyd Schwartz

The Calling - Sterling Watson

The Family Business - John DiNatale

Taking the Kids to Italy - Roland Merullo

The Winding Stream: The Carters, the Cashes and the Course of Country Music - Beth Harrington